W9-CFX-902

"Adam's back," Eve says quickly.

I hear him then, with the two boys. There is just time enough to slither under a bush. But this time Adam doesn't see me. The boys fall into some game with thread and polished stones. Sheitha toddles towards her daddy, grinning.

"We're just here to get somethng to eat," Adam says. "Ten minutes is all—what, Eve, isn't there anything to eat?"

Eve's face doesn't fall. But her eyes deepen in color a little, like skin that has been momentarily bruised.

When he and the boys have left again, I slither forward. "Eve," I say, "listen—"

I tell her how it will be for Sheitha after she marries Cain, who is not as sweet-tempered as her father. I tell her how it will be for Sheitha's daughter's daughter. I spare her nothing. Not the debate over whether women have souls. Nor the word "chattel." Finally, I finish, saying for perhaps the fortieth or fiftieth time, "Knowledge is the only way to change it. Knowledge, and truth. Eve, listen—"

From "Unto the Daughters"
by Nancy Kress

       (0451)

ENCHANTING REALMS

☐ **SCORPIANNE by Emily Devenport.** Lucy finds herself with a new identity on a new world at the brink of rebellion. Even here, she cannot escape the nightmare memories of the assassin who strikes without being seen, the one who has sworn Lucy's death, the stalker she knows only by the name Scorpianne.

(453182—$4.99)

☐ **THE EYE OF THE HUNTER by Dennis L. McKiernan.** From the best-selling author of *The Iron Tower* trilogy and *The Silver Call* duology—a new epic of Mithgar. The comet known as the Eye of the Hunter is riding through Mithgar's skies again, bringing with it destruction and the much dreaded master, Baron Stoke.

(452356—$5.99)

☐ **A SWORD FOR A DRAGON by Christopher Rowley.** The most loyal bunch of dragon warriors and human attendants ever to march on campaign had just been re-formed when Bazil Broketail and his human boy, Relkin, returned from a search for Bazil's beloved green dragoness. But when the Goddess of Death marks them both as her chosen victims for capture and sacrifice, they must face unexpected danger.

(452356—$5.99)

☐ **THE ARCHITECTURE OF DESIRE by Mary Gentle.** Discover a time and a place ruled by the Hermetic magic of the Renaissance, by secret, almost forgotten Masonic rites, a land divided between the royalists loyal to Queen Carola and the soldiers who follow the Protector-General Olivia in this magnificent sequel to *Rats and Gargoyles*.

(453530—$4.99)

Prices slightly higher in Canada.

Buy them at your local bookstore or use this convenient coupon for ordering.

PENGUIN USA
P.O. Box 999 — Dept. #17109
Bergenfield, New Jersey 07621

Please send me the books I have checked above.
I am enclosing $_____ (please add $2.00 to cover postage and handling). Send check or money order (no cash or C.O.D.'s) or charge by Mastercard or VISA (with a $15.00 minimum). Prices and numbers are subject to change without notice.

Card #_____ Exp. Date _____
Signature_____
Name_____
Address_____
City _____ State _____ Zip Code _____

For faster service when ordering by credit card call **1-800-253-6476**

Allow a minimum of 4-6 weeks for delivery. This offer is subject to change without notice.

Sisters in Fantasy

Edited by Susan Shwartz
and Martin H. Greenberg

A ROC BOOK

ROC
Published by the Penguin Group
Penguin Books USA Inc., 375 Hudson Street,
New York, New York 10014, U.S.A.
Penguin Books Ltd, 27 Wrights Lane, London W8 5TZ, England
Penguin Books Australia Ltd, Ringwood, Victoria, Australia
Penguin Books Canada Ltd, 10 Alcorn Avenue,
Toronto, Ontario, Canada M4V 3B2
Penguin Books (N.Z.) Ltd, 182–190 Wairau Road,
Auckland 10, New Zealand

Penguin Books Ltd, Registered Offices:
Harmondsworth, Middlesex, England

First published by Roc, an imprint of Dutton Signet,
a division of Penguin Books USA Inc.

First Printing, June, 1995

10 9 8 7 6 5 4 3 2 1

Copyright © Susan Shwartz and Martin H. Greenberg, 1995
"Women's Stories," copyright © by Jane Yolen, 1995; "Hallah's Choice,"
copyright © by Jo Clayton, 1995; "Wayfinder," copyright © by Janny Wurts,
1995; "The Way Wind," copyright © by Andre Norton, 1995; "Healer," copyright © by Josepha Sherman, 1995; "No Refunds," copyright © by Phyllis
Eisenstein, 1995; "Firstborn, Seaborn," copyright © by Sheila Finch, 1995;
"A Game of Cards," copyright © by Lisa Goldstein, 1995; "Courting Rites,"
copyright © by Kristine Kathryn Rusch, 1995; "Felixity," copyright © by
Tanith Lee, 1995; "Horse of Her Dreams," copyright © by Elizabeth Moon, 1995;
"Unto the Daughters," copyright © by Nancy Kress, 1995; "Babbitt's Daughter,"
copyright © by Phyllis Ann Karr, 1995; "*Remedia Amoris*," copyright © by
Judith Tarr, 1995; "The Bargain," copyright © by Katharine Kerr, 1995.
All rights reserved

 REGISTERED TRADEMARK—MARCA REGISTRADA

Printed in the United States of America

Without limiting the rights under copyright reserved above, no part of this
publication may be reproduced, stored in or introduced into a retrieval system, or transmitted, in any form, or by any means (electronic, mechanical,
photocopying, recording, or otherwise), without the prior written permission
of both the copyright owner and the above publisher of this book.

BOOKS ARE AVAILABLE AT QUANTITY DISCOUNTS WHEN USED TO PROMOTE
PRODUCTS OR SERVICES. FOR INFORMATION PLEASE WRITE TO PREMIUM MAR-
KETING DIVISION, PENGUIN BOOKS USA INC., 375 HUDSON STREET, NEW YORK,
NEW YORK 10014.

If you purchased this book without a cover you should be aware that this
book is stolen property. It was reported as "unsold and destroyed" to the
publisher and neither the author nor the publisher has received any payment
for this "stripped book."

To Stacey Davies

I wish you had stayed, to be more a part
of this book than the dedication.

CONTENTS

INTRODUCTION

The Women Whose Work We See—An Opossum's-Eye View of Fantasy

"Two of our opossums are missing," the late James Tiptree/Alice Sheldon/Raccoona Sheldon writes at the end of her chilling "The Women Men Don't See," as a mother and daughter choose to flee Earth with aliens rather than risk sexual oppression and growing backlash. In *Sisters in Fantasy,* I've assembled some of the stories that such opossums might have told if they had stuck it out at their home computers here on Earth.

When you picked up this book, you didn't just pick up an anthology, you know. What you are holding is also a thought experiment.

Is an anthology of fantasy fiction by women an idea whose time has *gone?* That's the question I asked Marty Greenberg when we first discussed this project.

Let's look back at the history of this idea. An anthology of fantasy stories by women writers—didn't Pamela Sargent do that in the 1970s, with *Women of Wonder* (1975), *More Women of Wonder* (1976), and

The New Women of Wonder (1978)? No, that was *science fiction.*

Well, then, what about Virginia Kidd's 1978 anthology, *Millennial Women,* which featured Ursula Le Guin and Joan Vinge, and offered early appearances of writers like Diana Paxson and Elizabeth Lynn? Also science fiction. And the controversial all-female *Analog* issue with the Joan Vinge cover story, "Eyes of Amber," which won a Hugo? Again, science fiction; and it, too, was published in the 1970s.

Well, what about fantasy, then? There's Jessica Amanda Salmonson's *Amazons* anthologies from the early 1980s, and there's Marion Zimmer Bradley's ongoing *Swords and Sorceress* series. There's even two of my own anthologies, *Hecate's Cauldron,* and *Moonsinger's Friends* (1985). But all of those anthologies have been open to male writers as well.

In other genres, Kathy Ptacek has edited two volumes of horror fiction by women, the *Women of Darkness* series; and women who write mysteries have enjoyed working on *Sisters in Crime,* which was one of the inspirations for this present volume.

Why are you editing an all-female anthology of fantasy stories now? (Apart, of course, from the fact that the writers we've gotten stories from are among the finest—male *and* female—in the field.)

Many people asked us that question as we collected the stories in this first volume. We even got the occasional reprimand. Some writers didn't find an all-women's anthology either necessary or desirable: all that had been done already; we would just be ghettoizing women writers further; the concerns of women writers were the concerns of *writers,* period, the end; it was unfair to our male colleagues.

Frankly, at one point, I might have agreed. Certainly, by the mid-1980s, I got tired of being regarded as a spokeswoman for all female writers and *very* tired, indeed, of being put on "Women in SF" and "Women in Fantasy" panels at conventions and academic conferences. At one point, in fact, a number of us had an attack of subversion and formally disbanded what we were pleased at the time to call the "Chix 'n' Fix" (Chicks in Fiction—sarcasm intended) panel.

What changed my mind? A number of things. First off, the stereotype of what a number of my colleagues call the FFW—the Female Fantasy Writer. This isn't just a woman—any woman—who writes fantasy, make no doubt of that. This is a stereotype every bit as invidious as the stereotype of the romance writer as a pink-clad, bonbon-eating moron—as anyone knows who's ever negotiated with one of those expert, contract-savvy women.

What does the so-called FFW write? Fluffy fantasy about bunnies, or unicorns . . . the "elfy-welfy" stuff, as it's called when people go into bash-FFW mode. Gentle, soppy, and all about rebellious young girls who want swords and horses and adventures so they can be tomboys forever.

Funny: no one I knew was writing that sort of thing—at least, not with a straight face. I began to wonder if this "FFW Syndrome" wasn't somehow akin to the reaction of which Susan Faludi writes in her provocative book *Backlash*.

The stories you're about to read disprove the charges of soppiness for once and for all, I think. No elves, no unicorns (not that I have any objections to either), and certainly no fluff.

Where did the perception of the "dreaded FFW" originate? We didn't know. We decided we'd find out. So, at a series of panel discussions, we revived the "Women in (fill in the blank) Fiction" panels, with a different emphasis. This time, we decided to ask different questions.

In the 1970s, people asked what women were writing fantasy and science fiction, why more than a few hadn't, and where we thought we'd all be going in the future. The emphasis was pretty much feminist; but then, the 1970s were pretty ideological times. Now, in the 1990s—an era to which the ambiguous label "postfeminist" has attached itself, and during which "I'm not a feminist" has become a leitmotif against charges of that revolting term "political correctness"—we are asking different questions.

Is women's fiction intrinsically *different*? Do different concerns emerge in it? Is the way a woman writer learns her craft different, somehow, from the way that a male writer does?

In short, as Jane Yolen declares in the poem that opens this book, "My stories are not your stories."

Where did we get *this* idea? Surely not from the Schenectady that all good SF is supposed to come from.

Where *did* we get it?

Ursula Le Guin's *Dancing at the Edge of the World* made me wonder if a woman artist doesn't indeed have different constraints upon her time and craft. That book sent me back to Virginia Woolf's *A Room of One's Own,* in which she argues that what a woman needs to write is an independent income and a space she can call her own. And the subsequent and wildly successful publication of Georgetown linguist Deborah Tannen's *You Just Don't Understand* convinced me, in any case, that women and men speaking together may both be speaking English—but may not be communicating because they consider different types and purposes of speech important.

Now, don't get me wrong, though it would be easy to do so right about now. I'm not an Amazon nor was I meant to be. Nor have I succumbed to the "I'm not a feminist" cop-out, and I don't plan to. However, I want to point out that *Sisters in Fantasy* is not a polemic or what Le Guin calls a "preachment" because, to my way of thinking, nothing ruins good fiction faster than a lecture. And what you're holding in this book is good fiction.

Instead, *Sisters in Fantasy* is intended to let readers and writers look at the questions I've been pondering—the thought experiment I mentioned at the beginning of this introduction. Make up your own minds whether or not these stories are any different from stories you'd find in "coeducated" anthologies.

Accordingly, I contacted other women who write fantasy. Write me, I said, a story. It must be fantasy. It needn't have a female protagonist or a female viewpoint character. You can write about anything you want. In fact, what I want you to write is the story you've *needed* to write and couldn't think of an appropriate market for before I contacted you.

And the stories began to come in. One thing I noted about them right away was their quality. This volume includes works by one Grand Master, one National Book award winner, at least one Nebula award winner and several nominees, World Fantasy and Campbell award nominees and winners, winners of the Compton Crooke award and the Crawford award, winners in young adult and children's fiction, and—apart from those pedigrees—outstanding writers.

Another thing I noticed that these stories were fantasy with a twist—not a gimmick, but a sea change on traditional themes. Take, for example, what I privately call the "yes, I can" theme in fantasy—the story of a woman or girl who is determined to prove that she too can be a warrior or a bard or anything else she has a gift for, despite parental or societal opposition.

Jo Clayton's "Hallah's Choice" presents a victim turned assassin, while Janny Wurts's "Wayfinder" shows a girl from a fishing village turned questing hero. These stories contain anger and fear—but their emphasis is on accomplishment and recovery, not stamp-your-foot defiance or, God forbid, spunkiness, that curse of the Gidget-with-sword adolescent heroine. The protagonists of such stories have long since proved to themselves their own competence.

Andre Norton and Josepha Sherman also adapt the conventions of traditional high fantasy to their needs. But Andre Norton's "The Way Wind" is far more than a "thou shalt not suffer a witch to live" story; it is a tale of quiet heroism, rather than fireworks—the daily struggle against despair and mounting odds that makes most battle stories seem, well, impatient. And Josepha Sherman's "Healer" uses the shamanic journey within to make important points not about power, but about love and family, told from the point of view of a healer who happens to be male.

I also selected a number of contemporary fantasies. In every case, these stories were fantasy with an ironic edge. Each of them—Eisenstein's "No Refunds," Finch's "Firstborn, Seaborn," Lisa Goldstein's "A Game of Cards," and Kristine Kathryn Rusch's "Courting Rites"—show women who are, in some sense, essentially alone and have been so for quite some time.

Eisenstein's fortune-teller is separated from her clients by a vast gulf of years. Finch's Maria (the name is given her) is constrained to be the good wife, the Christian mother; but she keeps her own secrets, reserving her most important decision until she sees a chance of not being thwarted by the men who have thwarted her—from the kindest of motives—until then. Lisa Goldstein's Rozal is a refugee and a survivor, dependent on, but isolated from her rich employers and their guests. And Kristine Kathryn Rush's

protagonist is that quintessential outside observer—
the private eye.

Each of these characters reaches a difficult and pre-
carious accommodation with her world and the people
in it. In each story, you get the sense that the protagonists are wary, as if sensing that outsiders may mean
well, but that they could, at any moment, turn on
them.

In these surroundings, the fantasy takes on a tinge
of horror at the psychological pain revealed in these
stories and in the sacrifices these women make just to
keep going. In some cases, we sense anger. In others,
the anger has been replaced by a deep compassion.
And in yet others, the accommodations have turned
subversive and downright sinister—as in Tanith Lee's
superbly decadent "Felixity," where an unattractive
woman takes power into her own hands, or in Elizabeth Moon's "Horse of her Dreams," in which the
father of a daughter "born to be sweet" (unattractive)
in a culture that prizes flamboyant beauty determines
to provide for the child he loves within the parameters
of the culture that rules him.

In a subversive fit of my own, I was also delighted
at the number of what I call revisionist stories. Fantasy
has always contained a very strong mythic component.
Logically enough, women's fantasy seems to make frequent use of women's myths and archetypes. As Jane
Yolen writes, "Job's wife has her own story." The
"revisionist" stories in *Sisters in Fantasy* make no
bones of examining the myths common to our culture
wryly, from the point of view of the outsider.

Take, for example, Nancy Kress's "Unto the
Daughters." It is the story of Lilith. Lilith, or Lilitu
in earlier accounts, is castigated in source material as
Adam's disobedient first wife or (therefore) as a
demon. But Nancy Kress presents her as the Mother
of Us All who sees clearly and ironically even her own

role in the story and the whole sorry state of affairs. Or Phyllis Ann Karr's complex "Babbitt's Daughter," which examines the notions of American Babbittry (no, that's not *Bobbitt*, but a figure out of Middle America as described by Sinclair Lewis), holiness, family values—and vampirism. Sheila Finch's "First-born, Seaborn" examines the transformation of the mother goddess into the Blessed Virgin, a symbol whom priests of the "uncle god" then use to trammel and control the protagonist of the story. Judith Tarr uses the power of sacrificial love to transform the randy Pan, while Katharine Kerr's "The Bargain" takes the archetype of the bard who goes off with the Queen of Faerie and turns it into a parable about love, wisdom, and maturity.

In each case, the writers know what they've been told all their lives about What Myths Really Mean and the Way Things Are. They've heard all that. For some years, they believed all that, perhaps, and maybe even hurt because their lives didn't fit within the confines of the "accepted truths." But, since they also know what their lives and experiences—and their art—have taught them, they may not think it's necessary to throw the traditional myths out (which would be wasteful), but they're not buying just the traditional interpretation.

I also think there's more to it than that. In *You Just Don't Understand*, Deborah Tannen describes "women's language" as "rapport-speech" as opposed to "report-speech," which is a speech register that she claims is used more by men. In other words, women speak to establish rapport; men speak to report information. (And yes, I know what appalling generalizations those are and that some men are empathic, while some women are information-oriented; what I'm reporting *here* is what Tannen writes.) Tannen knows that, too, and so do these writers. Nevertheless, as I read these stories, I was impressed by the degree of connectedness—of human caring and awareness—between even the most isolated character and his or her world.

In all of the stories in *Sisters in Fantasy,* you have protagonists who are simultaneously alone and part of various relationships. In each case, they know that, isolated though they may be in some ways, they cannot go it alone. They need the village, the husband, the friend, the client, the child, even the adversary, or the betrayers. No one is opting out because, even when the traditional themes of human relationships and loyalties go wrong, they're what you have—and all that you have—if you want to go on living . . . apart, of course, from the self-respect you work lifelong to build.

And all of the characters in these stories want not just to survive, but to endure in ways that will enable them to live with themselves.

Which brings me to what impressed me most about the stories you're about to read. Neither the writers nor the characters in these stories are whiz kids. The writers are all experienced, seasoned professionals. And their characters, by and large, are mature people. They have what T. H. White called in *The Once and Future King* the seventh sense that you get as you mature—the sense of balance. It calls for quiet virtues like patience, courage, endurance, and compassion. You may get some pyrotechnics, but mostly what you see is a subtly wrought chain of events, painstakingly linked by hand, then turned to the light so that you see the ordinary transformed and healed.

Not surprisingly, you'll find joy in these stories— but very little flash. In one way or another, all of the characters in these stories are veterans of their own wars. There's sadness to them—you don't endure this long without a few scars. Take, for example, the dedication of this book. Stacey Davies was a young woman on GEnie, my computer bulletin board, who died very young and very tragically. When that happened, a rose designed in ASCII characters was put up on the main banner of the computer board. That was the first time that happened. Ever since, when there has been a death in the "family," the rose has been put up to commemorate the person we have lost; and with each rose, we remember all of them. Our loss of Stacey—as person and as writer—has become part of our community in just the way that the losses of characters in the stories you're about to read have become parts of their lives.

As with all veterans, you don't push characters like this to talk. The losses and the old scars hurt; and maybe they don't quite trust you yet. But I'd be the last to deny that when they are in the mood, they have fine stories to tell.

And more than that. These stories, as I hoped, are not polemics or wish-fulfillments. Their characters *may* get their hearts' desires, long after those hearts have been broken, healed, and broken again—and whether or not those desires are any good for them. At the same time, however, you see characters setting about their lives with remarkably little bitterness, with great skill, and with increased knowledge of the world. They may even have healed a person or two—not to mention the readers or the writer herself.

I am not prepared—any more than are the writers in this volume—to argue that these are talents possessed only by women, or by women in particular. It would not only be prejudiced to argue that, it would be unrealistic. We have enough words without people putting words in our mouths: instead, listen to the words that *are* here.

I will, however, point out that these writers and their stories have the gift of creating rapport and seeking human connections, this seventh sense of balance, and this craft in full measure; and I am proud to present the writers, the craft, the stories, and the thought-experiment that comprises *Sisters in Fantasy*.

—Susan Shwartz

Women's Stories

Jane Yolen

Teacher, poet, novelist, short story writer, a magisterial figure in the world of young adult and children's writing, editor of a line her friends call HBJane, Jane Yolen is very definitely an elder of the fantasy and science-fiction community. "For I am the mother of all things," she tells people, "and all things should wear their sweaters." When she's not joking, however, she is thinking; and women's writing is one of the things she's thinking of.

Women's Stories

There are two fathers I do not understand:
the one at the bridge,
devil's bargain still warm on his mouth,
kissing his daughter first, saying:
"Do I have a husband for you";
and Abraham, with his traitor's hand,
leading Isaac up the hill to God.

1

These are not women's stories.
Even before I birthed my three,
and the one bled out before its time,
and the one encysted in the tube,
even before that I would have thrust the knife
in my own breast, before God;
I would have swallowed the kiss,
gone back to the beast myself.

Job's wife has her own story.
Lot's pillar of salt cried tears
indistinguishable from her eyes.
Who invented a glass slipper
never had to dance.

Do not try to climb my hair.
Do not circle me with a hedge of thorns.
My stories are not your stories.
We women go out into the desert together,
or not at all.

Hallah's Choice

Jo Clayton

From the Drytowns to Leigh Brackett Hamilton's Mars, mercenaries and assassins stride or skulk through exotic desert towns. They are violent and sinister, and, no doubt, each one of them has a history that we would wonder at—when we're not taking cover.

Hallah, Jo Clayton's protagonist, has a history more painful than most. Is she bent on revenge? Yes, but this is one assassin you can imagine singing a lullaby.

1
Into the web

Languorous late afternoon.

Heatwaves and a haze of yellow dust.

The Shiza'heyh of Yaanosin ride to the Betrothal Feast and Fealty Jubilee with their guards and dependents, their wives and daughters and their eldest sons, their equerries and orderlies and grooms, their harriers and farriers, their agents and their clerks, their stooges and their sycophants, their bath girls and bed-warmers, their tailors, their valets, their wardrobe masters, their cooks and their cupbearers, their food tasters and wine tasters, their scullions and slaveys.

The Shiza'heyh Kihyayti'an rides to the Betrothal Feast and Fealty Jubilee with all this and his un-matched pair of matchless assassins.

Zisgade Neisser the Shadowsnake, unfeeling as the polished ivory blades he wears up each sleeve—he is a thin grey man, yellow with dust, riding at his mas-ter's side.

Hallah Myur, with no epithet allowed—such things are a foolishness she is content to live without—a thin grey woman riding near the tail of the procession, a little woman yellow with the rolling dust, dark eyes narrowed to cracks. Sweat runnels cut through the dust plastered on her brow, baring streaks of lined light brown skin. Wisps of hair straggle from under her loosely wound headbands. She rides easily, slumped in the saddle of a dust-yellowed gelding, a longlegged, roughgaited, slabsided beast with enough energy and humor left to white his eyes at clots in the dust and shy at skittering shadows.

She is tired, hot, and bored, with no end of boredom in sight. For the next week or so she'll be nothing more than an attendant, a body to dress up the Shiza'-heyh's entourage. Katiang the Boar-rider and the other cursemen deal hardly with folk who break the Curse Truce, with the hand and the one-behind who hires the hand. Even Shiza'heyh Kihyayti'an in his maddest moods would not chance bringing the Curse on his head.

She expects to sleep a lot. She detests crowds, is bored by tumblers, street mimes, magicians, and their like. She seldom gambles, doesn't trust luck, only skill. Clothes are to cover her body, food is for fueling it. She prefers the tablewipe she buys for herself in hedge taverns to the delicate vintages the Shiza'heyh pro-vides for his favored hirelings. Beyond the highs of her work—which are fewer with every year that passes—her only real pleasure is a hard-fought game of stonechess. Since Atwarima is a busy riverport and the Jubilee/Betrothal should bring a flood of visitors from many realms, she hopes to locate an adequate opponent.

2
The first shock

In the Bath of the Toyaytay GuestHouse Hallah Myur stripped and stretched, sucking in the steamy air. She shook her head, her hair tumbling loose, fine long hair kinking into frizzy curls. Her body was limber as a child's but terribly scarred, nodules of keloid with streaks of white and pink running through the soft brown skin where her breasts had been; her back was laced with whip marks.

She sat on damp sacking bound over the bench beside the tub and combed the tangles and dust from her hair, singing softly to herself, clicking her tongue at how grey she was getting. When she was finished, she set the comb aside, twisted her hair into a knot atop her head, and slid with a soft purr of pleasure into the water.

Clean and relaxed, she pulled on her second-best tunic and trousers, tied on the grey silk formveil that masked her face eye to chin, bound her hair with grey silk bands, covering it completely. She gathered her dusty riding gear, paid the attendant, left the Bath and strolled toward the rooms assigned to the Shiza'heyh Kihyayti'an's entourage, humming a song she'd picked up somewhere, enjoying the warmth of her body, the easy shift of her muscles.

Though sunset was still half an hour off, in that maze of corridors and galleries within the massive walls of the GuestHouse, alabaster lamps were already lit, and their painted oils spread perfume on the drafts that coiled about her shoulders. She turned a corner.

A man walked toward her; his face and shoulders leapt at her as he passed a lamp.

She stopped walking. Stopped breathing.

His eyes passed over her, dismissed her. Under the Curse Truce, assassin's fangs were pulled. She was nothing to interest him. Nothing.

His footsteps faded.

Shudder after shudder passed along her body; she hunched over, beat her fists against her thighs, sucked in air in sharp, broken gasps. Shell twenty years thick shattered in that instant, twenty years of discipline gone.

But twenty years do have weight and reach.

After a moment she straightened her back, quieted her breathing. Almost running, drowning in memory, she hurried for the small private cubicle assigned to her.

Rosalie Zivan, fourteen years of mischief, spoiled by a doting father, her mother dead three years ago birthing Garro Zivan's last son, the spring moon like laughter in her blood, slipped into the Home-wood of Roka Membruda to gather herbs for her Auntee Rosamunda's simples and specifics: Mutes' tongue, love-at-ease, moonspurge, sowthistle, hop-over, bruisewort, poorfolks pepper, bee thumb, sucklings tit, wet-a-bed, shut-your-ear, flickwhittle, whistling fleabane, smartberry, creeping ninny, wart-weed, stinking willy.

Delighted by the edge of danger in her solitary windings through the wood, she prowled along the deer paths and in the scattered glades, grubbing in the thick black earth under the trees and along the noisy creek, knife flickering through the greens, the tubers, the brambles, the grasses growing on the banks and in the water, filling the gather sack she carried slung over her shoulder.

She ended her search when she reached the rowan pool in the heart of the wood, where the water ran deep and silent through ancient twisted trees, a place fragrant with the eddying sweetness of night-blooming jasmine and the acrid bite of riveroak, a place where it seemed to her the dreefolk must dance on their dreadnights.

She eased the sack onto rowan roots, careful to keep it from the damp dark earth, stripped off her blouse, her skirt, and her camisole, hung them on a rowan tree, then slipped into the water. The moon was a hair past full and directly overhead, turning the water to tarnished silver. She sculled dreamily about, watching the clouds swim by.

A young man came from the trees, blond hair blowing in an aureole about a beautiful lean face. She knew him. She'd seen him in the village, Membruda's Youngest Son. They said his name was Traccoar. "Rowan flower," he said to her, his voice like a wind in the trees. "Come bless me."

When she reached her room, she paced back and forth, back and forth, wall to door, around the end of the bed and back, shivering with reaction. After she'd calmed enough so she could stay still awhile, she stripped off her clothes, braided her hair, tied the ends, and slipped into bed.

Sleep came hard, and when she did at last drop off, the dreams came back, the ones she thought she'd left with her name.

Rosalie Zivan lay with hands clenched into fists as Traccoar's body moved on hers, as he whispered that she was the loveliest, the most magical being he'd ever known. Most women, he told her between grunts and other noises, are greedy whores, selling themselves for money and power. You're different, he told her, you're like the earth, rich and powerful, warm and giving.

She was only fourteen, and virgin, but she knew lies when she heard them. She lay like a stone, gathering herself to run when he rolled off her, before he remembered that he had to kill her so she couldn't put a Hammar Curse on him—that was what they believed, those beasts in the Rokas.

The Hammar of clan Gyoker-Zivan had no curses, only wise women and fast-fingered men.

He groaned, rolled over, and lay panting beside her.

She scrambled up, ran around a rowan tree when he leapt to his feet and lunged for her. "Dirty pig," she shouted at him. "May you never get it up again." She ran into the shadows and left him stumbling clumsily after her, cursing her.

Hallah Myur stirred in her sleep, ground her teeth, and whined like an angry cat; her hands moved up her body to touch the places where her breasts had been. Tears gathered in her sleeping eyes and leaked from beneath her lids.

3
The second shock

The Oath Hall was a vast domed cavity with eight sides and hanging galleries above a forest of arches. The walls shimmered with color, patterned tiles in red, blue, green. The dome itself was white and gold; it rested on scrolled, open arches, the morning sunlight

streaming through them, gilded with dancing dust
motes. Polished gold stairs rose to a two-level dais at
the western wall; a plain, heavy chair sat on the high-
est level, made from what rumor said was dragon
bones—the Alayjiyah's Throne. In front of the dais
was a square twenty feet wide of ivory tiles in a golden
matrix. On the north side of that square were three
backless ivory chairs with cushions of cloth of gold;
on the south side of the square were three more—set
there for the Six Shiza'heyh of Yaanosin.

Formveil hiding her impatience, Hallah Myur stood
behind the Shiza'heyh Kihyayti'an, Zisgade Neisser
the Shadowsnake at her left—which meant she was
the favored one today. She wondered vaguely what
Zisgade had done to annoy Kihyayti'an this time.
Quick work, but he was always doing it, eating his
feet. She didn't care about favor, it was just a job and
a tedious one at that—standing around and posing,
reminding Kihyayti'an's hopeful heirs of the sting in
the tail of ambition. Her indifference jabbed at Zisgade; he'd do anything he could to make trouble for
her. She wasn't worried; if she couldn't outthink that
twynt, she deserved to go down. Besides, the Guild
had uncomfortable ways of dealing with treachery. Except . . . She shifted uneasily. Groensacker gets wasps
in his cod when he thinks about me. Could be he's
hoping I'll get so antsy with this stint, I'll walk out on
it. Then he could fine me some serious gelt and mark
me unreliable. Viper.

She watched Zisgade a moment. He stood with his
hands clasped behind him, walking the muscles in his
arms and torso, his tunic shivering with their twitch.
She suppressed a yawn, fingered the stonebox in her
pouch. Get on with it, blump! This is *boring*. Kihyayti'an had promised his assassins a free day once the

rites were done, and she wanted a game, wanted it badly.

She glanced idly up at the northern gallery, which was filling with the guests come for the Betrothal. She scowled as she saw Traccoar standing on the edge of a cluster of men; their voices came down to her in a muted grumble, the words lost in the echoes.

!Maytre! he's gone to seed for sure. Look at the goat-son wag his tail and grin like a fool.

A newcomer pushed through them and stopped beside Traccoar, a tall, faded blonde whose hair had migrated from his head to a twin-tailed beard. Big brother, looks like. So Old Goatface is finally dead. Yes, of course. He would be. It's been more than twenty years, and he was older than the hills then. This one was ... She dredged through memory. Ah yes, Ardamoar the Eldest.

Naked except for a leather clout and a pectoral of seh'ki claws threaded on strands of kih-gut, their oiled bodies glistening in the sunlight streaming through the dome-arches, the Ghost Drummers came clattering in, hauling their tall drums on their backs.

They set the drums by the golden stairs, climbed on the stone stools, and began beating out a heart rhythm; the boombahms filled the chamber.

In the gallery, the clot of men was breaking apart as the guests sought their seats; behind them their dependents scurried about like startled waterbugs, negotiating places to stand.

As Ardamoar lowered his long bony body into a chair, a woman emerged from the throng and joined Traccoar, who was standing directly behind his brother.

Hair like new-minted copper.

Auntee Rosamunda's face on a long Lamenoor body.

Hallah swayed, clamped her teeth on her tongue.

Garro Zivan wept when Rosalie told him, warned her to say nothing to the other Hammar. With a little luck, he said, naught will come of this and we'll be as we were. That was how her father was, never a man to swallow bitters to keep a fever off. But as the Gyoker-Zivan Hammar moved their wagons across Membruda's Range and the months slid past, her body swelled and there was no hiding what had been done to her.

Auntee Rosamunda read the Weed Milk for her, but wouldn't say what she saw there. She emptied the bowl, shook her head. We have to leave her behind, she told Garro Zivan. Membruda will burn the wagons if he learns his blood is here.

Rosalie Zivan lived peacefully in that small mountain village where her people left her, supporting herself and her child with the box of medicines Auntee Rosamunda left with her.

One evening when Spring was new and her daughter was eighteen months and seething with curiosity and energy, Rosalie sat in deepening twilight on the doorstep of her cottage, rubbing the papery skins off a heap of flickwhittle bulbs and watching Rowanny toddle about, investigating toads and hoppers and stones and anything that caught her roving mind.

When she heard the rattle of hooves, she set her abrading cloth aside and went to snatch her daughter from the road.

Membruda's youngest son, face contorted with a hatred close to madness, rode at her, whip raised.

His brothers rode round and round her, yelling curses at her.

Her daughter was torn from her arms and thrown aside.

Her clothes were ripped off, Membruda's youngest son raped her, rolled off her, shouted his triumph, he was a man again. Cursing her, calling her dirty beast, witch, demon, bloodsucking whore, he hacked off her breasts, tossed them to one of his brothers.

After that the brothers stood in a ring about her, kicking at her, lacerating her back with their cattle whips.

Rowanny wailed. Someone, not Traccoar, but it might as well have been, said, "Shut the brat up, knock her head against a tree or something."

A bone flute played three notes over and over, the drumsounds came faster, with brushes and slides and taps weaving a complex texture through the deep resonant bahbooms. The drummers' bodies dripped sweat; their heads bobbed, muscles in their shoulders, arms, legs danced with the music of their hands.

The cursemen stamped their bone-shod feet, shook their rattles, and clashed the antlers strapped to their heads, chanting in their secret tongue. Katiang Boarrider danced in unbalanced spirals across and around the Ivory Floor, his thin wiry legs moving in and out of the musk censers hanging on bronze chains from the bone links of his girdle, never quite touching them; the streamers of blue-white smoke circled with him, mingled with smoke from the larger censer that sat atop the bronze cage he wore on his head.

Hallah Myur swayed with the music, flexed her toes, and began a muscle walk along her body; she had to move or she'd scream.

Zisgade was watching her. His eyes were the brown-black of strong coffee; it was always easy to tell where he was looking. !Maytre! He's smelled something. Weasel-face. I must've made more noise than I . . .

The Alayjiyah came in, a little round man with a sour face and thin hair stiffened with gel and swirled to a point. He was mostly robes thick with gold thread and embroidered with diamonds—robes and will; he was a hard man and dangerous. He settled himself on the dragon-bone chair, clapped his little hands, and six slave girls brought in his daughter.

The Yih Ma'yin Sa'aetinn was a cloud of fine linen, layer on layer of the translucent fabric, only her hands and feet showing. Her hands were heavy with rings, her feet were bare and elaborately jeweled.

Hallah sighed and set herself to endure a little longer, eyes on the floor, mind going round and round as she tried to sort out what she was going to do.

4
Tangled in the web

Hallah Myur ran.

In the streets around the Toyaytay Gardens where the Festival was well started, crowds were thick as clotted cream; there was noise and laughter, shouts, growls, clangs, music from dozens of players clashing and competing, smells of fried meats and hot bread, of candy and coffee, of perfumes and horse droppings and sweat, bright primal colors everywhere, flags and ribbons flapping from cords strung across the streets and between windows, the sequined and embroidered holiday costumes of the revelers.

She pushed impatiently through the revelers, passed into the alleys and winding ways of Atwarima's working quarters, then she ran and ran, words beating in her head to the beat of her feet. *Mem bru da's whore my Ro wan ny Mem bru da's whore my ba by Mem bru da's whore* . . .

She ran until her edginess was drained away, until even the words had faded and only the shift and play

of her body was left. Ran until she was exhausted
and gasping.

Hallah Myur leaned on a rope stretched between
bitts and watched the river eddying below her. An
aepha-gull dived past her, plunged into the dirty littered water, emerged with a long skinny fish flapping
wildly in its talons.

"If that's an omen, am I the fish or the gull?" She
shrugged and went looking for a tavern and a game.

Hallah Myur walked into the Seven Spinners,
stepped aside to clear the doorway, smiled behind the
formveil at the familiar noises, the smoke and murk,
the nosebite of homebrew. Two caravanners were
armwrestling by the bar; a beamdancer gyrated to a
tinny out-of-tune lute; a group of men and women sat
around three tables pushed together, shouting at each
other in a tongue she didn't recognize.

A tall vigorous woman with masses of blue-black
hair and large but shapely arms threaded through the
busy tables and stopped in front of Hallah; her green
eyes snapped with disfavor as she took in the assassin's grey and the veil. "I'm Thonsane, and this is my
House. If you're on business, no-name, take it and
yourself away."

Hallah untied the strings, pulled the veil away, and
tucked it down her shirt. "Not working," she said.
"It'd take a fool to break Truce, and I hope I'm not
that." She took the box from her pouch. "By your
favor, I'm looking for a game. I am Ivory cusping
Silver."

Thonsane relaxed. "By whose favor, eh?"

"Hallah Myur, Mistress."

"Hallah Myur, working or not, you're apt to make
my patrons nervous. I'll tuck you in an alcove . . .
mmm . . . over there, I think."

Thonsane plowed through the crowd, grabbed a snoring caravanner by his collar and belt, hauled him to the door, and dropped him on the steps outside, came striding back, waving a Pot Girl to her. She watched with a judging eye as the girl cleaned off the table, fetched a lamp, filled it with redeye oil, and lighted the floating wick. As the light brightened in the alcove, she rubbed a forefinger beside her nose. "If I can't scare you up a better, I'll give you a game myself, awhile on, say half an hour or so should you care to wait that long. I'm new Ivory looking to better myself. Wine, ale, or shag?"

Hallah Myur straightened her legs, slid down in the seat, cuddling the glass on her stomach, sipping at the dark brown shag whenever the glow it threw round her subsided a little.

There was a noisy surge as a mob of seamen came in and pushed toward the bar. A gap opened in the crowd, and she saw Zisgade Neisser sitting on a bench near the door; he'd shed his greys and was wearing nondescript laborer's clothing, his long hair was stuffed up under a knitted cap, though a ragged fringe was combed forward, sweeping across his eyes. Hallah looked quickly away, grinned down at the empty glass.

Another glass of shag and a pewter tankard in one hand, the other closed on the shoulder of a smallish man she urged along ahead of her, Thonsane came pushing through the crowd. The man's face was an assemblage of stains and bruises, wrinkles folded in on wrinkles, as if it has been lived in for several life-times, none of them easy, a hammered-thin, sun-faded, trouble-worn copy of her teacher.

Thonsane set the glass in front of Hallah, the pewter tankard across the table from her. "Aezel. Gold," she said. "Hallah Myur. Talk. Game or not, whatever's your choice." Shouting broke out across the room.

Muttering curses, Thonsane strode off, elbowing through the gathering spectators.

Aezel slid along the bench, gulped at the wine, set the tankard down. "Who taught you, Hallah Myur?" His voice was slow, soft, with an accent she couldn't place, a hint of a lilt in the words.

She opened the chess box out into the chessboard, set aside the cubbies with the stones, said, "Tarammen tai Peli, who earned his Mastery in Klymmavar from Ruska tyan ta Marssa, who earned hers from Zongari of Prena, who earned his from Andan Jarna." She smiled, her second genuine smile since she'd come to Atwarima. "I can go on for another half hour with the pedigree. Tarammen tai made sure I knew it. For three years I had to recite the list for him before he'd lift a stone." She touched the board with her fingertips, moved it across the table so he could see it. "The names are graved in the ivory squares, there's his"— she reached across the table, touched the tip of her forefinger to the penultimate name, then slid her finger to the last—"and that's mine; he passed the set to me as a Death Gift."

Aezel touched the ancient wood and the yellowed ivory with gentle fingers. "A fine thing," he said, pleasure husking his soft voice. He pushed the board into the middle of the table so both could reach it without straining, then he sat back, laced his fingers across his hard little paunch and began a litany of his own Masterline.

When he finished, they set up the game and began.

At first she was too aware of the noise around her, of the other customers drifting over to watch, of Zisgade moving in, his coffee eyes boring into her, of the circling memories. But as the game went on, all that vanished and she saw nothing but the stones and their patterning. Twice before she'd tipped into a state where her stones moved in a wave that built and built, sweeping the other stones away before them, but she'd never felt it so strongly as now.

It was not a slow game; there were no long, labored pauses on either side. Aezel was her match and more, a Gold in truth, keeping pace with her, doing all he could to check the wave and turn it aside.

And he did it. Her wave beat against his wall and fell away.

She'd overwhelmed him almost everywhere, yet he managed to preserve a handful of stones and herd them into the rare and powerful pattern called the Gorfellay, the ultimate defense of an ultimate Master.

Hallah Myur rubbed at her back and sighed; she could go on playing, hoping to catch him in a mistake, but the mistake would most likely be hers. She lifted her hand, let it fall. "Draw?"

"Agreed." He went limp, yawned, lay back with his eyes closed, exhausted but content.

Hallah looked around. The watchers that had collected about the alcove were scattering, stretching, yawning, wandering toward the bar, talking avidly about the game. Zisgade was gone; no doubt he left when he saw the game was going to last awhile. Stonechess gave him hives, he said; he hated the times when Kihyayti'an made him watch the play. She began tucking the stones into their cubbies. "Hah-hey," she said. "I loathe crowds."

"Ah." Aezel sucked up the last of his wine, raised a shaggy brow. When Hallah nodded, he summoned a Pot Girl to refill the tankard. When she'd gone, he tapped his thumbnail against the pewter in a monotonous clack clack clack clack . . .

Hallah Myur shuddered. "Stop that, will you?"

"You want something."

She scowled at him. His eyes had an odd shine to

them, a fugitive green phosphor. "Another game," she said warily. "By your favor, gold Aezel."

"That's not it."

"I don't understand."

"I offer a trade, silver Hallah. What you want for what I need." His thumbnail tap tap tapped against the pewter.

She leaned forward, her eyes on the thumb then lifting to meet his. She said nothing, but it was clear enough that Curse Truce or not he was going to lose that thumb if he kept on.

He flattened his hand on the table. "Will you trade?"

"Swear faith."

"By Koaysithe, I . . ."

"No! Swear by Stone."

"Why not." He laid his hand palm down on the ancient chess box. "I swear by Stone and my Master's Grave, what I say is true, what I say I do." He took his hand back, shifted his wrinkles in another smile. "Well, silver Hallah?"

"Why not." Whatever she did, she was up to her neck in carrion with the crows coming at her. "I have a daughter." To her annoyance, her eyes stung and her jaw started to tremble. She took a gulp of shag, set the glass down with a thump. "I lost her. Thought she was dead. She wasn't even two yet. I saw her today. At the Swearing. I want to know if she's happy . . . no . . . that's not right . . . if she's . . ." She rubbed her thumb along the heavy glass, but didn't drink this time; things were ragged enough. "I need to know without . . . intruding . . . I need to know . . . because . . ." She wiped at her mouth with a shaking hand and finished in a rush. "Because how she is, that's the fulcrum my future turns on, do you understand?"

"Yes." He sipped at the wine, wrapped his hands

around the tankard. "I can do that. I can show you
your daughter's state."

"What's the price?"

"You."

"My soul?"

He laughed, a deep rumbling chuckle. His eyes flattened, and his hooky nose grew more prominent. "A
shapeless drift of smoke? I want you. Hands and
head."

"There's the Truce."

"We know. That's not it."

"We?"

He lifted a hand, let it fall.

"Stone Oath binds you." Hallah slid along the
bench until she was near the end. "Only you."

"I and we"—he waggled his hand—"same thing. Up
to you. Yes or no?"

She was tired. That was bad. She got impatient and
reckless when she was tired. Take it slow, she told
herself. A step at a time. "One for one," she said
finally. "Find out for me how my daughter's doing,
and I'll cede you one service—your call. We can go
on from there."

"Done."

5
The last strands of the snare

Thonsane appeared at the alcove, waited without a
word until they slid from the booth, then led them up
the stairs at the end of the bar and into what at first
seemed an ordinary bedroom, perhaps a little cleaner
than most, lit by a single candle on a battered table
beside the bed.

When Thonsane pulled the door shut, the room changed.

The candle vanished. Points of light exploded about the dark undefined space, expanded into fist-sized globes that swam and bobbed about, clustering and moving apart like fireflies on a summer evening.

The walls were gone; trees marched to infinity on every side, merging in the distance into a murmuring darkness. A stream appeared from near where the door had been, spread into a pool, narrowed again and meandered on to vanish under the trees. Rowan trees bent over the pool, dropping their blossoms onto the quiet water.

There was the smell of woodlands, of grass and leaves and damp earth, punctuated by sharp peaks of pine and oak.

Aezel crouched on a hummock of grass, a wide shallow drum on his hairy thighs; grey-brown brindle hair, stiff, straight, and thick covered him from just below his ribs to the split hooves where his boots had been. He tapped at the drum with nails like claws and drew an odd, whispery rattle from the parchment head.

Thonsane laughed; it was a wild, eerie sound, deep-throated, frightening, and disconcertingly infectious.

Hallah turned.

Like Aezel, Thonsane had shed her clothes. Her hair was loose, long black tresses shifting about her body as she moved. Wide curving horns spread from her temples, alabaster horns glowing like the crescent moon.

"Look into the pool and think of her," Thonsane said, her voice a braiding of echoes.

Hallah shivered. They were showing her too much. She felt trapped. Stone Oath, that was her anchor, her one point of stability, and she clung to it as she took the two steps to reach the water. She was going to kneel, changed her mind, and squatted.

Something like a breeze brushed past her face and blew ripples on the pond, sending the rowan flowers scooting to the far bank. The water steadied, smoothed into a mirror.

She saw a bedroom with narrow windows set high in the walls and alabaster lamps sending out soft yellow light.

A woman was stretched out on a divan, propped up by pillows. She was sipping from a heavy, opaque glass, her face flushed, her coppery hair straggling loose from the elaborate braided crown she'd worn to the Oath Swearing. When the glass was empty, she fumbled among the pillows, pulled out a square bottle, and filled it again, tilting the bottle and shaking it to get out the last drops. She gulped at the liquid, shuddered, coughed, went back to sipping.

A door opened and a girl came in, a tall, tender girl still on the child's side of puberty, with red-gold hair fairer than the woman's hanging down past her waist.

Hallah gasped, closed her hands into fists. Her daughter's daughter. !Maytre!

The girl stopped, clamped her wide mouth into a grim line as she saw Rowanna. "You promised," she said, her voice trembling, angry. "You said you wouldn't. He'll do it, you know he will. You want to get put out the door?"

Rowanna's hand started shaking, spilling the liquor on her hand. She set the glass on the table beside the divan, spilling more in the process. "You—" she cleared her throat, wiped her mouth—"you don't understand, Bree. Baby . . ." She started crying, held out her hand. "Baby, he's going to . . ." The girl didn't move, so she pulled her hand back, got clumsily to her feet, and stood swaying. "He's sold you, Briony."

"What?"

"He told me this morning. He dangled you on the ship, and the Vramheir took the bait. The Bridegroom." She laughed unsteadily. "Don't you think that's funny, Bree? All the way from the Pearl Isles to meet his bride, and he picks up a trinket for himself on the way."

The breeze blew again and broke the mirror.

A moment later the bedroom was back. Aezel was sitting on the bed looking tired and sleepy, Thonsane was standing with her arms folded, her back against the door. Hallah Myur got to her feet.

Aezel cleared his throat. "Was it enough?"

"Yes. What do you want from me?"

He smiled, the wrinkles of his face spreading and sliding back. "We can look into the Toyaytay if we're careful, but we can't get past the Curse." He shrugged, spread his hands. "And there's no one we could trust who's inside right now. We want you to carry something to the Yih Ma'yin Sa'aetinn."

"Is she apt to scream at shadows?"

"No. She has asked a question. She awaits an answer."

"Do you have a plan of the Toyaytay or must I jump blind?"

"We have. You'll see it."

I'm a fly in a spider's web, she thought, and I can see only a little of it. I don't like this. Do I have a choice? No. "One for one," she said aloud. "That was a joke, wasn't it. !Maytre! I'm a fool. Let it be done. Hands and head. If you get my daughter out of there, and my daughter's daughter, and swear to keep them safe and in comfort, I swear by Stone I will serve you till my life's end."

"And if we ask you to do something you don't like?"

Hallah laughed. It was a hard unhappy sound. "Considering how I've earned my bread, there's not much I find beyond me. Distasteful, yes, impossible no." She moved impatiently, clasped her hands behind her. "I'm not a puppet to dance to your strings; if you want work done well, you'll let me do it my way. Set me goals and turn me loose."

"There might be complexities that can't be explained, complexities that require a certain style of act."

"Tchah! You couldn't choose a needle to pry up a stone. Use me right and the job is done, wrong and I break and ruin the work."

"Yes. I see. Speaking of ruin, you have a choice before you, Hallah Myur. Pay Membruda's Son for what he's done to you or bring your daughter out. You can't do both." He held up his hand to stop her protest. "We aren't being arbitrary; it's a matter of what we can do, not what we want."

Hallah stared past him at the dull grey wall, shadows from the candle dancing on it. "Membruda's son," she said softly. "As a matter of abstract justice, the blat needs his throat cut." She shook her head, wiped her hands down her sides. "He's gas on the belly; one fart and he's gone." She managed a small smile. "My daughter's more important. So. Show me the plan of the Toyaytay and let's get started."

6
The first delivery

Feltsoled busks groping for a toehold, Hallah Myur wriggled backward through the small window over her cot. She found one of the cracks between the courses of stone she'd seen from the outside, worked the rest of her clear, and started moving cautiously along the wall.

Clouds were thickening across the face of the moon, and she could smell damp on the air; she spent a thought on hoping it wouldn't rain until she got down, then concentrated on working around the nearest cor-

ner and up the turret wall. When she reached the roof,
she rolled over the parapet and went swiftly along it,
bent over to keep her head from showing, until she
came to the lacy iron spires that marked the family
gardens of the Alayjiyah.

She pulled on her leather palms, caught hold of the
top crossbar, and swung over, then went cautiously
down the wall, shifting from crevice to crevice, dropping the last dozen feet into the soft loam of a flower
bed. She scratched the earth over the marks of her
busks, rearranged the flowers, then flowed along the
wall until she reached a window.

"I mean no harm to anyone within," she whispered
before she touched it. "I am only a messenger."

Say that to yourself and to the air, Aezel told her.
Over and over. And believe it. And the Curse will
slumber while you work.

A slide and wiggle of a thin blade took care of the
catch; she eased the casement open and slipped inside.
For several breaths she stood listening intently while
her eyes adjusted to the increased darkness. No problem. Aezel was right. Once she was past the outer
walls of the Toyaytay, there wasn't much security to
worry about. Except the Curse. Always excepting the
Curse. She crossed the room, a sewing room the plan
called it, charging the blowpipe with black kumunda
dust as she moved.

"I mean no harm," she whispered to the dark. "I
am only a messenger."

She eased the door open a hair and pressed the
bulb. A moment later she heard a muted thump. She
nodded, pressed filters into her nostrils, and left
the room.

She stepped over the last guard, tried the door.
Locked.

She ran her fingers around the latch, located the

lock plate—and the key protruding from it. Key on the outside. !Maytre! Joyful betrothal, this. I begin to smell a pattern. She turned the key and eased the door open, slipped inside, collapsing the blowpipe and sliding it into a pocket.

The Yih Ma'yin's breathing came soft and steady from behind curtains yellowed by the glowcandles on the bedstead. Her busks soundless on the stone floor, Hallah hurried across the room, pushed aside the bed curtains, and bent over the sleeping girl.

The Yih Ma'yin had her father's nose, which was not a blessing, but she'd found the rest of her bones in another place; and while she wasn't pretty, Hallah suspected she was attractive enough when she was awake. She slept clenched in a knot. Stubborn, angry maiden, ready to run from a wedding she didn't want. Hallah pressed her palm over the girl's mouth, pinched her earlobe. "Wake up," she whispered. "I'm sent by friends. You know who."

The Yih Ma'yin's eyes snapped open, and she managed a nod, her head moving under Hallah's hand.

"Don't say anything, just listen." Hallah took her hand away, peeled the spelled khihy leaves from the small white pebble Aezel had given her. "Put this in your mouth and walk out. No one will follow you. The taste's the guide. Sweet means you're on trail, sour means you've strayed. It'll take you where you want to go." She set the pebble in the Yih Ma'yin's hand, folded her fingers over it. "Count twenty after I'm gone. Safer for you that way, less chance guards or a curseman will light on you by accident. Oh yeah, here's your door key." The Yih Ma'yin's eyes glinted as Hallah dropped it on the bed. "Lock the door and leave the key in it, maybe they'll think you're still inside."

Hallah Myur left, pulling out the sections of the blowpipe as she went, chanting Aezel's litany under her breath: I mean no harm, I am only a messenger. Around the litany she thought: It's going to be one holy mess when they find her among the missing. !Maytre! And on my head. Weasel face'll make sure of that.

A guard stood at the entrance to the GuestHouse, but a puff of kumunda dust sent him folding gently to the floor.

"I mean no harm, I am only a messenger."

Hallah Myur hauled him up, propped him against the wall, his iron-bound batoule laid across his thighs. With a little luck, he'd wake confused and keep quiet about his lapse; guards who slept on duty got nine stripes from the kou and swelled like blowfish from the nettle soup the lash was soaked in. She'd seen it often enough. Kihyayti'an was fond of applying kou discipline to anyone who annoyed him.

She slipped inside, moved swiftly and silently through the maze of halls until she reached the suite where the Membrudas were staying. The lamps had burned low, some of them were out in this back-of-behind area of the GuestHouse, and there were no Toyaytay servants about. The guests out here were barely important enough to be invited; they certainly weren't going to be cosseted at the Alayjiyah's expense.

Her mouth twitched into a smile as she knelt and inspected the lock. Membruda's Sons must be sore as snag teeth at treatment like this. "I mean no harm, I am only a messenger." She inserted a pick into the lock and began feeling for the wards.

When she was in, she stood for a dozen breaths with her eyes closed to regain her nightsight, then went looking for her daughter and her daughter's daughter.

7
The second delivery

Briony lay curled up on a pallet in a cramped cubicle with three serving maids; she slept like a small neat kitten, her mouth opening and closing in tiny sucking movements, her hands kneading at the pallet.

Hallah edged past the maids and knelt beside the child. "I mean no harm, I am only a messenger." Once again she peeled a pebble—a grey one striped with black—from its khihy leaves, then slipped it into Briony's mouth, easing it under her tongue. "Come," she murmured. "Come away, come away, baby." She shivered as she took Briony's hand. It was small and hot and a little sticky. She pushed away the things it made her feel and eased the spelled child onto her feet, led her out the door.

It will be as if they walk in their sleep, Aezel said; keep them calm, talk to them as you would a fractious horse, and they'll follow wherever you lead. But be quick about it. These ca'o'in aren't like the Yin Ma'yin's ca'o. They could trip alarms if the cursemen are awake enough. So hurry.

"Wait," she murmured when she reached Membruda's bedroom. "Wait until I call you, Briony."

"I mean no harm, I am only a messenger." She peeled the leaves from the last pebble, pushed it into her daughter's mouth, wrinkling her nose at the stink of black rum. "Come," she whispered. "Come away, baby. Follow and be free."

She stepped back, watched Rowanna crawl clumsily from the bed. No clothes. !Maytre! It only needed that. "Stay, baby," she said. "Stand there while I . . ."

Ardamoar grunted, mumbled, and groped about for Rowanna, not awake yet, but close . . .

Hallah ran on her toes around the bed, laid her sap neatly alongside his head, muttering, "I mean no harm, I am only a messenger." He grunted again, went limp. Hastily she thrust her fingers under his jaw, relaxed as she felt the pulse beating strongly. "Wait. Be quiet. No need to fuss." She darted around the bed again, heading for a chest by the door and almost tripped as her foot caught in a pool of cloth. She swept the thing up, shook it out. Bedrobe. Thick wool and dark. No wonder I didn't notice it. !Maytre! it's amateur time . . .

Rowanna was more than three spans taller than she, but she got the robe over her daughter's head, her arms in the sleeves, and tugged her down so she could tie the lacings at the neck, her fingers faltering as memories fought to surface. She forced them down and finished the job. "I mean no harm," she murmured again, "I am only a messenger. Good. You'll do for now. Come, baby, come, follow me, come, sweetee, Mama's going to take you home . . ."

There was tension in the air as she tolled the two through the hallways of the GuestHouse. The Curse was stirring, they were an irritant inside it. She hurried as much as she dared, murmured words flowing in a muted stream to draw the sleepers after her.

Yawning and scratching her head, a maid stepped into the hall just as Hallah came ghosting along. The girl gaped, started to yell, collapsed in a heap on the floor as Hallah used the sap again.

Witnesses everywhere! !Maytre's Nails! even when I was a greenling, I never laid a trail like this.

"As soon as you're out," Aezel had said, "go straight east through the Gardens until you reach the river. We'll be waiting for you there."

"Come, babies, come, steady now, step and step,

one foot swings, the other follows, come babies come . . ." Hallah Myur had no magic in her, only dry precision and an obsession with detail, but it didn't take magic to smell the Curse or feel it seeking them. A long time ago, just after she'd started Guild training, she'd been trapped underground with a huge cave spider, white as death and blind. She'd never forgot the way it turned and turned on those hideous white legs, searching for her.

They moved through the heavy, oscillating shadow beneath the trees, shadow broken by the tall lamps set at intervals throughout the Garden. "Come along, babies," Hallah murmured. "Quiet and quick, come along, babies, come ah come . . ."

The pressure from the Curse grew stronger; the air was thick with the stink of threat. The bubble was close to popping. Any minute, something could happen . . .

Hallah Myur rounded a large thorny bush, whipped up the blowpipe, and puffed the black dust at the curseman before he got his bones lifted; in almost the same move, she flung a waxy breakstone at his middle. It caught him in the diaphragm, knocked the wind out of him, forced him to breathe in the dust.

The Curse twanged.

Hallah swore and dropped to her knees as a sudden gust of wind blew the cloud of dust back at her. She switched ends and scrabbled for Rowanna, but she was too late. Her daughter got a whiff of dust and folded gracefully to the grass. Briony was off to one side and farther away; the backblow missed her.

The twanging increased enormously, the soundless sound hammered at Hallah. Briony trembled, blinked blind, blank eyes. She started away, hands groping before her.

The drums in the drum tower began sounding. Men were shouting; there was the clank of metal on metal.

"!Maytre!" Hallah ran after the girl, brought her back to Rowanna's limp body. "Stay there." She caught hold of Rowanna's wrists, hauled her up until she was sitting. Grunting and straining, she got her daughter over her shoulder and staggered to her feet. She bent her knees, straightened, bouncing her daughter on her shoulders, shifting the weight to a marginally better balance. "Come along, baby," she sang, and reached for the child's hand. "Come, baby, come with Mama and Gramma, come baby, come . . . gods, daughter, you weigh a ton, come, baby, come, easier to carry you last time we were together, come, baby, come, I wish, I don't know what I wish, come, baby, come, quiet and quick, sweet and saucy, come, baby, come . . ."

The smell of the garden changed to the wild forest odors she remembered from the tavern bedroom. Grey-white forms flitted through the trees; elongated and eerie, they circled around her. She kept moving and tried to ignore them.

The drums grew muted, all sounds were muted, the trees turned translucent and insubstantial; she might have been moving through a dream.

Her knees hurt, her back hurt, she was straining for breath, sweat dripped into her eyes, and the dream went on and on; she didn't know how long, time was elsewhere.

Aezel stepped through the ring of shades. He lifted Rowanna from Hallah's shoulder, cradled her in his arms, her red hair like a fall of fire. He smiled. "It's only a few steps more."

8
Fly on a long leash

The river flowed around the sandy spit, silent and powerful, black ink in the clouded moonlight. A single oak leaned out over the water, roots exposed, the earth washed away on the riverside. Rowanna lay on the sand; Briony stood beside her.

The moonwraiths wavered in the shadow of other trees, nervous pillars of mist, their features smudges of grey on curdled white.

Aezel and Thonsane stood together, hand in hand, spoke together. "Hallah Myur, you must be behind us. What comes is not for you."

Weary in body and mind, Hallah walked into the shadow of the oak. She lowered herself onto one of the roots, sat with her hands on her thighs, waiting for the thing to be finished.

Their braided voices riding on the rising/falling drone of the moonwraiths' *hum*, Aezel/Thonsane intoned, "You who walk the Dark Ways, I and I are the Opener of Doors, I and I call to you, O Sulkahayn, O Pathspinner. Open the GhostWay. I and I call to you. Show the DarkPath to this mother and child."

A knot of darkness deeper and blacker than the night expanded into a tall oval, and a path black on black shone without light.

Hallah shivered as Rowanna rose to her feet and with Briony turned to face the Door.

"The Way is open," Aezel/Thonsane sang. "Go into it."

Rowanna and Briony stepped into the dark and glided away.

Hallah watched, thumb rubbing nervously across her fingers; it seemed to her they took only a single step, then they were out the far side, standing on a mountain slope in early morning sunlight, looking down into a valley filled with springtime. A small neat village was tucked into a bend of a blue, bouncing river winding through the valley. Smoke rose from the chimneys, and children were bringing in cows for the morning milking.

A tall woman stepped from behind a tree, held out her hand to Rowanna, spoke. Hallah couldn't hear the words, but she could see Briony smiling.

The Dark Way closed.

The wraiths faded into the trees.

Thonsane left without speaking.

Aezel came to squat beside her. "Is it well-done, Hallah Myur?"

"I suppose. They'll be cared for?"

"Yes. Did you want to go with them?"

"No. What I am, I'm not ashamed of it, but . . ." She shook her head. "What now?"

"There's a ship waiting out there"—he nodded at the river—"it's sending a boat for you. It'll take you to a city called Gorjo Xil. Wait there till we call you to service."

She thought briefly about asking him why he and his had worked to bring war on this land—because it would be war when the Vramheir of the Pearl Isles found his bride had run out on him—but she was too tired to care. "The Guild will be hunting me."

"There's gold waiting on ship; use it to dig yourself a hole."

Wearily she shook her head. "No hole would be deep enough. It'll take them awhile to sort things out, so I should be safe for a month or two. After that, I'll have to keep moving."

"We'll work that out." He touched her arm, stood. "The boat's here. It's time to go. Farewell, silver Hallah. We'll play again."

"I'd like that, gold Aezel." She gathered herself,

stood without touching the hand he held out, and walked down the sand to the boat with its dark oarsmen. Before she waded over to it, she turned, saluted him. "Farewell and take care," she called. "I will win one of those games. One day."

Wayfinder

Janny Wurts

In heroic and high fantasy, the questing hero has a
counterpart—the questing heroine, who seeks not only
help for her people, but a value for herself. Tough,
unselfish Sabin, apprentice to a hard life, is an excel-
lent example of the breed. But, as you might expect,
having set up that pattern, author Janny Wurts tran-
scends it, liberating Sabin to find her own way.

Ciondo had blown out the lanterns for the night
when Sabin remembered her mistake. Lately arrived
to help out on the sloop for the summer, she had
forgotten to bring in her jacket. It lay where it had
been left, draped over the upturned keel of the dory;
wet by now in the fog, and growing redolent of the
mildew that would speckle its patched, sun-faded
shoulders if someone did not crawl out of warm blankets and fetch it up from the beach.

The wind had risen. Gusts slammed and whined
across the eaves, and moaned through the windbreak
of pines that lined the cliffs. Winter had revisited since
sundown; the drafts through the chinks held the scent

of northern snow. The floorboards, too, were cold under Sabin's bare feet. She looked out through the crack in the shutter, dressing quickly as she did so. The sky had given her a moon, but a thin, ragged cloud cover sent shadows chasing in ink and silver across the sea. The path to the harborside was steep, even dangerous, all rocks and twined roots that could trip the unwary even in brightest sunlight.

Stupid, she had been, and ever a fool for letting her mind stray in daydreams. She longed to curse in irritation as her uncle did when his hands slipped on a net, but she dreaded to raise a disturbance. The household was sleeping. Even her aunt who wept in her pillow each night for the son just lost to the sea; Sabin's cousin, who was four years older than her undersized fourteen, and whose boots she could never grow to fill.

"A girl can work hard and master a boy's chores," Uncle Ciondo had summed up gruffly. "But you will never be strong enough to take the place of a man."

Yet the nets were heavy and the sloop was old, its scarred, patched planking in constant need of repairs. A girl's hands were better than going without, or so her mother insisted. Grudgingly, Uncle Ciondo agreed that Aunt Kala would do better if an empty chair no longer faced her through mealtimes. Sabin was given blankets and a lumpy cot in the loft, and cast-off sailor's clothing that smelled of cod and oakum, poor gifts, but precious for the fact they could ill be spared.

Her lapse over the jacket could not go unremedied. She fumbled and found her damp boots in the dark. Too lazy to bother with trousers, she pulled on the man-size fisher's smock that hung halfway to her knees. The loose cuffs had to be rolled to free her hands. She knotted the waist with rope to hold it from billowing in the wind, although in the deeps of the night, no one was abroad to care if she ran outside half-clothed.

The board floor squeaked to her step, and the outer latch clanged down as she shut the weathered plank door. "Sabin," she admonished as she hooked a heel on the door stoop and caught herself short of a stumble, "Don't you go tripping and banging, or someone will mistake you for trouble and shoot you in the back for a troll."

Except that no one in her village kept so much as a bow. The fisherfolk had only rigging knives and cutlery for the kitchen, and those were risky things to be throwing at trolls in the dark. Given any metal at all, and a troll will someday do murder with it; or so her mother used to threaten to scare out her habit of mislaying things. Sabin sighed at her failure, since her jacket was not hanging as it should to dry on the hook by the hearth.

Cloud cover smothered the moon. Past the garden gate, the trail to the sea plunged deep into shadow. She stubbed her toes on corners of slate, and cursed like a fishwife, since her uncle was not there to scold. The path switched back once, twice, in tortuous descent. Westward it was faced by sheer rock cliffs, moss-grown, and stuffed with old bird nests in the niches. The moon reemerged. The pines that clawed foothold in on the lower slope moaned in the lash of the winds, their trunks in stark silhouette against silver-lace sheets of spent breakers as they slid in fan curves back to sea. Sabin tossed tangled hair from her eyes. The night was wild around her. She could feel the great waves thud and boom over the barrier reefs even through the leather of her bootsoles.

A night to bring boat wrecks, she knew, the sea in her blood enough now that her ear had attuned to its moods. She hurried as the slate path leveled out and gave way at last to sand, ground of the same black stone, and unpleasant with chill in the dark. The last fringe of trees passed behind, and she started across the crescent beach. The moon went and came again. Out on the reefs, the high-flying spindrift carved up by the rocks tossed like the manes of white horses; great herds there seemed to be, galloping with arched necks, the surf roll became the thunder of churning hooves. Sabin forgot the folly of the daydreams that had forced her out of bed. As if someone's voice had addressed her, she stopped very still and stared. For a second the horses seemed *real*. There, the red flare of nostrils in the moon-whitened planes of wedged faces, and now, a ringing neigh on the wind that tore past her ears.

Impossible, she insisted, and yet—

A cloud scudded over the moon. Her wonder vanished, and she chided herself. There was nothing. Only the tide-swept sand of the beach and herself, a scarecrow figure of a girl with mussed hair and no sense, gawping at a span of wild waters. The village idiot knew horses did not run in the sea. Sabin shivered and felt cold. The dory lay beached above the tideline, a brisk walk distant up the beach. She turned that way, determined to fetch back her jacket without another lapse into silliness.

But before she had gone half the distance, something else caught her eye in the surf. Not a horse, but a dark clot of rags that at first she mistook for flotsam. Then the crest of a wave rolled it over, and she saw a man. He was floundering to keep his face above water, and only a hairsbreadth from drowning.

Fear and memory drove her. She spun and plunged into the sea. Cousin Juard had been lost to the waves, ripped from the decks of her uncle's boat during the fury of a storm. As the racking, retching coughs of the man who struggled reached her, she wondered if Juard had died as miserably, his body bent into spasms as the cold salt water stung his lungs.

Then the swirl of a comber cascaded over her boot-tops and foamed up around her chest, and her gasping shudder killed thought. The castaway born along by the tide tumbled under, and the weight of him slammed her in the knees.

She dropped, clutching at a shoulder whose shirt was all tatters, and skin underneath that was ice. As the rough sands scoured under her shins, she hooked his elbow, and braced against the drag of the ebb.

Her head broke water. Through a plastering of hair, Sabin huffed what she hoped was encouragement. "This way. The beach."

His struggles were clumsy. She labored to raise him, distracted by a chink of metal: iron, she saw in the flash of bared moonlight. He was fettered in rusted chains, the skin of both wrists torn raw from their chafing.

"Mother of mercy," she blasphemed. He had found his knees, an old man, white-haired and wasted of body. His head dangled with fatigue. She said, "Nobody could swim pulled down by all this chain!"

"Didn't," he husked; he had no breath to speak. He thrashed in attempt to rise, and fell again as the water hit and dashed in fountains around his chin.

She gripped him under his flaccid arms and dragged mightily. Despite her best effort, his head dipped under the flood. He swallowed a mouthful, gagging on salt, while she grunted in tearful frustration. The wave sucked back. He dragged his face free of its deadly, clinging currents with the dregs of his failing strength. His feet seemed fastened to the shoaling sands as if they were moored in place.

Belatedly suspicious, Sabin kept tugging. "Your ankles. Are they in irons also?"

He made a sound between a laugh, a sob, and a cough. "Always."

His floundering efforts managed to coordinate for a moment with hers. Together they stumbled a few yards shoreward, harried on by flooding water. Again the wave ebbed, and he sank and bumped against the sand. Panting, Sabin locked her fingers in his shirt. She held him braced against the hungry drag of the sea, desperate, while her heart raced drumrolls with the surf. Something was not quite right, she thought, her stressed mind sluggish to reason. The incoming tide carried no flotsam, not a stick or a plank that a shipwrecked man might have used to float his way ashore. "You never swam," she accused again, as he regained the surface and sputtered.

Weak as he was, her sharpness stung him. He raised his chin, and eyes that were piercingly clear met hers, lit by the uncertain moonlight. "I didn't." His voice held a roughness like harpstrings slackened out of tune. "I begged help from the seaborne spirits that can be called to take the shape of horses. They answered and drew me to land, but they could not see me safe. To lead one even once from the water dooms it to mortal life ashore."

The interval between waves seemed drawn out, an unnatural interruption of rhythm like a breath too long held suspended. Even disallowing for chains, his weight was too much for a girl; but it was a spasm of recognition like fear that locked Sabin's limbs and tongue—until those cut-crystal eyes looked down. As if released from bewitchment, she blurted, "Who are you?"

She thought the wind took her words. Or that they were lost in the grinding thunder of the sea as she scrabbled the last yards to dry sand. But when, safe at last, he collapsed in bruised exhaustion, he answered. "I am a wayfinder, and the son of a wayfinder." His cracked tone broke to a whisper. "And I was a slave for more time than I care to remember."

He spoke nonsense, she determined, and said so. He was a madman and no doubt a convict who had fled in the shallows to hide his tracks from dogs. A denial she did not understand closed her eyes and her heart against the logic that argued for him: that the road ran high above the cliffs, and those few paths that turned shoreward were much too steep for a captive to negotiate in chains. Had he come that way, he should have fallen, and broken his legs or his neck. Through teeth that chattered, Sabin waited. Yet the refugee stayed silent. She poked him in the ribs with her toe and found he had succumbed at last to the beating the sea had given him; either he slept or had dropped unconscious. The wind bit at wet flesh, made cruel by driven spray. The tide rose still, and the sand where he lay would very soon be submerged. Forced by necessity, Sabin arose. The jacket she had left on the dory would have to serve the old man as a blanket until Uncle Ciondo could be fetched from his bed.

Sabin awakened to sunlight. Afraid of her uncle's gruff scolding, she shot straight, too fast. The blood left her head. Dizziness held her still and blinking, and she realized: Uncle Ciondo *was* shouting. His voice drifted up through the trapdoor to the ladder, though he probably stood in the kitchen by the stove, shaking a fist as he ranted.

"A condemned man, what else could he be! Or why should anyone have chained him? Those fetters were not closed with locks. They were riveted. We cannot shelter such a man, Kala."

The castaway, Sabin remembered. She pushed out of bed, and tripped in her haste over the wet smock she had discarded without hanging last night. From the clothes chest she grabbed her only spare, and followed with the woolen britches every fisher's lad wore to sea. She left her boots. Even if they were not drenched and salt-stiff, they would make too much noise and draw notice.

Masked by the murmur of her aunt's voice, declaiming, Sabin set bare feet on the ladder. At the bottom, the door to Juard's room lay cracked open, beyond the stairwell, which funneled the bellow of her uncle's protest. "Kala, that's daft and you know it! He could be dangerous, a murderer. I say we send him inland in the fish wagon and leave his fate to the King's bailiff."

Sabin's uncle was not hard-hearted, but only a sailor, and the sea rewards no man for sentiment. Ciondo would care very little if the rescued man could hear the rough anger in his voice. But as a girl not born to a fisher's trade, Sabin flinched. She tiptoed down the hall and slipped through the opened door, a ghost with mousy, tangled hair and a sailcloth smock flocked at the cuffs with the rusty blood of gutted cod.

The man the sea had cast up was asleep. Chain lay on him still, looped at wrists and ankles with spare line that tied him spread-eagled to the bedposts. Ciondo had taken no chances, but had secured the refugee with the same half hitches he might use to hold a dory against a squall. Still, the undyed wool of the blankets hung half kicked off, as if the prisoner had thrashed in nightmares. His rags were gone. Daylight through the opened shutters exposed a history of abuse, from the salt-galled sores left by shackles to a mapwork of dry, welted scars. He was not old after all, Sabin saw, but starved like a mongrel dog. His skin was sun-cured to teak and creases, and his hair bleached lusterless white. He looked as weatherworn as the fishing tackle on the sloop's decks, beaten by years of hard use.

Aunt Kala's voice filtered through the doorway,

raised to unusual sharpness. "Ciondo, I'll be sending no man on to the bailiff before he finds his wits and tells his name! Nor will any needy stranger leave our roof hungry, the more shame to you for witless fears! As if anybody so starved could cause harm while bound up in metal chains! Now, be off! Go down to the beach with the rest, and leave me in peace to stir the soup."

A grumbling followed, and a scrape of boots on the brick. Few could stand up to Kala when she was angry, and since Juard's death, none dared. She was apt to weep when distressed, and if anyone saw her, she would throw cooking pots at them with an aim that could flatten a pigeon.

Cautious in the quiet after the door slammed, Sabin crept to the window. The sun threw slanting bars of yellow through gently tossing pines. Yet if the vicious, tearing winds had quieted, the sea mirrored no such calm. Beyond the spit off the point, the breakers still reared on the reefs, booming down in tall geysers of spray. The surge rushed on untamed, through the harbor gates where the round-bottomed boats rolled at anchor, an ominous sign. Sabin bit her lip. She squinted against the scintillant brightness of reflections and saw wreckage scattered amid the foam: the sundered masts and planking of ships gutted wholesale by the reefs.

No one had shaken her awake at dawn because today the twine would not be cast out for fish. When the wrecks littered the beach, men plied their nets to glean a storm's harvest from the waves. Custom barred girls and women from such labor, lest the nets bring up dead bodies, and the sight of drowned flesh sour the luck of their sons, born and unborn, and curse them to the horror that had befallen cousin Juard, to be taken alive by the sea.

The man on the bed had escaped that fate, just barely. He had come in on a ship that was now ripped

to fragments, Sabin knew for a surety. He had not
swam; not in chains. And horses did not run in the sea.
Unwilling to risk misfortune by looking too closely at
the waves, or what tossed and surfaced in the whiten-
ing tumble of foam, Sabin spun away from the window. She shivered in the sun that fell on her back,
and shivered again as she saw that the man on the
bed had awakened. He studied her, his eyes like fine
flawed crystal broken to a razor's edge.

"You do not trust me," he said in his rusty whisper.
He flexed one wrist, and immediately grimaced in
pain.

"My uncle thinks you're a murderer."

He ground out a bitter, silent laugh. "Oh, but I am,
though my hand has never taken life."

She frowned, a plain-spoken girl who dreamed, but
had always hated riddles. "What is a wayfinder?"

Riddles came back in answer, as he regarded the
beams of the ceiling. "One who hears the sea. One
who can read the earth. One who can travel and never
be lost."

"I don't understand." She stepped back, and sat on
the clothes chest that had once held the shirt she was
wearing, when it had been Juard's, and she had spent
days spinning thread for her father's loom. Now her
hands had grown horny and tough, and fine wool
would catch on the callus. But the incessant lapses of
attention had not left her; she forgot to mind sheet
lines as readily as she had faltered at spindle and
wheel. She curled her knees up and clasped her hands
to bury that recognition. "Anyone can be lost."

He stirred in the faintest impatience, jerked back
by the cut of his chains. "Inland to the east, there is
a road, a very dusty road with stone markers that
winds through a forest. Beyond lie farmlands, and
three villages, and lastly a trader's town. Beyond brick
walls are wide sands, called by the desert people who

live there Dei'eh'vikia." His head tipped sideways toward Sabin. His eyes now were darkened as gray sapphires, and he considered her as though she should be awed.

She was not. "You could have spoken to someone who passed that way," she accused. "Perhaps you lived there yourself." But she knew as she spoke that he did not. His vessel had broken on the reef, and never sought harbor in these isles. Few ships did, for the rocks gave hostile greeting to mariners from afar.

He looked at her in sadness or maybe pain, as if he had offered riches to the village halfwit who had use for no coin at all. He kept staring until she twisted her fingers together, embarrassed as if caught at a lie. For all his foreign accent, he *had* pronounced the place-name as crisply as the nomads who made the desert their home. Townsmen and traders slurred over the vowels and called it Daaviki, in contempt for the troublesome native speech.

He perceived that she knew this. He saw also that stubbornness kept her silent.

He looked at her still, his gaze heavylidded, almost glazed as a drunk's. The angle of his neck must have pulled at his shoulders and wrists, but he shed any sign of discomfort as he said, "Sabin, outside this room, there is a passage covered with braided rugs. It leads to a stairway that winds around itself twice. Downstairs, to the right of the kitchen lies a door that leads to a springhouse. Purple flowers grow by the path, and seven steps to the left lead to the sea cliff where there is a little slate ledge. You like to sit there on sunny mornings, in what you call your chair seat. But the people who inhabited these coasts before yours used the site as a shrine." His grainy voice was almost gentle as he finished. "They left carvings. You have seen them, when you scratched at the moss."

Sabin jumped up with her mouth opened like a

fish's. He had been carried into this house, unconscious. Ciondo had brought him through the front
door. Someone might have mentioned her name in his
hearing, but there was no way he could have seen the
springhouse, or have known of her fondness for that
ledge. Her aunt and uncle did not know, nor her own
mother and father.

"I am a wayfinder," he said simply, as if that sealed
a truth that she realized, shivering, could not be other
than magic. Her need to escape that room, and that
compelling, mesmerizing gaze came out in a rush of
speech. "I have to go, now."

The Wayfinder let his head fall back on the pillow.
At a word from him, she would have fled; she waited,
tautly poised on one foot. But he made no sound. He
closed his eyes, and curiosity welled over her fear and held
her rooted. "Still there?" he murmured after a while.

"Maybe." Sabin put her foot down, but quietly.

He did not open his eyes. "You have a piece of the
gift yourself, you know, Sabin."

She quivered again, as much from anger. "What gift!"

His hands were not relaxed now, but bunched into
white-knuckled fists. One of his sores had begun to
bleed from the pressure; he was trying her uncle's
knots, and finding them dishearteningly firm. "You
came to the beach at my call."

She stamped her foot, as much to drive off uneasiness. "You called nothing! I forgot my jacket. That
was all."

"No." His hands gave up their fretting. "You have
given your jacket as the reason. But it was my call
that caused you to forget it in the first place. When I
asked the spirits for their help, you heard also. That
was the true cause of the forgetfulness that drew you
outside in the night."

"I've been scolded for carelessness all my life," she
protested, "and my jacket was forgotten at twilight!"

"And so at that hour I called." He was smiling.

She wanted to curse him, for that. He seemed so smug. Like Juard had been when he teased her; and that remembrance called up tears. Sabin whirled violently toward the doorway and collided headlong with her aunt.

"Sabin! Merciful god, you've spilled the soup." Kala raised the wooden tray to keep it beyond reach of calamity, and her plump face dimpled into a frown. "What are you doing here anyway? A sick man has no need for prying girls."

"Talk to him," Sabin snapped back. "He's the one who pries."

"Awake, is he?" Kala stiffened primly. She glanced toward the bed and stopped cold, her chins sagging beneath her opened mouth, and the tray forgotten in her hands. For a moment she seemed to breathe smoke as she inhaled rising steam from the soup bowl.

Then she exploded. "My fool of a husband! Rope ties! The cruelty and the shame of it." She stepped sideways, banged her tray down on the clothes chest, and in a fit of total distraction, failed to bemoan the slopped soup. "Sabin, run out and fetch our mallet and chisel." She added to the stranger on the bed, "We'll have you free in just minutes."

For an instant, the Wayfinder's cut-crystal eyes seemed to mirror all of the earth. "Your goodman thinks I'm a murderer."

"My goodman is a fool who thinks in circles like a sand crab." Kala noticed that Sabin still lingered in the doorway. "Girl, must you always be idling about waiting for speech from the wind? Get along! Hammer and chisel, and quickly."

Kala had matters well in hand before the last fetter was struck. "You're taking up no space that's needed," she insisted with determined steadiness. "Juard's bed is yours, he's dead and at rest in the sea, and if you care to lend a hand at the chores, we could use the help, truly. Sabin belongs home with her family.''

She ended with a strike of the mallet. As the last rivet sheared away, and rusted metal fell open and clanged in a heap on the floor, the Wayfinder raised his freed wrists. He rubbed at torn skin, then looked up at Kala, who stood over him gripping the tools with both fists braced on broad hips. In profile, Sabin saw the stranger give her aunt that same, heavy-lidded gaze that had earlier caused her the shivers.

"He's not lost, your Juard," the broken voice announced softly.

Kala went white. She dropped the tools with a clatter and clapped her palms behind her back to distract bad luck, and avert the misfortune of hearing false words. "Do not spin me lies! Respect our loss. Ill comes of wishing drowned men back from death, for they hear. They rise in sorrow and walk the sea bed without rest for all of eternity.''

The Wayfinder cocked up his eyebrows in sad self-mockery. "I never lie. And no such lost spirits walk the sea, nor ever have." At Kala's shocked stiffness, he thumped his marred fist on the mattress in frustration. "Your boy is not dead, only washed up on a beach, as I was.''

Aunt Kala turned her back, which was as near to an insult as anyone ever got from her. The Wayfinder glared fiercely, his ice-gray eyes lit to burning. Then his jaw hardened until the muscles jumped and his speech scraped out of his throat. "Your son fetched up on the Barraken Rock, to the west. At this moment, he is gutting a fish with a knife he chipped from a mussel shell.''

"My son is dead!" Kala snapped back. "Now say no more, or when Ciondo comes back, you will go trussed in the wagon to the bailiff's. I'll hear your word."

The Wayfinder sighed, as though sucked down in a chasm of weariness. "Woman, you'll get no word from me, but neither will you hear any, either, if that is your desire."

"It is." Kala stamped out through the doorway without looking back. "Sabin," she yelled from the threshold at the head of the stairwell. "You'll see that yon man eats his soup, and bring down the tray when he's finished."

But Kala's bidding was impossible to carry out, Sabin found. On the bed, the Wayfinder had closed his eyes and fallen deeply asleep.

The house stayed quiet for the rest of the morning, with Kala beating quilts with a ferocity that outlasted the dust. At noon Uncle Ciondo returned from the beach, swathed in dripping oilskins, his boots caked to the ankles with damp sand. The bull bellow of his voice carried up through the second-storied window where Sabin kept vigil with the invalid. "Kala! Where is that man?"

The thwack of the broom against fabric faltered. "Where else would he be, but in bed? The shame on you, Ciondo, for leaving him trussed like the felon he certainly isn't." Smack! went the broom at the quilts.

When only the cottage door hammered closed in reply, Sabin gripped her knees with sweaty hands. She all but cowered as her uncle's angry tread ascended the stairs; bits of grit and shell scattered from his boots and fell pattering against the baseboards as he hurried the length of the hall. The next instant his hulking shoulders filled the bedroom doorway, and his sailor's squint fixed on the empty shackles that lay where they had fallen on the floor.

"Fool woman," he growled in reference to his wife. He raised hands scraped raw from his labors with net and sea, and swiped salt-drenched hair from his temples. Then he noticed Sabin. "Out, imp."

Her chin jerked up to indicate the man on the bed. "I found him."

"So you did." Ciondo's grimness did not ease as he strode closer, but he did not send her away. Sabin watched as he, too, met the uncanny gaze of the stranger who had wakened again at the noise. The sword-edged clarity of that stare arrested her uncle also, for he stopped, his hands clenched at his sides. "Do you know that all morning we have been dragging in bits of burst ships? Not just one, but a fleet of them."

The Wayfinder said a touch tartly, "Karbaschi warships."

"So you know them." Ciondo sighed. "At least you admit it." His annoyance stayed at odds with his gesture as he noticed his boots, and the sand left tracked in wet clumps. Hopeful as a miscreant mongrel, he bent and scuffed the mess beneath the bed where Kala might not notice. He dusted his fingers, ham-pink and swollen from salt water, on the already gritty patches of his oilskins. "You were a criminal? Their prisoner perhaps?"

The Wayfinder's lip curled in a spasm of distaste. "Worse than that."

Ciondo straightened. "You'd better tell me. Everything. Our people fear such fleets, for where they go, they bring ruin."

The man propped up by the pillows seemed brown and wasted as stormwrack cast up and dried on the beach. In a whisper napped like spoiled velvet, he said, "I was their Wayfinder. Kept bound in chains to the flagship's mast, to guide them on their raids. When I refused to see the way for their murdering, or led them in circles at sea, they made sure that I suffered. But by the grace of your kindness, no more."

Uncle Ciondo's square face looked vacant with astonishment. "You!" He took a breath. *"You?* One of the *in'am shealdi,* the ones who are never lost? I don't believe it."

"Then don't." The Wayfinder closed his eyes. His lashes were dark at the roots, and bleached white at the tips from too much sun. "Your wife named me liar also."

"Storm and tide! She'll fling any manner of insult at a man, if she thinks it will help make him listen." Ciondo shifted stance in disgust. "And I did not say you spoke falsehood, but only that I can't believe you."

At this, the Wayfinder's eyes flicked open. Though he tensed no muscle, Sabin felt warning charge his presence that swept the room like cold wind. "Is it proof you want? You shall have it. Leave me blindfolded on any of your fishing sloops, and give me the tiller, and I will set you an accurate course for the spit called the Barraken Rock."

"A wager?" Ciondo covered uneasiness with a cough. Thoughtfully, he added, "The trial would have to be at night, or the sun on your face might guide you."

"Be it night, or in storm, I care very little," the Wayfinder challenged. "But if I win, I'd have your promise: not a word of my gift shall go beyond this village. Your King, if he found me, would send me back as a bribe to plead for an exemption from tribute. Greedy traders anywhere would sell the secret of my survival. The Karbasch make unforgiving masters. If they learned I still lived, a warrior fleet would sail to collect me, and killing and looting would follow. If your people have no riches to adorn Karbaschi honor, your houses would burn, and your daughters know the miseries of slavery."

Ciondo went pale, even to the end of his nose that

seasons of winds had buffed red. He stepped back from the edge of the mattress and sat without care for soggy oilskins on the cushion by the windowseat. "If you are *in'am shealdi*, then you steered those ships afoul of the currents. Was it you who set your Karbasch overlords on our reef to drown and then took your chance in the sea?"

The Wayfinder denied nothing, but regarded his wrists as if the weals dug by fetters could plead his testimony for him. A tight-drawn interval followed, broken at last by the rattle of pots in the kitchen; Kala had relented enough to oversee the noon meal. Her industry spoiled the quiet, and forced the Wayfinder to raise his burred voice to be heard.

"Men travel the land, but they do not hear it. They sail the waters, yet they do not know the sea. The Karbaschi warships carve paths of destruction, and the peoples they conquer grieve for slain husbands and sons. But where the Karbasch stay to settle, they bring cruelties more lasting than death to the flesh. The lands they rule will wither in time, because they are a race who take and give nothing back. Their habit of pillage has deafened them, until they plow up forests for fields and raise towns without asking leave. The rituals mouthed by their priests are empty of truth, and without care for the still, small needs of the earth." Here, the invalid lifted his wasted, leathery shoulders in a shrug. "*In'am shealdi* are actually guardians. We nurture the spirits that the Karbasch run over roughshod, because they love only the desires of humanity. It is such spirits that show me the way. If I call, they answer, though the Karbasch ruled my body as a man might course a hunting dog. The guidance given to me in trust was forced to ill-use, and inevitably brought the earth sorrow. The day came when I could not endure its pain, or my own, any longer."

The Wayfinder sounded wistful as he finished. "I expected to die in the sea. Since I did not, I should like very much to stay. To live simply, and make use of my talent very little. I wish for nothing beyond your leave to guide your village sloops back to anchorage each night for the rest of my life."

Secure in the belief she was forgotten where she sat on the clothes chest, only Sabin caught the half glance he flicked in her direction. As if his cracked voice informed her, she knew: because of her he begged sanctuary—because of the gift he claimed she shared; and not least, for the sake of Juard, *who was dead, who had to be dead, else magic and spirits were real and horses ran wild in the sea.*

If in truth such beauty existed, she would never shed the distraction of dreams, but helplessly become consumed by them until the small inattentions that cursed her grew monstrous and took over her life.

Spooked by strangeness that threatened to draw her like some hapless moth to a flame, Sabin sprang to her feet and fled. Out and through the hall she pounded, and on down the stair beyond. Kala called out as she passed through the kitchen, to say the noon meal was waiting. But the girl did not stop until she had left the house, and raced at reckless speed down the cliff path to the place she called her chair seat.

There she spent the afternoon, while the Wayfinder slept. She did not return for supper, though Kala called from the back door to say that their guest had risen for the meal. By that Sabin understood that her uncle had accepted the Wayfinder at his word; an outsider who spoke false might stay because he was ill and had need, but he would not be invited to table. One supposed that Kala and the stranger had settled their hostilities by not speaking.

At nightfall, when most folk gathered at the tavern,

the beachhead glittered with torches. Word had passed round of a wager, and every boy with the sea in his blood turned out to ask Ciondo's leave to man the sloop, never mind that the craft was handy and needed little crew. The commotion as boasts were made and shouted down, and lots were finally drawn to keep the choice fair, enabled Sabin to sneak past and hide under the nets in the dory. Certain she had not been seen, she peered out cautiously and saw the tight knot of men stepping back. They left the Wayfinder standing alone with black cloth muffling his head. He turned unerringly toward the tender that was Ciondo's. If his steps were unsteady due to weakness, the line he walked was straight. He crossed and found the thwart without fumbling, and spoke so no others could hear. "Your good aunt does not know where we sail. I never mentioned to your uncle that I know your cousin Juard to be alive. Before we arrive at the Barraken Rock, I give you the burden of telling him."

"Aunt Kala would curse you for putting your lies in my mouth," Sabin accused from under damp nets, the reek of which suddenly made her dizzy. She was trembling again, and that made her angry, for he sensed her fear, she was certain. She could feel those pale eyes burning even through their veiling of cloth as he said, "But you are not Kala. You are the child of a weaver, and your fears are not ruled by the sea."

"They are when I sit in a boat!" she snapped back, more like her aunt than herself.

He laughed in his broken, rasping way, and because there was no malice in him, she wanted to hit him or scream. Instead she shrank into a tight huddle. Light and voices intruded, and the boat lifted, jostling, to be launched. As the keel smacked the water, and blown spray trickled through her cocoon of nets, she tasted warm salt with the cold. Tears: she was crying. The man seemed so certain that poor, lost Juard still breathed.

Sabin felt the rampaging buck of the surf toss the dory over a swell. The alternative terrified, that her cousin had rightly drowned, and that this stranger who lured the people laughing to their boats to follow his blindfolded quest was a sorcerer who could swim in iron chains. They might rescue Juard, or else join him, leaving more bereaved families to weep and to curse at the sea.

Sabin rubbed the stinging cheek her uncle had smacked when he found her, and smacked again when she told what the Wayfinder had said of her lost cousin. While the wind shifted fitfully, slapping sails and stays in contrary gusts, and moonlight silvered the wavelets, she braced against the windward rail, away from the men by the binnacle. Their talk grew ever more sullen as Juard's fate was uneasily discussed, and shoreline and lights shrank astern.

"Nothing lives on the Barraken Rock but fishing birds that drink seawater!" cried Tebald over the wear of patched canvas. Young, and a friend of Juard's, his jutted chin and narrowed eyes were wasted.

Blind behind swaths of black rag, the Wayfinder stood serene before aggression, his thin hands draped on the tiller as if the wood underneath were alive.

Darru argued further. "Without a fresh spring, a castaway would perish."

"It has rained twice in the past week," the stranger rebuked. "Oilskins can be rigged to trap water, and the seabirds are plentiful enough to snare." Ciondo's spare smock flapped off his shoulders like an ill-fitting sail, the cuffs tied back to keep from troubling his sores. The linen bindings covering his wrists emphasized prominent bones; a man so gaunt should not have been able to stand up, far less command the muscle to mind the helm. But Sabin could see from where she stood that the sloop held flawless course. The wake carved an arrow's track astern.

Ciondo glowered and said nothing, but his hand strayed often to the rigging knife at his belt.

"We should put about and sail back," Tebald said.

Darru was more adamant. "We should let you swim back, stranger, for your lies."

The Wayfinder answered in the absent way of a man whose thoughts are interrupted. "If I prove wrong, you may kill me."

At this came a good deal of footshifting, and one or two gestures to ward ill luck. No one voiced the obvious, that they could kill him only if malfortune went elsewhere and they lived to make good such a threat.

The night wore on, and the stars turned. The wind settled to a steady northeast, brisk and coldly clear. Moonset threw darkness on the water, and the land invisible astern. Once, Darru repeated the suggestion that the wager be abandoned, that the sloop seek return by the stars. He spoke to Ciondo by the mainmast pinrail, but was answered in gruff-voiced challenge by the Wayfinder aft at the helm. "Would you take such a chance, just to keep Juard's doom a clear certainty?"

Darru spun in vicious anger, jerked back by Ciondo's braced hand. "Don't provoke him! He is *in'am shealdi*, or how else does he steer without sight? Find faith in the straight course he sails, or else give the decency of holding your tongue until you have true cause to doubt."

"Grief for your son has turned your head," Darru muttered, shrugging himself free. But he could not argue that lacking clear stars or a compass, no ordinary man could keep a heading hour after hour without mistake.

Night waned. Sabin slept through the dawn curled

against a bight of rope. She dreamed of waves and white horses, and the rolling thunder of troubled seas until Tebald's shout awakened her. "The Barraken Rock! Dead off our bow, do you see!"

She opened her eyes to a dazzle of sunlight, and the soured smell of seaweed beached and dried. "Juard," she whispered.

No one noticed. Ciondo stood as a man frozen in place by the foremast stay; the more volatile Darru gave back laughter and cried to his fellow crewman, "Where were you an hour ago when the spit rose out of the sea?"

"Sleeping," Tebald confessed. His awed glance encompassed the scarecrow figure who guided the tiller with a feather touch, and whose eyesight was yet swathed in cloth. The mouth that showed underneath seemed turned up in detached amusement. Tebald leaned down and ruffled Sabin's hair as he passed, his discomfort masked by a shrug.

Peevish and oddly unrefreshed, she tried a kick that missed at his ankle. "Don't do that. I'm not a little girl anymore."

Tebald ignored her as if she were a bothersome younger sister. To Ciondo he said, "The wager's won, I'd say. Your *in'am shealdi* should take off his blindfold. It's probably making him sweat."

"I said so," Ciondo admitted. With one hand fastened to the head stay, he kept his eyes trained on the rock that jutted like a spindle from the sea. "Tell him again if you want."

But with the arcane powers of the helmsman now proven, no one seemed anxious to speak. Sun glared like molten brass off the wet shine of the deck, and the sheet lines creaked under their burden of sail. The pitiless isolation of the sea seemed to amplify the wind and the mingled cries of seabirds that squabbled and flew above the rock. The deeper shout that was human seemed to rend the day's peace like a mortal blow to the heart.

On that gale-carved, desolate spit, splashing in seawater to the knees, a raggedy figure ran, dancing and gyrating to a paean of reborn hope.

"It's Juard!" Darru gasped. He glanced nervously back at the Wayfinder, ashamed for his unkind threats. Tebald at his side held his breath in wordless shock, and Ciondo just buried his face in his hands and let the tears spill through his fingers.

It was Sabin who moved to free sheetlines when the Wayfinder threw up the helm. While Tebald and Darru roused belatedly to set the anchor, the girl unlashed an empty bait barrel. She stood it on end by the sternpost, climbed up, and as the Wayfinder bent his head to receive her touch, she picked out the knots of his blindfold. The cloth fell away. Hair bleached like bone tumbled free in the breeze, and she confronted a face set level with hers that had been battered into pallor by exhaustion. The eyes no longer burned, but seemed wide and drugged as a dreamer's. Almost, she could plumb their depths, and sense the echoes of the spirits whose guidance had led without charts.

"You could hear them yourself, were you taught," the Wayfinder murmured in his grainy bass. Yet before those eyes could brighten and tempt her irrevocably to sacrifice the reality she understood, she retreated to a braced stance behind the barrel.

"The moment Juard can sail with his father, I'll be sent back home. Whether or not there are horses in the sea, I shan't be getting lost behind a loom." Her bare feet made no sound as she whirled and bounded off to help Ciondo, who was struggling in feverish eagerness to launch the tender by himself.

The sloop was met on her return by men with streaming torches. Juard's reappearance from the lost brought cries of joy and disbelief. Kala was fetched from her bed for a tearful reunion with the son miraculously restored to her. For Juard was alive; starved thin, his hair matted in tangles so thick they could only be shorn, and his skin marred everywhere with festering scratches that needed immediate care. The greedy sea had been forced to give back its plunder, and the news swept like fire through the village.

A crowd gathered. Children in nightshirts gamboled on the fringes, while their parents jabbered in amazement. The Wayfinder, whose feat had engineered the commotion, stood aloof, his weight braced against the stempost of a dry dory, as if he needed help to stand up. From farther back in the shadows, outside the ring of torchlight, Sabin watched him. She listened, as he did, to the noise and the happiness, and she alone saw him shiver and stiffen and suddenly stride into the press with his light eyes hardened to purpose.

He set a hand marked as Juard's on Ciondo's arm, and said, "No, I forbid this," to the fisherman who had been boasting the loudest. "You will not be repeating this tale to any traders, nor be offering my service to outsiders. This is my bargain for Juard's life."

Silence fell with the suddenness of a thunderclap. Surf and the snap of flame remained, and a ring of stupefied faces unfamiliarly edged with hostility. "Which of us made any such bargain?" shouted someone from the sidelines.

The Wayfinder's peaked brows rose. "Ciondo is my witness, and here is my warning. For yourselves, you may ask of me as you will. The guiding and ward of your fleet I shall do as I can; but let none beyond this village ever know that I am *in'am shealdi*. Say nothing, or sorrow will come of it."

Finished speaking, or perhaps too weary to stay standing, the Wayfinder strode out of the pack. He left all the village muttering and wondering as he moved in slow steps toward the path. On the chill sands outside the torchlight, Sabin watched him vanish in the darkness under the pines. She did not follow; nor did she feel moved to join the villagers. The waking dream had touched her. Curiosity no longer drove her to discuss the stranger Kala sheltered.

"Was he a felon, to want such secrecy?" one goodwife muttered from the sidelines.

Ciondo replied in indignation. "Does it matter?" Then good sense prevailed over argument, and Kala scolded the gawkers roundly for keeping poor Juard from his bed.

A month passed, and seven days. Juard recovered his health and returned to fishing on the sloop. The Wayfinder who had brought his recovery took a longer time to mend. Kala pressed food and comforts on him constantly, until he complained of her coddling. Unlike anybody else, she listened, and left him alone. His white hair grew out its natural color, a golden, honey-brown, until Sabin sitting in her chair seat on the cliffside could no longer pick him out from the villagers who manned the sloops. She saw him seldom, and spoke with him not at all. Winding the skeins of wool and stringing the looms in her father's craft shop in furious concentration, she avoided walking the beach. Since the night she forgot her jacket, she could not bear to watch the combers. She heard them, felt them, even indoors with her ears filled with the clack of shuttle and loom—the thunder of what might be hooves, and the tumble of white, upflung spray that pounded the beaches in procession. She swept cut threads from the floor, and helped her mother bake, and each night begged her sleep to show her silence.

It did not. She misplaced socks and tools, and once, let the fire burn out. The waking world came to seem as a dream, and herself, strangely separate, adrift. She was scolded more often for stargazing, and seemed more than ever to care less.

The Wayfinder laughed in the tavern at night, accepted, but with a reverence that marked him apart. Two boats he saved from ruin when storms caused shoaling off the reefs. Another smack was recovered with a damaged compass after squall winds blew it astray. No one knowingly broke the Wayfinder's faith, but his presence loomed too large to shelter. Sabin understood this, her hands fallen idle over wool she was meant to be spinning. She twisted the red-dyed fibers aimlessly, knowing: there were traders who had heard of Juard's loss, and who saw him back among the men. They asked questions. Driven by balked curiosity, they pressured and cajoled, and won themselves no satisfaction.

The silence itself caused talk.

Summer passed. The winds shifted and blew in cold from the northeast, and the fleet changed quarter to follow the shoals of fish. The looms in the weaver's shop worked overtime to meet the demand for new blankets. Sabin crawled into bed each evening too tired to blow out the lamp; and so it chanced that she wakened in the deeps of night by the blood-dim glow of a spent wick. This time no forgotten jacket needed recovery from shore. The restlessness that stirred her refused to be denied.

She arose, dressed in haste, and let herself out the back door. Lights still burned in the tavern, and a few drunken voices inside argued over ways to cure sharkskin. Sabin slipped past, down the lane toward her uncle's cottage. Once there she did not knock; every window was dark. Instead she went on down the cliff path. Her shins brushed the stalks of purple flowers, dried now, and rattling with seedheads in the change of season. Wind snatched her clothing and snapped at the ends of her hair. A wild night, yet again, the kind that was wont to bring wrecks. She completed the last, familiar steps to the chair seat, dreading what she might find.

The horizon was clearly delineated under a waning half moon. Clouds scudded past like dirty streamers, muddling the swells pewter and gray, and against them, like pen strokes in charcoal, an advancing forest of black masts. Where peaceful craft would have plied sails, this fleet cleaved against the wind, lashing up coils of foam beneath the driving stroke of banked oars.

War galleys, Sabin identified, though the Karbasch to her were just talk. The Wayfinder's secret was loose in the world, and his overlords returned now to claim him. Poised to run and rouse the town, Sabin found she could not move. Her flesh became riveted by a cry that had no sound, but ripped between the fabric of the air itself to echo and ring through her inner mind.

The vibration negated her scream of terrified surprise, and filled her unasked with its essence: that of rage and sorrow and mystery, and a wounding edge of betrayal.

Dizzied almost to sickness, she clawed at the rocks for a handhold to ward off a tumbling fall. The summons faded but did not leave silence. The grind of the sea overwhelmed her ears with a mauling crescendo of sound. Cowering down in the cleft of the chair seat, Sabin saw the sea roll back. It sucked in white arrows of current off the tide flats until slate, shingle, and reef were laid bare. Fish flapped in confused crescents across settled streamers of weed, and the scuttled, half-rotted hull of a schooner turned turtle with a smack in the mud. Fishingboats settled on their anchor chains, and townside, the bell in the harbormaster's house began steadily tolling alarm.

Faintly, from the cottage behind, Sabin heard her uncle's bellow of inquiry as the clangor aroused him from bed. Juard, also, would be tossing off blankets, and stumbling out with the rest.

Sabin did not move. She, who had been born in a village of seafarers, and should have been, *would have been,* one of them, could only stare with her joints locked immobile. She alone did not flee in blind concern toward the beach path to stave off the threat to the boats.

Had she gone, it would not have mattered; the chair seat offered an untrammeled view as the horses thundered in from the sea.

They came on in a vast, white herd, manes tossing, and forehooves carving up arcs of flying spray. The water swirled under their bellies and legs, and rushed in black torrents behind uncountable upflung tails. Wave after wave, they surged in, plowing up weeds and fish and muddy gouts of seabottom, and milling the shells of galleys and sloops into shreds and splinters as they passed. Spars of fishing smacks entangled with snapped-off oars and the dragon-horned timbers of Karbaschi shipwrights; the cries of warriors and oarsmen entangled in the flood mingled with shouts from the villagers who saw their fleet and that of the raiders become smashed to kindling at a stroke. The horses swept on in a boil of foam that boomed like a god-wielded hammer against the shore. Spindrift sluiced across the cliffs. Ancient pines shivered and cracked at the blow, and boulders broke off and tumbled.

Drenched to her heels by cold water, Sabin cowered down, weeping for the beauty of a thousand salt-white steeds that reared up and struck at the windy sky. And with that release came understanding, at last, of what all along had been wrong: her heart held no

sorrow for the terrible, irreversible destruction that
rendered her whole village destitute.

Lights flickered through the pines at her back, as
angry men lit torches. Shouts and curses carried on
the wind, and the tolling bell fell silent, leaving the
seethe of the seas a scouring roar across the reef.
Sabin pressed her knuckles to her face. The Wayfinder
was going to be blamed. This ruin was his doing, every
man knew, and when they found him, they would tear
him in pieces.

Pressed into her cranny by a weight of remorse she
could not shed, Sabin saw the wild horses swirl like a
vortex and turn. Back, they plunged into the sea that
had spawned them, leaving churned sand and burst
wood and snarled bits of rope. Amid the roil of foam,
a lone swell arose and broke; one mare spun away
and parted from her companions.

Sabin saw her stop with lifted head, as if she listened
to something far away. She tossed her mane, shedding
spray, then raised up one forehoof and stepped, not
into water, but most irrevocably, out onto wrack-
strewn sand.

Sabin cried out at that moment, as if some force of
nature wrenched her, spirit from flesh. Reflex over-
turned thought, and she was up and running inland at
a pace that left her breathless. Voices called out to
her as she reached the lane, people she knew, but she
had no answer. The torchlight in the market did not
slow her, nor the press of enraged men who gathered
to seek their revenge. Scraps of conversation touched
her ears and glanced away without impression—the
in'am shealdi and his vicious, unfair bargain—Juard's
life, in exchange for the livelihood of all the village.
Boats had been broken and sunk. Folk would starve.
The Wayfinder would be made to pay, made to burn;
they would pack him off in chains to rot in the dun-
geons of the King's bailiff. A hangman was too good

for him, someone yelled, his words torn through with the sounds of a woman's crying.

Sabin stumbled and kept going, past the cedar shingles of the wool shop where her mother stood on the door stoop. "Girl, where are you off to, there's salvage work to be done, and soup to be fixed for the men."

But the rebuke of her parent was meaningless, now, and had been for quite some time.

Deep darkness wrapped the hollow where the crossroads met the town and the lane led inland through forest. Sabin went that way, her lungs burning, and her eyes streaming tears. The terrible truth pursued her: she did not weep for loss. The village was nothing to her, its hold inexorably diminished since the moment she left a jacket on the beach.

By the stone marker on the hill above the market, the Wayfinder waited, as she knew he would. He sat astride a mare whose coat caught the moonlight like sea-foam, and whose eyes held the darkness and mystery of water countless fathoms deep. She tossed her head at Sabin's arrival, as if chiding the girl for being tardy, and her mane lifted like a veil of spindrift; subsided like falling spray.

The Wayfinder regarded Sabin gravely, the burning in his eyes near to scalding. "You heard my call," he said. "The mare came, and you answered also."

Sabin found speech at last. "You knew I would."

He shook his head, his unbleached honey-colored hair veiling his weatherbeaten face. "I wasn't sure. I hoped you might. Gifts such as yours are needed sorely."

The white mare stamped, impatient. She blew a salty, gusty snort. New tears welled in tracks down Sabin's cheeks, and she reached out trembling fingers and touched the shimmering white shoulder. It was icy as sea-water; magical and terrifying and beautiful enough to bring madness. The words she struggled to shape came out choked. "If the horse cannot return, then neither will I."

"You are both my responsibility," the Wayfinder admitted. "And will be, to the end of my days." He extended his hand, no longer so thin, but disfigured still with old scars. "You must know the Karbasch would have burned more than boats, and slaughtered and raped did they land."

Sabin felt as if she had swallowed a stone. "You spared the whole village, and they hate you."

He sighed, and the mare shifted under him, anxious to be away. "Oh my dear, it could not be helped. What is a boat? Or a man? New trees will grow and be fashioned into planks, and women will birth babies that age and grow senile and die. But just as this mare can't return to the waves, so an earth spirit that is maimed can never heal. The Karbasch shed more than mortal blood. I could not allow myself to be captured, however bitter the price."

"You could have died," Sabin said, her gaze transfixed by the horse.

And he saw it was not his exile, but the fate of the mare that she mourned. The two of them, man and girl, were alike to the very core.

A shout knifed the quiet, and torches shimmered through the trees. The mare stamped again, and was restrained by a touch as the Wayfinder said in measured calm, "I can still die. But you must know, the mare should be cared for. She is not of mortal flesh. If I give myself up, hear warning. Your talents will blossom with time. A horse such as this will draw notice, and the Karbasch will send another fleet. Their craving for conquest is insatiable as the ocean is vast, and *in'am shealdi* to guide them, most rare."

She made no move, and her rejection seemed to shatter his detachment. He lifted his head as the noise of the mob came closer. The edgy, unaccountable wariness that every offered kindness had not softened gentled very suddenly into pity. *"In'am shealdi,"* he murmured in the grainy, musical voice that had commanded the horse from the sea. "This mare left the water at my call, you are right, but her sacrifice was never made for me."

Sabin looked up, stricken. "For my life?" she gasped, "or my gift?"

"Both." His eyes were not cold. Inside the serenity lent by power lay a human being who could bleed. "If you treasure the beauty of the horses, heed this. We are the only ones who know their kind. Others see no more than surf and foam. It is our protection, Sabin, that keep this spirit-mare alive, our call that lends her substance."

The torches reached the crossroad, and light flared and arrowed between the trees.

"There he is!" someone shouted, and the note of the mob quickened like the baying of hounds that sight game.

To her dream-filled ears, the pursuers uttered no words, but made only a cacophony of vicious noise. The roll of the sea held more meaning, and from this time forward, always would.

Sabin grasped the Wayfinder's hand. Clinging as if to a lifeline, she let him pull her up astride the mare. As the villagers burst into the clearing, they lost their quarry in a half-glimpsed flash of white. The clearing resounded to what could have been hoofbeats, or the enduring thunder of a comber pounding the pebbles of the shore.

The Way Wind

Andre Norton

Andre Norton's imaginary Kingdom of Estcarp, surrounded by enemies, one foot in twilight, the other in the long night of defeat, has always struck me as the metaphor for a kind of patient courage: those who hold the gates, those who wait, those who hope, and those who guard not only against outward enemies, but against their own despair.

"The Way Wind" is a story of how the winds of change come to gatekeepers if their courage holds firm.

The crumbling walled fortress and the dreary, ragged town, which had woven a ragged skirt about it during long years, stood at the end of the Way Pass. It was named l'Estal, which in a language older than legend, had a double meaning—First and Last.

For it was the first dwelling of men at the end of Way Pass along which any traffic from the west must come. And it was also the end of a long, coiling snake of a road stretching eastward and downward to Klem, which long ago it had been designed to guard.

There could have been another name for that straggle of drear buildings also—End of Hope.

For generations now it had been a place of exile. Those sent from Klem had been men and women outlawed for one reason or another. The scribe whose pen had been a key used too freely, the officer who was too ambitious—or at times, too conscientious, the rebel, the misfit, those sometimes fleeing the law or ruler's whim, they came hither.

There was no returning, for a geas had been set on the coil road, and those of lowland blood coming up might only travel one way—never to return. There had been countless attempts, of course. But whatever mage had set that barrier had indeed been one of power, for the spell did not dwindle with the years as magic often did.

Through the Way Pass there came only a trickle of travelers, sometimes not more than three or four in a season. None of them lingered in l'Estal; there was that about the place which was like a dank cloud, and its people were grim of face, meager of livelihood.

During the years they had managed to scrape a living, tilling small scraps of fields they terraced along the slopes, raising lean goats and small runtish sheep, hunting, burrowing into the rock of the heights to bring out stores of ore.

The latter was transported once a year to a certain bend in the descending road, and there traded for supplies they could not otherwise raise—salt, pigs of iron, a few items of what was luxury to them. Then it was also that the Castellan of the fort would receive the pouch bearing the royal arms containing, ever the same, orders. And now and again there would be another exile to be sent aloft.

The trickle of travelers from the west were mostly merchants, dealers in a small way, too poor to make the long journey by sea to the port of Klem itself.

They were hunters with pelts, drovers of straggles of lean mountain cattle or sheep, small, dark people who grunted rasping words in trade language, kept to themselves, and finished their business as soon as possible.

Of the Klemish exiles, none took the westward road. If there was a geas set upon that also, no one spoke of such. It was simply accepted that for them there was only one place to be longed for, dreamed of, hopelessly remembered—that that lay always eastward.

There had been many generations of exiles, and their children had known no other place; yet to them l'Estal was not a home but a prison of sorts, and the tales told of the eastern land made of that a paradise forbidden, changed out of all knowledge of what it had been or was.

Still there was always one point of interest that stirred the western gate sentries each year—and that was the Way Wind. At the very beginning of spring, which came slowly and harshly in these gaunt uplands, a wind blew strongly from west to east, souring the pass, carrying with it strange scents. It might last a single day; it might blow so for three or four.

And by chance, it always brought with it some one of the western travelers, as if it pulled them on into the line of the pass and drew them forward. Thus, in a place where there was so little of the new and strange, the Way Wind farers were a matter of wager, and often time not only the armsmen at the gate but their officers and their women gathered, along with townspeople, when they heard the outer horn blast, which signaled that the wind herded a traveler to them.

This day there were four who stood on the parapet of the inner wall, not closely together as if they were united in their company, but rather each a little apart.

The oldest of that company, a man who had allowed the hood of his cloak to fall back so the wind lifted tuffs of steel gray hair, had the paler face of one who kept much indoors. Yet there was a strength in his features, a gleam of eye which that about him had not defeated, nor ever would. At the throat of his cloak was the harp badge of a bard. Osono he had named himself ten years before when he had accompanied the east traders back from their rendezvous. And by that name he was accepted, eagerly by the Castellan and those of his household.

Next to him, holding her own thick cloak tightly about her as if she feared the wind might divest her of it, was the Lady Almadis, she who had been born to the Castellan's lady after their arrival here. Her clothing was as coarse as that of any townswoman on the streets below, and the hands that held to that cloak were sun-browned. There was a steady look to her, as if she had fitted herself to the grim husk housing her.

At pace or so behind her was a second man. Unlike the other two he had no cloak, but rather dressed in mail and leather, sword-armed. But his head was bare also as he cradled a pitted helm on one hip. His features were gaunt, thinned, bitter, his mouth a mere line above a stubborn jaw—Urgell, who had once been a mercenary and now served as swordsmaster in the fortress.

The fourth was strange even in that company, for she was a broad-girthed woman, red of face, thick of shoulder. Her cloak was a matter of patched strips, as if she had been forced to sew together the remains of several such in order to cover her. A fringe of yellow-white hair showed under the edge of a cap covering her head. For all the poverty of her appearance, Forina had a good position in the town, for she was the keeper of the only inn, and any of the Way Wind brought would come to her for shelter.

"What is your wager, my lady?" Osono's trained bard's voice easily overreached the whistle of the wind.

Almadis laughed, a hard-edged sound which lacked any softening of humor.

"I, sir bard? Since my last two wind wagers were so speedily proved wrong, I have learned caution. This year I make no speculation; thus I shall not be disappointed again. Think me over-timid of my purse if you will."

Osono glanced at her. She was not looking toward him but rather down the wind road. "Lady," he returned, "I think you are over-timid in nothing."

After a moment she laughed again. "Bard, life in l'Estal makes for dull acceptance—perhaps that gives root to timidity."

"There is the priest." The observation from the mercenary cut through their exchange. He had moved forward, as if drawn by some force beyond his own understanding, to look down at the cluster of townspeople and guards by the gate.

"Thunur," Osono nodded. "Yes, that crow is well on the hop. Though if he tries to deliver his message to either herdsman or trader, he will not get the better of them. Shut-mouthed they are, and to all of them I think we are Dark-shadowed—they would listen no more to one of us than to the bark of a chained hound."

Urgell had put his hand to the edge of the parapet wall, and now his mail and leather gauntlet grated on the stone there. Chained hound, Almadis thought, proper term not only for such as this man, but perhaps for all of them. But then a Bard was trained in apt word choice.

"That is one as makes trouble—" Forina had come forward also on the other side of the soldier. "He has a tongue as bitter as var, and he uses it to dip into many pots. T'would be well to keep an eye on him."

Urgell turned his head quickly. "What stir has he tried to set, Goodwife?"

"More than one. Ask Vill Blacksmith what a pother made his sister sharp-tongue him. Ask of Tatwin why three of those snot-nosed brats he strives to beat learning into no longer come to his bidding, ask Solasten why she was pelted with market dung. Ask me why the doors of the Hafted Stone are now barred to him. A troublemaker he is, and this is a place where we need no one to heat old quarrels and pot new ones!"

"If he is a brawler, speak to the guard," Osono suggested. "But I think he is perhaps something even more to be watched—"

"What may that be?" The bard had all their attention now, but it was Almadis who asked that question.

"A fanatic, my lady. One so obsessed with his own beliefs that he is like a smoldering torch ready to be put to a straw heap. We have not an easy life here; there were many old hatreds, despairs, and these can be gathered up to fuel a new fire. Ten years ago, one of his nature arose in Salanika—there was such a bloodletting thereafter as the plains had not seen since the days of Black Gorn. It took full two seasons to quench that fire, and some brands still smoldering may have been scattered to blaze again—"

"Such a one as Thunur, you think?" Almadis demanded. "L'Estal has answers to such—have we not?" The bitterness in her voice was plain. "What are we all but outlaws, and we can exist only as we hold together." She did not turn her head, but she loosed one hand from her cloak hold and motioned to that dark, ill-fortuned spread of age-hardened timbers which surmounted the wall of the shorter tower. "That has borne fruit many times over."

"He has a following," Urgell said, "but he and they are under eye. If he tries aught with the western travelers, he will be in a cell within an hour. We want no trouble with them."

Certainly they could afford no trouble with the few who came the western road. Such wayfarers were their only real link with a world which was not overshadowed by the walls about them and the past which had brought them here.

The gray-robed priest had indeed been roughly jostled away from the gate. He was making small hops, for he was a short man, trying to see over the crowd before him the nature of the wayfarer who was now well within sight.

"It—it is a child!" Almadis was shaken out of her composure and came with a single step to stand beside the mercenary. "A child—! But what fate has brought her here?"

The wayfarer was slight, her bundle of travel cloak huddled about her as if it were intended for a much larger and stouter wearer. Hood folds had fallen back on her shoulders, and they saw hair that the wind had pulled from braids to fly in wisps about her face. She was remarkably fair of skin for a wilderness traveler, and her hair was very fair, though streaked here and there by a darker strand closer to the gleam of red-gold.

There was no mistaking, however, the youth of that slight body and those composed features. She walked confidently, and at her shoulder bobbed the head of a hill pony, still so thick with winter hair that it was like an ambling mound of fur.

Bulging panniers rode on either side of a pack-saddle. And that was surrounded in the middle by what looked to be a basket half covered by a lid.

Contrary to all who made this perilous way through the high mountains, the girl carried no visible weapons

except a stout staff which had been crudely hacked
from some sapling, stubs of branches yet to be marked
along its length. This was topped, however, with a
bunch of flowers and leaves, massed together. Nor did
any of them look wilted; rather it would seem they
had just been plucked, though there were yet no
flowers to be found in the upper reaches where reluc-
tant patches of snow could be sighted.

"Who—what—" Almadis was snapped out of her
boredom, of that weariness which overshadowed her
days and nights.

As the girl came to the gate, there was a sudden
change. The Way Wind died, there was an odd kind
of silence as if they all waited for something; they did
not know what.

So complete was that silence that the sound Osono
uttered startled them all.

"Who—what—?" Almadis turned upon the bard almost fiercely.

He shook his head slowly. "Lady, I have seen many
things in my time, and have heard of countless more.
There is said to be—somewhere in the western
lands—those who are one with the land in a way that
none of our blood can ever hope to be—"

The sentries at the gate seemed disinclined to ask
any questions. In fact they had fallen back, and with
them the townspeople withdrew to allow her a way
path. In their doing so, Thunur won to the front rank
and stood, his head stretched a little forward on his
lank neck, staring at her, his teeth showing a little.

Almadis turned swiftly but Osono matched her,
even extending his wrist in a courtly fashion to give
her dignity. Forina, closest to the stairway, was already
lumbering down, and behind them Urgell seemed as
eager to catch a closer sight of this most unusual
wayfarer.

They gained the portion of street just in time to

witness Thunur's up-flung arm, hear his speech delivered with such force as to send spittle flying.

"Witchery! Here comes witchery! See the demon who is riding in such state!"

The crowd shrunk back even more as there was a stir to that half-covered basket on the top of the pony pack.

"Fool!" Forina's voice arose in the kind of roar she used to subdue a taproom scuffle. For so large a woman she moved very fast, and now she was halfway between the slavering priest and the girl, who watched them both serenely as if she had no cause to suspect that she was unwelcome.

"Fool! That is but a cat—"

The rust-yellow head with pricked ears had arisen yet farther from within its traveling basket, and green eyes surveyed them all with the same unconcern as that of the girl.

But such a cat. One of those pricked ears was black, and as the cat arose higher in its riding basket, they could see that there was a black patch on its chest. There was such a certain cockiness about it, an air of vast self-confidence, that Almadis laughed; and that was a laugh that had no edge of harshness.

Her laugh was quickly swallowed up by a chuckle from Osono, and a moment later there sounded no less than a full-lunged bellow from Vill Blacksmith.

The girl was smiling openly at them all as if they were greeting her with the best of goodwill.

"I am Meg, dealing in herbs and seeds, good folk. These traveling companions of mine are Kaska and Mors—"

The hair-concealed head of the pony nodded as if it perfectly understood the formalities of introduction, but Kaska merely opened a well-fanged mouth in a bored yawn.

Now the sergeant of the guard appeared to have

recovered from the surprise that had gripped them all. He dropped his pike in a form of barrier and looked at the girl.

"You are from—, mistress?" he demanded gruffly.

"From Westlea, guardsman. And I am one who trades—herbs—seeds."

Almadis blinked. The girl had moved her staff a fraction. That bouquet of tightly packed flowers which had looked so fresh from above now presented another aspect. The color was still there but faded— these were dried flowers surely, yet they preserved more of their once life than any she had ever seen.

"There be toll," the pike had lowered in the sergeant's hold. " 'Tis a matter of four coppers, and there be a second taking for a market stall."

Meg nodded briskly. Her hand groped beneath her cloak and came forth again to spill out four dulled rounds of metal into his hand.

Those who had gathered there had begun to shift away. Since this stranger the wind had brought was going to set up in the marketplace, there would be plenty of time to inspect her—though she was indeed something new. None of her kind of merchant had entered l'Estal before in the memories of all.

Only Thunur held his place until the sergeant, seemingly unaware that he was close behind him, swung back the pike and the priest had to skip quickly aside to escape a thud from that weapon. He was scowling at the girl, and his mouth opened as if to deliver some other accusation when Urgell took a hand in the matter.

"Off with you, crow— You stand in the lady's way!"

Now the priest swung around with a snarl, and his narrowed eyes surveyed Almadis and the bard. There was a glint of red rage in that stare. But he turned indeed and pushed through the last of the thinning crowd, to vanish down one of the more narrow alleys.

"Mistress," the mercenary spoke directly to the young traveler. "If that fluttering carrion eater makes you trouble, speak up—his voice is not one we have a liking for."

Meg surveyed him as one who wished to set a face in memory. "Armsman," she inclined her head, "I think that here I have little to fear, but for your courtesy I give you thanks."

To Almadis's surprise, she saw Urgell flush and then he moved swiftly, leaving as abruptly as the priest had done.

"You'll be wantin' shelter," Forina said. "I keep the Halfed Stone—it be the trade inn."

Again Meg favored the speaker with one of those long looks, and then she smiled. "Goodwife, what you have to offer we shall gladly accept. It has been a long road and Mors is wearied. Our greatest burden has been his—sure foot and clever trail head that he has."

She reached out to lace fingers in the puff of long hair on the pony's neck. He gave another vigorous nod and snorted.

"If you have spices—or meadowsweet for linens—" Almadis had an odd feeling that she did not want this girl to disappear. A new face in l'Estal was always to be hoped for, and this wayfarer was so different. She had kept stealing glances at the bouquet on the staff. It seemed so real, as if, at times, it had the power of taking on the freshness it had had when each of those blossoms had been plunked.

"Your flowers, Herbgatherer, what art gives the dried the seeming of life?"

"It is an art, my lady, an ancient one of my own people. In here"—Meg drew her hand down the side of one of those bulging panniers, "I have others. They be part of my trade stock. Also scents such as your meadowsweet—"

"Then surely I shall be seeing you again, Herbgatherer," Almadis said. "A good rest to you and your companions."

"My lady, such wishes are seeds for greater things—"

"As are ill wishes!" Osono said. "Do some of your wares come perhaps from Farlea?"

Meg turned now that measuring look to the bard.

"Farlea is sung of, sir bard. If it ever existed, that was many times ago. No, I do not aspire to the arts of the Fair Ones, only to such knowledge as any herbwife can know, if she seeks always to learn more."

Now it was her turn to move away, following Forina. Kaska had settled down again in her basket until only those mismatched tips of ears showed. But there were those who had been in the crowd at the gate who trailed the girl at a distance as if they did not want to lose sight of her for some reason.

"Farlea, Osono? I think with that question you may have displeased our herbwife," Almadis said slowly. "You are a storer of legends; which do you touch on now?"

He was frowning. "On the veriest wisp of an old one, my lady. There was a tale of a youth who followed my own calling, though he was of a roving bent. He vanished for a time, and then he returned hollow-eyed and wasted, saying that he sought something he had lost, or rather had thrown away through some foolishness, and that his fate was harsh because of that. He had been offered a way into a land of peace and rare beauty, and thereafter he sang always of Farlea. But he withered and died before the year was done, eaten up by his sorrow."

"But what makes you think of Farlea when you look upon this herbwife?" Almadis persisted.

"Those flowers on her staff—fresh plucked." His frown grew deeper.

"So I, too, thought when first I saw them. But no,

they are rather very cleverly dried so that they are preserved with all their color, and I think their scent. Surely I smelled roses when she held them out a little. That is an art worth the knowing. We have no gardens here—the rose walk gives but a handful of blooms, and those are quickly gone. To have a bouquet of such ever to hand"—her voice trailed off wistfully and then she added—"yes, such could even fight the grim aging of these walls. I must go to the market when she sets up her stall."

Meg did set up her stall on the following day. From the market mistress she rented the three stools and a board to balance on two of them, to form the humblest of the displays. Mathe, who oversaw the trading place, watched the girl's sure moves in adjusting the plank to show her wares. He lingered even a fraction longer, though it was a busy day, to see her unpack bundles of dried herbs, their fragrance even able to be scented over the mixed odors, few of them pleasant, which were a part of market day.

There were packets also of yellowish, fine-woven cloth which gave forth even more intensified perfumes, and small, corner wrapped, bits of thin parchment such as were for the keeping of seeds. While in the very middle of that board was given honored place to that same bunch of flowers as had crowned Meg's trail staff.

Kaska's basket was set on the pavement behind the rude table. And Mors stood behind. The cat made no attempt to get out of her basket, but she was sitting well up in it surveying all about her with manifest interest.

Two small figures moved cautiously toward the stall. Beneath the grimed skin and the much-patched clothing, one face was the exact match of the other. Between them strutted a goat, each of his proud curl of horns clasped by a little, rough-skinned hand.

They proceeded slowly, darting glances to either side as if they were scouts in enemy territory. Only the goat was at ease, apparently confident in his ability to handle any situation which might arise.

"You—Tay—Tod—take that four-legged abomination out of here!" A man arose from the stoop behind one of the neighboring stalls and waved his arms.

The goat gave voice in a way which suggested that he was making a profane answer to that, and refused to answer to the force dragging at him from either side. The boys cowered, but it was apparent they had no idea of deserting their four-legged companion to run for cover.

Meg was on her feet also, smiling as if the two small herds and their beast were the most promising of customers. When her neighbor came from behind his own stall table, a thick stick in his hand, she waved him back.

"No harm, goodman," she said. "This beast but seeks what is a delicacy for his kind. Which he shall be freely given." She selected a stalk wrapped loosely around with its own withered leaves and held it out to the goat. For a moment he regarded her and then, with the neat dexterity of one who had done this many times before, he tongued the proffered bit of dried stuff and drew it into his mouth, nodding his head up and down, as if to signify his approval, with a vigor to near shake free the grip of his two companions.

The other tradesman stared, his upraised club falling slowly to his side. But there was a wariness in his look when he shifted his glance toward Meg, then he withdrew behind his own table, as if he wished some barrier against a threat he did not truly understand.

However, Meg paid no attention to him. Rather now, she reached behind her and brought out a coarse napkin from which she unrolled thick slices of bread with green-veined cheese between—the food she had brought for her nooning.

Two pair of small eyes fastened upon that, as she broke the larger of the portion in half, holding it out to the boys. Though they did not entirely loose their hold on the goat's horns, their other hands shot out to snatch what she held, cramming it into their mouths as if they feared that it might be demanded back.

"Tay—Tod." She spoke the names the man had spoken.

The one to her right gave a gulp that left him choking, but his twin was the quicker to answer. "I be Tod, lady—this be Tay."

"And your friend—" Meg nodded gravely to the goat, as if indeed the beast were a person of two-legged consequence.

"He be Nid!" There was pride in that answer such as a liege man might show in naming his lord.

"Well met, Tod, Tay, and Nid," Meg nodded gravely. "I am Meg, and here are my friends, Kaska and Mors." The cat only stared, but the pony uttered a soft neigh.

A valiant swallow had carried the food down, and Tay was able to speak:

"Lacy-lorn"— he gestured toward the bouquet of dried flowers—"But too cold now—" He shook his head.

"Lacy-lorn," Meg repeated with a note of approval in her voice, "and hearts-ease, serenity, and love-light, Kings-silver, Red-rose, Gold-for-luck, Sorrows end, Hope-in-the-sun—maiden's love and knight's honor, yes." The old country names came singingly from her as if she voiced some bard's verse.

"Bright—" Tod said before he stuffed his mouth with another huge bit.

"You see them bright?" Meg's head was cocked a little to one side. "That is well, very well. Now, younglings, would you give me some service? My good Mors needs some hay for his nooning, and we had too much to carry from the inn to bear that also. Can you bring me such? Here is the copper for Mistress Forina."

"Nid—" began Tod hesitantly.

"Nid will bide here, and there will be no trouble." There was complete assurance in her answer.

Tod took the proffered coin and with his twin shot off across the marketplace. Meg turned to the man who had warned off the boys and the goat.

"Of whose household are those two, if you please, goodman?"

He snorted. "Household? None would own such as those two. Oh, they make themselves useful as herds. They be the only ones as can handle beast Nid," he shot a baneful glance at the goat. "Three of a kind they be, stealing from stalls and making trouble."

"But they are but children."

The man flushed, there was that he could read in her voice and eyes which he did not like.

"There are a number such. We had the green-sick here three seasons agone, Herbwife. Many died, and there were fireless hearths left. Mistress Forina, she gives them leftovers and lets them sleep in the hay at the stable. More fool she; they are a plaguey lot." He turned away abruptly as a woman approached his stall, glad to have done with Meg's questions.

The goat had shifted to one side and touched noses with Mors. Kasha gave a fastidious warn-off hiss just as a thin man in a shabby cloak paused before Meg's narrow table.

He was eyeing the flowers.

"I thought them real." He spoke as if to himself.

"Real, they are, good sir. But this is what you wish—for your daughter." Meg's hand was already on a small packet. "Steep it in apple ale, and let her have it each morning before she breaks her fast."

"But—herbwife—you did not ask me—I did not tell—"

"You saw," Meg answered slowly and firmly, as one might speak to a child learning its letters, "and I am a healer. We all have gifts, good sir. Even as you have yours. Out of love of learning, you have striven hard and given much—"

Never taking his eyes from hers, he fumbled in the pouch at his belt and brought out a coin.

"Herbwife, I know not what you are—but there is good in what you do, of that I am sure. Just as"—his eyes had dropped as if against his will to the flowers and he gave a start—"just as those are real! Yet it is out of season, and some I have not seen for long. For such grew once in a garden eastward where I can no longer go. I thank you."

Meg was busy with the bouquet, freeing from its tight swathering a spike of flower violet-red. As she held it up, it did in truth seem to be fresh plucked.

"This for your hearth-home, scholar. May it bring you some ease of heart for not all memories are ill ones."

He seemed unable for a moment or two to realize that she meant it. And when he took it between two fingers, he was smiling.

"Lady, how can one thank—"

Meg shook her head. "Thanks are worth the more when passed along. You had one who has given much, scholar—therefore to you shall be given in turn. Remember this well"—and there was force in those three words.

It was almost as if he were so bemused by the flowers that he did not hear her. For he did not say one word in farewell as he turned away from her stall.

Those shadows awakened in the afternoon from the walls about the market square were growing longer when Almadis came. As usual Osono was at her side, and behind her Urgell. Though she had been free of l'Estal since childhood, taking no maids with her, it was insisted that she ever have some guard. And usually the armsmaster took that duty upon himself.

There were feuds brought into l'Estal, for men of power arose and fell in the lowlands, and sometimes a triumphant enemy suffered the same fate as his former victim. Lord Jules had been a mighty ruler of a quarter of Klem before his enemies had brought him down. His lordship became this single mountain hold, instead of leading armies he rode with patrols to keep the boundaries against the outlaws of the western heights; his palace was this maze of ancient cold and crooked walls, and warrens of rooms. But he was still remembered and feared, and there were those who would reach him even if they must do so through his only child.

So Urgell went armed, and Almadis carried in her sleeve a knife with which she was well trained. There was a sword also sheathed by Osono's side, though as a bard he supposedly had safe conduct wherever he might go. Might go—that was no longer true—there was only l'Estal. No man or woman asked of another what had brought one to exile here, so Almadis did not know the past tale of either of the men pacing with her now, but that they were of honor and trust she was sure, and she welcomed their company accordingly.

Meg's stall had been a popular one this day. Most of those coming to buy had been dealt with briskly, but there were some with whom she spoke with authority, and twice more she had drawn flowers from that amazing bouquet and given them to the amazement of those with whom she dealt. So it had been with Vill Blacksmith, who had come seeking a herb known to be helpful against a burn such as his young apprentice had suffered. He went off with not only his purchase, but a sprig of knight's honor gold bright in the hand of his bonnet. And there was Brydan the embroideress, who wished a wash for aching eyes, and received also a full-blown heart's-ease, purple and gold as a fine lady's gem when she fastened it to the breast of her worn grey gown.

Oddly enough it seemed that, though Meg plundered her bouquet so from time to time, it did not appear to shrink in size. Her neighbor began to watch her more closely, and his frown became a sharp crease between his eyes. Now and again his own hand arose to caress a certain dark-holed stone which hung from a dingy string about his throat, and once he muttered under his breath while he fingered that.

He was the first to sight Almadis and her companions, and his frown became a sickly kind of smile, though there was no reason to believe the Castellan's daughter would be interested in his withered roots of vegetables, the last remaining from the winter stores.

Indeed she crossed the market as one with a definite mission in mind, heading straight to Meg's stand.

"Goodwill to you, Herbwife," she said. "I trust that trade has been brisk for you. We have but very few here who follow such a calling."

Meg did not curtsey, but smiled as one who greets an old friend.

"Indeed, lady, this is a fair market, and I have been well suited in bargaining. We spoke of meadowsweet for the freshening before times—"

"Lad's Love—dove's wings"— Osono paid no attention to the women, his was all for the bouquet— "Star fast—"

"Falcon feather!" Urgell's much harsher voice cut across the smooth tones of the bard.

"You are well learned, good sirs," Meg returned, and her hand hovered over the bouquet. "Those are names not common in these parts."

Osono's gaze might be aimed at the flowers, but yet it was as if he saw beyond them something else—as might grow in a meadow under that full, warm sun, which never even in summer seemed to reach into these stark heights.

Meg's fingers plucked and brought forth a stem on which swung two white blooms, star-pointed. She held that out to the bard, and he accepted it as one in a dream. Then she snapped thumb and forefinger together with more vigor and freed a narrow leaf, oddly colored so that it indeed resembled a feather.

"For you also, warrior." And her words held something of an order, as if to make sure he would not refuse. Then she spoke to Almadis:

"Meadowsweet, yes." She swept up a bundle of leaves and wrapped them expertly in a small cloth. "But something else also, is it not so?"

"Red-rose," Almadis said slowly. "My mother strove to grow a bush, but this land is too sere to nurture it. Red-rose—"

The flower Meg handed her was not full opened yet, and when Almadis held it close to her, she could smell a perfume so delicate that she could hardly believe such could come into the grayness that was l'Estal.

"Herbwife," she leaned a little forward, "who are you?"

"Meg, my lady, a dealer—a friend—"

Almadis nodded. "Yes, of a certainty that."

She brought out her purse. "For the meadowsweet"—she laid down one of the coins.

"Just so," Meg agreed. "For the meadowsweet."

Osono was fumbling at his own purse with one hand, the other carefully cupping the starflower. Then he caught Meg's eye, and flushed. Instead he bowed as he might to the lady of some great hall where he had been night's singer.

"My thanks to you—Herbwife."

Urgell's bow was not so low or polished, but there was a lightening of his harsh features. "And mine also, mistress—your gifts have a value beyond price."

There were others who sought the herb dealer after the castle's lady had departed. But few of them were favored with a gift of bloom. Perhaps six in all bore away a leaf or flower, but still the bouquet appeared to grow no smaller. When Meg, in the beginning twilight, gathered up her wares and repacked them, two small figures appeared.

Behind them still ambled their horned and bewiskered companion. For the second time Nid touched noses with Mors, who was hardly taller than he. And Kaska voiced a small hiss.

"Help you, mistress?" Tay shuffled a bare foot back and forth in the straw which strewed the market square in marketing days.

"But of course. Many hands make light of work." Meg swung one of her cord-tied bundles to the boy, and he hurried to fit it into the panniers, which his brother had already placed on Mors.

"You are not out with the herds, youngling?" she added as she picked up as the last of her supplies, that bouquet.

Tod hung his head. "They will not have Nid now—he fought with Whrit, and they say he has too bad a temper—that any of his get are not wanted. They—set the dogs on us and Nid savaged two, so—so they talk now of—" He gulped and his brother continued:

"They talk of killing him, mistress."

"But he is yours?"

Both small faces turned toward hers, and there was a fierce determination in the chorus of their answer.

"Before times, he was herd leader, mistress. When Lan, our brother, was herder. But"— now their voices faltered—"Lan died of the green-sick. And the herd went to Finus—they said as how Lan had told him so—that we were too young— And Finus—he said as how there was much owed him by Lan, and that he had the rights. Only Nid would come with us, and he stayed. But—" Tod stopped as if to catch breath, however Tad's words gushed on:

"They won't let us to the pasture anymore. Finus, he lives in our house and says it is his."

"What have you then as shelter?" asked Meg quietly. She was holding the flowers close to her, beneath her chin, as if she breathed in for some purpose the faint scents.

"Inn mistress Forina—she lets us in the stable—but they say that Nid is bad for the horses."

"Not for this one," Meg nodded to Mors. "Let he and Nid bed down together, and we shall see what can be done."

They made a small procession of their own out of the marketplace. Meg carried the flowers and humped Kaska's basket up on one hip with the familiar gesture of a countrywoman bearing burdens. Mors trotted after her, no leading rein to draw him on, and he was matched by the goat, the two forming a guard, one to each side.

There were those who watched them go, narrow-eyed and sour of face. It would seem that just as there were those who had been drawn to the stall during that day, so also there were those who shunned it. Now a darker shadow moved forward to stand beside the stall which had neighbored Meg's.

"You have kept eye on her, goodman?" it hissed a question.

"I have, priest. There is that about her which is not natural right enough. She is weaving spells, even as a noxious spider weaves a web. Already she has touched some here—"

"Those being?" The voice was hot, near exulting.

Now the stall keeper spoke names, and those names were oddly companioned—lady, bard, soldier, smith, scholar, needlewoman, a laborer in from one of the scanty hill farms, a gate sentry off duty, a washerwoman, the wife of a merchant and her daughter—

And with the speaking of each name, Thunur nodded his head. "You have done well, Danler, very well. Continue to watch here, and I shall search elsewhere. We shall bring down this slut who deals with the Dark yet! You are a worthy son of GORT, the Ever-Mighty."

Within the keep the ways were dark and damp as always. Though in some of the halls there were dank and moldy tapestries on the walls, no one had made any attempt to renew them, to bring any hint of color into those somber quarters. Even candles seemed here to have their halos of dim light circumscribed so that they could not reveal too much of any way.

Almadis tugged at her heavy trained skirt with an impatient hand. She had but little time, and this was a way which had not been trodden for long. She could remember well her last visit here, when rage at all the world had seemed to so heat her, she had felt none of the chill thrown off by the walls. The loss of her mother had weighed both heart and spirit.

Now the pallid light of her candle picked out the outline of the door she sought. But she had to set that on the floor and use both hands in order to force open the barrier, which damp had near sealed beyond her efforts.

Then she was in, candle aloft, looking about. No one had cared—there had probably been no one here since last she left. Yet the mustiness was still tinged with a hint of incense. The room was small, its floor covered with the rotting remnants of what had once been whortle reeds, which trodden upon, gave back sweet scent.

There was a single window, shuttered tight, a bar dropped firmly in place to hold it so. Beneath that stood a boxlike fixture which might be an altar.

That was shrouded with thick dust, a dust which clouded the round of once-polished mirror set there, gathered about the bases of three candlesticks.

For a long moment Almadis merely stood and looked at that altar and its furnishings. She had turned her back on what this stood for, told herself that there was nothing here beyond what she could see, touch, that to believe in more was folly—a child's folly. Yet her mother—

Slowly Almadis moved forward. There were still half-consumed candles in those sticks, grimed, a little lopsided. She used the one she carried to touch the wicks of those into life. Then, suddenly, she jerked her long scarf from about her shoulders, and, in spite of its fine embroidery, she used it to dust the mirror free, dropping its grime-clogged stuff to the floor when she had done.

Lastly she turned to that window. Straining, she worked free the bar, threw back the shutter, opened the room to the night, in spite of the wind which wove about this small side tower.

For so long it had not mattered what rode the sky; this night it did. And what was rising now was the full moon in all its brilliance and glory. Almadis returned to the altar. She could not remember the forms. Those other times she had merely repeated words her mother had uttered without regard for their meaning. There were only scraps which she could assemble now.

But she stationed herself before that mirror, leaning forward a little, her hands placed flat on either side. On its tarnished surface she could see reflected the light of the three candles—but nothing else. There was no representation of her own face—the once-burnished plate was too dim.

Nor had she that learning which could bring it alive. Yet she had been drawn here and knew that this had meaning, a meaning she dared not deny.

Tucked in the lacing of her bodice was that rose Meg had given her. Dried it might be—with great skill—yet it seemed to have just been plucked from a bush such as her mother had striven to keep alive.

The girl moistened her lips.

"One In Three," she began falteringly. "She who rules the skies, She who is maiden, wife, and elder in turn, She who answers the cries of her daughters in distress, who reaches to touch a land and bring it into fruitfulness, She who knows what truly lies within the heart—"

Almadis's voice trailed into silence. What right had she to ask for anything in this forsaken place, return to a faith she had said held no meaning?

There was certainly another shadow of something on the mirror—growing stronger. It was—the rose!

Almadis gasped, for a moment she felt light-headed, that only her hold on the altar kept her upright.

"Lady"—her voice was the thinnest of whispers—"Lady who was, and always will be—give me forgiveness. Your messenger—she must be one of your heart held— Lady, I am not fit—"

She raised her hands to that flower caught in her lacing. Yet something would not let her loosen it as she wished, to leave it as an offering here.

Instead there was the sweetness of the rose about her, as if each candle breathed forth its fragrance. She looked down—that flower which had been yet half a bud was now open.

Quickly, almost feverishly in her haste, Almadis reached again for the altar. There had been something else left there long ago. The dust had concealed it, but she found it— Her fingers caught the coil of a chain, and she held it up, from it swung that pendant—the flat oval of silver (but the silver was not tarnished black as it should have been) on it, in small, raised, milky white gems, the three symbols of the Lady in Her waxing, Her full life, Her waning.

It seemed to Almadis that the candlelight no longer was the illumination of that chamber, rather the moon itself shown within, brighter than she could remember it. She raised the chain, bowed her head a fraction, slipped those links over it, allowing the moon gem-set pendant to fall upon her breast. Then she did as she remembered her mother had always done, tucked it into hiding beneath her bodice, so that now the pendant rested between her breasts just under the rose. Though it did not carry the chill of metal to her flesh, it was rather warm, as if it had but been passed from one who had the right to wear it to another.

Now she gathered courage to speak again.

"Lady, you know what will be asked of me, and what is in me. I cannot walk my father's way—and he will be angry. Give me the strength and courage to remain myself in the face of such anger—though I know that by his beliefs he means me only well."

She leaned forward then, a kind of resolution manifest in her movements, to blow out the three candles. But she made no move to bar away the moonlight before she picked up her journey candle to leave the room.

Though it was day without, the guardroom was grimly dusk within.

"Three of them we took," a brawny man in a rust-marked mail coat said to one of his fellows. He jerked a thumb at a rolled ball of hide. "Over the gate to the west he says."

The older man he addressed grunted. "We do things here by my Lord Jules's ordering."

"Don't be so free with words like that hereabouts,

Ruddy," cautioned the other. "Our Knight-Captain has long ears—"

"Or more than one pair of them," retorted Ruddy. "We've got us more trouble than just a bunch of lousy sheep raiders, Jonas. While you've been out a-ridin', there's a stew boilin' here."

The bigger man leaned on the edge of the table, "Thunur, I'm thinkin'. That one came at dawn light a-brayin' somethin' about a witch. He's a big mouth, always yappin'."

"To some purpose, Jonas, there's more n'more listen to him. An' you know well what happened below when those yellin' 'GORT, come down' broke loose."

"Gods," snorted the city sergeant. "We be those all gods have forgot. Perhaps just as well, there was always a pother o' trouble below when priests stuck their claws into affairs. There are those here who are like to stir if the right spoon is thrust into the pot, too. Thunur is gettin' him a followin'— Let him get enough to listen an' we'll be out with pikes, an' you'll remember outlaw hunting as somethin' as a day's good ramble."

"Well, I could do with a ramble—over to the Hafted Stone to wet m' 'gullet an' then to barracks an' m'bunk. His Honor is late—"

"Right good reason." A younger man turned from the group of his fellows by the door and leered. "Hear as how it was all to be fixed up for our Knight-Captain—wed and bed the lord's daughter—make sure that he is firm in the saddle for the time when m'lord don't take to ridin' anymore. They have a big feastin' tonight just to settle the matter, don't they?"

There was no time for an answer. Those by the door parted swiftly to allow another to enter. He was unhelmed, but wore mail, and over that a surcoat patterned with a snarling wolf head. His dark hair was cropped after the fashion of one who wore a helm much, and it was sleeked above a high forehead. The seam of a scar twisted one corner of his mouth, so that he seemed to sneer at the world around.

He was young for all of that, and once must have been handsome. His narrow beak of a nose gave him now the look of some bird of prey, an impression his sharp yellowish eyes did nothing to lighten. Otger, Knight-Captain under the Castellan, was no man to be taken lightly either in war or council. Now he stalked past the men who crowded back to give him room, as if they were invisible, even Jonas pulled away quickly as his commander fronted Ruddy face-to-face.

"There is trouble, Town Sergeant?"

Ruddy had straightened. His face was as impassive as that of a puppet soldier.

"Sir, no more than ever. Th' priest of GORT is brayin' again. Some are beginnin' to listen. This mornin' he came here—"

"So!" Otger turned his head but a fraction. "Dismissed to the courtyard."

They were quick to go. Only Jonas and Ruddy remained. The Knight regarded them with the hooded eyes of a predator biding time.

"He is still here?"

"Sir, he spilled forth such blather that I thought it best you hear. He speaks of those above him in a manner which is not fit."

Otger moved past him, seated himself on the single chair behind that table, as a giver of justice might install himself in court. His hand went to his cheek, the fingers tracing that scar. Jonas edged backward another step. That was always a trouble sign. Young as Otger was, he had gained such influence here as to be served swiftly.

It was the Castellan who had advanced him swiftly—and in a way, who could blame Lord Jules? The years spun by only too swiftly, and a man aged

with them. The lord had no son—but there was a
daughter. One wedding her would surely rule here.
Those of the east plains would take no notice, if all
was done properly, and there had been no exile of
high blood now since Otger himself had ridden in as
a gold-eyed youth five seasons back.

"Bring the priest," he ordered now. And Jonas went
to fetch Thunur.

The man did not cringe as he came. Instead, he was
bold at this fronting, his head up, and eyes blazing
with the fire of the rage that always burned in him.

"I hear you wish to see me," Otger's gaze swept
the fellow from head to foot and back again. Just so
had he looked two days before at that wounded outlaw they had taken.

"Witchery, Sir Knight. Foul witchery has come by
the Way Wind into l'Estal. It must be routed out.
Already it has ensorcelled many—many, Sir Knight.
Among them"— Thunur paused for a moment to
make his next statement more portentous, "The Lady
Almadis—"

"And who is this dealer in witchery?" Otger's voice
was very calm. Ruddy hitched one shoulder. This
priest would soon learn his lesson by all the signs.

Thus encouraged, Thunur spoke his tale, so swiftly
that spittle accompanied the words he spewed forth.
He ended with the listing of those who had borne
away tokens of Meg's giving. And at the saying of
some of those names, Otger's eyes narrowed a
fraction.

"It is laid upon all true men and women to deal
with witches as GORT has deemed right—with fire.
This—this sluttish whore, and those brutes she
brought with her—they must be slain; and those whom
she has entoiled must be reasoned with—'less they too
are tainted past cleansing."

"You name some who are above you, priest.

Tongues that wag too freely can be cut from jaws. I would advise you to take heed of the need of silence for now—"

"For now?" Thunur repeated slowly.

"For now." Otger arose. "You seem to have an eye for such matters. Out with you to use that eye, but not the tongue, mind you!"

Thunur blinked. And then he turned and went. But Otger spoke to Ruddy. "Have the patrol keep an eye to that one. I have seen his like before—they can be well used if they are handled rightly, but if they are not under rein, they are useless and must be removed."

The market was alive. Though some of the sellers noted that there were more men at arms making their ways leisurely among the booths. However, since the border patrol had just returned, that might be expected.

Again Meg had taken her place, Mors behind her and Kaska's basket carefully out of the way. Her bouquet centered her table board. But those who came to look over her stock this day did not seem to note it particularly, nor did she all the morning lose any bloom from it for gifting.

Tod and Tay came by just before the nooning bell and brought her a basket Forina had promised. This time Nid walked behind them, his heavy-horned head swinging from side to side, as if he wished to keep a close eye on all about.

Just as he stepped up to exchange polite nose taps with Mors, one of the guards halted before Meg's display. He had the weather-roughened and darkened skin of a man who had spent many years around and about, and there was a small emblem caught fast in the mail shirt he wore that marked his rank.

"Fair day to you, Herbwife." He studied her, and

then his eyes dropped to her wares. "You have Ill-bane, I see."

"You see and you wonder, Guard Sergeant? Why?" She took up the bundle of leaves. "It stands against evil, does it not—ill of body, ill of mind. What do they say of it? That if those of dark purpose strive to touch it, they are like to find a brand laid across their rash fingers."

"You know what they say of you, then?"

Meg smiled. "They say many things of me, Guard Sergeant Ruddy. It depends upon who says it. I have already been called witch—"

"And that does not alarm you?"

"Guard Sergeant Ruddy, when you are summoned to some duty, would any words from those not your officers turn you aside?"

"Duty—" he repeated. "Herbwife, I tell you that you may well have a right to fear."

"Fear and duty often ride comrades. But fear is the shadow and duty the substance. Look you"— she had laid down the bundle of leaves, turned her hand palm-up to show the unmarked flesh, and carried that gesture on so that as his eyes followed they touched the bouquet.

"Rowan leaf and berry," he said.

"Such as grow in hedgerows elsewhere." Meg pulled out the stem to show a pair of prick defended leaves, a trefoil of berries.

Slowly he reached out and took it from her.

"Watch with care, Herbwife." He did not tuck her gift into full sight as had the others who had taken such, but rather closed his fist tightly upon it and thrust that into his belt pouch.

Almadis stood by the window. One could catch a small sight of the market square from this vista. But she could not sight Meg's stall. She was stiff with anger, and yet she must watch her speech. It might be that she was caught at last, yet she could not bring herself to believe that.

"He rode in," she tried to keep her words even in tone, not make them such as could be used against her. "And with him he brought *heads*—heads of men! He would plant those as warnings! Warnings!"

"Against raiders, outlaws. They only understand such." That answering voice held weariness. "Their raids grow bolder—oftener. The land we hold, which supplies us with food, with that very robe you are wearing, cannot yield what we need when it is constantly under raid. Now, with the upper snows fast-going, we shall have them down upon us more and more. I know not what presses them these past few seasons, but they have grown bolder and bolder. We lost a farm to fire and sword—Otger collected payment. They deal in blood, thus we must also."

Almadis turned. "He is a man of blood," she said flatly.

"He holds the peace. You call him man of blood— well, and that he is in another way also. We are of ancient family, daughter—thrown aside though we may be. Rank weds with rank. Otger is the son of a House near equal to our own. Whom you wed will rule here afterward; he must be one born to such heritage. There is no one else."

She came to stand before her father where he sat in his high-back chair. And she was suddenly startled, then afraid. Somehow—somehow he had aged—and she had not seen it happening! He had always remained to her, until this hour, the strong leader l'Estal needed. He was old and to the old came death.

So for the moment she temporized. "Father, grant me a little more time. I cannot find it in me to like Otger—give me a little time." Her fingers were at her breast pressing against the hidden pendant, caressing the rose which still held both color and fragrance.

"Where got you that flower, Almadis?" There was a sharpness in his tone now.

Swiftly she told him of Meg, brought by the Way Wind, and of her stall in the market.

"I have heard a tale of witchery," he returned.

"Witchery? Do some then listen to that mad priest?" Almadis was disturbed. "She came with the Way Wind—from the west—she brings herbs such as we cannot grow—for the soothing of minds and bodies. She is but a girl, hardly more than a child. There is no evil in her!"

"Daughter, we are a people shunned, broken from our roots. There is shame, pain, anger eating at many of us. Such feelings are not easily put aside. And in some they take another form, seeking one upon whom blame may be thrown, one who may be made, after a fashion, to pay for all that which has caused us ill. Eyes have seen, ears have heard, lips reported—there are those who cry, witchery, yes. And very quickly such rumors can turn to action. This Meg may be a harmless trader—she may be the cause of an uprising. There is the ancient law for the westerners, one which we seldom invoke but which I turn to now—not only for the sake of town peace but for her safety also. This is the third day in the market—by sundown—"

Almadis swallowed back the protest she would have cried out. That her father spoke so seriously meant that indeed there might be forces brewing who take fire in l'Estal. But on sudden impulse, she did say:

"Let me be the one to tell her so. I would not have her think that I have been unmindful of her gift." Once more she touched the rose.

"So be it. Also let it be that you think carefully on what else I have said to you. Time does not wait. I

would have matters settled for your own good and for
my duty."

So once more Almadis went down to the market
and with her, without her asking, but rather as if they
understood her unhappiness about this matter, there
came Osono and Urgell. She noted in surprise that
the bard had his harp case riding on his shoulder, as
if he were on the way to some feast, and that Urgell
went full armed.

It was midday, and Almadis looked about her somewhat puzzled for the usual crowd of those in the market, whether they came to buy and sell, or merely to
spend time, was a small one. The man whose stall
had neighbored Meg's was gone, and there were other
empty spaces. Also there was a strange feeling which
she could not quite put name to.

Ruddy, the guard sergeant, backed by two of his
men, were pacing slowly along the rows of stalls. Now
Urgell came a step forward so that he was at Almadis's right hand. His head was up, and he glanced right
and left. Osono shifted the harp case a little, pulling
loose his cloak so that the girl caught sight of his
weapon, a span of tempered blade between a dagger
and a sword in length.

If there had been a falling away of the crowd, that
was not so apparent about the stall where Meg was
busied as she had been since she first came into l'Estal.
But those who had drifted toward her were a very
mixed lot. Almadis recognized the tall bulk of the
smith, and near shoulder to him was Tatwin, the
scholar, his arm about the shoulders of a slight girl
whose pale face suggested illness not yet past, while
by her skirts trotted a small shaggy dog with purpose
which seemed even more sustained than that of the
two it accompanied.

There was also, somewhat to Almadis's surprise,

Forina of the inn, and behind her wide bulk of body came Tod and Tay, once more grasping the horns of Nid with the suggestion about them that they were not going to lose touch with that four-footed warrior.

Others, too, a shambling-footed laborer from the farmlands, with one hand to the rope halter of a drooping-headed horse that might have drawn far too many carts or plows through weary seasons.

Just as they gathered, so did others in the market-place draw apart. That feeling of menace which had been but a faint touch when Almadis trod out on this cobbled square grew.

There was movement in the alleyways, the streets, which led into that square. Others were appearing there who did not venture out into the sunlight.

Urgell's hand was at sword hilt. Almadis quickened pace to reach Meg's stall.

"Go! Oh, go quickly!" she burst out. "I do not know what comes, but there is evil rising here. Go while you can!"

Meg had not spread out her bundles of herbs. Now she looked to the Castellan's daughter and nodded. She picked up her staff and set to the crown of it the bouquet of flowers. The twins suddenly loosed their hold on Nid and pushed behind the board of the stall, shifting the panniers to Mors's back. Meg stooped and caught up the basket in which Kaska rode, settled it firmly within her arm crook.

"Witch—get the witch!" The scream arose from one of the alley mouths.

In a moment, Vill was beside Urgell, and Almadis saw that he carried with him his great hammer. Osono had shifted his harp well back on his shoulder to give him room for weapon play. There were others, too, who moved to join that line between Meg and the sulkers in the streets and alleys.

"To the gate," Almadis said. "If you bide with me,

they will not dare to touch you!" She hoped that was true. But to make sure that these who threatened knew who and what she was and the protection she could offer, she pushed back her cloak hood that her face might be readily seen.

"To the gate," Ruddy appeared with his armsmen, added the authority of his own to the would-be defenders.

They retreated, all of them, bard, mercenary, smith, sergeant forming a rear guard. Only before the gate there were others—

A line of men drawn up, men who had been hardened by the riding of the borders, Otger's chosen. Before them stood the knight-captain himself.

"My lady," he said as they halted in confusion. "This is no place for you."

Almadis's hand went to Meg's arm. "Sir, if you come to give protection, that is well. But this much I shall do for myself, see an innocent woman free of any wrong—"

"You give me no choice then—" He snapped his fingers, and his men moved in, he a stride ahead plainly aiming to reach Almadis himself.

"Sir Knight," Almadis's hand was on her breast, and under it the moon token was warm. "I come not at your demand or that of any man, thank the *Lady*, save at a wish which is my own."

Otger's twisted mouth was a grimace of hate, and he lunged.

Only—

From the staff Meg held, there blazed a burst of rainbow-hued light. Otger and those with him cried out, raising their hands to their eyes and stumbled back. From behind Almadis and Meg moved Mors and Nid, the ancient horse, whose head was now raised, and those three pushed in among the guard, shouldering aside men who wavered and flailed out blindly.

Then Almadis was at the gate, and her hands were raised to the bar there. Beside her was the scholar, and with more force than either of them came Forina. So did the barrier to the freedom without fall. And they came out into the crisp wind without the walls, the very momentum of their efforts carrying them into the mouth of the Way Wind road.

There were cries behind them, and the screeching of voices, harsh and hurting. Almadis looked behind. All their strangely constituted party had won through the gates, the rear guard walking backward. Urgell and Osono had both drawn steel, and the smith held his hammer at ready. There were improvised clubs, a dagger or two, Ruddy's pike, but none were bloodied. Urgell and Ruddy, the smith beside them, slammed the gates fast.

Almadis could still hear the shouting of Otger, knew that they had perhaps only moments before they would be overwhelmed by those who were ready for a hunt.

Meg swung up her staff. There was no wide burst of light this time—rather a ray as straight as a sword blade. It crisscrossed the air before them, leaving behind a shimmer of light the width of the road, near as high as the wall behind them.

As she lowered her staff, she raised her other hand in salute to that shimmer, as if there waited behind it someone or thing she held in honor.

Then she spoke, and, though she did not shout, her words cried easily over the clamor behind them.

"Here is the Gate of Touching. The choice now lies with you all. There will be no hindrance for those going forward. And if you would go back, you shall find those behind will accept you again as you are.

"Those who come four-footed are comrades—the

choice being theirs also. For what lies beyond accepts all life of equal worth. The comradeship of heart is enough.

"The choice is yours, so mote it be!"

She stood a little aside to give room, and Tod and Tay, laying hands once more to Nid's horns, went into the light. Behind them, his hand on the old horse's neck, the laborer trod, head up and firmly. Almadis stood beside Meg and watched them pass. None of them looked to her or Meg, it was as if they were drawn to something so great they had no longer only any knowledge of themselves, only of it.

At last there were those of the rear guard. Osono and Vill did not glance toward her. But Urgell, whose sword was once more within its sheath, dropped behind. Somehow her gaze was willed to meet his. The leaf Meg had given him was set in his battered helm as a plume, the plume that a leader might wear to some victory.

Almadis stirred. She stepped forward, to lay her hand on the one he held out to her as if they would tread some formal pattern which was long woven into being.

Meg steadied Kaska's basket on her hip, and looked up to the glimmer as Castellan's daughter and mercenary disappeared.

"Is it well-done, *Lady*?"

"It is well-done, dear daughter. So mote it be!"

With staff and basket held steady, Meg went forward, and when she passed the gate of light it vanished. The Way lay open once again to the scouring of the wind.

Healer

Josepha Sherman

"Do these stories have to have a female protagonist?" I can't tell you how many times I was asked that question. It's every bit as much a stereotype as the ones surrounding fantasy, science fiction, or the men and women who write it.

Archaeologist, folklorist, and novelist Josepha Sherman didn't bother with that question, being busy with other, more pressing ones.

In this story of courage and initiation, Josepha moves out of the area of Russian folklore, in which she has made a name for herself, and into the realm of shamans whom she asks: Is there life beyond power? Dr. Faustus said no, and traded life and soul for a dream of magic.

In this story, the author offers her healer Faustus's choice: the power of love, or the love of power. Who says a man can't choose right? Not Josepha Sherman.

The night had been wet and chill with the promise of winter, and as Osheoan crept through the narrow entrance of his small, solitary lodge, body still and mind weary from a broken, troubled sleep, the morning air was still dank enough to make him shiver and grab his fur robe about himself. As he moved, the little Power signs of shell and bone and metal woven into it jangled shrilly together. At the high, thin sound, folk turned briefly to look at him, tensing or smiling or nodding politely according to their natures. Osheoan, Spirit-Speaker of this, the Wind Bird Clan, drew himself up to his full lean height in slightly self-conscious pride.

Ohe, yes, the people still did show him the respect due one who spoke with spirits. Even if he had produced no miracles in these many years, nothing more than the small marvels of healing torn flesh or broken bones.

Not, thought Osheoan wryly, that there was anything wrong in minor healings: seeing young Ashewan walking without a limp on the leg he had splinted or plump Esewa cuddling her latest baby, cured of the nagging cough that had threatened to drain the flesh from her. When Osheoan, then little more than a boy, had first been struck by Power, his initial feeling— aside from sheer terror at being set aside from the norm—had been delight that now he could do something to help those in pain.

Pride had come later.

Osheoan put aside thoughts of his troubled sleep (no messages there, no hidden dream-warnings), and made his circuit of the lodges, pleased to find no injuries, no illness. Hunters returning to the lodges, luck charms jingling from robes and braided hair, antelope or strings of hares borne on their backs, paused beneath their burdens to dip their heads in courtesy. Women weaving the tribal blankets or gathering herbs and roots, black hair and copper ornaments glinting in the sun, took a moment to touch hand to heart when he passed, a tall, quiet shadow in Spirit-Speaker's grey. And Osheoan admitted, deep within himself, that the respect shown him was sweet, still sweet.

Sweetness with a faintly bitter undertaste: secret shame, secret sorrow.

No one saw Osheoan's sudden flinch, no one saw him clench his teeth against unwelcome memories. Had the Power ever been real? Once, surely, he'd been that young, earnest boy, once he'd been believing. Once he had walked with spirits (ah, or had those been nothing more than waking dreams, forced on a boy dizzy from smoke and dazed by drums?), learned the true, deep way of healing. The way now closed to him.

Once, too, he had loved: Seshawa. Gentle Seshawa with a wit like the sharpness of berry-tang beneath honey. Seshawa of the laughing eyes and heart: she, his wife, his own.

Seshawa, who had died in birthing, for all her husband's Power, leaving a son, Mikasha, and an empty, bitter man.

Osheoan gave a silent, humorless laugh. Being Spirit-Speaker was still sweet, yes. And so he still went through the trappings of Power, the rituals that kept the others of the clan in awe of him. He still healed. But no one save he knew no spirits were roused by those rituals, that the healing was of simple herbs and time, nothing more. Fortunate, fortunate, that the Wind Bird Clan was a healthy one, that there had been no devastating illnesses or wounds, nothing to deeply harm them and destroy him. The day would come, though; the thought of it lingered, quivering, just at the back of his mind. Someday disaster would—must—strike, and he, the so-mighty Spirit-Speaker, would try, and fail, and be revealed as false.

Osheoan stirred, impatient with himself. Yes, the Power had spilled away from him with Seshawa's death (if, indeed, he'd ever truly borne it) and with it, belief in the gods. But life continued, the here, the now, the real.

The loneliness—

No. Enough self-pity.

Osheoan knew he'd hidden his loss of Power well. No one suspected, not even his son. Least of all his son, handsome Mikasha, with his father's height and mother's laughing eyes. Osheoan winced, remembering the boy who had been, face still pudgy with childishness but ablaze with near-adult eagerness, staring fiercely up at him, asking, *"Why won't you teach me? I'm your son, your blood. Why can't I be your apprentice?"*

How could he answer that fierceness? *Because I'm a sham. A liar, with nothing to teach you.* No, no, he had never said that, he had forced the blame onto Mikasha instead, putting the boy off with stories, telling him at first, year after year, *"Later. You are still too young."* Then, when at last Mikasha was old enough to know his father lied, Osheoan had heard himself speak the cruelest lie of all: *"I cannot teach you. It would be too dangerous, impossible. I'm afraid you have no gift for Power at all."*

And in lying to his son, he'd lied to himself as well, insisting, *The boy will forget what he cannot have. He will make himself some bright new life as warrior or wise man. He has no need of Power.*

Osheoan stared bleakly out past the circle of lodges, blindly out to the vast, cold plains. How could it have come to this? He had never thought himself a coward, had undergone the rites of manhood and the harsher, grimmer rituals of Power—scarring mind instead of merely body—without a qualm. He had risked the very essence that was Osheoan without hesitation. Yet, when a handful of words would have put Mikasha's mind at ease—Mikasha, his son!—fear had shaken his heart, stopped his tongue. Fear of losing the last trace of what he'd been, the pride, the awe if not the reality of Power.

He'd kept silent. And by that silence, Osheoan knew he had taught his son all too well: bitterness at what the boy could only think his own fault, his own inner shortcomings. He had taught Mikasha unhappiness.

And in the end, he had driven his son away. Once the boy had become adult, passing the rituals of manhood without a word to his father, Mikasha had quietly abandoned his home, his clan, setting out to hunt for his own purpose in being.

A sudden chill gust of wind swept wet off the plains, and Osheoan shivered. "Mikasha," he murmured, aching. "Oh, my son . . ."

His dreams had been about the boy, full of trouble, of pain . . .

But dreams held no secret messages, not for him, not anymore.

Osheoan started, jarred out of his inner darkness by shouting. There on the flat horizon stumbled a lone figure, staggering its way toward the lodge circle. Warriors snatched up their spears, staring, alert as wolves.

"One man alone hardly constitutes a threat," Osheoan said mildly. "Why not go out there and see what he wants?"

The warriors dipped their spears in compliance. Some of them raced out from the lodges, using the swift, loose-limbed, ground-devouring jog that could wear down a running antelope. Osheoan, watching, suffered a moment's doubt. He'd judged wisely, hadn't he? Surely one man couldn't be an enemy, not alone. And plainly injured, judging from that hesitant gait.

Injured? Or ill?

Oh, you idiot! What if he's bringing disease toward the lodges?

Osheoan snatched up his curing bundle and started

after the men, determined to stop the stranger before he got too near. But then Osheoan froze, staring, feeling his heart leap painfully.

"Mikasha . . . ?" It was a wisp of sound.

Taller now, a man's body, no longer a boy, but—
"Mikasha!"

Osheoan didn't remember breaking into a run. He knew only that his son was here, his son had returned, and when Mikasha, face drawn and painfully thin, sagged suddenly, eyes closing, it was his father who caught him and eased him gently to the ground. *Grey robe,* Osheoan noted abstractedly, vaguely surprised, *Spirit-Speaker's robe,* though no Spirit-Speaker's ornaments, not yet, only the plain spirals of bone marking an apprentice. That Mikasha should be wearing them would mean something later, he knew it, something painful, but right now Osheoan could focus only on the sweetly stale smell of illness hovering about his son, the stain of old blood across Mikasha's chest.

With the aid of the wary, respectful warriors, Osheoan brought his son home, had him laid gently down on the Spirit-Speaker's own bed of soft furs. Staring down at Mikasha's thin, still face with its lines of suffering, remembering the plump, joyous little boy now forever lost, Osheoan blindly waved the warriors away. Alone with Mikasha, he knelt by his son's side, delicately peeling back the worn, stained robe, dreading what he might find.

The breath hissed between his teeth as he inhaled in shock. *Ohe,* bad.

A fiery weal cut across Mikasha's chest, the flesh on either side swollen and puffy, streaked with sullen red: the scar of what would have been a jagged wound, such as stone dagger might make (though who would deliberately harm a Spirit-Speaker?), or perhaps a miscast splinter of metal shattering at the cooling. Osheoan reached out to gently trace its length, then drew his hand back, alarmed at the fever heat he'd felt. This was no fresh injury. The skin had had time to close over it, deceptively, dangerously imitating true healing, hiding the sickness festering within, the slow, sure death.

Osheoan started, suddenly realizing that Mikasha was awake and watching him from fever-glazed eyes.

"Lie still," Osheoan murmured. "I . . . will do what I can."

"I thought the wound had healed." It was the driest whisper of sound. "Shattered . . . knife shattered in the ritual . . . Power burst free . . ."

"What were you doing toying with Power?" Osheoan heard his voice come out too harsh, too sharp, but couldn't stop himself from babbling on. "I told you, you have no Gift"—flinching inwardly at the familiar lie.

Mikasha stirred restlessly. "No. You were wrong. Too close to me, maybe. Power *is* there, burning . . . Had to learn to use it." He drew a deep, shuddering breath. "Found another Spirit-Speaker. Torik of the White Snake Clan . . . Said he would teach me, even if I was Wind Bird . . . not Snake . . ."

Mikasha's eyes closed. "Enough," Osheoan said softly. "Rest."

But his son continued, forcing out the words, "Hadn't taught me healing, though. Not Power healing. No time, before he . . . before the knife broke . . . killed him, hurt me. White Snake Clan tried to kill me, too. But I escaped." The feverish eyes snapped open, staring at Osheoan. "Came to Clan summer grounds, hoped lodges would still be here . . . Where else could I go? Father . . ."

His eyes closed again, voice trailing into silence. His thin form seemed to collapse in on itself, and Osheoan cried in sudden terror, "Mikasha?" then sighed in relief to see that his son still breathed. Grimly, the man forced himself under control and bent to examine the wound again, desperate for some reason for hope.

The wound had slashed across Mikasha's ribs and down, though how deep it had cut into the flesh, he couldn't tell by mere sight. It might have come perilously close to a lung ... But Mikasha showed none of the terrifying blood froth on his lips that would mean a death wound. Still, who knew what other damage might have been done within?

And Osheoan's mind answered him cruelly, *A Spirit-Speaker would know.*

A true Spirit-Speaker. Not a Sham. The Power would stir within such a one and tell him what to do. The Power would guide his hand and heart, help him draw out the poison and heal the sick flesh ...

"Power," Osheoan muttered.

Here was the heart of his fear, come before him at last: the one patient he might not aid by simple herbs, the one patient who, by dying, was going to reveal him as an imposter— And that one was his son, his son ...

And what are you going to do? Osheoan's mind asked relentlessly. *Let Mikasha die? All because you are afraid?*

"No."

At least he still did have his basic knowledge of healing. It ... must be enough.

But as Osheoan bent over his son's body, knife in hand, prepared to reopen the wound and let the poison drain, he was shaken by a spasm of pure terror. If only he *knew* exactly where to cut! What if his hand slipped? What if he cut too deeply, or nicked one of the vital, blood-carrying vessels? Other men could call on the gods for help, but for him, the disbeliever, there was nothing, no one. And suddenly he could have wept like a child for his loneliness. Suddenly he ached in every twist of his being for belief, for any sign at all that he was not alone.

Please, oh please, help me.

"Now, why should we?"

Osheoan twisted wildly about. There in the lodge was ... a fox, nothing more than one of the scrawny, silvery-furred foxes, stolen in from the plains. The man cried out as much in loss as in anger, and looked for something to hurl at the little scavenger.

"So quick to be rid of me?"

The non-voice tickled his mind. Osheoan froze, staring, slowly realizing what he faced. "You ... can't be ..."

"Can't I?" The fox shook itself and trotted forward a few deft paces, coming to a stop just out of his reach. *"Not elegant enough for you? You'd prefer an eagle, maybe, all talons and pride?"* Mocking amber eyes glanced up at him. *"Mm, yes, you'd like that, wouldn't you? Sorry. I'm all you get."*

"I'm not—I mean—You can't be here," Osheoan told the spirit-animal flatly. "Not now. Not after all this time."

"Why not?" The fox sat without ceremony and began to nibble at its hind leg like a dog after a flea. *"Ah,"* it said, satisfied, *"got him."* It looked up at Osheoan across its outstretched leg, gaze suddenly disconcertingly steady. *"Seems to me, it's you to blame for 'all this time,' not us."*

"Liar!" The word blazed out before Osheoan could block it.

The amber gaze hardened. *"Foolish. We never lie."*

There was a world of warning in the suddenly cold voice, but the dam of Osheoan's self-control had already shattered. Unable to stop himself, he felt all the years of pent-up bitterness come pouring out in a torrent of words. "Oh no, you never lie. You are too far above us poor little human folk for that. Too far above us for mercy, or pity— Standing by and watching a woman die ..." But the first anguished frenzy was already ebbing. "Why?" Osheoan asked softly. "She was young, lovely, happy. Why did you take my Power from me just when I needed it the most?"

"We never did that." Was that the faintest touch of sympathy in the wry non-voice? *"Come, use your head, man. Remember your training. Were you ever taught that, even with Power, you could save everyone?"*

"No, of course not. Some folk come sooner than others to the end of their life thread, no matter what a Spirit-Speaker may do to ..."

Osheoan trailed to a stop. The fox laughed as a dog laughs, tongue lolling.

"So now! The man shows the dawning of wisdom."

"It ... was Seshawa's appointed time? Is that what you're saying?" Shaking, Osheoan gasped out, "Are you trying to tell me I didn't lose my Power, but— myself?"

The fox shook itself impatiently. *"I'm not trying to tell you anything. Go ahead."* It gestured toward Mikasha with its head. *"Your son is waiting."*

A wave of renewed fear surged through Osheoan. "I—I can't, I don't have—"

"Keep saying that often enough, and you'll make it true." The fox gave a long, gaping yawn. *"Seems to me,"* it said, fixing Osheoan with a suddenly chill stare, *"that all I've heard from you is 'I,' 'I', 'I.' You like being Spirit-Speaker, don't you? You like Being Someone."*

With an effort, Osheoan wrenched his gaze away. "I take pride in what I do. What's wrong with that?"

"Did I say there was anything wrong? So now, here is a riddle for you: What if saving Mikasha here meant giving it all up, stopping being Spirit-Speaker now, totally, forever? What would you do?"

"What do you think?" Osheoan snapped. "I'd save my son!"

"Would you, now? Go ahead, then. Save him."

Trying to ignore the mocking amber stare, Osheoan turned to his son and picked up his knife, studying Mikasha's wound, forcing himself to decide where and how to begin. If he cut there . . . No. Too risky, too near the throat. There, then . . . No, no, if his hand slipped it would—His hand was sure to slip, shaking as it was, and—

"Stop staring at me!" he shouted at the fox.

"I?" the spirit-animal said blithely. *"I am doing nothing. I am only here."*

Osheoan turned fiercely to his son again. But the fox's riddle had insinuated itself into his mind, repeating tauntingly over and over: *"What if saving Mikasha meant giving up being Spirit-Speaker forever? What would you do?"*

Osheoan looked down at Mikasha's pale face, seeing the unfinished softness of boy still hinted at beneath the firm lines of man, remembering that boy, all youth and earnestness, bubbling with laughter till his father had to laugh with him. And such a rush of warmth swept over Osheoan that he could have wept, thinking of the wasted years after he'd driven Mikasha away . . .

And yet, and yet . . . To Osheoan's horror, he found himself remembering the people of the Clan watching him in awe, heeding every word he spoke, worshiping him, their wonder warm as love. To give it all up, to see folk eyeing him in scorn, despising him for being nothing—

As they had once despised Mikasha.

And I did nothing to stop them. Ah no, Osheoan cried in sudden silent agony, *no more! I've hurt my son enough. I will not sacrifice his life to me!*

"Guide my hand," he prayed, and began.

And Power rushed up to enfold him.

*   *   *

Osheoan slowly came back to himself, trembling with exhaustion, drained of Power, wondering dimly if it would ever return. Mikasha—

"It is done," said a quiet non-voice, and Osheoan turned to see the fox, all mockery gone from its eyes. *"The poison is drained, the wound healing. Your son shall live."*

"Thank you."

"I?" The fox sat abruptly and scratched its ear with a busy hind claw. *"I did nothing.* You *chose, Spirit-Speaker. You chose."* It scrambled to its feet, laughing. *"Now, choose again. Your son will make a fine Spirit-Speaker. If he is trained. Finish his training."*

"Or?"

"Or not."

"Will I lose my Power if I don't?"

"Maybe. Maybe not. Who can say? Does it matter to you?"

Osheoan looked down to where Mikasha lay deep in healing slumber and thought of the difficult time ahead. He would be truthful to his son; he must. But would Mikasha understand? Could he forgive his father for the long, bitter lies of the past?

To his surprise, Osheoan heard himself give a soft, joyous laugh. Whatever happened, whether his Power ever returned, whether Mikasha forgave him or not, at least there was this: his son would live.

The fox, unnoted, had faded into empty air. But its final question still hung lightly in the air: *Does the loss of Power matter to you?*

"No," Osheoan said softly, and knew he spoke the truth. "It doesn't matter at all."

No Refunds

Phyllis Eisenstein

I'm sure Phyllis Eisenstein, living in Chicago as she does, has seen the leaflets. Solemn children hand them out on street corners or stick them into the advertisements tacked up on buses or rapid transit: Mrs. So and So, or Madame X, or Sister Y—"readers and advisers" to tell your future, solve your problems, stop your pain.

Or she's seen the Tarot readers sit in parks and in shabby-curtained rooms two floors up, visited by women (mostly) in suits out for an evening's fun, who giggle about rip offs as they wait to hand over their palms and their money for a peek into a magic they don't really believe in.

But maybe, just maybe, these readers have other clients, too, slipping in quietly. They believe—or they're desperate. And who knows what price they pay for their fortunes?

In many ways, "No Refunds" reminds me of O. Henry's "Gift of the Magi." Is it more blessed to give than to receive? As Phyllis Eisenstein shows, the blessing is never unmixed.

She knew he was a junkie before he opened the door. She knew that he lived on the street, cadging change from strangers, eating out of garbage cans,

117

shooting up with people who were his friends when they had the junk and his competition for returnable bottles the rest of the time. She knew because *knowing* was what she was, and what she purveyed—knowing what had been, what was, what would be. The small sign in the curtained plate glass window said READER AND ADVISER, but that was only because the police would arrest anyone who bluntly claimed to tell fortunes.

The junkie opened the door, and the little bell above his head jangled to announce him.

"Madame Catherine?" he said in a hoarse, uncertain voice. He squinted toward the drapery of beads that half-obscured the rear two-thirds of the narrow room.

She waited a moment, letting him take in her carefully cultivated ambience—the floor covered with worn, grayed-out tiles; the walls and ceiling festooned with dusty silks and velvets; the small table draped with faded satin, the pitted crystal ball sitting on a brass pedestal at its center; the gypsy fortune-teller swathed in skirts and scarves and junk jewelry. This was the decor she kept going back to, far better than the wood-paneled high-rise office and the chic suit, or the black-and-white New Age studio and the designer jeans. Clients came most readily to this shabby storefront, their basest carnival expectations confirmed by it. The right kinds of clients.

She raised a hand toward the junkie. "Come in, Steven," she said.

He pushed a few strings of beads aside and leaned into the inner sanctum. "You know my name."

"Of course." Finding his name among the myriad voices he had heard in his life hardly took any effort at all. His mother had used it, his father, his friends, his wife, a vast, echoing chorus of *Steven*. Catherine gestured toward the overstuffed chair on the far side of the table. "Won't you sit down?"

He hesitated another moment, then slipped sideways through the beads and slowly limped to the chair. He dropped to its worn cushions and sat there in silence, his head, his whole body, drooping. He was painfully thin, the skull visible behind the papery skin of his face, the cheeks deeply hollowed above a short straggling beard, the sunken eyes rimmed with dark circles. Multiple layers of clothing partly camouflaged his frailty, hanging slack at shoulder and hip, so that he looked a little like a child trying on an older brother's discards; but above his shirt and sweater collars, every cord of his neck was visible, and his Adam's apple stood out like a half-swallowed peach pit. And he stank of sweat and rotten teeth, with a sharp overtone of bleach.

He had cleaned a needle with that bleach an hour ago, she knew. Volunteers from the local settlement house had been showing the junkies how to do it, to protect themselves from AIDS. Too late for Steven, of course—she saw that the doctors had told him so weeks ago—but there was kindness in his doing it for others. He had not lost his humanity on the street, along with everything else.

She brushed a twinge of pity aside. Her business had nothing to do with pity or kindness. The kindly and the pitying died along with the wicked when the plagues came; that had always been the way of the world. Only the careful and the lucky survived. And Catherine.

When he had sat in the chair for a minute without speaking, she said, "What brings you to me, Steven?"

"Don't you know that, too?" he muttered.

She made a sweeping gesture with her open palm. "I read events, not thoughts, Steven. There is a difference. You must tell me what you want."

He looked up at her then, and there was despair in his bloodshot eyes. "I'm ill, Madame Catherine. I've been down to County Hospital, in and out, lately. They say there isn't much they can do for me."

She waited for him to go on.

He sighed again. "I've heard ... that you can do things."

She stroked the pitted surface of the crystal ball. "I can't cure you," she said quietly. "I give people advice about their lives, nothing more."

"I've heard ... that you tell people how to get money."

She inclined her head slightly. "Sometimes."

He took a deep breath, as if gathering courage to speak, then suddenly pressed his elbow against his side. He made tight fists of both his hands, and then slowly, slowly opened them, over the course of a long exhalation.

"Perhaps you should be back at the hospital," she said.

He shook his head. "I've heard about the price for the money. I'm willing to pay it."

She leaned forward, putting her elbows on the table and steepling her fingers under her chin. "And what do you think the price is, Steven?"

"Time," he said.

She said nothing.

"It's pretty obvious that if you can tell other people how to get money, you can get it for yourself, too. You don't need to collect it from your customers. But *time* ... that makes sense. You take years of life and give money in return. It's a bargain a lot of people would jump at."

"It is," Catherine said softly.

"Then you must be very old."

"I am." She watched him search her face for signs of that age, but she knew all he would see was a woman in her early forties, with crow's-feet crinkling her eyes and a touch of gray in her dark hair. A woman not much older than himself. She had looked that way for a very long time.

He eased forward in his chair. "Someone I know won the lottery. Not the big prize, but a good one. Good enough to get him off the street. You gave him the number, two months ago. His name was Charlie."

She thought back for a moment. A tall man, sallow with incipient jaundice, jobless, and without prospects. He had been living on gin, in a cardboard box, for quite some time before he found her. "I remember Charlie."

"He said he traded you six months for it."

She nodded.

"He got twenty thousand dollars."

"Twenty-one thousand six hundred dollars, precisely."

"And he'll live six months less than he would have if he hadn't come to you?"

She let her fingers interlace on the crystal ball. "It's a little more complicated than that. If he stops drinking and starts taking proper care of himself, he could live quite a long time. Perhaps even the span he would have lived if he had never started drinking. Less the six months he traded to me. If he stays on the booze, his liver will kill him six months sooner than it would have if he'd never come to me. So this life span depends on his own behavior."

"But you get that six months."

"Yes."

Steven's knobby throat bobbed as he swallowed. "Is that your standing offer? Twenty grand for six months?"

"There are many offers, Steven," she said.

"Tell me about them."

"The basic rate is five dollars an hour. The number

of hours involved is up to the client. For a day, a hundred and twenty dollars; for a year, forty-three thousand eight hundred; for twenty years, eight hundred and seventy-six thousand."

He was staring at her. "Has anyone ever given you twenty years?"

"You might be surprised, Steven," she said, thinking of one evening in the high-rise office, and a man who wanted to be rich more than he wanted to have an old age.

"And how much will you give me?" Steven asked.

She looked down into the crystal ball, as if there were something inside to see, but there was only glass, and the familiar effects of reflection and refraction. The surface was pitted and scratched from years of being knocked about, moved from city to city, country to country. Several times, she had dropped it, but it hadn't smashed. Good quality glass, but still only glass. The answer to Steven's question was inside Steven, waiting to be found.

The future was always harder to know than the present or the past. It was a changeable thing, and she herself had changed it for many a client, simply by giving away money via lotteries, racetracks, casinos, and the stock market. Catherine took almost a full minute to find Steven's future.

"How much?" he repeated.

She looked up into his eyes. The whites were yellowing, the rims reddened and watery. She knew the doctors had asked him to stay in the hospital. But he had limped his way out and come to her. "Steven," she said quietly, "I can't give you anything."

He straightened slowly in the chair.

"Not anything," she said.

He opened his mouth, but for a moment no sound emerged, then in a strangled voice he said, "Are you telling me that I don't have any time left?" He pressed his elbow against his side once more, and he clutched it with his other hand. "Am I going to die here, now?"

She shook her head. "You have a little time—a few days. But if I take them, what good will the money do you?"

"How many days?"

"Do you really want to know?"

"Yes!"

She hesitated for just a moment, and then she said, "Six."

His throat bobbed again. "You're sure?"

"Yes."

He squeezed his eyes shut and covered his face with his hands.

"I'm sorry," she said softly.

When he lowered his hands, they quivered. "Do you have a piece of paper and a pencil?" he whispered.

She drew a memo pad and a ballpoint pen from a pocket of her skirt and passed them over. Shakily, he scribbled a name and address.

"Take the six days and send the money to her," he said.

Catherine looked at the name. "Your wife?"

He nodded.

She tore the sheet off and pushed it across the table toward him. "No. I won't take the time you have left."

"It's all I have to give her," said Steven.

She looked into him again and saw that three years had passed since he had last seen his wife. She saw their final moments together—Steven looking long at the sleeping woman and then leaving without waking her. She saw farther back, to tears and poverty, to job loss and home loss. It was a familiar story: half the people who lived on the street could tell something like it.

"Listen to me, Steven," she said. "I'm an Adviser as well as a Reader. Take my advice and call her. Tell her you love her. It will mean more to her than a few hundred dollars."

He stood up. "You won't give me the money?"

She shook her head.

"Damn you," he muttered, but without force. Then he turned and limped out, leaving only the jangling bell to show that he had been there. In a moment, even that sound was gone.

Catherine closed her eyes and rested her forehead against the cool surface of the crystal ball. She was tired. Looking inside people was wearing, especially when there was no compensating gain of lifetime. Merely dealing with the kinds of clients who came to the storefront was wearing—the desperate, the destitute, the bottomed-out. Yet the high-rise office and the New Age studio were not better, just different—they delivered the debt-ridden rich who didn't want to lose their lifestyles, the entrepreneurs who would rather pay her in time than pay interest to a bank or venture capital company, the embezzlers, the market manipulators, the wheeler-dealers temporarily out of the wherewithal to wheel and deal. They were fewer than the clients of the shabby storefront, but wearing, too, in their way. Sometimes she felt like chucking them all, top to bottom. But she couldn't, because in all these long years, she had never stopped wanting to live.

Madame Catherine no longer remembered precisely when she was born, or where. It hadn't been much of a time and place anyway—a winter between wars in some duchy or principality that was always changing hands. Her mother had been the village wisewoman, using her skill at *knowing* to help others sow and reap, endure storm and drought, and find lost lambs. She had been well-respected ... until some of her neighbors decided it would be a good idea to burn her. The family had fled then, to become itinerant peddlers, wagon menders, tool sharpeners, any means her father could find to put bread in their mouths. Finally, in the great city of Genoa, where he had thought to find his fortune, he died of the plague, leaving Catherine and her mother to fend for themselves. Catherine did remember the gorgeous blue of the Mediterranean at Genoa, and the fish-stink of its docks. And she remembered the year as well, the first year whose number she had any awareness of—1348, the year of the Black Death.

Her mother had known, of course, that he would die. But knowing had not helped, because the plague could not be evaded like angry peasants, like some pillaging army. One third of the population of Europe was winnowed by plague that century. Catherine and her mother, though, were lucky and lived. But they had no land, and no man. They had only the *knowing* to support them—in Catherine, too, by that time; and so they wandered through Europe, gypsy-like, telling fortunes wherever someone would listen, to earn their bread and bed, and sometimes a little silver.

Catherine's mother had only the *knowing,* no more, for she died of old age, a white-haired, bent-backed crone: half blind, half deaf, toothless. But shortly after that death, Catherine discovered that she herself had an additional skill—she could steal time.

She was beginning to go gray by then, and to find an ache in her back in the mornings. And one day as she told fortunes in an inn on the road from Trier to Koblenz, she found herself jealous of a customer. The customer was young, beautiful, a woman just-married and spending her merchant husband's money on the foolish fantasies, as she called them, of a fortune-teller. She tossed Catherine a gold coin for those fantasies, because they had been of beautiful children and long life and prosperity. And as Catherine caught the coin to her bosom, she yearned with all her heart to have a piece of the new bride's youth.

In the next moment, she realized that her prediction for the woman had not been exactly right, that her life would not be quite so long. That, in fact, it would be five years shorter than Catherine had first thought. But she didn't say anything about it, because the fortune was told and the gold paid. She only wondered why her skill had so betrayed her. The next morning, there was no ache in her back; nor did it return; and some weeks later she saw that her gray hair was growing out dark once more. At that, she knew what she had done, and she felt a little remorse—but only a little, because the woman had called her skill foolish. Afterward, though, she never stole as many as five years from a single person. Instead, she took a month here, a week there, whenever she needed them, her age bobbing up and down, from a few gray hairs to none at all.

A woman who never grew old could not stay in one place very long, but neither could a fortune-teller, so her gypsy life went on as before. The years passed, the decades, and the decades piled into centuries. Sometimes she found a lover, though she always left him. Sometimes she found a patron, though she always left him, too, or her. She grew familiar with many places, many customs, many languages. It was not a bad life, as long as she was young.

In the seventeenth century, she finally found a way to make her own fortune. Foreseeing the success of the Dutch East India Company, she saved up a few gold coins and went to Amsterdam to invest them in a ship that she knew would come home heavy-laden with spices. Within a few years, she no longer needed to ask coin or food for telling the future. The economics of the world had changed, money could breed money, and a woman who could see tomorrow could become rich.

That was when she stopped stealing time and started taking it as pay for *knowing*.

Now, nearly three hundred years and four thousand miles from that first investment, she had all the wealth she would ever need, in stocks, bonds, precious metals and stones, and bank accounts. For nearly three hundred years, she had found people willing to trade their time for the assurance of money. Not everyone would do it, of course. Ninety-nine percent would not. But Catherine had become very good at finding that other one percent, or at enabling them to find her.

READER AND ADVISER.

She raised her head from the crystal ball. It was still early, but she decided to go home, perhaps watch a few videotapes, listen to a little music. Just now, she lived in a condominium on the lake, a pleasant place she planned to keep for four or five more years, before she moved to anther part of the city. She took a bus to the public garage where she had left her minivan, changed clothes in the van, and drove home, an ordinary-looking middle-aged woman, nothing like the gypsy of the shabby storefront.

The next day, when she arrived at the store, Steven's wife was waiting outside.

"Madame Catherine," she said. "I'd like to speak to you."

Beth was her name, the name that Steven had scribbled on the memo pad. She was thinner than his memories of her, and her face was tired around the eyes; Catherine knew she had not slept the previous night. And there was Steven, focused sharply within her life—Steven as he once had been, Steven as he was now. She had seen him eighteen hours ago.

"Come in, Beth," said Catherine, pushing the door open.

They settled on either side of the table, Beth with her hands folded in her lap, the gypsy fortune-teller behind her crystal ball.

"You know who I am?" said Beth.

Catherine nodded. "Your husband was here yesterday. I see that he followed my advice and called you."

Beth's folded hands tightened. "Thank you for getting him to do that. When he left, I tried to find him, but . . ." She shook her head. "So thank you. For giving him back to me."

Catherine waited, knowing there would be more.

Beth stared at the crystal ball. "He thinks you really can tell the future."

"I can," said Catherine.

"And he tells this . . . this really wild story about you giving away winning lottery numbers, in return for years of a person's life."

"I do that sometimes," said Catherine. "Do you want a winning lottery number?"

Beth shook her head. "I want Steven."

Catherine leaned back in her chair. "I don't give away lives here. I give away money. If that would help you . . ."

"It won't. I wish it could, but it won't. He's going to die. And I don't want him to. I don't want him to!" Her eyes squeezed shut, and tears started down her cheeks. Then she gulped and knuckled the wet streaks away with both hands.

"I'm sorry," said Catherine, and she sighed. How many wives, she thought, had said those words, in plague after plague? Even her own mother, so very long ago.

"Look," said Beth, and she was leaning forward now, touching the crystal ball with one hand, her voice tightly controlled. "What happens if somebody gives you the time and takes the money and then changes his mind. Can you give the time back?"

Catherine frowned slightly. "It's not my policy to give refunds."

"But *can* you? Are you *able* to do it?"

Catherine nodded.

"And does that mean that you could sell someone time. Extra time?"

"You mean for money?"

"For anything."

"Why would I want to do that, Beth? I haven't any desire to shorten my own life. Quite the contrary."

"But *could* you?"

Catherine looked at her narrowly. "Do you mean, would I sell Steven time?"

"Yes. Yes."

"I could," said Catherine, "but I won't. He doesn't have anything that I would accept in exchange."

"But I do," said Beth. She gripped the edges of the table. "I'm young. I have a lot of life ahead of me. Take some of it—some for yourself and some for Steven."

Catherine shook her head. "Think of what you're saying, Beth."

"Don't I have a lot of life left?"

Almost unwillingly, Catherine looked into Beth's future. There was indeed a good deal of life left to her, on the ordinary human scale. "You're all right," Catherine told her. "You'll last into your eighties, as things stand."

"Then split it between him and me. And take a fee for yourself, a broker's fee. Isn't that a good deal? You gain something from it. We all gain."

"I don't think so, Beth."

"Yes, we do!"

"Beth . . ."

"Don't you see—that way, we can be together again."

"He has more troubles than AIDS, Beth. It wasn't AIDS that drove him away from you."

"We can do something about those troubles if he lives. But if he dies, we can't even try." The tears had started again, and this time she made no move to stop them. "Please, Madame Catherine. We don't have anyone else to turn to."

Catherine looked down at the satin-draped tabletop, at the corroded brass pedestal that held the crystal ball. From the corners of her eyes, she could see Beth's hands to either side, white-knuckled. "You're making a terrible choice, Beth. There's no guarantee that he'll come back to you."

Beth's voice shook. "There's a guarantee now. If you don't do something, he's going to die. Guaranteed."

Catherine reached out to her again, to look at her past, at the better times, to see Steven as she saw him. He had been handsome, once, forty or fifty pounds ago, and he had laughed easily. He had held Beth's hand a great deal, even after they had been married for a dozen years. His last gift, when he still had a job, was a gold pendant with their initials entwined; she was wearing it now.

"You must love him very much," Catherine said at last.

"Very much," said Beth.

Catherine met her eyes. "All right. I can offer you a compromise. In five years, there will be a cure for AIDS. I'll give him six, to make sure he has time to take it."

Beth's eyes were wide. "Will you?"

Catherine nodded.

"And ... your fee?"

"There won't be any fee."

"No?"

"No. I think you'll be paying enough as it is."

"Oh, Madame Catherine ..." She found some tissues in her purse and wiped her face and blew her nose. "I'm sorry to be like this in front of you, but ... you can't know how grateful I am." She balled the tissues up and clutched them in one hand. "When can we ... ?"

"Can you bring him here at four o'clock?"

"Any time you say."

"Four." She waved toward the door. "Go on, now. Go back to him."

Beth stood up. "This is so kind of you."

Catherine looked up at her, thinking that in six hundred years she had never loved anyone as much as Beth loved Steven. Not anyone, except perhaps herself. "What will you tell him," she said, "about this deal?"

"The truth. But only afterward. Until then, I'll tell him you've agreed to give me a lottery ticket in return for the time he has left. You don't mind, do you?"

"Will he believe you?"

"I think so. He ... begged me to ask you for it."

The bell jangled her departure.

When they came back at four, Steven seemed very calm and said very little, and Beth, too, was subdued. He had bathed and put on clean clothing; but he didn't look better—the clothes, Catherine knew, were his own old ones, and they hung just as loose on him as his rags had. And she knew also that he had shot up less than two hours ago, coaxed the money out of his wife, making no secret that he was going to use it to buy junk. His argument had been that he would be dead soon, so it didn't make any difference.

The transfer of time from Beth to Catherine and then to Steven took less than a minute, and only Cath-

erine was aware of it. Afterward, she gave Beth a slip
of paper, the supposed lottery number.

"You're finished here," she said. "Go home."

Hand in hand, they left.

Occasionally, over the next few days, she wondered
if Beth had finally told him the truth, or if she was
just letting him discover it for himself as he lived on,
day after day, feeling less and less sick, gaining weight,
recoiling from the death that had almost claimed him.
She also wondered how long Beth's job at the super-
market would support Steven's habit. But she put her
curiosity aside. It had never been her policy to follow
a client after striking a bargain.

Two weeks after their bargain, a week after he
would otherwise have been dead, Steven came back
to the shabby storefront. He waited outside for a few
minutes because Catherine was with someone else, but
when that client left, he slipped in before the door
had even closed.

He thrust the beads aside roughly, and they clicked
and clattered as they swung to behind him. "You
shouldn't have done it," he said.

He looked better—anyone could have seen that. He
had gained a little weight in his face, and the whites of
his eyes had cleared. And his clothes were still clean.
Catherine saw that he was living with Beth; she
guessed that he had expected to die with her.

"You shouldn't have done it!" he said again, and
his mouth twisted angrily.

"Sit down, Steven," she said softly.

Instead, he stood behind the chair, gripping its upholstered back. Then he pounded its cushioned arm
with his fist. "How could you *do* that to her?"

Catherine saw that Beth had only told him the truth
that morning. That they had had a fight over it, culmi-
nating in Steven storming out. Two weeks before,
Catherine reflected, he wouldn't have had the strength

to slam that door. "It was her choice, Steven," she said. "I gave her what she wanted."

"She tried to tell me you were wrong about the time I had left. She tried to tell me you were a fake. As if I didn't know better!" His fingers dug hard into the chair. "Give her back those years! I don't want them!"

Catherine shook her head. "Our bargain is done. I don't give refunds. I told her that."

Steven let go of the chair abruptly. "I never agreed to that bargain."

"Your agreement wasn't required," said Catherine. "The bargain was between Beth and me."

He pointed at her, jabbing the air with his rigid forefinger. "You stole those years from her. She didn't know what she was doing!"

"You know that isn't true, Steven."

"It *must* be!"

"Then you don't know her very well. And you don't know how much she loves you."

He lowered his hand slowly. Then his shoulders slumped, as if the act of pointing had drained his strength. He leaned on the chair, shaking his head. "I can't let this happen to her."

"She'll have a long life anyway," Catherine said. "Even without those few years."

He kept shaking his head. "You don't understand. I can't take those years from her."

Catherine looked at him long and hard, though only with her eyes. She didn't want to look at him any other way anymore. Finally, she said, "Steven, don't you want to live?"

He walked around the chair and sat down. He put one hand on the table, beside the crystal ball. "What will you give me for those years? In money."

"You can live till they find a cure, Steven," she said. "You have the time now."

"What will you give me?"

"Are you sure this is what you want?"

"How much!"

She did the calculations in her head, then looked into the near future for a match. She found one in Saturday's newspaper. "Friday's lottery has a four-digit jackpot for two hundred and fifty thousand dollars," she said. "That would leave you with three and a half months to spare."

He frowned. "I meant for everything."

She looked again. "The three-digit game can give you an extra ten thousand, with fifteen days left over. That's my best offer."

"It's a deal."

"Steven—"

"It's a deal!"

Catherine shrugged. "It's your life," she said, and she pulled out her memo pad and wrote the numbers down. "Don't buy the tickets in this neighborhood. Take the bus down Ashland a couple of miles; you'll find plenty of vendors." She drew a five-dollar bill from her blouse and passed it over with the sheet of paper. "Here's your seed money and bus fare."

He tucked the paper and the bill into his shirt pocket. "I'm ready now," he said. "For the other side of the bargain."

It took only a moment for Catherine to draw five years and fifty weeks from him. "Go on, now," she said when it was done. "You have traveling to do."

He hesitated. "Have you . . . ?"

"Yes."

"I didn't feel anything."

"Do you ever feel time passing?"

He swallowed. "Sometimes." He pushed himself out of the chair. "Thanks, Madame Catherine."

"Don't come back," she said.

His lips made a thin white line. "I won't."

Catherine sat watching the beads sway after he had gone, listening to the echo of the bell. No, he wouldn't be back. She knew that even without reading him.

Three days later, Beth came.

She had been crying, crying till her eyes were swollen and discolored. She slammed the beads aside, stalked to the table, and threw something at Catherine. But that something was only a couple of pieces of paper, and instead of hitting their target, they fluttered wildly and sank to the floor. Lottery tickets.

"He's dead!" she choked, her voice roughened from the crying. "You killed him with these!"

"Sit down, Beth," Catherine said softly.

"Why did you do it? Why did you give them to him?"

"Please. Sit down."

Beth fell into the chair and stared at Catherine with her wide, raw eyes.

Catherine bent to pick up the tickets. She set them on Beth's side of the table. "He wanted you to have these," she said.

Beth shook her head. "It's blood money."

Catherine looked into her then and saw that the police had called at her apartment, had taken her down to the morgue to identify the body, had told her it was a case of overdose. And in the morning she had gotten an envelope in the mail, with these pieces of paper in it, and a note saying that he loved her.

"Yes, it's blood money," said Catherine. "It's always blood money. That's what I sell."

"How *can* you?" Beth moaned.

"He knew what he was asking for."

Beth shook her head sharply. "I don't want it. Take it back."

Very quietly, Catherine said, "I told you, I don't give refunds."

"Then just keep it!" She got up abruptly, and one

thigh struck the table so hard that the crystal ball rocked off its brass pedestal and, before Catherine could stop it, fell to the floor. It struck with a loud dull thud, which made Beth gasp and fall back into her chair. Then the ball rolled slowly across the tiles to the nearest wall, where it rebounded gently at an angle and went on rolling.

"I didn't mean—" Beth began. "I didn't . . ."

After a second rebound, the ball came to rest almost at Catherine's feet. She scooped it up with both hands and set it back on its pedestal.

"It's all right," she said. "Glass is tougher than you might think."

Beth looked at the scratched and pitted crystal ball, then she reached out a hand and touched it. "I wish I were made of glass," she whispered. "I wish I were tough."

Catherine picked up the lottery tickets, which had fallen to the floor again with the jostling of the table. She set them near Beth's hand. "Take these," she said. "They belong to you."

Beth closed her reddened eyes, as if something shining in the glass hurt them, something more than just the usual complex of reflection and refraction. "They aren't what I want," she said.

"They're the best he could do," said Catherine.

Beth stood up at last, slowly this time, not hitting the table again, and she picked up the tickets, as Catherine had known she would. The bell over the door jangled as she took them away with her.

The next day, Madame Catherine closed her shabby storefront and moved to a spacious modern office in a downtown high-rise.

Firstborn, Seaborn

Sheila Finch

I have always thought of the stories and ballads of the great silkies, their brides, and their children as a product of cold weather, cold water, and rocky coasts. Sheila Finch, as is typical for her, has thought longer and more deeply on the subject, and blended into her story the California that is her adopted homeland and the medieval iconography she has studied.

"Stella Maris," star of the sea, is one of the loveliest names used to praise the Virgin Mary. But before the Blessed Virgin was the Goddess, tied to the all-enveloping rhythms of the sea. As "Firstborn, Seaborn" shows, it is difficult to remember Her in a world ruled by a God and men who seek to bind what must be free.

The lights of the bus that brought her to this lonely stretch of California coast dwindled away in the distance, leaving her to the frozen constellations of December overhead and the luminous curls of foam below. She walked down the steps to the rocky beach, her feet sure on the familiar path. She held her breath. Except for the slow hiss of waves sucking at pebbles, the beach lay silent.

Five miles away in the small house in the city, the youngest infant would be whimpering, she knew, seeing it in her mind's eye. And the man, come home to a cold house and an empty plate, waiting for his woman, drowsing in the chair beside the cradle, another child on his lap. She could not love them, though she had often tried, but she could not hate them, either. She did not have the strength.

She let out her breath and gazed out to the horizon, as empty of feeling now as the night was of sound. A full moon climbed, laying a white path across the water. She took off her shoes and felt the bite of ocean on her bare feet. She hesitated, pulling the thin denim jacket over her stomach, covering the new life flickering in her belly; a spark too small to attract a moth now, later it would be a fire to consume her with its need, as the others had done.

Except for the firstborn.

The Pacific Ocean spread its mosaic of drowned stars before her. Memories slid through her mind like bright fish through a fog of loneliness and despair.

Once, she had been more alive in the water than she would ever be on land. She had worked with dolphins at the marine park, swimming with them, socializing them, readying them to work with the park's trainers. She had known their kind since her childhood in Mexico, friendly spirits who played beside the children in the warm surf. It was good work, though it grieved her to think of this animal held captive, and she often thought they must yearn to be free.

The marine park made money, the city thrived on the taxes the park paid, and the management expected the staff to keep their doubts and their worries to themselves. The tourists returned again and again with their children and their children's children; the entrance turnstiles clattered hungrily. The dolphins splashed and smiled and squeaked in their cartoon voices all summer long, and if they entertained any thoughts at all about the situation, their thoughts were silent.

But night after night she lay alone in her narrow bed in a rented room and thought of one dolphin in particular, leaping from flashing water, the sun flaming on his back. She could not forget one windy March day as the seasons turned, feast day of her own naming, when everything had changed. She had entered his pool a dozen times before, but this day was to be different. She had hardly slipped into the water when it turned suddenly to liquid fire, so bright she could hardly see him anymore. She cried out in fear as something ancient and immortal enveloped her in golden haze, a spray of stars flying upward from sea to sky. She sensed its presence covering her, but it did not hurt her. Something that could not be explained away on Sunday morning consumed her at that moment, in a sacrament of light and water. Then it was gone, leaving her with no words to explain or understand what it had given or what it had taken away.

After a while, the park's director noticed the bulge growing beneath her narrow rib cage. In time, he said, his white hand patting her brown one softly on the polished desktop, she might have become one of the best trainers the park had ever known, even if she was a woman. But company rules and the insurance policy give him no choice. He had to let her go. Of course, if she considered—if she would perhaps—well, there were ways. And what, after all, were the options for a poor Latina like herself if she did not take his advice? He waited for her answer, but when none came he said he hoped she would understand how much he regretted this.

She accepted his decision silently, gazing out past the dolphin pens to the sweep of ocean at the park's

boundary, opalescent in the setting sun. The director
turned away and shuffled papers on his desk. He
counted out the bills that were owed for her services.
Then he added a few more because he felt sorry for
her.

She ran from the director's office and stumbled
down the path to the dolphin pen in flooding darkness.
The tourists had all gone home. Only the plastic cups
rolling over the path, the discarded candy wrappers,
the canceled tickets spoke of their visit, and a child's
pink shoe forlorn under a bench. She had seen these
signs a thousand times before, but today she read
them as messages from a world that waited for her
outside the gates of her watery Eden.

Along the way, the park's cleanup crew leaned on
their brooms and watched her. Last in the line was
Manuel, who stood directly in front of her so that she
had to step off the path to pass him. He smiled, small,
even teeth showing white against his dark brown skin,
and put out his hand to catch her arm.

"Where are you going, Maria?"

That was not her name. She had never told any of
them her name, except the director when she applied
for the job, and he had probably forgotten. It was not
that she felt herself superior to the others who worked
in the park. But it had seemed unimportant to have
a name; there was no one who cared, no place that
it mattered.

Manuel had named her Maria, explaining that he
had to call her something. He often waited for her
after work, lounging in the shadows by the staff gate,
catching her arm and walking with her to the bus stop.
Sometimes he persuaded her to let the bus go by, and
they walked together in the sunset that turned the
highway bloodred. Those nights he spoke to her of
Mexico. He had come from the Sonoran Desert, but
she from a seaside town in Oaxaca, and it was as if

they had been born in different countries. She remembered the sound of bells on Sundays that seemed to her as a child to speak of so much glory that never came to pass. She thought the god who lived on those altars must be like an uncle who made rich promises he could not keep at Christmas, then crept away ashamed. She had left home as soon as she was able, making her way to *El Norte*, where it was said some glory could still be found by those who believed.

This evening, when she did not answer him, Manuel released the grip of his fingers, letting his hand slide gently down to brush against the curve of her belly. One finger remained on her body like the admonition of a priest.

"The little one, Maria," he said, "is not mine. ¡*Malisimo!*"

She went on past him, hearing the scratch of brooms on the path in the twilight, the muffled, jeering laughter of the others, catching the scent of their hair oil over the clean salt of the ocean's breath.

The water in the dolphin pen was dark and turbulent, a swirl of creamy foam marking the place where the dolphin had submerged. She sat on the wall, her knees tucked under her chin, and waited. He came up directly in front of her in a shower of drops that took the light of the setting sun like a spray of blood. He was a large dolphin, the largest the marine park had ever captured, and the director had named him Rex, and though that was not his name, either, there was a rightness to it the director never dreamed. But he was only a creature of the sea, after all, and perhaps she had imagined anything else. She saw herself caught for a moment in his unblinking left eye, like a caged seabird. He nudged at her toes, and she let herself carefully down into the pool beside him.

At once he rolled over and slid his body along hers,

shoving his hard beak between her swollen breasts. She felt the pulsing strength in him, the powerful tail fin thrusting against her thighs. She put her arms about him, and he swam slowly with her around the pen. Now his beak probed her gently, and she let him touch her without fear. The bruises he had inadvertently marked on her arms and legs in the first days of their learning to know each other had long since faded, and she did not doubt he knew what grew beneath her breastbone. His touch on her skin was as gentle as a lover's, and she leaned her cheek against him, feeling the sleek underbelly sliding over her hips. She felt as if she were alone with him in a timeless infinity of ocean, under a sky so full of sunset colors she could feel the weight of it on her brow. She laid her hand lightly on his blowhole, their signal. One last time, she thought, they would twist and curve in the eddying water, diving and surfacing in the late afternoon light.

But today he jerked away from her touch, so that for a moment she floundered in the tumult of the waves, kicking her feet till she was buoyant again. He swam in tight circles about her, his gaze spearing her like a fish as she trod water, gasping for breath. She opened her arms to him, reaching out with all her senses, yearning to communicate her confusion and her regret, but there was no contact this time. Instead, something rose between them; she heard voices whispering in the dark corners of her mind, felt them like the spidery touch of silk, gone when she turned to look.

Suddenly afraid, she clasped her arms about the dolphin again, and they hung suspended, bubbles beading her legs and his fins like seed pearls. The voices whispered of the sea and its ways which were not the ways of the land, and of a folk who existed long before the painted god came to sit on his altar in her village. She sensed again the power that scoffed at mission bells and human laws, more ancient than either, something that never made promises, whose gifts were dangerous and strange.

"*¿Que pasa?*" Manuel's voice wrenched her back. "Someday that fish will drown you!"

Lights pooled yellow among thick shadows in the marine park. Manuel's face was dark under a halo of lamplight, but she knew he was frowning. Pride smoldered beneath his easy smile at all times, swift to explode in flame. The big dolphin slipped out of her embrace and darted close to the pen's rim where Manuel stood, challenging him with a quick squirt of water. The man stepped back, brushing drops from his cheek.

"Come out, Maria. That one is dangerous."

The water was icy, and already she was tiring more quickly than before. She pushed herself through the foamy wake the dolphin had left and reached the edge. Manuel stepped forward and pulled her out. He picked up a towel that lay in a puddle of amber light and draped it over her, covering her belly from view.

"You are a strange woman, Maria! Why do you waste your time with a fish when you can have a man?" He waited for her reply. When she gave him none, he frowned. "One day he will not be here when you come to him! And then you will have to look at me."

Icy water lapped against her knees, shocking her out of the past. All about her, the tips of waves flashed like shattered crystals, as if someone had taken an axe to stained-glass windows. She turned her gaze outward, away from the memories, to the bright road of possibilities the moon created.

They were out there tonight, the voices, the Old Ones who had once spoken to her of their secrets, the hidden lore beyond anything the good fathers in their brown robes could speak of with authority. She knew that, although she could not see them. They waited at the other end of the moon's white bridge between the worlds of land and ocean. They called to her across the chasm that separated their kingdom of myth and mists from the reality of a woman's life taken and then abandoned. She had not accepted this at first, and in her loss and her despair, she had sought to replace what had been snatched from her, as if it was only a nightmare that could be chased away in a mortal man's arms.

She thought about this as she always did at this time of year. He was a good man, even if she could not love him. He was patient with her, expecting less than the priests had taught was her duty to give, and she could not truthfully say she was unhappy. The small house was warm enough and filled with simple, necessary things, and the comfort of children's voices that almost banished ghosts. But he had carried each one in its turn to the church in the city, ignoring her tears, and dedicated it to the uncle god with empty hands.

It was no more than a dream that haunted her, a bright fantasy she yearned for, she thought, as the Pacific sucked at her legs. The merest moment when something primeval had brushed against her, used her, and gone its way again, leaving her like a shell cast up on the dry sand, out of reach of the tide whose touch it would never forget. There was neither cruelty nor love in the act, which was why it was so hard to be rid of. But how was this better than the priests' god who lived only in pictures on walls and windows?

Yet the moon's path spread its silver coins before her each year, beckoning, and one day she must surely follow it or she would die. Perhaps, she thought, she had died already, consumed in that one explosion of cold fire that had shredded the fabric of her life.

The child fluttered mothlike below her ribs, and for

a moment she could not remember which child it was. Then the face of her firstborn rose in her mind.

On the day at the end of December when the last of the money had gone, an icy wind raged in from the northwest, whipping the waves into a fury, battering the foot of the low cliffs of the peninsula on which the marine park stood. In an evening without sunset, grey sky tangled with grey sea at the jagged horizon as she made her way to the dolphin pen. No job, no rent money, meant she no longer had a home; and the city's shelters were full. She did not know where else to go.

The pen was empty. The dolphin was gone.

She did not stay to ask what had happened to him. She never asked for anything, fearing they would not tell her if she did. Or worse, they would wonder why she wanted to know, and then they would begin to ask questions she could not answer. There was nothing she could explain even if she had wanted to. Perhaps the dolphin had sickened and died, as so many of them did. Perhaps Manuel had made good on his threat.

She left the park in darkness and walked on the beach below the cliffs, slow and heavy now, seeking a place that would give her shelter. At one point the cliffs rose straight up from the water's edge; rocks tumbled across the sand and out to sea, breaking the waves' headlong gallop onshore. One of the larger rocks curved across the sand, preserving a little warmth in the crook of its arm, and here she sat. Exhaustion dragged her down below the surface of fitful sleep.

She dreamed of window glass blazing with winged archangels trampling demons with scales and fins, and of young girls gathered in stiff white communion frocks, dark eyes darting one to the other and lips

whispering of boys, while their hands folded dutifully
on missals and rosaries, and of the mission priest who
spoke to them of Eve's sin and the uncle god's vengeance on Eve's kind.

She awoke abruptly to a tidal wave of pain, and she
clung to the sheltering rock till it subsided. The voices
of the Old Ones chittered anxiously in her mind, but
there was no time to listen to them now. Another
wave of pain rolled over her, threatening to tear her
apart. She shut her eyes against it. Again and again
the force of the child's arrival battered at her, and the
voices of the Old Ones argued, cajoled, persuaded, till
she gave in, let go and let be.

Eyes closed in a moment's calm, she drifted back
into sleep and saw the broken-tiled roofs of the town
of Puerto Angel where she had been born, the patched
and faded sails of the fishing boats on the Gulf of
Tehuantepec, the dusty squares full of scrawny chickens, a mule clopping tiredly around a well, old women,
squatting against the mission wall—grandmothers who
talked of death and birth and death again in a litany
older than the doctrines of the brown-robed fathers.
And beyond the town she saw the dark sea itself
where her people had once known the Old Ones and
both had prospered, before the coming of the priests
who smashed the ancient contract, dooming the fish-
ermen to guilt and the Old Ones to despair.

As the winter moon rose full out of the black water,
the life within her gathered itself and broke free, gush-
ing out of her into the night. The voices of the Old
Ones rose in triumph, then hushed suddenly, as if
afraid of their own eagerness. Weak and almost deliri-
ous, she fell back against the rock, colder than the
stone of the communion table.

The thin cry of the child roused her, and she looked
down at it on the sand between her legs. Moonlight
frosted the soft fuzz of its head. Its eyes were tightly

closed, and its mouth sought from side to side. She lifted it and wiped away sand and blood, then severed the cord with her teeth. She brushed its face free of the caul that clung to it like a frond of gray kelp. She put the child against her breast, but there was no milk in her yet. She let it suck the dry teat, feeling the strangeness. It closed a tiny fist over her fingers and opened dark eyes to gaze at her. She felt as if she were drowning.

At last the child was satisfied, its eyes closed, its mouth went slack with sleep. She stood up, cradling it in one arm, the other holding the rock, for her legs were as weak as seaweed, and looked out over the ocean.

The Old Ones lay half in and half out of the surf in the shelter of the rock, watching her. Starlight slipped like a mantle over their white arms and crowned their heads, turning their hair to silver flame. They did not move and neither did she. Just beyond the ring of waiting Old Ones, a dolphin leaped, the light radiant on its back.

She stumbled forward over the sand, and at once the Old Ones yearned toward her, hands outstretched in their eagerness for the life which they could not produce alone. She looked down at the infant asleep in her arms, a child that had been given to her to bear but was not hers to keep. She brushed the tip of its moon-washed head with her lips, disengaging the tiny fingers clasped about her own. Then she held it out to them. The moon glinted on the child's naked body, drawing a line of light from the small head, down the arms, over the little chest, to the gentle curve of the tail.

At that, they sighed, a sound like surf hissing over a multitude of small stones. One of the Old Ones, silver hair streaming over her full breasts, took the child from the woman and cradled it. For a moment

none of them stirred. Then as if at some signal only
they heard, they turned and darted out to sea in a
flurry of white arms and scaly tails. But the one that
carried the child held it aloft for her to see for the
last time before they disappeared under the waves.

"*¡Madre de Dios!*" Manuel's voice said behind her.
"What have you done, Maria?"

She turned and saw him cross himself against the
horror. She stepped back from the revulsion on his
face, clasping trembling arms over her slack belly.

"You have killed the child!"

She turned her back on him at that. Westward, a
dark shape rose out of the water, blocking the moon,
and she thought of the soft face of her firstborn. Regret stabbed sharply through her. She floundered
through the surf toward the dolphin.

"No, Maria, no! You must stay! It was I who let
Rex go so that you would stay here with me!"

Urgently she flailed at the man's arms that pinned
her, imprisoning her in his world. Strained toward the
dolphin, Manuel only locked her tighter. Now she saw
other dolphins attending the first. But he was larger
and stronger than any of them, a primeval spirit who
mocked the mission fathers and their painted images.
She yearned to go with him until she thought her heart
would burst. The man and the woman struggled silently at the edge of the sea while the stars flared
overhead and the moon's path beckoned.

"Perhaps it was well-done," Manuel said at last,
panting with the effort of holding her. "The child was
not healthy. Even I could see there was something
not right."

Far offshore, the dolphin reared up hugely out of
the waves, balancing himself on his tail in a blaze of
light. She cried out in desperation, and Manuel
clapped a hand over her mouth to silence her.

"The police, Maria! What would they think?"

Then the dolphin sank beneath the waves, the others with him, and the child was gone. She leaned against Manuel's shoulder and wept.

"Come home with me, Maria," he said. "I shall give you fine babies, if that is what you want."

The sea was up to her armpits.

So long ago now, she thought, yet the pain still stung like salt water on an open wound. Tears filled her eyes as she remembered how Manuel had crushed her to him that night, banishing the secrets of the sea and anchoring her to the land. The dolphin was gone, the marine park itself was gone now, and California had settled into years of drought and loss. Or was it only she who had sinned and lost? She did not know. Something fierce and awful had gone out of the world and left behind this terrible gaping sadness. She felt as if she knew the answer but was afraid to speak it.

Her skin shriveled from the water's icy touch like the fingers of death. Then she opened her eyes and found his face a hand's breadth away.

"It is the night, *mamacita*. I, too, remember," he said. "But you have never been so far out before!"

He gripped her shoulders and turned her toward the shore, supporting her when she would have stumbled and fallen beneath the waves. The worn blanket he had brought, the same one he carried to her every year like an absolution, lay folded in its usual place on the beach. He wrapped her in it, ignoring his own wet clothes, then led her up the path to the road where the battered sedan stood with its plastic Virgin and Child on the dashboard.

At the top of the cliff she stopped and looked back at the sea. He waited patiently beside her, slowly, grudgingly with the passage of the years accepting there were mysteries he would never understand. The moon was high overhead, but the white path burned between the worlds. Far out on the ocean, a speck moved, a brief flash of fin or tail, and was gone again.

The door's rusted hinges protested as Manuel opened it. The toddler gazed drowsily up at her from the backseat, thumb against his lips, the baby wakeful beside him. Their mouths moved, innocent as birds, their urgent hunger ready to consume her, like the baby pelicans in the fable the good fathers told that sucked the blood from their starving mother.

She hesitated, thinking of her firstborn, seaborn child, but her eyes were caught by the infant god on the dashboard. He was smiling.

"A woman does not thrive in this world, Concepcion," her *abuela* had said, in the shadow of the mission wall at dusk. "She endures in the cracks between past and present, church and village, sea and land, this world and the other." She had been eight years old and had not understood the old woman's words.

Manuel said softly, "I am trying to make it better. But I am a man, not an angel! Is this so hard to accept?"

She knew he spoke the truth.

"And you are my woman." He patted her stomach, settling her into the car beside him. "We will go home now, Maria Concepcion."

She sagged against the seat, shivering with cold, thinking of men whose promises were worth nothing because they had nothing, of gods who made promises they could not keep, and of that which never made promises but took what it needed at will.

And she thought of the strength a woman must find to endure against them all.

A Game of Cards

Lisa Goldstein

It all looks so civilized. A dinner party in the film community, attended by civilized, cultivated people, served by a dark-haired woman who might well be a refugee from the Third World. Family problems, problems with work, relaxation with a game of cards.

What's wrong with this picture?

Only the eyes, flicking from face to face, counting up the betrayals. And the refugee, hoping to survive for another day.

"A Game of Cards" frankly reminds me of the game "Get the Guests" in *Who's Afraid of Virginia Woolf?* The question is, however, who gets them?

The doorbell rang at seven. Rozal looked through the peephole and saw two guests framed as in a picture, a woman with short brown hair and a tall gangly man carrying a bottle of wine. Helen and Keith—they'd been at the house before. Rozal opened the door.

"Beautiful house," Helen said, coming in and slipping off her coat. Rozal nodded, not sure how to take this. Of course they knew the house belonged to Mr. and Mrs. Hobart.

She hung the coats in the closet; they had a faint perfume scent, and the smell that water brings out in wool. Was it raining, then? In the bustle that surrounded the preparations for dinner, Rozal had not been able to go outside all day.

Helen paused at the framed mirror in the entryway and patted her hair. Keith scowled and grinned at his reflection, as if resigned to what he saw. The bottle of wine hung from his hand as though attached to it; he seemed to have forgotten it was there. Rozal watched as they made their way through the thick off-white carpet in the living room, leaving footprints as they went. The carpet had been vacuumed just minutes before the party, and would have to be vacuumed again tomorrow.

She couldn't resist a quick glance in the mirror herself. Most Americans took her for older than her twenty-four years, but then most Americans looked far younger than their actual age. Her hair and eyes were brown and her complexion dark; they had called her skin "olive" at the immigration office, and she had looked the word up as soon as she got home, but she'd been none the wiser. She smiled at the reflection; she had not looked so healthy, so plump, in many years.

The doorbell rang, and she hurried to answer it. A young blond woman stood on the doorstep, Carol, another frequent visitor to the house. As soon as Rozal hung up her coat, she heard the bell again. This time when she opened the door, she saw a good-looking dark young man, balancing on the balls of his feet in impatience. He had an amused, quizzical expression, as if he had put on a face to greet Mrs. Hobart.

Rozal had never seen him in the house before, but she recognized him immediately from the movies she watched on her days off. He looked shorter than she would have expected. He said something to her in Spanish, but she smiled and shook her head: no, she was not Spanish.

Mrs. Hobart had seated Keith and Helen and Carol on the sectional couch, and now rose to greet the new arrival. "Steve!" she said. "So glad you could make it."

"Drinks!" Mr. Hobart said, coming into the living room and clapping his hands. Carol called for something Rozal didn't catch. Keith stood to hand over his bottle of wine, and Mr. Hobart pretended to be angry at him; somehow it had been both right and wrong for Keith to bring the wine.

At a signal from Mrs. Hobart, Rozal hurried through the dining room to the kitchen for the appetizers. The kitchen was at least ten degrees hotter than the living room: both ovens were on, and the cook had set a teakettle on the stove for tea. Rozal nodded to the cook, who sat on a high stool near the stove and fanned herself with a magazine, but the other woman seemed not to notice her. There was some question of status between her and the cook that Rozal did not quite understand.

Rozal took the tray of appetizers out of the refrigerator and went back to the living room. The party had already divided itself into groups: Mrs. Hobart was deep in conversation with Steve, waving her cigarette smoke away from his face, and Keith and Helen sat a little uncomfortably on the couch next to Carol. "And what do you do?" Keith asked. His face was too long, and his jaw and forehead protruded a little.

"Keith!" Helen said, and leaned to whisper something in his ear. Rozal offered them an appetizer, trying not to look amused. She had seen Carol come up to the house and talk to Mr. Hobart; money and small plastic bags were exchanged. "I thought she had something to do with video," Keith said, unrepentant. Carol laughed, and after a while Helen joined in.

Rozal returned to the kitchen for more appetizers. As she passed the wet bar that divided the kitchen from the dining room, she heard a voice raised in anger, and she glanced around quickly. In the three months she had been with the Hobarts, she had learned that though they rarely became angry, it was best to pay attention when they did. But the shouting she heard was not directed at her. Mr. Hobart sat at the bar, speaking to someone on the phone.

"I just want to know where he is," Mr. Hobart said. "No, he isn't here—that's why I called you. Well, how the hell should I know where he is?"

Rozal hurried back to the living room and began to pass around the appetizers. "Thank you, Rozal," Mrs. Hobart said. The shouting from the bar grew louder; surely everyone in the living room could hear it by now. Mrs. Hobart raised her voice to cover it.

"No, she isn't Hispanic," she said. She laughed a little, but Rozal could see that she was getting worried. She glanced at her watch. "Why don't you ask her yourself? Rozal, Steve wants to know where you're from. Do you understand?"

"From Amaz," Rozal said.

"Amaz?" Steve asked. "Where's that?"

"Oh, you must have seen it on the news," Mrs. Hobart said. "There was a coup and then a countercoup—no one's really sure who's running the country now. It was horrible. But Rozal managed to get out—she was one of the lucky ones."

"Yes," Rozal said. She had found a pack of cards somewhere on the long terrible road to the United States, and they had told her what Mrs. Hobart was saying now, that she would be fortunate, she would reach her destination. "Great abundance," the cards had said, and she had certainly come to the land of abundance, a place where even the candy bars were encased in silver.

The doorbell rang, and she set down the tray of appetizers and went to answer it. Peter Hobart, Mr. and Mrs. Hobart's son, stood in the doorway. By the streetlight behind him Rozal could see the rain she had sensed all day, coming down now in a black sheet like a slab of stone. She looked for Peter's wife, but did not see her anywhere.

"John!" Mrs. Hobart called. "John, he's here."

Peter took off his leather jacket, revealing a ponytail that fell nearly to his waist, and handed the jacket to Rozal. It shone like silk from the rain. Mr. Hobart came into the entryway as she was putting it away. "Finally," he said. "Don't you think you're taking the concept of fashionably late a little too far?"

"He wants to shout at me but he doesn't dare," Peter said to Rozal. "Not with all these people here."

Rozal smiled at him, not too wide a smile because her first loyalty, after all, was to her employers. Still, she couldn't help but like Peter; over the months she had discovered that most people did.

"We can start eating now," Mr. Hobart said, going into the living room. "My son has decided to grace us with his presence."

"Kill the fatted calf," Peter said. He did not follow his father but remained behind to whisper to Rozal. "I've got something for you, Rosie my love. You'll like it."

Rozal closed the door to the closet, pleased. She remembered the loud dissatisfied tourists she had seen in Amaz, traveling in groups like fat geese, and she thought how lucky she was to be here, in this house, working for people as kind as the Hobarts. She had never heard that employers gave gifts to their servants. What could Peter possibly have for her? The pocket of his jacket had felt heavy.

The guests moved in an undisciplined group toward the dining room. "I'm sure everyone needs their drinks refreshed," Mr. Hobart asked, going behind the bar. "I would have asked before, but I was busy trying to find my son."

"Were you?" Peter asked. He sat at one of the two remaining places at the table; the other was probably for his wife. "There was no reason to bother Debbie— you know I always turn up sooner or later."

Rozal went to the kitchen and began ladling the soup. "Does Mr. Hobart hate his son?" she asked the cook.

The other woman looked at her so oddly that for a moment Rozal thought she had gotten a word wrong, and she went over what she had said in her mind. Then the cook said, "It's none of our business what they get up to. My job is to cook the food, and yours is to serve it, and that's all we have to know." Chastised, Rozal took the first bowls of soup out to the dining room.

"Looks wonderful," Keith said. "Is this Amaz cuisine? Amazian cuisine?"

There was silence for a moment; Keith had made another social error by not knowing that the Hobarts had a cook in addition to a maid. Rozal began to like him. "I'm sure Amaz cuisine would be wonderful," Mrs. Hobart said graciously. "We're stuck with plain old American tonight, I'm afraid. Does anyone object to lamb?"

Rozal went back to the kitchen for more soup. She had never heard of Amaz cuisine; since the drought and the disruptions on the farms, most people had had enough to do just finding food to eat. A friend of hers, a man who had come to America with her, had opened a restaurant in the refugee neighborhood near downtown. He'd told her that no one here really knew what people ate in Amaz; he could serve anything he liked.

The talk at the table grew boisterous. Rozal knew that Mr. and Mrs. Hobart were in something called the "entertainment industry," and the idea of a business formed solely to entertain greatly appealed to her. But she could barely understand anything the guests said, with their talk of points and box office and percentages.

Steve began to talk about a movie he'd seen lately. Carol, seated next to him, was watching him intently. Keith tried to say something but Steve interrupted him, his voice growing angrier and louder. "You've got to look at the numbers!" Mr. Hobart said, pitching his voice to drown out everyone else's. "Look at the numbers!" Rozal wondered what numbers Mr. Hobart meant. She didn't think she could ask anyone; certainly the cook wouldn't know.

At last the meal ended, and Rozal went to the kitchen to prepare the tray of coffee cups. Loud laughter came from the pantry; Rozal looked through the doorway and saw Carol and Mrs. Hobart standing there. "He's gorgeous!" Carol said. "Wrap him up— I'll take him home! Did you invite him for me?"

"Of course I did." Mrs. Hobart waved the smoke from her cigarette away from her face. "You were complaining for so long about never meeting any good men that I thought it was our duty to find you one. Go in there and be charming."

"What's wrong with him? Is he married?"

"Never been married, as far as I know."

"What does that mean? Is he afraid of commitment? Oh, no—I bet he's gay!"

Mrs. Hobart laughed. "I don't think so. He was dating someone for six months—they just broke up."

"It's drugs, then."

"You'd know that better than I would."

"I don't sell the hard stuff, you know that."

"Listen—why don't you ask him yourself if you're so curious?"

"Oh, sure. Excuse me, but do you have any antisocial habits I should know about? And by the way, you wouldn't happen to have any horrible diseases, would you?"

Mrs. Hobart shepherded Carol into the dining room, and Rozal followed them. "You don't know how lucky you are, being married," Carol said, turning back to her hostess.

The guests in the dining room seemed to have talked themselves out; Carol and Mrs. Hobart took their places in silence. Rozal could hear the rain beating on the roof. Peter leaned back in his chair. "Oh, yeah," he said. "I brought something you might be interested in."

Rozal set down a coffee cup and looked up at him, wishing she had some pretext to stay in the dining room. Or could this be the present he said he'd gotten her? As if in answer to her question he said, "Stay here, Rosie—you'll like this."

He stood and went to the living room. Mrs. Hobart exchanged glances with a few of the guests, her eyebrows raised above her china coffee cup. Mr. Hobart whispered something to her, and she said, "Well, I certainly have no idea. He never tells me anything, you know that."

Peter returned with a flat box the size of a book. "Oh . . ." Rozal said involuntarily.

He winked at her. "I thought you'd like this, Rosie my love," he said. "You've seen these before, then?"

She reached her hand out to touch the box, but Peter had already turned to show it to Steve. "I found these in that new neighborhood downtown, where all the refugees live," Peter said. "They said it's the first time they've gotten a shipment of cards from Amaz."

"What are they?" Carol asked. "Are they like tarot cards?"

"Apparently you're supposed to play a game with them," Peter said. "That's what the man who sold them to me said, anyway. Isn't that right, Rosie?"

Rozal shook her head, wishing she had the words to explain. "They say—they tell us what happen in my country. In Amaz."

"What do you mean?" Mrs. Hobart asked.

"Like on television. We have no television, so we read the cards."

"You mean like the news?" Carol asked.

"*Beka*," Rozal said, so grateful for the word she reverted to her own language. "Yes. They tell us the news."

"Actually you're supposed to play a game with them," Peter said, frowning a little. "See? It looks like Bingo." He opened the box and took out little boards, which he passed around to everyone at the table.

Carol laughed, delighted. Keith turned his board over and studied the elaborate pattern on the back. "Come on, Helen," he said to his wife, who had not touched her board. "Let's play awhile." Helen looked around the table, seeming anxious that her husband not make another blunder, but when she saw the others collect their boards, she relaxed.

Rozal looked on, feeling wretched. This was not the way you treated the cards at all. You had to read them for the latest news first; it was only when they became outdated, when all the timeliness had gone out of them and another pack was issued, that you played games with them. Or you told fortunes; she had been the best in her village for coaxing meaning out of the cards.

She ached for news of Amaz, something to counter the rumors she and every other immigrant heard every day. Who had come to power while she had been struggling to find her way in America? Which faction had triumphed? Were the famines finally over?

Peter began to read the instructions. Was this the present he had promised her? She felt cheated, so bitterly disappointed that she could barely pay attention.

But Peter had said that a shipment of cards had come in. She could buy one the next time she went downtown to visit her friends. She relaxed and began to watch the game. It seemed odder than she could say to look on while these people, most of them strangers, played a game familiar to her since childhood.

"'Announcer will take card from deck and read face,'" Peter read. Everyone laughed. "Rosie! Hey, Rosie, what does this mean? Look, it's written in Amazian, too. Here, translate this for us, will you?"

The language she spoke was called Lurqazi, not Amazian. She took the instructions from Peter but did not try to read them; she had had to leave school when she was eight. "You have to take the card from—from here—"

"The deck," Mrs. Hobart said, encouraging her.

"Yes, the deck, and read what it says. And then if you have that picture on your card, you cover it with a stone. And if you have these pictures here—" She drew lines on the card with her hands, vertical, horizontal, diagonal.

"See, it's Bingo," Peter said. "Where do we get all those stones, though?"

"Poker chips," Mrs. Hobart said. "John, where did you put the poker chips?"

Mr. Hobart stood heavily; he had had a little too much to drink. Carol studied her card. "Look, there's a picture of a cactus here. And ugh, look—here's a snake."

Mr. Hobart returned with the case of poker chips. "Now what?" he asked.

"Now I take card from deck and read from face," Peter said. "Okay. Okay, it looks like a house. Anyone have a house?"

"I do," Keith said.

"My man!" Peter said. "One poker chip for you— here, pass it down. And the next card—"

"No," Rozal said. Everyone turned to look at her. "Now you read the—here. Read what it says."

"Hey, look at this," Peter said, unfolding the instructions. "It's got—they look like fortunes. House, let's see. House—here it is. 'Beware of build on unstable land.' There you are, Keith—beware of build."

Everyone laughed but Helen. Now Rozal remembered that Keith and Helen had talked a little about their new house during dinner. The card must mean that they couldn't afford it. She glanced at Helen; the tightness around the other woman's mouth told her everything she needed to know.

These people weren't that different from the ones whose fortunes she had read in Amaz. They had the same hopes and fears and desires, and their bodies gave away what they tried so hard to hide with words. But she saw that they didn't understand the power of the cards, that they had no idea what they were doing. If she said something, would they stop? She didn't think so.

"Okay, next card. Cactus. Hey, good one, Carol." Someone passed Carol a chip. "And the cactus means—"

"Don't tell me, I don't want to know," Carol said. "Prickly, right? Sharp and unpleasant."

"Cool water in a dry country," Peter said, reading.

Everyone turned to look at Carol, who blushed. "Not bad," Mrs. Hobart said. "Come on, do another one. I want to see what they say about me."

Rozal had sagged forward a little in relief. The cactus meant that the drought in Amaz had ended. She had seen it on Carol's board but that didn't mean that it would turn up in the deck. So—unstable land meant that the country was still in the hands of bad leaders, but at least the water had come, and the famine might end.

She glanced at the well-fed group at the table and saw that they had guessed none of this. They were only interested in what the game might say about themselves; they didn't realize that the cards held more than one meaning. A story they could not guess at unfolded all around them.

Peter drew another card from the deck. "Looks like—scales." He showed it to the rest of the party. "Scales of justice. Do you have that in Amaz, Rosie?"

Rozal nodded, unable to speak. Justice would come to Amaz, then. She was crying a little, and she wiped her eyes quickly so that no one would notice.

"Here!" Keith said, looking up from his board.

"Keith!" Peter said. "Who said you're supposed to win this game? I haven't gotten a single one yet."

Keith grinned. "Read it."

"Justice, balance. A wise man speaks unwelcome words."

"A wise man," Keith said, still grinning. "What do you know."

"What do they mean by unwelcome words, though?" Carol asked.

"You did tell me my last picture sucked," Mr. Hobart said.

Helen stirred, and with that gesture Rozal understood a great many things. Keith needed to write for Mr. Hobart's next picture; he had bought the house on the strength of his expectations and then had antagonized Mr. Hobart by speaking frankly to him. Helen, sitting beside Keith and squeezing his hand, meant to make certain he said nothing unpleasant the entire evening.

"I'm sorry, I shouldn't have—"

Mr. Hobart waved his hand. "No, no—you've groveled quite enough for that already. And look at Steve here—he's spent dinner telling me how much my current picture sucks."

"Yeah, but he's an actor," Keith said. "Everyone knows actors don't know anything."

He had meant to be charming, Rozal saw, but because there was some truth in what he said—Mr. Hobart listened to screenwriters far more than he listened to actors—Keith had managed instead to insult Steve as well as Mr. Hobart. Helen saw it, too, and she tightened her grip on her husband's hand.

"Is that so," Steve said flatly. "Did you know I have a master's degree in philosophy?"

"No—look, I'm sorry. Do you really?"

"No," Steve said, and everyone laughed.

Keith sat back with relief. He thought the crisis had passed; he had missed the fact that no one had really relaxed. Mrs. Hobart lit another cigarette, though her last one still smoldered on the saucer in front of her. Steve glanced at his watch, and Carol looked at him anxiously, clearly hoping he would stay. The rain sounded loud on the roof.

"Whew," Peter said. "Next card. Or should I just give it up entirely?" Everyone called for him to continue. "Okay. The lion."

"Yo!" Steve said. "That's me—the lion. What does it say?"

Peter looked at the instructions and laughed. "Cruel," he said.

"What?"

"Cruel. That's all it says. Here, look."

"That can't be me—I'm a pussycat. It's got to be a mistranslation. Here, Rozal. What does this say?"

Rozal moved forward to take the instructions from

his hand. There was a growl of thunder from outside, and all the lights went out.

Someone laughed; she thought it might be Peter. "Get the candles!" Mrs. Hobart said, sounding a little frightened. "Rozal, you know where the candles are, don't you?"

"Yes," Rozal said. She felt her way toward the kitchen. Lightning jumped outside, briefly illuminating her way, and the thunder roared again. "Hey, it's the lion," Mr. Hobart said, behind her. "Just what the card said."

A few people laughed, but Rozal knew Mr. Hobart was right; the cards predicted small truths as well as large ones, current events and things that might not happen for years. A light glimmered ahead of her, and she saw that the cook had managed to find the candles and light one. She took the silver candelabrum and four candles from the cabinet, lit the candles and set them in the candelabrum, and headed back.

"Can you read this by candlelight?" Steve said as she came up to the dining room table.

She took the instructions from him. "*Kaj*, cruel," she read. Perhaps she should lie and tell him it meant strong, or manly. But by the shivering light of the candles, she saw Carol looking at him, wide-eyed, and she knew that she couldn't lie for Carol's sake. "Cruel, yes," she said.

No one spoke for a moment. Then Carol said, "What the hell—it's only a pack of cards."

Suddenly Rozal saw a brief glimpse of the future, something that had happened to her once or twice before when she read the cards. Steve and Carol would become lovers; she would be water in a dry country to him for a little while, until his temper and jealousy got the better of him. She wanted to warn Carol, but she knew the other woman wouldn't believe her.

The lightning struck again. Each face stood out as sharp and meaningful as a card. She saw the patterns and currents swirling among them, and she knew from the way they looked at her that now they saw her for what she was, a fortune-teller and wisewoman.

Peter took a long breath and turned over the next card. "Garden," he said.

"I've got that one," Mrs. Hobart said.

Peter squinted in the candlelight and read the instructions. "A shelter shaded by leaves, a place of protection," he said. Then he laughed, almost involuntarily. "Refugee," he said.

No one laughed with him. Everyone sat hunched over his or her card, drawn in tight against what might be coming. "Let me see that," Mrs. Hobart said, reaching out for the instructions.

"Refuge," said Keith, the writer. "They mean refuge."

"Oh," said Mrs. Hobart. "Oh, thank God."

"Next card," Peter said, speaking quickly as if anxious to finish. "Looks like a beautiful woman. Anyone have this one?"

"I do," Mr. Hobart said.

"Good. Beautiful woman, let's see. Here it is."

"Well?" Mr. Hobart said. "What does it say?"

Peter looked up at his father. His face was expressionless in the candlelight, all his good humor leached away. "I'm not going to read it," he said.

"What?" Mr. Hobart said. "What do you mean—you're not going to read it? Give me that."

"No."

"Peter—"

Silently, Peter gave his father the instructions, and in that motion Rozal saw twenty-five years of similar gestures between father and son. Mr. Hobart scanned the list of cards, looking for the beautiful woman.

" 'Treachery, betrayal,' " he said. " 'The woman

does not belong to the man.' " He looked up at his son. "So? What does that mean? Why wouldn't you read that?"

"You know perfectly well."

"I'm afraid I don't—"

"Do you want me to tell everyone? I will if I have to. I've certainly got nothing to lose."

Mr. Hobart laughed. "Peter, if you've got something to say—"

"You slept with Debbie, didn't you? And you didn't even have the decency to do it before we got married—you had to wait until afterward—"

"Peter, you can't believe—"

"It was more fun to wait, more exciting, wasn't it? More of a conquest—see, the old man's not quite dead yet, not if he can interest his son's lawfully wedded wife—"

"Peter, stop that. You have no right to say those things—you have no proof—"

"Of course I have proof. She told me. She felt so bad about it that she finally came out and told me. Why do you think she isn't here tonight? She never wants to see your face again."

Mr. Hobart turned to his wife. "Janet, I never— You have to believe me—"

"Of course I believe you," Mrs. Hobart said. The gaiety was gone from her voice; she sounded almost as if she were talking in her sleep. "Peter, why are you saying these dreadful things?"

"I'm not saying anything, Mom," Peter said. "It's the cards talking. The cards just told you everything you need to know."

"It's only a game, Peter," Mrs. Hobart said. She reached for a cigarette.

The lights came on. All around the table people blinked against the brightness. One by one they dared to glance at each other, seeing in each others' faces a harshness that hadn't been there earlier. "Well," said Carol, pushing back her chair, "it's late—I've really got to go."

"Me, too—" "Thank you for a wonderful dinner—" "We'll see you again—" Rozal hurried to the entryway closet to get their coats.

As she went she saw a last picture of Mrs. Hobart, the smoke spiraling up from her cigarette as she stared bleakly at the board in front of her. It would take awhile, Rozal knew, but after all the accusations were spoken, after Mr. Hobart had moved out and started the divorce proceedings, she would learn to be, finally, a shelter shaded by leaves, a place of protection.

Courting Rites

Kristine Kathryn Rusch

Humphrey Bogart used to star in the sort of hard-edge, black-and-white film that ``Courting Rites'' could easily be made into. But let's cast Lauren Bacall or Mary Astor as the detective this time (if we don't opt for Kathleen Turner as V.I. Warshawski)—a gumshoe who isn't as tough as her trade, but who's as smart as any of the movie detectives who wait behind those glass doors for clients to walk in with problems that are always, always more than they seem. Maybe even smarter. Those detectives usually turn up in Los Angeles and New York. Ms. Winters works out of Nevada, where the rents are cheap.

From this winner of the John Campbell, the Hugo, and the World Fantasy Awards, we have the tale of the hard-boiled detective with a heart that's soft—but not *that* soft.

I should have known the case would be difficult from the start. He walked into my office, sure as you please, confident he could charm any woman within range. Maybe he could have once; he had a face that even at his age registered beauty. Problem was, the face should never have grown old. His silver hair and startling blue eyes only accented the idea that this man should have died young.

"Miss Winters?"

I nodded. I allowed men of his age certain liberties when it came to addressing me. Any man under forty-five would have been reminded curtly that the proper title is "Ms."

"How may I help you, Mr."—I glanced at the appointment book—"Silas?"

He smiled. "Silas is my first name."

"And your last?"

"Doesn't matter." He took the chair in front of my desk. His clothes, dated and slightly formal, carried the faint scent of pipe smoke. It added an exotic feel to my rather staid office.

There are, perhaps, a thousand P.I.s in LA, which is why I left. I took all my ready cash and set up shop in Nevada, where the land and the rents are cheaper by hundreds—sometimes thousands—of dollars. I set up a fancy office—plush blue upholstered chairs, matching carpet, framed prints on the wall, all-important air-conditioning, and room for my part-time secretary in the months I needed her. I had hoped it would give clients the idea that I was well-off—a woman who knew what she was doing. It helped with tourists. But I got the sense that this man was not a tourist.

"So," I said again. "How may I help you?"

"You may find my banjo."

Whatever I had expected, it wasn't this. "Your banjo?"

"It may sound trivial to you, Miss," he said. "But to me, it is of the utmost importance."

I folded my hands on my clean desk. I hadn't had a client in weeks, and the last had been a skip-trace

out of Vegas. Certainly not the most interesting kind
of case, nor the most lucrative. "What is it, a collec-
tor's item?"

He smiled, and I saw a flash of that once-powerful
charm. "It's one of a kind."

"Pictures, records, serial number?"

"No, none." He waved a hand, dismissing my comment. "It was made by my grandfather. The banjo
looks like a normal banjo, but when you touch it, it
feels warm—elastic, as if a live thing were stretched
across the drum instead of dried skin. It will not play
for you. In fact, it will not play for anyone except the
person who owns it."

I scrawled notes, pleased that I also had the tape
running inside my desk. I couldn't decide if this man
was a nutcase or not. He seemed rational, but then,
so did Ted Bundy. "So what happened to it?"

I expected him to shake his head. Instead, his entire
expression softened. "It's a bit of a story," he said. "I
fell in love." He took a picture out of his wallet and
slid it across the desk. A professionally done job: black
windblown hair, wide painted eyes, and a glossy
mouth. A beauty.

"Her name is Mariah Golden. She lived at Fifth and
Fremont. I had occasion to visit next door. We struck
up an acquaintance, and eventually, she convinced me
to stay with her. A week later, I awoke one morning
to discover that she and the banjo had disappeared."

"Not kidnapped? No ransom?"

"Oh, no," he said. "And the police say they can't
do anything."

"I suppose not." I tapped my pencil on the desk,
then quit when I remembered the tape recorder. "I
take a $500 retainer, and charge $25 per hour, plus
expenses."

He took the money—cash—from his wallet, and set

it between us. "I'm staying in her house, waiting for her. You can reach me there."

I nodded, knowing I should have asked a dozen more questions, but deciding that I would rather wait until later. Until I had investigated a bit on my own.

He got up, straightened his pants legs, and nodded once.

"Tell me," I said. "What is the importance of this banjo?"

He walked to the door, as if he hadn't heard me, then paused. When he turned, he watched me for a moment, as if he were assessing me. Finally, he said, "I'll die without it," and then let himself out of the room.

No chemicals bleached the Nevada sky. The sun was pure here, hot and radiant. The highway looked like a sharp heat vision against the desert brown. Even my new car, with its fancy air-conditioning system and loud-playing stereo, faded a little in the heat.

I came out here once a day to view the vast emptiness. The desert reminded me of life—little patches of growth fighting against an overwhelming army of death. Death and I were constant companions. In LA, it was part of my job—always a gunshot away. And here, here my finger rested on the trigger.

I pulled to the side of the road, and shut off the car. Whirling dirt surrounded me—not a dust storm—just dust devils, playing with my mind. The way that man had, Silas, the one who wanted the banjo.

He probably wanted the woman, too.

I got out, stretched, and sucked in the dry air. The desert consoled me. It was the only place where I could admit my unhappiness. I had run away to this small Nevada town. I had left LA not because of those thousand other detectives, but because I got to the point where I imagined Death beside me.

It happened late one afternoon, in an alleyway near Graumann's Chinese. I had cornered a young pimp who wouldn't let me take a fourteen-year-old girl—the one it had taken me nearly a month to find—because, he said, she was his best "lady." He was mouthing off to me when I pulled out my pistol. The gun didn't make him quit—maybe he thought a lady wouldn't use one—so I let a shot ricochet off the wall. The second wasn't as well-timed—the pimp let out a grunt and slid to the garbage-strewn pavement.

Then everything froze. Street noise I hadn't thought I heard disappeared. Cars stopped in their tracks, and the pimp paused in mid-groan. A man stood over the pimp, a slender man, longish dark hair and startling blue eyes. A man who hadn't been there before.

"I'm going to stop this," he said. He had the most beautiful voice I had ever heard. "You're way past your limit."

He ran his hand over the pimp's wound. A gout of blood and pus leaked out, followed by the bullet. The wound closed itself, leaving only a scratch. The man smiled, tipped his hat at me, and then the sounds came back—the honking horns, blaring music, nattering tourists. The pimp completed his moan, touched his shoulder, and looked surprised when no blood coated his fingers.

The man had disappeared.

I cuffed the pimp, left him, and took the girl home. She ran away again, not a week later. Maybe the vision had been right. Maybe I killed too many and had sympathy for too few.

I came to Nevada to find solace. Instead, I found a loneliness so deep that not even the desert would soften it. I would dream of the man in black, his beautiful voice and his striking eyes, and in the morning, I would wake, my gun clutched in my hand, wondering how the barrel would taste against my tongue.

The dream hadn't come in nearly a month.

I missed it.

The heat made my skin prickle. I watched the dust devils swirl around me, wondering if they were lonely, too. Finally I decided they weren't—they always worked together, in company of two. I went home to an empty house. No one had kept me company for a long, long time.

Mariah Golden spent her days at the hospital, holding the hand of an old man dying of cancer. His room had that putrid stink of flesh gone bad, but she didn't seem to mind. She read to him, watched television with him, or sat quietly beside him, a presence, nothing more.

I had no trouble finding her. She lived in the family home just outside of town—alone, from what I could tell. She used her credit cards regularly to send flowers to the old man, and she made no effort to hide her appearance around town. Odd thing for a thief, but then, a banjo was an odd thing for a wealthy woman to steal.

I waited until she went on one of her hospital runs, then used the lock set to let me into her house. The security alarm was a familiar one—I had been the consultant for the LA firm that developed it—and so I knew I had thirty seconds to disable it before the cops arrived, guns in hand.

It took me fifteen.

Two steps down let me into the sunken living room, done in cream with Navajo blankets for color. Designer books stood on the wall, a framed Chagall hid from the light. I assumed the small objets d'art decorating the tables were also worth a small fortune.

I took two steps back up and stopped in the dining room to admire the stained-glass chandelier and the mahogany table. The dishes in the hutch were Wedgwood—predictable, I thought—and a Dali original dominated that room.

No banjo.

Not that I expected it to hide in plain sight.

The walls were thin. Neither the bookcase nor the painting could hide more than a shallow money safe—and money didn't concern me. I glanced in the kitchen, approving of the stove island, the expensive hanging pots, and the more reasonably priced (and obviously used) stoneware. The stereo lived in this room, which was probably where Mariah spent most of her time.

I went out the side kitchen door and into a narrow hallway, lined with track lighting focused on more framed, expensive art. The master bedroom looked as if no one lived there. The bed had a regulation military feel to it, and nothing cluttered the end tables. I opened closets and drawers, finding nothing except men's clothing—much of it silk, and much of it dated.

The master bath smelled dry and even lonelier than the bedroom.

Across the hall stood the only other bedroom. It was small, and lived in. Clothes scattered all over the chair and desk, empty hangers in the closet, an unmade water bed in the corner, and well-thumbed paperbacks stacked on the headboard. I searched this room slowly, careful not to disrupt the mess.

Nothing.

The trapdoor to the attic delivered dust and mice droppings. The attic itself was empty, as was the crawl space under the house. I walked back to the sunken living room, turned and surveyed the place, worried that I missed something.

My search was fine. If Silas had been right, and she had stolen his banjo, she certainly wasn't hiding it here.

I sighed. I had more questions for him.

* * *

He looked even older when he answered the door at the house on Fifth and Fremont. His hands were palsied, and age spots had appeared on his skin. His beautiful silver hair was thinning.

"Come in," he said, as if my presence annoyed him.

I stepped into the house and saw that the same person had decorated both houses. They shared a creamy, expensive Southwestern look, a taste in modern art, and a penchant for exact detail.

"She's not difficult to find," I said, refusing to move away from the door so that he could shut out the sunshine. "She spends every day at the hospital. She has no need of money, and she has no banjo hiding in her house. In fact, when she bought this house five months ago, the realtor said she bought it with a man in mind. You, maybe?"

"Most likely," he said.

"It's time to tell me what you know."

"You won't believe me," he said.

"I've been known to believe some pretty strange things."

"Yes," he said. "You have."

He took me inside, and closed the door. The room grew dark, but not as dark as I had feared. Sunlight filtered through the mini-blinds. He pushed aside some cushions on the couch, as if he expected me to sit. I didn't. He walked over to the fireplace and turned his back to me.

His silver hair curled against his collar. He had a young man's body, slender, broad-shouldered, slim-hipped. From the back, I would have guessed him to be in his thirties.

"We've met before," he said.

I frowned. Surely, I would remember a man as old and as beautiful. "I don't remember."

"I know," he said. He picked up a poker, jabbed it

at the carefully stacked wood. The logs crumbled into ash. "I looked different then, but I've been beside you from the moment you shot that man trying to rob your friend's convenience store."

I had been alone in that convenience store. Me and the thief. Not even Suzy saw it. She had been in back dialing 911.

He set the poker down and turned, his hands shaking more than ever. "The last time, I stopped you from killing a man in an alley in Hollywood. You got trigger-happy, toward the end."

The overlay fell across him like a two-part transparency. Same slim body, same beautiful hair—now silver, same startling blue eyes.

"No," I whispered.

He shrugged. Either I accepted him or I didn't.

"What happened to you?" I asked.

"There are maybe a hundred of us working this world," he said. "Each with our own tools, our own abilities. I'm one of six who handle the Southwest." He saw the look on my face. "They can't help, either. We must each work our own people in our own way. If we fail, we can blame no one but ourselves." He smiled. "And the only admonition I got when I started—the only one—was to let no one else touch my tools."

"Your banjo."

He nodded.

"Without it you age?" I asked.

"Without it I die," he said.

"Why would Mariah want to kill you?" I did believe him, against my will. His voice was the same.

"She doesn't. She wants to save someone."

The picture came clear, then. "The old man."

He nodded. "Her father."

And suddenly I was back five years, fifteen pounds lighter, and six hundred strands of gray darker. Not the lone gumshoe of the mystery novelists, but a detective with the LAPD, like my father and grandfather before me. Only a girl born to the Winters family, but still she had to follow tradition.

That afternoon, I hurried through the halls of the hospital, late as usual. We had a last-minute call, third convenience store robbery in a week, and arrived too late to do anything but mop-up. I figured by the time I got there, he would already be out of post-op, and comfortable in his room again.

I wasn't worried. The operation was routine.

I stopped at the nurse's station and let the ambiance wash over me. Intercom voices, a bit too measured, a bit too calm. Televisions, playing clashing programs. Beeping equipment, and hushed whispers. The squeak of rubber soles against tile. Lights blinking in the background, and underneath it all the too-strong smell of disinfectant.

A nurse set her clipboard aside, looked up at me with a fake smile, prepared for trouble. I told her my name, told her who I had come to see. Her face blanched a bit.

"Next of kin?" she asked.

"Daughter," I said.

She nodded. The routine had not gone according to plan. She hustled me through back corridors and side doors, ending up in a room I had never seen before, would probably never see again.

My father looked smaller, diminished somehow, tubes up his nose and in his mouth. An oxygen tent over his face. His hair was wispy and gray, his hands skeletal. The monitors beside him beeped at intervals even I knew weren't natural.

"I'm sorry," she said. "It was worse than we thought."

Later they told me. Later they said they opened him up and found that the single small tumor was a growth that extended through his entire body. The growth hadn't shown up on any tests. They closed him immediately, but the procedure sapped what strength he had. They were hoping that he would live until morning. I think he managed to live until he saw me.

His eyes flickered once. I caught a glimpse of them, brown and cloudy. I knew the look, had seen it too many times on the street. He smiled, just a little, and for a moment, I thought I heard music. Then it stopped—and so did he.

I sat there for what seemed like hours, but it must have been only minutes. Then I realized that I was completely alone. No one left. No family, no lover. No one to hold me when I cried.

"Miss Winters?" A man beside me, dressed in black. An old-fashioned suit, a banjo on his back, and the prettiest blue eyes I had ever seen. He extended his arms to me, and I went into them, let him hold me while sobs shivered through my body. Then when I was done, when the wave had passed, I was sitting on the chair again, my father's body before me, businesslike nurses invading the room like ants.

I quit the force. Too much death, I said. Then I went out and courted him my own way.

Hospitals were never quiet. This one was no exception. The halls were wide and expansive, more like those in a Hyatt Regency than a small Nevada hospital. Someone had painted them kelly green, and placed a plush carpet on the floor. I missed the squeak of rubber soles against the tile.

I left Silas in the lobby, staring at the terrarium. I didn't trust him. He had fallen in love with this woman, had trusted her with the very thing that would, if improperly handled, destroy him. I didn't want him to do it again.

I stopped at the door to the room and stared inside.

The television blared. The old man huddled on the bed, eyes closed. As I watched, I realized that he was probably no older than my own father had been. Sickness had diminished him. In Mariah's eyes, he was probably a giant of a man, immortal and all-powerful. What kind of life would she have without him? If death came to her father, it would come to her, too. If death could defeat a man as powerful as that, it could defeat anyone.

But Mariah had outsmarted death. She had traded her father's life for Silas's, and for it, all she had to show was this hospital room that stank of decaying skin.

I closed my eyes. If I had had Silas's banjo, would I have given it up? Even knowing that our existence would be a kind of never-ending purgatory of bad television, lime green walls and disease?

I took a deep breath, forced myself out of the memory, and scanned the room. The banjo sat beside the bed, looking as fragile as Silas himself. I stepped inside, no plan in mind, my only goal to pick up the banjo and hold it tight against myself.

Mariah sat up. The old man started, breath rasping rapidly through his half-open mouth. I grabbed the banjo, shocked at its warmth. It was a live thing, as Silas had said. I could feel the power trapped within it, running up and down the strings like an arpeggio.

"You can't do that," Mariah said, and reached for the banjo. I swung around, keeping it out of her grasp.

"She can do whatever she wants." Silas stood at the door. I wondered how long he had been there, if he had followed me from the moment I left the lobby.

Mariah gasped. She froze, looking at him, then looking at her father. Of course, she had never seen Silas old. She had only seen the young man, the one who had held me. It was easy to make love to death when he was the most beautiful man you had ever seen. Difficult when he was caving inside himself, only eyes, hair, and voice remaining.

"Give me the banjo," Silas said, that voice carrying more power than I had ever heard—even more than the day he had admonished me for taking too many lives.

"No," Mariah whispered. She extended her hand to me. It shook.

But I didn't look at her. I looked at her father. Tubes shoved into his arms, the cords of his neck exposed, eyes sunken into a skeletal face. If I gave it back, he would live, but he would never be the powerful man he had been, the man who made his bed with military precision, who probably dominated any room he stood in. She was clinging to a shell and he, he was too far gone to know it.

I had been lucky. My father had died quickly, by comparison.

"Give me the banjo," Silas repeated.

But life was life. And there it was, staring up at me from the depths of a hospital bed, as wispy and tenacious as greenery in the desert.

Silas made these decisions every day. Every hour of every day. I could not.

I extended one hand to him, letting the banjo pass in front of Mariah. This was their fight, not mine.

Mariah lunged for it, but Silas was quicker. He snatched the banjo from me, hugging it like a long-lost friend. On the bed, the father made a strange keening sound—and I couldn't tell if it was from fear or pain.

The years shed off of Silas like fur off a cat. As he crossed the room, Mariah wrapped herself around him. The sounds of the hospital had faded into nothing.

"Let him live," she said.

Silas, young, black-haired, slim, the beautiful man I

had first seen, ran his hand along her face. He kissed her forehead and cupped her chin, as if he had never held anything so precious. "You should have asked that in the first place," he said.

"I didn't mean to hurt you." Her voice sounded desperate. I wanted to look away, but couldn't.

"I'm as familiar with hurt as I am with anything else," he said. "The banjo takes the hurt away."

"But only for him."

"Yes," Silas said. "Only for him."

He walked beside the bed, took the old man's hand. The old man stared up at him, keening stopped. I could see fear in the old man's rheumy eyes, but his gaze never wavered. "You can live like this for years," Silas said, "or you can come with me."

Mariah was shaking. She hadn't moved another step. All through this, she had thought of no one but herself.

"I'm sorry," the old man said to her.

She nodded, unable to speak. A lump rose in my throat, too. I wanted out, but didn't dare move. Silas let go of the old man's hand, swung the banjo to the front of his chest, and played.

I didn't quite hear the music, although I felt it, rollicking through me. For a moment, the old man's face lit up, and I saw him, strong and young, a baby girl on his shoulder, a beautiful woman beside him. Then the image faded, and with it, the sparkle in his eye. Silas finished playing, swung the banjo back into position, and reached for the old man's face.

Mariah pushed him aside, knelt beside her father. Silas stumbled backward, then stared at her for a moment, and I saw longing so intense that it burned me. What was it like to be outside time, human but not human, loving, but unlovable? I hoped I would never know.

He saw me watching him. Color touched his cheeks. "Come on," he said.

We walked into the corridor. People flowed around us like water around a rock.

"You lied to me, you know," I said. "You were there when my father died."

He stopped near the elevator. "The first time you summoned me was in that convenience store."

"I was courting you."

He smiled a little, but the smile was sad. I liked his beauty. I liked his compassion. I liked him. "I'm not the kind of lover you want," he said. "I'll never leave you, but I'll never make you happy."

He reached into his pocket, pulled out an envelope and handed it to me. Then he leaned forward and kissed my forehead. "Silas," I said—but he disappeared. One moment there, one moment gone. A man who was lonelier than I could ever be.

I stood there for a while, then I remembered to pocket the envelope. When I got downstairs, I would donate the money to the hospice center. They had to have one, every hospital did, for cancer care for families and patients. Then I would go to the desert and stare at the greenery.

The dream would never come again. Nor would he ever have to admonish me anymore.

The courtship had ended. We were, and we would remain, just good friends.

Felixity

Tanith Lee

The name sounds a little like "felicity," or happiness, and a little like "felix," or luck. Felixity, the quintessential poor little rich girl, seems to be neither happy nor lucky. In any fairy story, such a girl would have compensations of brain or talent and marry a handsome prince. Felixity can't even do good watercolors. And when she chooses a husband—don't even ask.

Let Tanith Lee tell you in this ironic and elegantly decadent story. I could compare "Felixity" to the works of Oscar Wilde or Angela Carter—but I think I'll say that this is Tanith Lee at the top of her form, and leave it at that.

Felixity's parents were so beautiful that everywhere they went they were attended by a low murmuring, like that of a beehive. Even when pregnant with her child, Felixity's mother was lovely, an ormolu madonna. But when Felixity was born, her mother died.

Among the riches of her father, then, in a succession of elaborate houses, surrounded by gardens which sometimes led to a cobalt sea, Felixity grew up, motherless. Her father watched her grow—he must have—although nannies tended her, servants waited on her, and tutors gave her lessons. Sometimes in the evening, when the heat of the day had settled and the stars had come out, Felixity's father would interview his daughter on the lamplit terrace above the philodendrons.

"Now tell me what you learned today."

But Felixity, confronted by her beautiful and elegant father burnished on the dark with pale electricity, was tongue-tied. She twisted her single plait around her finger and hunched her knees. She was an ugly child, ungraceful and gauche, with muddy skin and thin unshining hair. She had no energy, and even when put out to play, wandered slowly about the garden walks, or tried tiredly to skip, giving up after five or six heavy jumps. She was slow at her studies, worried over them, and suffered headaches. She was meek. Her teeth were always needing fillings, and she bore this unpleasantness with resignation.

"Surely there must have been something of note in your day?"

"I went to the dentist, Papa."

"Your mother," said Felixity's father, "had only one tiny filling in her entire head. It was the size of a pin's point. It was gold." He said this without cruelty, more in wonder. "You must have some more dresses," he added presently.

Felixity hated it when clothes were bought for her. She looked so awful in anything attractive or pretty, but they had never given up. Glamorously dressed, she resembled a chrysalis clad in the butterfly. When she could, she put on her drabbest, most nondescript clothes.

After half an hour or so of his daughter's unstimulating company, Felixity's father sent her away. He was tactful, but Felixity was under no illusions. Beneath the dentist's numbing cocaine, she was aware her teeth were being drilled to the nerve, and that shortly, when the anesthetic wore off, they would hurt her.

Inevitably, as time passed, Felixity grew up and became a woman. Her body changed, but it did not improve. If anyone had been hoping for some magical transformation, they were disappointed. When she was sixteen, Felixity was, nevertheless, launched into society. Not a ripple attended the event, although she wore a red dress and a most lifelike wig fashioned by a famous coiffeur. Following this beginning, Felixity was often on the edges of social activities, where she was never noticed, gave neither offense nor inspiration, and before some of which she was physically sick several times from neurasthenia. As the years went by, however, her terror gradually left her. She no longer expected anything momentous with which she would not be able to cope.

Felixity's father aged marvelously. He remained slim and limber, was scarcely lined and that only in a way to make him more interesting. His hair and teeth were like a boy's.

"How that color suited your mother," he remarked to Felixity, as she crossed the room in a gown of translucent lemon silk, which made her look like an uncooked tuber. "I remember three such dresses, and a long fringed scarf. She was so partial to it." Again, he was not being cruel. Perhaps he was entitled to be perplexed. They had anticipated an exquisite child, the best of both of them. But then, they had also expected to live out their lives together.

When she was thirty-three, Felixity stopped moving in society, and attended only those functions she could not, from politeness, avoid. Her father did not remonstrate with her, indeed he only saw her now once a week, at a rite he referred to as "Dining with my

Daughter." Although his first vision of her was always a slight shock, he did not disenjoy these dinners, which lasted two hours exactly, and at which he was able to reminisce at great length about his beautiful wife. If anyone had asked him, he would have said he did this for Felixity's sake. Otherwise, he assumed she was quite happy. She read books, and occasionally painted rather poor watercolors. Her teeth, which had of necessity been overfilled, had begun to break at regular intervals, but aside from this her life was tranquil, and passed in luxury. There was nothing more that could be done for her.

One evening, as Felixity was being driven home to one of her father's city houses, a young man ran from a side street out across the boulevard, in front of the car. The chauffeur put on his brakes at once. But the large silver vehicle lightly touched the young man's side, and he fell in front of it. A crowd gathered instantly, at the periphery of which three dark-clad men might be seen looking on. But these soon after went away.

The chauffeur came to Felixity's door to tell her that the young man was apparently unhurt, but shaken. The crowd began to adopt factions, some saying that the young man was to blame for the accident, others that the car had been driven too fast. In the midst of this, the young man himself appeared at Felixity's door. In years he was about twenty-six, smartly if showily dressed in an ice-cream white suit now somewhat dusty from the road. His blue-black hair curled thickly on his neck; he was extremely handsome. He stared at the woman in the car with amontillado eyes. He said, "No, no, it was not your fault." And then he collapsed on the ground.

The crowd ascended into uproar. The young man must be taken immediately to the hospital.

Felixity was flustered, and it may have been this which caused her to open her door, and to instruct the chauffeur and a bystander to assist the young man into the car. As it was done, the young man revived a little.

"Put him here, beside me," said Felixity, although her voice trembled with alarm.

The car door was closed again, and the chauffeur told to proceed to a hospital. The crowd made loud sounds as they drove off.

To Felixity's relief, and faint fright, the young man now completely revived. He assured her that it was not essential to go to the hospital, but that if she were kind enough to allow him to rest a moment in her house, and maybe swallow a glass of water, he would be well enough to continue on his way. He had been hurrying, he explained, because he had arranged to see his aunt, and was late. Felixity was afraid that the drive to her house would prolong this lateness, but the young man, who said his name was Roland, admitted that he was often tardy on visits to his aunt, and she would forgive him.

Felixity, knowing no better, therefore permitted Roland to be driven with her to the house. Its electric gates and ectomorphic pillars did not seem to antagonize him, and ten minutes later, he was seated in the blond, eighteenth-century drawing room, drinking bottled carbonated water with slices of lime. Felixity asked him whether she should call her father's doctor, who was in residence. But Roland said again that he had no need of medical attention. Felixity believed him. He had all the hallmarks of strength, elasticity, and vitality she had noted in others. She was both glad and strangely sorry when he rose springingly up again, thanked her, and said that now he would be leaving.

When he had left, she found that she shook all over,

sweat beaded her forehead, and she felt quite sick. That night she could not sleep, and the next morning, at breakfast, she broke another tooth on a roll.

Two days after, a bouquet of pink roses, from a fashionable florist, arrived for Felixity. That very afternoon Roland came to the gates and inquired if he might see her. The servants, the guards at the gate, were so unused to anyone seeking Felixity—indeed, it was unique—that they conveyed the message to her without question. And, of course, Felixity, wan with nauseous amazement and a hammering heart, invited Roland in.

"I've been unable to stop thinking about you," said Roland. "I've never before met with a woman so gracious and so kind."

Roland said many things, more or less in this vein, as they walked about the garden among the imported catalpas and the orchids. He confessed to Felixity that his aunt was dead; it was her grave he had been going to visit; he had no one in the world.

Felixity did not know what she felt, but never before had she felt anything like it. In the dim past of her childhood, when some vague attempts had been made to prepare or alter her, she had been given to understand that she might, when she gained them, entertain her friends in her father's houses, and that her suitors would be formally welcomed. Neither friend nor suitor had ever crossed the thresholds of the houses, but now Felixity fell into a kind of delayed response, and in a while she had offered Roland wine on the terrace.

As they sat sipping it, her sick elation faded and a mute sweetness possessed her.

It was not that she thought herself lovable; she thought herself nothing. It was that one had come to her who had made her the center of the day. The monumental trees and exotic flowers had become a backdrop, the heat, the house, the servants who brought them things. She had met before people like Roland, the gorgeous magicians, who never saw her. But Roland did see her. He had fixed on her. He spoke to her of his sad beleaguered life, how his father had gambled away a fortune, how he had been sadistically misled on his chances of film stardom. He wanted her to know him. He gazed into her eyes, and saw in her, it was plain, vast continents of possibility.

He stayed with her until the dinner hour, and begged that he might be able to return. He had not told her she was beautiful, or any lie of that nature. He had said she was good, and luminously kind, and that never before had he met these qualities in a young woman, and that she must not shut him out as he could not bear it.

On his second visit, under a palm tree, Felixity was taken by compunction. "Six of my teeth are crowned," she said. "And this—is a wig!" And she snatched it off to reveal her thin cropped hair.

Roland gave a gentle smile. "How you honor me," he said. "I'm so happy that you trust me. But what does any of this matter? Throw the silly wig away. You are yourself. There has never been anyone like you. Not in the whole world."

When Felixity and Roland had been meeting for a month, Felixity received a summons from her incredible father.

Felixity went to see him with a new type of courage. Some of her awe had lessened, although she would not have put this into words. She had been with a creature of fires. It seemed she knew her father a little better.

"I'm afraid," said Felixity's father, "that it is my grim task to disillusion you. The young man you've made your companion is a deceiver."

"Oh," said Felixity. She looked blank.

"Yes, my child. I don't know what he has told you,

but I've had him investigated. He is the bastard son of a prostitute, and has lived so far by dealings with thieves and shady organizations. He was in flight from one of these when he ran in front of your car. Obviously now he is in pursuit of your money, both your own finances and those which you'll inherit on my death."

Felixity did not say she would not hear ill of Roland. She thought about what her father had told her, and slowly she nodded. Then, from the patois of her curtailed emotions, she translated her heart into normal human emotional terms. "But I love him."

Felixity's father looked down at her with crucial pity. It was a fact, he did not truly think of her as his daughter, for his daughter would have been lovely. He accepted her as a pathetic dependent, until now always needing him, a jest of God upon a flawless delight which had been rent away.

"If you love him, Felixity," he said, "you must send him to me."

Felixity nodded again. Beings of fire communicated with each other. She had no fears.

The next day she waited on the terrace, and eventually Roland came out of the house into the sunlight. He seemed a little pale, but he spoke to her brightly. "What a man he is. We are to marry, my beloved. That is, if you'll have me. I'm to care for you. What a golden future lies before us!" Roland did not detail his conversation with Felixity's father. He did not relate, for example, that Felixity's father had courteously touched on Roland's career as crook and gigolo. Or that Felixity's father had informed Roland that he grasped perfectly his aims, but that those aims were to be gratified, for Felixity's sake. "She has had little enough," said Felixity's father. "Providing you are kind to her, a model husband, and don't enlighten her in the matter of your real feelings, I am prepared to let you live at her expense." Roland had protested feebly that he adored Felixity, her tenderness had won his heart. Roland did not recount to Felixity either that her father had greeted this effusion with the words: "You will not, please, try your formula on me."

In the days which succeeded Roland's dialogue with Felixity's father, the now-betrothed couple were blissful, each for their own reasons.

Then Felixity's father flew to another city on a business venture, the engine of his plane malfunctioned, and it crashed into the forests. Before the month was up, his remarkable but dead body had been recovered, woven with lianas and chewed by jaguars. Felixity became the heiress to his fortune.

During this time of tragedy, Roland supported Felixity with unswerving attention. Felixity was bewildered at her loss, for she could not properly persuade herself she had lost anything.

The funeral took place with extreme pomp, and soon after the lovers sought a quiet civil wedding. Felixity had chosen her own dress, which was a swampy brown. The groom wore vanilla and scarlet. When the legalities were completed, Roland drove Felixity away in his new white car, toward a sixty-roomed villa on the coast.

As she was driven, a little too fast, along the dusty road, Felixity was saturated by an incoherent but intense nervousness.

She had never had any female friends, but she had read a number of books, and she guessed that her unease sprang from sexual apprehension. Never, in all their courtship, had Roland done more than press her hands or her lips lightly with his own. She had valued this decorum in him, even though disappointment sometimes chilled her. At the impress of his flesh, however light, her pulses raced. She was actually very passionate, and had never before had the chance of realizing it. Nevertheless, Roland had told her that, along with her kindness, he worshiped her purity. She knew she must wait for their wedding night to learn of the demons of love.

Now it seemed she was afraid. But what was there to dread? Her reading, which if not salacious, had at least been comprehensive, had given her the gist of the nuptial act. She was prepared to suffer the natural pain of deflowerment in order to offer joy to her partner. She imagined that Roland would be as grave and gentle in lovemaking as he had always been in all their dealings. Therefore, why her unease?

Along the road the copper-green pyramids of coffee trees spun past, and on the horizon's edge, the forests kept pace with the car.

By midnight, Felixity thought, I shall be different.

They arrived before sunset at the villa, where Felixity had spent some of her childhood. Felixity was surprised to find that no servants came out to greet them. Her bafflement grew when, on entering the house, she found the rooms polished and vacant.

"Don't concern yourself with that," said Roland. "Come with me. I want to show you something."

Felixity went obediently. Roland had somehow given her to understand that, along with kindness and purity, he liked docility. They moved up the grand stairway, along corridors, and so into the upper regions of the house, which were reached by narrow twining flights of steps. Up here, somewhere, Roland unlocked and opened a door.

They went into a bare whitewashed room. A few utilitarian pieces of furniture were in it, a chair or two, a slender bed, a round mirror. In one wall a door gave on a bathroom closet. There was a window, but it was caged in a complex if ornamental grill.

"Here we are," said Roland.

Felixity looked at him, confused.

"Where?" she asked.

"Your apartment."

Felixity considered this must be a joke, and laughed falsely, as she had sometimes done in her society days.

"I have you at a disadvantage," said Roland. "Let me explain."

He did so. This room was where Felixity was to live. If there was anything else she wanted—he knew she was fond of books—it could be supplied. Food would be put in through that flap, there, near the bottom of the door. She should return her empty trays via the same aperture. She would find the bathroom stocked with clean towels, soap, and toothpaste. These would be replaced at proper intervals. Whatever else she required, she should list—see the notepad and pencil on the table—and these things too would be delivered. She could have a radio, if she liked. And perhaps a gramophone.

"But—" said Felixity, "but—"

"Oh, surely you didn't think I would ever *cohabit* with you?" asked Roland reasonably. "I admit, I might have had to awhile, if your father had survived, but maybe not even then. He was so glad to be rid of you, a letter from you every six months, dictated by me, would have sufficed. No, you will live up here. And I shall live in the house and do as I want. Now and then I'll ask you to sign the odd document, in order to assist my access to your money. But otherwise I won't trouble you at all. And so, dear Felixity, thank you, and au revoir. I wish you a pleasant evening."

And having said this, Roland went out, before Felixity could shift hand or limb, and she heard the key turning in the lock. And then a raucous silence.

At first she did not credit what had happened. She ran about like a trapped insect, to the door, to the window. But both were closed fast and the window looked out on a desolate plain that stretched away beyond the house to the mountains. The sun was going down, and the sky was indelibly hot and merciless.

Roland would come back, of course. This was some game, to tease her.

But darkness came, and Roland did not. And much later a tray of bread and chicken and coffee was put through the door. Felixity ran to the door again, shrieking for help. But whoever had brought the tray took no notice.

Felixity sat through her wedding night on a hard chair, shivering with terror and incipient madness, by the light of the one electric lamp she had found on the table.

In the villa, far off, she thought she heard music, but it might only have been the rhythm of the sea.

Near dawn, she came to accept what had occurred. It was only what she should have expected. She wept for half an hour, and then lay down on the mean bed to sleep.

For weeks, and probably months, Felixity existed in the whitewashed room with the grilled window.

Every few days books were put through her door, along with the trays of meals. The food was generally simple or meager, and always cold; still it punctually arrived. A radio appeared, too, a few days after Felixity's internment. It seemed able to receive only one station, which put out endless light music and melodramatic serials, but even so Felixity came to have it on more and more. At midnight the station closed down. Then it was replaced by a claustrophobic loud silence.

Other supplies were promptly presented through the door on her written request. Clean towels, new soap, shampoo, toothpaste and toothbrushes, Felixity's brand of analgesics for her headaches, and her preferred form of sanitary protection.

There was no clock or calendar in the room, but the radio station repeatedly gave the day and hour. At first Felixity noticed the progress of time, until eventually she recognized that she was counting it up like a prisoner, as if, when she had served her sentence, she would be released. But, of course, her freedom would never come. Felixity ceased to attend to the progress of time.

In the beginning, too, she went on with her normal routines of cleanliness and order. In her father's houses, her bathrooms had been spectacular, and she had liked using them, experimenting there with soaps and foams, and with preparations which claimed they might make her hair thicker, although they did not. With only the functional white bathroom at her disposal, Felixity lost interest in hygiene, and several days would sometimes elapse before she bathed. She had also to clean the bathroom herself, which initially had proved challenging, but soon it became a chore she did not bother with. Besides, she found the less she used the bathroom, the less cleaning it needed.

Felixity would sit most of the day, listening with unfixed open eyes to the radio. Now and then she would read part of a book. Occasionally she would wander to the window and look out. But the view never changed, and the glare of the distant mountains tired her eyes. Often she found it very hard to focus on the printed word, and would read the same phrase in a novel over and over, trying to make sense of it.

After perhaps three months had gone by, an afternoon came when she heard the key turn in the lock of her door.

She was now too apathetic to be startled. Yet when Roland, gleaming in his ice-cream clothes, came into the room, she knew a moment of shame. But then she

acknowledged it did not matter if he saw her un-
washed in her robe, her thin hair and unpowdered
face greasy, for he had never cared what she looked
like; she was nothing to him.

And Roland approached with his usual charm, smiling at her, and holding out some papers.

"Here I am," he said, "I won't keep you a minute.
If you'd just be kind enough to sign these."

Felixity did not get up at once only because she was
lethargic. But she said softly, "What if I refuse?"

Roland continued to smile. "I should be forced to
take away your radio and books, and to starve you."

Felixity believed him. After all, if he starved her to
death, he would inherit everything. It was really quite
good of him to allow her to live.

She went to the table and signed the papers.

"Thank you so much," said Roland.

"Won't you let me out?" said Felixity.

"Obviously I can't." He added logically, "It's much
better if you stay here. Or you might be tempted to
run away and divorce me. Or if you didn't do that,
you'd be horribly in my way."

Roland had, prior to their drive to the villa, sacked
the original servants and installed a second set, all of
whom were bribed to his will, served him unquestion-
ingly, and held their tongues. Roland now lived the
life which ideally suited him, answerable to no one.
He lay in bed until noon, breakfasted extravagantly,
spent the day lazily, and in the evening drove to the
nearest city to gamble and to drink. Frequently he
would return to the villa in the small hours with beautiful women, to whom, in a great scrolled bed, he
made ferocious love, casting them out again at dawn,
in their spangled dresses, like the rinds of eaten fruits.

"But," said Felixity, "you see I'm afraid—if I have
to stay here—I may lose my mind."

"Oh, don't worry about that," said Roland. "The

servants already think I locked you up because you were insane."

Then he left her, and Felixity went to gaze from her window. The mountains looked like the demarcation line at the end of the world. Felixity turned on her radio.

That night, as she ate a piece of hard sausage, she broke a tooth.

She felt curiously humiliated by this, yet she had no choice but to set the fact down on a page of the notepad, and append a request for a dentist. This she slipped out through the flap in the door with a pallid misgiving. She did not suppose for an instant Roland would permit her to leave the house and what kind of mechanic would he send in to her?

For nine days, during which the broken tooth tore at her mouth and finally made it bleed, Felixity awaited Roland's response. On the tenth day she came to see he would not trouble to respond at all. He had spared her what suffering he could, under the circumstances, but to put himself out over her teeth was too much to ask of him.

This, then, was where she had sunk to.

Four hours passed, and Felixity sat in her chair listening to a serial about a sensational girl who could not choose between her lovers. Behind her the window became feverish, then cool; and darkness slid into the room.

Suddenly something strange happened. Felixity sprang to her feet as if she had been electrically shocked. She rushed toward the cheap mirror on the wall, and stared at herself in the fading crepuscule. She did not need light, for she knew it all. She reached up and rent at her thin hair and a scream burst out of her, lacerating her mouth freshly on the sharp edge of broken enamel.

"Nononononono!" screamed Felixity.

She was denying only herself.

She jumped up and down before the mirror, shrieking, galvanized by a scalding white thread inside her.

Only when this huge energy had left her, which took several minutes, did she crawl back to the chair and collapse in it, weeping. She cried for hours out of the well of pain. Her sobs were strong and violent, and the room seemed to shake at them.

At midnight, the radio station closed down and the shattering silence bounded into the room. Felixity looked up. Everything was in blackness, the lamp unlit, and yet it seemed there had been a flash of brilliance. Perhaps there was a storm above the mountains. Or, incredibly, perhaps some human life went over the plain, a car driving on the dirt tracks of it with headlights blazing.

Felixity moved to the window. Night covered the plain, and the mountains were like dead coals. Above, the stars winked artificially, as they had done in the planetarium where once she had been taken as a child.

The whip of light cracked, again. It was not out on the plain but inside the room.

Felixity was still too stunned for ordinary fear.

She walked back slowly to her chair, and as she did so, she saw her reflection in the round mirror on the wall.

Felixity stopped, and her reflection stopped, inevitably. Felixity raised her right arm, let it fall. Her left arm, let it fall. The reflection did the same. Felixity began to walk forward again, toward the mirror. She walked directly up to it, and halted close enough to touch.

Earlier, in the twilight, the mirror had reflected Felixity only too faithfully. It had shown the apex of her ungainly figure, her drab, oily complexion, her ugly features and wispy hair. Now the mirror contained something else. It was illuminated as if a lamp shone on it out of the dark room. In the mirror, Felixity's reflection was no longer Felixity.

Instead, a woman stood in the mirror, copying exactly every gesture that Felixity made.

This woman, to judge from her upper torso, was slender, with deeply indented breasts. Her skin, which was visible in the low-cut bodice, at the throat, and the lower part of the face, was the mildest gold, like dilute honey. Her tightly fitting gown was a flame. On her upper face, across her forehead and eyes, she wore a mask like yellow jade, from which long sprays of sparkling feathers curved away. And above the mask and beneath ran thickly coiling gilded hair, like golden snakes poured from a jar.

Felixity put both her hands up over her mouth. And the woman in the mirror did as Felixity did. She wore long gloves the color of topaz, streaked with scintillants.

The flash of brilliance snapped again. It was up in the black air above the woman. A lyre of sparks came all unstrung: A firework. As it faded, an entire scene was there at the woman's back.

It was a city of steps and arches, plazas and tall buildings, through which a brimstone river curled its way. But over the river, slim bridges ran that were fruited with lamps of orange amber, and on the facades all about roared torches of lava red. All these lights burned in the river, too, wreathing it with fires.

Figures went across the levels of the city, in scarlet, brass, and embers. Some led oxblood dogs, or carried incandescent parrots on their wrists. A bronze alligator surfaced from the river, glittered like jewelry, and was gone.

Felixity saw a large red star hung in the sky.

Within the woman's mask, two eyes glimmered. She lowered her hands from her mouth, and Felixity found that she had lowered her hands. But then the woman turned from the mirror and walked away.

Felixity watched the woman walk to the end of a torchlit pier, and there she waited in her gown of flame, until a flaming boat came by and she stepped into it and was borne off under the bridges of lamps.

After this the scene melted, all its fires and colors spilling together downward, and out by some nonexistent gutter at the mirror's base.

Felixity took two or three paces back. In sheer darkness now she went and lay on her bed. But the afterimages of the lights stayed on her retinas for some while, in flickering floating patches. The mirror remained black, and in it she could dimly see the room reflecting. Felixity closed her eyes, and beheld the alligator surfacing in a gold garland of ripples, and as it slipped under again, she slept.

In the morning, when she woke, Felixity did not think she had been dreaming. It did occur to her that perhaps Roland had played some kind of trick on her, but then she quickly dismissed this idea, for Roland had no interest in her; why should he waste effort on such a thing? Had she then suffered an hallucination? Was this the onset of madness? Felixity discovered that she did not thrill with horror. She felt curiously calm, almost complacent. She took a bath and shampooed her hair, ate the meals that were shunted through the door, ignoring as best she could the difficulty with the broken tooth, and listened to the radio. She was waiting for the darkness to come back. And when it did so, she switched off the radio and sat in her chair, watching the mirror.

Hours passed, and the mirror kept up its blackness, faintly reflecting the room. Once Felixity thought there was a spark of light, but it was only some spasm in her eyes.

Eventually Felixity put on the radio again. It was midnight, and the station was closing down. Felixity became alert, for it was at this moment on the previous night that the mirror had come alive. However, the station went off the air and that was all. Felixity watched the mirror from her bed until sleep overcame her.

Somewhere in the markerless black of early morning, she awakened, and over the mirror was flowing a ribbon of fire.

Felixity leapt from the bed and dashed to the mirror, but already the fire had vanished, leaving no trace.

Felixity set herself to sleep by day and watch by night. This was quite easy for her, for, rather like a caged animal, she had become able to slumber almost at will. In the darkness she would sit, without the lamp, sometimes not looking directly at the mirror. She let the radio play softly in the background, and when the closedown came, she would tense. But nothing happened.

Seven nights went by.

Felixity continued her bat-like existence.

Only one magical thing had ever taken place in her life before, her betrothal to Roland; and that had been proved to be a sham. The magic of the mirror she recognized, as sometimes a piece of music, never heard before, may seem familiar. This music was for her.

On the eighth night, just after the radio had announced it was eleven o'clock, the mirror turned to a coin of gold.

Without a sound, Felixity got up, went to the mirror, and stared in.

It was a golden ballroom lit by bizarre chandeliers like the rosy clustered hearts of pomegranates. There on the floor of obsidian a man and woman danced in

an austere yet sensual fashion. His were sophisticated
carnival clothes of black and blood, and he was
masked in jet. She was Felixity's reflection, and now
she wore a dress of sulfur beaded by magma rain.
There was a tango playing on the radio, and it seemed
they moved in time to it.

Felixity felt herself dancing, although she did not
stir, and the man's arm around her.

In a tall window was a sort of day, a sky that was
coral pink and a huge red sun or planet lying low.

The tango quivered to its end.

The man and woman separated, and all the colors
pooled together and sluiced down the mirror. Felixity
made a wild motion, as if to catch them as they flushed
through the bottom of the glass. But, of course, nothing ran out.

In the blackness of her room then, Felixity solemnly
danced a tango alone. She was stiff and unwieldy, and
sometimes bumped into the flimsy furniture. She knew
now a raw craving and yearning, a nostalgia as if for
an idyllic childhood. She had come to understand who
the woman was. She was Felixity, in another world.
Felixity's brain had made the intellectual and spiritual
jump swiftly and completely. Here she was a lump,
unloved, unliked even, so insignificant she could be
made a prisoner forever. But there, she was a being
of fire.

Oh, to go through the mirror. Oh, to be one with
her true self.

And at last she touched the mirror, which was very
warm against her hand, as if the sun had just shone
on it. But otherwise it gave no clue to its remarkable
properties. And certainly no hint of a way in.

After the vision at eleven o'clock on the eighth
night, a month elapsed, and the mirror never altered
by night or day.

Felixity grew very sad. Although she had been thrown into an abyss, idly tossed there, her reaction had been mostly passivity rather than despair, for she was used to ill-treatment in one form or another. But the images in the mirror had raised her up to a savage height, to a plateau of lights she had never before achieved. That she grasped almost at once their implication demonstrated how profoundly she had been affected. And now she was left with the nothing which had always encompassed her and which Roland had driven in beside her, into her cage.

She ceased to eat the scanty meals and only sipped the coffee or water. In order to hide what she did—she was incoherently afraid of force-feeding—she dropped the portions of food into the lavatory. Felixity became extremely feeble, dizzy, and sick. Her head ached constantly, and she could not keep down the painkillers. She lay on the bed all day, sinking in and out of sleep. She could hardly hear the radio for the singing in her ears. At night she tried to stay conscious, but the mirror was like a black void that sucked her in. Her head whirled and spots of light burst over her eyes, deceiving her, for there was nothing there. She cried softly, without passion. She hoped she would die soon. Then she could sleep indefinitely.

On the first morning of the new month, before sunrise, Felixity raised her gluey lids and saw the woman who was herself standing up against the inside of the mirror in her mask of yellow jade, a dress like naphtha and the glinting vipers of her golden hair.

Felixity's heart palpitated. She tried to get up, but she was too weak.

Behind the woman who was the real Felixity, there was, as at the start, only blackness. But now the mirror-Felixity lifted her ruby glove, and she held in her fingers a single long coppery feather, the plume of some extraordinary bird.

If she would only take off her mask, Felixity thought, I'd see that she is me. It would be my face, and it would be beautiful.

But the woman did not remove the mask of yellow jade. Instead she turned her head toward the feather, and she blew gently on it.

The breath that came out of her mouth was bloomed with a soft lightning. It enveloped the tip of the feather, which at once caught fire.

Felixity watched, dazzled, until the flame went out and the woman dissolved abruptly into glowing snow, and the mirror was only a mirror again. Then Felixity turned on her side and fell asleep.

When it was light, she woke refreshed, and going into the bathroom, bathed and washed her hair. Presently when the tray of food came, she ate it. Her stomach hurt for some while after, but she did not pay any attention. She put on the radio and hummed along with the melodies, most of which she now knew by heart.

In the afternoon, after the lunch tray, from which she ate everything, the door was unlocked and Roland entered the room.

Felixity stood up. She had not realized he would arrive so quickly.

"Here I am," he said, "I won't detain you a moment. Just some more of these dull papers to sign."

Felixity smiled, and Roland was surprised. He expected acquiescence, but not happiness.

"Naturally I'll sign them," said Felixity. "But first, you must kiss me."

Roland now looked concerned.

"It seems inappropriate."

"Not at all," said Felixity. "I'm your wife."

And at this, the gigolo must have triumphed over the thief, for Roland approached Felixity and gravely bowed his head. Indeed, at the press of her flesh on his, after the libidinous life he had been leading, his lips parted from force of habit, and Felixity blew into his mouth.

Roland sprang away. His face appeared congested and astonished. He went on, stumbling backward, until he reached the door, and then he turned as if to rush out of it.

So Felixity saw from the back of him, the tailored suit and blue-black hair, and two jets of white flame which spouted suddenly from his ears.

Roland spun on the spot, and now she saw his face, with yellow flames gouting from his nose and purple gases from his mouth. And then he went up in a noiseless scream of fire, like petrol, or a torch.

The doorway was burning, and she could not get out of it. Flames were darting around the room, consuming the sticks of furniture as they went. The bed erupted like an opening rose. The mirror was gold again, and red.

How cold the flames were. Felixity felt them eating her and gave herself eagerly, glad to be rid of it, the vileness of her treacherous body. The last thing she saw was half the burning floor give way and crash down into the lower regions of the house, and the mirror flying after it like a bubble of the sun.

The servants escaped the blazing villa, and stood in the gardens of the house above the sea, wailing and exclaiming. It was generally concluded that their employer, Roland, and his mad invalid wife, had perished in the inferno. With amazing rapidity, the house collapsed, sending up a pillar of red smoke that could be seen for miles.

Unseen by anyone, however, Felixity emerged out of the rubble.

She had not a mark or a smut upon her. She had instead the body of a goddess and the face of an angel.

Her skin was like honey and her hair like a cascade of golden serpents and in her mouth were the white and flawless teeth of a healthy predator.

Somehow she had had burned on to her, also, a lemon dress and amber shoes.

She went among the philodendrons, Felixity, out of sight. And so down toward the road, without a backward glance.

Horse of Her Dreams

Elizabeth Moon

Think of a parade on Main Street, any Main Street, in a small Texas town. Think of the horses, and riding them, tall "Texas girls" with the brilliant smiles and flowing manes of hair you've seen on television and in magazines—more spectacular than cheerleaders, more vibrant than California surfers.

A stereotype, you say? Maybe, or a fantasy—most deeply held by those who can never, never possess it.

Elizabeth Moon, who rides and lives in a small town in Texas, has seen those parades and the shadows they cast across even the most sunlit lives.

It was just another little wide spot in the road. One of those towns with a hot shadeless Main Street, some old brick or rock buildings on each side, and a big ugly new government building intended to look modern and urban and progressive, but clunky as a cinder block in a display case of Chinese porcelain. Here it combined City Hall, Fire Station, Library, and Community Center, all in one big chunk of beige precast-concrete panels that hadn't had time to mellow, but had been there long enough for rust streaks to come down the sides. Three spindly little oaks in planters out front hadn't really taken hold.

We knew the town's reputation as the county scapegoat—it's our business to know—but that's not why we came. We—the Frontline News team, Channel 8—had come to cover their annual festival, producing a thirty-second clip for our Weekend Previews on the Friday-night six-o'clock news. So on this July Wednesday, there we were square in the middle of that two blocks of Main Street, in trouble.

What you want is local color, and what the locals think is color isn't what you want. Which meant the big sign draped across the City Center saying "Welcome Frontline News!" wasn't it. Nor the pair of girls in shorts and clogs who stared at us through the windows of Clara's Café and then sauntered out, flipping their long out-of-date hair and pretending to ignore us. Obviously they didn't understand what a long lens does to a rear view ... anyone's rear view.

Main Street had been modernized back in the Fifties or Sixties, more stucco and plate glass than stone or brick. No old hitching rails, no antique streetlights. There weren't any shady benches for old men to sit and talk and look rural on—so of course we didn't see any local-color kind of old men. The fiberglass horse over the door of Sim's Western Wear and Saddlery would have done, except that the week before we'd used a fiberglass horse over the door of another western wear somewhere else. And *that* one had had a fancy saddle on it.

Aside from Main Street, all two blocks of it, the town had something under two thousand inhabitants living on maybe sixteen miles of streets. I know, because we drove up and down every single damn street, looking for local color. We found what you always find: a few neat brick houses maintained by fanatics (curtains matching, grass plucked with tweezers at the sidewalk, freshly tarred drive), many more comfortable-looking old brick or frame houses with shaggy yards and big hairy dogs lying in the shade, a few backyards enlivened by a sheep, calf, or pony, and some much older but very dilapidated old shacks that were the wrong sort of local color if we ever wanted to come back.

Then Joe stepped hard on the brakes and said "God bless," under his breath, which isn't his usual expletive.

She was the kind of local color you almost never find. Not too young, not at all old, shaped perfectly for the camera, and a true honey blonde. She moved well, too, and she was heaving a big old parade saddle (black with silver trim) onto a palomino horse as pretty as she was—for a horse, that is. White blaze and four white stockings, and they sure looked like a pair, her in those tight jeans and tall white boots and blue western shirt with a little white pinstripe.

There's a lot that happened later that I don't understand, but I can't believe that it was Kelly's fault. She's just a normal, healthy, flat-out *gorgeous* hunk of Texas womanhood, getting ready to lead a parade in three days and happening to catch our eye. Which of course she did.

Turned out she was a junior (at the university, I figured) and wanted to be a schoolteacher, and thought her mom and dad were wonderful, and wouldn't miss a—well, I can't tell you the name of the festival, or you could find the town, now, couldn't you? But she wouldn't miss it, and if she married and had to move to (her blue eyes rolled up as she thought about someplace outrageous) *New York,* even, she'd come back every summer and lead the parade the way she had since . . . a short pause, and I thought she was counting years, but she said, "Since I got Sunny."

Well, people do tend to name horses stupid things like Brownie and Black Beauty and Sunny, and you don't have to have more sense than that to be married in your senior year to someone headed for law school or medical school, which was clearly her destiny.

She wasn't camera shy at all—knew all the tricks, and no wonder, having led the parade all those years. She clucked, and Sunny put those ears forward like a pro. Joe got her talking to the horse, and waving at her mom on the porch. Her mom didn't look anything like her, but lightning doesn't strike twice in families, either. My wife's a showstopping redhead, but our daughter has my hair. And nose. Then he asked her if she'd ride for us, and she beamed, and bounced up on that horse as slick as butter, and pranced him back and forth. It was then I noticed the spurs.

I don't pretend to be much of a cowboy, but one thing I do know is that those big old roweled spurs you see pictures of aren't in use anymore. The humane society had something to say about it, I think. But she had these blued-steel spurs with rowels as long as my fingers, and needle-sharp, or looked like it. Wicked things, that could have hurt if you'd just bumped into them. And she was digging them into that sleek golden horse like he had no nerves at all, with a pretty smile on her lovely face. I looked at the bridle. Sure enough, hung on that fancy black and silver parade bridle was a blued-steel bit that would have held a charging grizzly.

Funny thing is, that gold horse just pranced back and forth, never jumping sideways when she jabbed the spurs in, never gaping its mouth when she gave a little yank to the reins. And that's not natural. A horse that'll prance like that is usually the kind that's pretty touchy about having its reins yanked and spurs stuck in its sides. I wondered did she have it tranquilized, but the horse's eye was a clear shining ... *green.*

It's a wonder I didn't grab Joe's arm in the middle of a shot. Green! Horses don't have green eyes, and if they did it wouldn't be that bright, clear emerald green, wickedly alight with mischief. Horses are (forgive me, ladies) *stupid.* I mean, any animal that could buck people off, but prefers to carry them around on its back ... any animal that runs back into a burning barn and sticks its dumb legs in fences and then fights to get loose, tearing itself to shreds ... that's *stupid.* Black Beauty and all those horse stories aside. Besides, my cousin Don's horse ran under a tree with me and scraped me off when I was ten or so, and any animal with brains would have known that I was lighter than anyone else around, and if it got rid of me it would only mean more work. I live on the edge of the city, and my ranchette came with a two-stall stable and corral (courtesy of the previous owners who had two teenage daughters) but we don't have a horse even though Marcy's as horse-crazy as any other girl.

Joe didn't notice, but then Joe's from Houston, and where he grew up he never saw a horse in real life till he moved away. For all Joe knows, horses might have eyes every color of the rainbow. Joe just nodded and swung the camcorder around as usual, and let me do the interview.

Kelly kept chattering away, telling us about her friend named Charlene—she thought maybe we'd like a shot of both of them on their horses. Charlene had always ridden right behind her in the parade, she said. I guess Joe and I both were thinking the same thing: girls like Kelly had girlfriends with names like Charlene, and the girlfriends were always a lot less pretty but very energetic and *sweet.* Sweet, out here, means nothing to look at, and not enough spunk to leave. I tried not to let myself think about Marcy, my Marcy, who was born to be sweet ...

Charlene, Kelly went on, wrote poetry and painted

pictures, and was going to be a famous writer someday. Joe and I looked at each other and managed not
to sigh, and said, Sure, we'd be glad to meet her
friend, but the folks back at the station couldn't ever
use all we'd shot. We always had that excuse. So Kelly
rode off down the street, and for once, a back view
looked good in the long lens. Joe caught some of it,
just for us.

When she came back, we had another shock. Charlene could have been Kelly's twin for size and shape,
with long curly black hair and a face out of an art
book. Kelly was pretty—Kelly was typical golden-girl
all-American long-legged gorgeous—but Charlene had
bone to keep her beautiful for years, while Kelly
would find out in her thirties that a round chin can
double all too easily. Charlene had a black horse to
match her hair, the blackest, shiniest horse I ever saw
outside of a china figurine, not a brown hair on him.
And green eyes.

Now one green-eyed horse would be a marvel, the
sort of thing that's a freak. *Two* green-eyed horses—
one black, and one palomino, and both with the prettiest girls I'd seen in years on their backs—that's something else. The black horse gave me the same
mischievous sidelong glance as the golden one had,
and I noted that Charlene also wore wickedly roweled
spurs and had one helluva long-shanked bit, like Kelly's, in that beast's mouth. I got a cold feeling on the
back of my neck, and decided not to worry about it;
it wasn't my business, and the girls were easy to look
at. That *was* our business.

"Charlene used to lead the parade," said Kelly,
throwing her friend one of those smiles that cuts your
hand if you touch it. "But then I got Sunny."

I think I'd have let them lead it together—it must
be spectacular anyway, with two gorgeous girls on
those two handsome horses—for horses—and why not

both in front? But Charlene was giving Kelly a smile to match the one she'd been given, and her voice, when she spoke, was husky and warm and in keeping with that face.

"I didn't want to hog it forever," she said. "Besides, the Texas flag looks better with a black horse. And I know you'll be just as generous when someone else is ready to take over." Kelly smiled back, a little stiffly, and I figured they weren't really friends. How could they be? Two pretty girls in such a small town are born rivals, and if they don't know it, everyone makes it clear to them. About the time that one beat the other out for class sweetheart or most beautiful, *friend* had become an empty term. You don't, right out loud, talk about enemies.

When I got home, I told Marcy about the horses. Like so many girls her age, she thinks anything with four legs and a mane is wonderful. For years she's been saving her allowance and birthday money to buy her own horse and take lessons at the stable up the road.

"Could we go see them, Daddy?" I should have expected that. I looked at Denise. Mothers have rights, I'd learned, and besides we had planned to go to Hal's poolside barbecue on Saturday. I had hoped Marcy would learn some things from his daughter. Suzi wasn't a patch on those gorgeous girls with their horses, but she did have style, and Marcy was going to need all the help she could get.

Denise gave me one of those inscrutable glances she'd been giving me lately and shrugged. "If you want . . ." She'd already told me she didn't much like the party idea, back when I made the mistake of saying I thought Suzi was pretty sharp for a kid her age. Denise said yes, like a knife, and Marcy was a wonderful girl who needed to be recognized for what she was.

We hadn't exactly argued, but I'd felt uncomfortable. She should know I love Marcy more than anything else; I just want her to have a happy life, and pretty girls are happier. Denise should know that; she was a stunner.

So I said, "If it's clear," and Marcy grinned at me, half braces and half teeth.

We ran the spot Friday, on schedule. I'd noticed on the monitor that the horses' green eyes didn't show up well, and decided not to mention it. The girls were pretty enough, one all gold and blue on a gold and white horse, and one all black and green (did I mention that Charlene wore a green western shirt, something that glittered, with black jeans and boots?) on a black horse. Not quite as gorgeous as I remembered—in fact, not more than middling pretty—but things rarely look the same on tape, and I'm used to it. After all, we'd had to shoot the spot in midafternoon in July. Maybe those little lines came from squinting at the bright sun—the camera sees what's really there; it doesn't make allowances for lousy lighting. Kelly's voice I'd figured wouldn't tape well—breathy, a little too high—but I was surprised at Charlene's—it sounded more hoarse than husky. But again—a hot day, midafternoon—maybe she'd been thirsty. Marcy thought the horses were great; I don't know if she even looked at the riders.

Saturday morning, traffic held us up north of the city, and if Marcy hadn't been humming tunelessly beside me, I'd have turned back. It was nothing but a little pissant country town with two pretty girls riding horses in a tacky parade; we'd get hot and dusty, and eat too much cheap greasy food—Hal's pool would be a lot more fun. But Denise had sent us off smiling; she wouldn't like it if I changed plans on her now.

We had to park at the far end of a dusty field beside

the town's rickety little football stadium, crammed in
between a pickup truck with its bed full of assorted
junk, and a rusty barbwire fence. It was a two-block
walk to the parade route, nothing much in the city,
but here a hot, sweaty trek past sunburned yards and
houses flaking ancient paint. They looked even older,
more faded, today than they had on the Wednesday
before. Two people came out of one house, and
glanced at us without speaking.

We got to the main street a little late, and had to
crowd in behind a double row of others. A little boy
rode by on a bicycle decorated with crepe paper, holding a red ribbon in his teeth. I glanced at my watch.
Time and more for the parade to start. Sweat trickled
down my sides; I could smell the hair spray from the
huge bouffant arrangement on the tall woman next to
me. A puff of wind blew a wiry strand of it across my
nose; I batted it away, blinking at the dust, just as
another, sharper puff spanked my other cheek. Marcy
shook her head, but when I looked down, she flashed
her metallic smile at me. One thing about her, she's
no complainer, our girl. If she had the looks she de-
serves, she'd be a match for anyone. I squeezed her
shoulder, and felt my heart contract at the look she
gave me. I didn't deserve that kind of trust—no man
could.

More little gusts of wind, carrying the smells of a
summer celebration: bubble gum baked on the pavement, horses, barbecue. Scraps of paper lifted from
the street; a small child chased one, was captured by
a tired-faced woman wearing an apron over her dress.
It crossed my mind I hadn't seen a woman wear an
apron like that in years. Then the dust hit, a soft fist
pummeling our faces, our eyes, stinging; wind jerked
my shirt and hair first one way then the other. Marcy
grabbed my arm and squealed "Daddy!" then
coughed. I could hardly breathe myself. For an instant,

sight and hearing blurred, caught in a whirl of wind-noise and grit. Then I could hear the chokes, coughs, children crying, even screams.

The wind went as it had come, without warning or reason; I watched the tawny blur of the dust-devil follow the road out of town, as steadily as a drunk driver trying to be careful.

But the crowd's noise yanked my attention back to the street. Something had happened. I cursed myself for coming without even a pocket 'corder, but I'd promised Denise the trip was for Marcy. Still I edged us leftward, back toward the disturbance.

Another news team stood where I usually stand, in the middle of things. How was I going to explain *this* at work? With Marcy clinging to my hand, a little nervous in the crowd, I couldn't push my way through as I usually did. I went up on tiptoe, trying to see. There was an opening: that usually meant someone was on the ground. Just beyond the gap, a well-polished pickup had both doors open; behind it was the parade's first float, and the girl who should have been perched on a throne waving was stepping across the trailer hitch from the float to the pickup, hampered only slightly by her formal gown, intent on seeing what had happened.

Suddenly a siren went off in my ear, and I jumped. It was the fire engine that should have cleared the way for the parade; we had come around it, with the rest of the crowd, hardly noticing it—now its lights flashed, and the siren beeped and squealed. The volunteers, in their blue shirts with lots of insignia, began pushing the crowd back, and I saw another flashing light coming along a side street: the ambulance.

Of course, everyone was talking about what happened, but already there were five or six stories just in those few minutes. Only a few, it seemed, had been on the spot, and they'd been squinting against the sud-

den dust storm the same as anyone else. The girls
were hurt; the girls were killed; the girls had been
bucked off; the horses had run away . . . I figured then
who it had to be, of course. We backed up with the
others, as requested, and let the ambulance through; I
couldn't see any more than the stretchers being loaded
aboard it. Then the siren whooped again, and the parade went on, just as parades always do go on in spite
of accidents.

Marcy was less disappointed than I'd expected.
There were other horses to exclaim over, and after
all, she never had seen the palomino and black that
weren't there anymore except on tape. I felt it more;
I'd really looked forward to seeing those two girls ride
by, all proud and beautiful in the sunlight, and without
them the parade was a predictable mixture of senti-
mentality and cheap glitter. The girls on the homemade floats, the pride of each little town in the festival
circuit, were pretty enough, but nothing like Kelly and
Charlene on horseback.

But I set myself to being a good father, and Marcy
enjoyed herself. I even waited patiently while she
walked around talking to the people who had ridden
in the parade. She petted their horses, flashed that
metallic grin more than I'd seen in months. I caught
myself thinking that if she looked like Kelly, I'd buy
her a horse and let her ride in parades—she looked
so happy. And that was almost enough for the day,
except that I really did want to know about Kelly
and Charlene.

The late news that night had coverage from our
competition; I sipped my drink as I watched, and tried
to figure out how to salvage my part in it while criticiz-
ing the camera angles the competition used. The announcer said it was Kelly and Charlene, but the
pictures certainly didn't do them justice. Kelly's
golden hair looked dusty, and I guess it's hard to be

cute and pretty when someone's splinting your broken wrist. Charlene must have been hurting, too; she looked almost gaunt, those gorgeous bones ready to break through the skin. Nothing was said about their horses on one channel; the next, when I flipped to it, had already done the story, and the other one stuck it on last and mentioned that the horses had run off in terror at the "sudden storm." Our station ran the tape we'd done before, and a brief shot of their faces, and Melanie, who has the evening news spot on Saturday and is trying for more, said what a horrible ordeal for two such pretty girls.

I don't read the paper all that often, unless I'm researching something, but the Sunday paper had it on the front page—mostly because their Congressman had been there. I could have shot the old buzzard at City Hall, for not telling me he was coming when I picked up the brochure; if I'd known, I'd have brought a 'corder no matter what. Mysterious disappearance of famous parade horses, they called it. I quirked my mouth over that "famous" but let it ride. Anyone who'd seen Kelly on that palomino wouldn't have forgotten it. I wondered then if she'd ever ridden in anyone else's parades, or if she'd been content to reign in a small realm. The horses, the story ended, had not been found.

It occurred to me that I could salvage our station's position by getting a human-interest continuation. That would justify seeing them again, and (my fatherly conscience being tender) I could even ask their advice about Marcy: would riding in parades do anything to help a girl get along in high school? So about midweek, I took a camcorder and told my boss I might get an interview, and he raised his eyebrows but nodded. I also took a present I didn't tell him about, two copies of the original tape we took of Kelly and Charlene (all but the rump shot, of course).

Kelly's mom didn't look real friendly when she opened the door, and I was glad I'd come in my own car, not the station van. I told her I'd heard about it, and thought maybe Kelly would like a copy of the pictures we'd gotten before her horse was lost. The woman's eyes glittered dangerously.

"*Her* horse!" she said, with an emphasis I couldn't quite understand. "That—!"

But then Kelly walked in, her not-really-golden hair pulled back and her eye shadow a bit too blue. The cast on her arm still had her off balance; I could see the difference in her walk. No girl is as pretty when she's hurt, and tired, and miserable about losing a favorite horse. You can see what they'll look like in ten years. But she smiled at me, and the dimples were still there, and the white teeth. I handed her the tape, and told her how sorry I was, and maybe this would help. Her eyes were a little red, and now the tears started. That didn't bother me: I've seen plenty, for better reason and none at all, in my business. But I said I was sorry again, and she choked on a thank you, and her mom huffed loudly and walked out. Kelly waved an arm at the living room, and I sat down.

"He'll never come back," she said softly, with a wary glance at the door. I opened my mouth to say something about searches being made, and she interrupted the first word.

"No. They'll never find him. He's gone back"—and then her head jerked up and her eyes widened, tear-smeary as they were. "I—I'm sorry—I'm so upset. I don't really know what I'm saying, and besides—" I felt a jolt of glee—my instincts had been right; there *was* a story here.

"I used to have a horse." I lied, trying for empathy. Her face relaxed slightly.

"Not like Sunny," she said.

"No. But I wouldn't have believed it then." I felt

my way into my role as bereft horse lover, and like all roles, it came easily to me. "He was a plain old brown horse you wouldn't look at twice, but to me—" I shook my head, and she nodded. Whatever else she was or wasn't in the realm of beauty, Kelly had a normal amount of sentiment.

"How long did you have him?" she asked, good manners overcoming grief.

I pondered a moment. Could I remember enough incidents from my uncle's place to flesh out a long horse ownership? "Five years," I said, shaking my head again. "Then my family moved, and we—we had to sell him." I glanced at her; a little color had come into her face. "How long did you have Sunny?"

It was the wrong question. She stiffened and paled, as if I'd hit her cast with a bat. "I—it's hard to think right now. My arm—" I looked at it dutifully, not impressed with her intelligence. A broken wrist five days old is a nuisance, no more. With my eyes safely away from hers, she said softly, "I got him with . . . from Charlene. She got hers first."

So I stood up, and smiled at her, and told her I'd brought a tape for Charlene, too, if she'd tell me where Charlene lived. And she told me in the way that country people give directions, all relating to things you only know about if you live there, but I finally figured it out when she came out on the front porch and pointed.

I'd thought before Charlene was the smart one of the pair, and so it turned out. She had on dark glasses that day, and had propped her bandaged ankle on a couch, but her voice was as lovely as the first time I'd heard it.

Charlene was, she told me straight out, just over two years older than Kelly, and at fourteen, she'd been a long, gawky girl with lank hair and no self-confidence. Smart, but the local school had no scope for her kind of smart, and she knew that she'd never qualify for a really good scholarship. But she could ride anything on four legs, and she'd seen an article about barrel racers' winnings in a western riding magazine. That would be her ticket out. She'd sold her old sorrel horse that didn't have enough speed, and gone looking for a new mount.

She relaxed enough to slip the dark glasses up, and I could see Charlene at fourteen. Bones that might have character someday, but missed beauty by a slight margin almost worse for being slight. Well-placed collarbones with too deep a hollow above and below them. She'd have had thin muscular wrists and long thin hands, and she'd have pulled her dark hair back to a plain plastic clip. And the money from the sale of the sorrel horse would have been folded tightly into a wad, and tucked deep in the pocket of jeans worn thin at the knees.

She'd come to the farm—she didn't say where it was—still looking for a barrel-racing prospect. A brisk little woman, dark-skinned and gray-haired, had come out, looked her up and down, and offered only one horse: the black. The price was what she'd jammed deep in her pocket. And she'd taken one look and known she'd pay it, though she wasn't the kind of girl to buy a horse for its looks. The woman took her money, and followed her home in a pickup with the black horse in the trailer. There, with the horse in Charlene's lot, the woman gave her roweled spurs and spade bit, and told her she must never mount the horse without them.

At that point, Charlene explained, she'd have decided not to buy the horse, because there are rules about spurs and bits in barrel racing, but the horse was there, and the woman had driven off with her money before she could argue. So she saddled up, strapped the unfamiliar spurs on her boots, and mounted.

That began the happiest years of her life, she said, beginning to cry. When a boy she knew, who had ignored her for years, stopped her even as she rode down the street that first day, and stared, wide-eyed. When she looked in the mirror. When she dressed the next day for school and things were tight and loose in different places. When she got more looks, and more attention, than she'd ever had before . . . and she knew it was wrong, she said, sobs blurring the words, but she couldn't stop once she knew what she had.

She didn't drive back out to the farm to demand her money and return the horse. She didn't even think of it, or of the barrel racing that had been her plan of escape. By midsummer, she had become the acknowledged town beauty, overshadowing the older girls. And she was asked to lead the parade on her beautiful black horse, carrying the American flag down the center of Main Street as everyone cheered. After that first parade, after she had the taste of it in her mouth, the odd little woman had visited, and explained the dangers and limitations of the gift. Charlene didn't tell me what they were right then, or if she did I didn't hear her. I had a sudden vision of Marcy, sitting tall on such a horse, no braces on her teeth, and a crowd waving. Maybe a red horse, and her hair the color Denise's had been, a vivid flame. My vision blurred. Maybe I had more than a story.

For three years, Charlene and the black horse graced the town, and the honors she couldn't win by being smart and hardworking came easily to the town beauty, the most popular girl in school. Then she noticed Kelly, down the block, standing forlorn in the yard and watching her ride by. Kelly was not quite cute, the way Charlene had not been quite beautiful.

To seventeen, fourteen doesn't seem like competition. Charlene never thought of the older girls she'd displaced, but she remembered her own miseries. First she thought she'd let Kelly ride the black horse. That didn't work: Kelly couldn't even get on. But somewhere in the conversation, Charlene let slip to Kelly that the horse was her secret, the way she had become what she was. And for Kelly, that was enough. She pestered, and warted, and fretted, and pleaded, and finally Charlene gave her certain directions, and two days later Kelly rode down the street on a golden palomino that matched her now-golden hair. Charlene wanted me to know that she had *offered* to let Kelly lead the parade that summer, but I was sure that Kelly would have been asked anyway. No one could resist that golden image.

And that had been ... Charlene closed her eyes, counting. That had been twenty years ago, the first year that Kelly led the parade. I must have moved or something, for her eyes flicked open, and her mouth quirked. "You don't believe me?"

I looked at her face, now every bit of thirty-seven years old, if not more, and nodded slowly. I wasn't sure what I believed, but I wanted Charlene to go on talking. Questions could come later.

"I would have quit before," she said slowly. "I had had my high school triumphs; that's all I wanted. I had two scholarships—not big, but big enough to get out of town—and I planned to go. I could give up being the local beauty, to gain the world. But then—" Her longer fingers moved restlessly in her lap. "There was Kelly, and Sunny—"

Kelly had never wanted anything more than to be a golden girl leading a parade on a golden horse. To freeze time in that moment of triumph, to be forever prancing down the street with everyone watching her, a light breeze rippling the flag she carried. I found myself nodding: that's what any girl would want, if she could get it. Perfectly natural. Kelly, though, had scoffed at the warning she received, as Charlene had not scoffed. Maybe Charlene would have to quit, but she wouldn't. She would ride that parade every year of her life. She would step out of time, and take the world with her.

I still didn't understand. "What warning? How do you mean, the gift had limits? And what was it about in the first place?" More questions clogged my head: how and why and who and when and where. Especially where.

"Five years, or my twentieth birthday, whichever came first. That's what the woman said, after my first parade: I was to ride the horse back out there before then. If I didn't, he'd disappear, and I'd have that to explain. And as for why . . . I never knew. I never asked." She saw my doubt and insisted, "I never asked why: there were answers she might have given that I didn't want to hear. Why did I buy that horse in the first place? It had to be some kind of magic—dangerous, maybe even wrong . . . *wicked*. I can imagine what the preacher at church would have said, if he'd known about it. You don't question things like that. If you find out it's something really bad, then you can't do it, but if you don't know then it's not your fault."

That I could understand—even though my business is looking for answers, there are some things I don't question, some rocks I don't turn over. So I could do without answers, except that there were horses that made girls beautiful, and Marcy—who wasn't beautiful—loved horses. I found myself agreeing with Charlene: the rest really didn't matter. "How did Kelly do it? Where did she get the power to overcome . . . whatever it was?"

Charlene gave me a look far too old for the age she had been until this past week, a look Denise might have given me. "It took me years to figure that out, but ... it wasn't just Kelly who wanted it." I must have looked as confused as I felt; she sighed and went on. "Look—she wanted to lead the parade. But the others—everyone in town, just about—wanted to *see* her lead it. Wanted her to be that perfect, golden image. Never aging, never sick, never faded, always up there with the flag, the dream that came true." She sighed again. "And we couldn't any of us get free of it. What it came down to, it's what people really wanted, wanted bad enough to lose ... whatever we lost."

She fell silent, and I thought of the town as it had been ... as it was. That squatty ugly building—had it been new when Kelly rode in her first parade? I asked, and Charlene nodded. So the move to restore old buildings to their original stone and brick had by-passed this town, and new industries had settled elsewhere, and those here could not manage to move away. Things faded, grew vaguely shabby, blurred or frayed at the margins like a tape played too many times, but never progressed in normal aging. Other people? Charlene nodded. "Those closest to us slow down, but they can wear out and die. My parents did. People we didn't know much, they seem pretty normal."

"And did you finish school?" I asked, suspecting the answer. "Go on to college?"

"No." The dark glasses went back on. "No, I didn't do anything, but ride in that parade once a year behind Kelly and Sunny."

Whatever she could have been, whatever Kelly could have been, in those twenty years ... all gone to feed the dream of glory, the yearly spectacle. Kelly, I figured, had had nothing much to look forward to; Charlene could have been anything. A tragedy, if you look at things that way. But it had been an accident, surely. If it hadn't been for Kelly's mistake, Charlene would have had nothing to complain of—in fact, she'd been a lot better off as a beauty than she had been plain and shabby and ignored. It was really her fault, for telling Kelly about the horse. I wondered what had broken the spell, or whatever it was—if we, with our camera, perhaps, had done it, by broadcasting the reality—but it didn't matter now. It wasn't as if I had a story; I didn't need to tie up all the loose ends. Something else mattered more.

I opened my mouth to ask her where the horse farm was, and stopped just in time. She'd want to know why I asked, and if I told her about Marcy she'd probably get mad. It had been a tragedy for her; she would be sure it couldn't work right for anyone else. She probably never thought of it as wrong, or maybe wicked, until it turned bad for her. Women are like that: everything's so personal to them. But Marcy was different. I could protect her, make sure nothing like this happened to her. Whatever the intent of this mysterious woman with magic horses, whatever the nature of the spell, it couldn't possibly hurt Marcy with me to look out for her. I didn't have to understand it; I just had to watch out for Marcy. I said good-bye and went back for a last visit with Kelly.

Like I said, you can't really blame Kelly. She's too old for cute, but she's still got that all-American grin with the dimple in the corner of her mouth, and if the gold in her hair will come from a bottle from now on, so what? I used a little subtle highlighting myself. She's a good girl, a good wholesome small-town girl who liked all the right things: Mom, Pop, apple pie, the Tigers on the ten-yard line with a first down . . . and riding a golden horse down Main Street once a year with the American flag in her hand. It wasn't Kelly's fault that she got too much power too soon, that she had such limited dreams to freeze in the amber-gold of that palomino horse. She only wanted what we all want, to make the good times last forever.

She understood that I only wanted the best for my daughter; if her father had been like me, things would have been different. She said Marcy sounded sweet, and she told me the truth when I asked her where the place was.

I have this daughter I love so much it hurts, a girl brave and tough and wise beyond her years. She's already learned to think of herself as homely. When the pretty girls walk by, when she sees the boys look after them, I can see her face stiffen, holding back the longing she's too brave to show. She's going to be fourteen next spring, and she wants a horse for her birthday.

Unto the Daughters

Nancy Kress

Like Sheila Finch, Nebula award winner Nancy Kress deals with religion in a revisionist vein. All those millennia of theologians telling women what to believe and how to behave—and then the women go off and talk by themselves. "Unto the Daughters" would probably give such religious authorities nightmares (take *that*, John Milton!), but it seems perfectly reasonable—and hilarious in an ironic sort of way—to me.

Ever want to know what the women are talking about when they're alone? Read on, but at the risk of your assumptions.

This is not the way you heard the story.

In the beginning, the tree was young. White blossoms scenting the air for a quarter mile. Shiny succulent fruit, bending the same boughs that held blossoms. Leaves of that delicate yellow-green that cannot, will not, last. Yet it did. He always did have gaudy taste. No restraint. Just look at the Himalayas. Or blowfish. I mean—really!

The woman was young, too. Pink curling toes,

breasts as barely budded as the apple blossoms. And the man! My dear, those long, firm flanks alone could make you ache inside for hours. He could run five miles and not even be winded. He could make love to the woman five times a day. And did.

The flowers were young. The animals, tumbling and cavorting on the grass, were young. The fucking *beach sand* was young, clean evenly shaped grains that only yesterday had been igneous rock. There was virgin rain.

Only I was old.

But it wasn't that. That was the first thing that came to your mind, wasn't it? Jealousy of glorious youth, revenge by the dried-up and jaded. Oh, you don't know, you sitting there so many centuries ahead. It wasn't that at all. I mean, I loved them both.

Looking at them, how could one not?

"Go away," Eve says. "I'm not going to eat one."

She sits cross-legged, braiding flowers into a crown. The flowers are about what you'd expect from Him, garish scarlet petals and a vulva-shaped pistil like a bad joke. Braiding them, her fingers are deft and competent. Some lion cubs tumble tiresomely on the grass.

"I want to give you a reason why you should eat one," I say, not gently.

"I've heard all your reasons."

"Not this one, Eve. This is a *new* reason."

She isn't interested. She knots the crown of flowers, puts it on her head, giggles, tosses it at the lions. It settles lopsided over one cub's left ear. The cub looks up with comic surprise, and Eve explodes into laughter.

Really, sometimes I wonder why I bother. She's so stupid, compared to the man.

I bother because she's so stupid compared to the man.

"Listen, Eve. *He* withholds knowledge from you two because He's selfish. What else would you call it to keep knowledge to yourself when you could just as well share it?"

"I don't need knowledge," Eve says airily. "What do I need knowledge for? And anyway, that's not a new reason. You've said that before."

"A tree, Eve. A fucking *tree*. To invest knowledge in. Doesn't that strike you as just a teeny bit warped? Mathematics in xylem, morality in fruit pulp? Astronomy rotting on the ground every time an apple falls. Don't you wonder what kind of a mind would do that?"

She only stares at me blankly. Oh, she's dumb. I mean!

I shout, in the temper of perfect despair, "Without knowledge, nothing will change!"

"Are *you* here again?" Adam says. I hadn't heard him climb over the rock behind us. He has a very quiet footstep for someone whose toenails have never ever been cut, and a quiet, penetrating voice. Eve jumps up as if she's been shot.

"I thought I told you not to talk to this ... thing ever again," Adam says. "Did I tell you that?"

Eve hangs her pretty head. "Yes, Adam. You did. I forgot."

He looks at her, and his face softens. That blooming skin, those sweet lips. Her hair falls forward, lustrous at night. I don't think my despair can go any deeper, but it does. She is so pretty. He will always forgive her. And she will always forget everything he says two minutes after he says it.

"Be gone! You don't belong here!" Adam shouts, and throws a rock at me. It hits just behind my head. It hurts like hell. One of the lion cubs happily fetches it back, waggling a golden tail. The other one is still wearing the lopsided crown of flowers.

As I slither away, half blind with pain, Eve calls after me. "I don't *want* anything to change! I really don't!"

The hell with her.

"Just listen," I say. "Just put your entire tiny mind on one thing for once and *listen* to me."

Eve sits sewing leaves into a blanket. Not cross-legged anymore: She is six months pregnant. The leaves are wide and soft, with a sort of furry nap on their underside. They appeared in the garden right after she got pregnant, along with tough spiderwebs that make splendid thread. Why not a bush that grows little caps? Or tiny diapers with plastic fastening tabs? Really, He has such a banal imagination.

Eve hums as she sews. Beside her is the cradle Adam made. It's carved with moons and numbers and stars and other cabalistic signs: a lovely piece of work. *Adam* has imagination.

"You have to *listen*, Eve. Not just hear—*listen*. Stop that humming. I know the future—how could I know the future unless I am exactly what I say I am? I know everything that's going to happen. I told you when you'd conceive, didn't I? That alone should have convinced you. And now I'm telling you that your baby will be a boy, and you'll call him Cain, and he—"

"No, I'm going to call him Silas," Eve says. She knots the end of her spider thread and bites it off. "I *love* the name Silas."

"You're going to call him Cain, and he—"

"Do you think it would be prettier to embroider roses on this blanket, or daisies?"

"Eve, listen, if I can foretell the future, then isn't it logical, isn't it reasonable for you to think—"

"I don't have to think," Eve says. "Adam does that for both of us, plus all the forest-dressing and fruit-tending. He works so hard, poor dear."

"Eve—"

"Roses, I think. In blue."

I can't stand it anymore. I go out into the constant, perpetual, monotonous sunshine, which smells like roses, like wisteria, like gardenia, like woodsmoke, like new-mown hay. Like heaven.

Eve has the baby at nine months, thirty-two seconds. She laughs as the small head slides out, which takes two painless minutes. The child is perfect.

"We'll call him Cain," Adam says.

"I thought we might call him Silas. I love the na—"

"Cain," Adam says firmly.

"All right, Adam."

He will never know she was disappointed.

"Eve," I say. "Listen."

She is bathing the two boys in the river, in the shallows just before the river splits into four parts and leaves the garden. Cain is diligently scrubbing his small penis, but Abel has caught at some seaweed and is examining how it hangs over his chubby fists. He turns it this way and that, bending his head close. He is much more intelligent than his brother.

"Eve, Adam will be back soon. If you'd just listen . . ."

"Daddy," Abel says, raising his head. He has a level gaze, friendly but evaluative, even at his age. He spends a lot of time with his father. "Daddy gone."

"Oh, yes, Daddy's gone to pick breadfruit in the west!" Eve cries, in a perfect ecstasy of maternal pride. "He'll be back tonight, my little poppets. He'll be home with his precious little boys!"

Cain looks up. He has succeeded in giving his penis the most innocent of erections. He smiles beatifically at Abel, at his mother, who does not see him because she is scrubbing Abel's back, careful not to drip soapstone onto his seaweed.

"Daddy pick breadfruit," Abel repeats. "Mommy not."

"Mommy doesn't want to go pick breadfruit," Eve says. "Mommy is happy right here with her little poppets."

"Mommy not," Abel repeats, thoughtfully.

"Eve," I say, "only with knowledge can you make choices. Only with truth can you be free. Four thousand years from now—"

"I am free," Eve says, momentarily startled. She looks at me. Her eyes are as fresh, as innocent, as when she was created. They open very wide. "How could anyone not think I'm perfectly *free?*"

"If you'd just listen—"

"Daddy gone," Abel says a third time. "Mommy not."

"Even thirty seconds of careful listening—"

"Mommy never gone."

"Tell that brat to shut up while I'm trying to talk to you!"

Wrong, wrong. Fury leaps into Eve's eyes. She scoops up both children as if I were trying to stone them, the silly bitch. She hugs them tight to her chest, breathing something from those perfect lips that might have been "Well!" or "Ugly!" or even "Help!" Then she staggers off with both boys in her arms, dripping water, Abel dripping seaweed.

"Put Abel down," Abel says dramatically. "Abel walk."

She does. The child looks at her. "Mommy do what Abel say!"

I go eat worms.

The third child is a girl, whom they name Sheitha.

Cain and Abel are almost grown. They help Adam with the garden dressing, the animal naming, whatever comes up. I don't know. I'm getting pretty sick of the whole lot of them. The tree still has both blossoms and fruit on the same branch. The river still flows into four exactly equal branches just beyond the garden: Pison, Gihon, Hiddekel, Euphrates. Exactly the same number of water molecules in each. I stop thinking He's theatrical and decide instead that He's compulsive. I mean—really. Fish lay the exact same number of eggs in each river.

Eve hasn't seen Him in decades. Adam, of course, walks with Him in the cool of every evening. Now the two boys go, too. Heaven knows what they talk about; I stay away. Often it's my one chance at Eve, who spends every day sewing and changing diapers and sweeping bowers and slicing breadfruit. Her toes are still pink curling delicacies.

"Eve, listen—"

Sheitha giggles at a bluebird perched on her dimpled knee.

"Adam makes all the decisions, decides all the rules, thinks up all the names, does all the thinking—"

"So?" Eve says. "Sheitha—you precious little angel!" She catches the baby in her arms and covers her with kisses. Sheitha crows in delight.

"Eve, listen—"

Miraculously, she does. She sets the baby on the grass and says seriously, "Adam says you aren't capable of telling the truth."

"Not *his* truth," I say. "Or His." But, of course, this subtlety of pronoun goes right over her head.

"Look, snake, I don't want to be rude. You've been very kind to me, keeping me company while I do my housework, and I appreciate—"

"I'm not being kind," I say desperately. Kind! Oh, my Eve ... "I'm too old and tired for kindness. I'm just trying to show you, to get you to listen—"

"Adam's back," Eve says quickly. I hear him then, with the two boys. There is just time enough to slither under a bush. I lie there very still. Lately Adam has turned murderous toward me; I think he must have a special dispensation for it. *He* must have told Adam violence toward me doesn't count, because I have stepped out of my place. Which, of course, I have.

But this time Adam doesn't see me. The boys fall into some game with thread and polished stones. Sheitha toddles toward her daddy, grinning.

"We're just here to get something to eat," Adam says. "Ten minutes, is all—what, Eve, isn't there anything ready? What have you been doing all morning?"

Eve's face doesn't fall. But her eyes deepen in color a little, like skin that has been momentarily bruised. Of course, skin doesn't stay bruised here. Not here.

"I'm sorry, dear! I'll get something ready right away!"

"Please," Adam says. "Some of us have to work for a living."

She bustles quickly around. The slim pretty fingers are deft as ever. Adam throws himself prone into a bower. Sheitha climbs into his lap. She is as precocious as the boys were.

"Daddy go back?"

"Yes, my little sweetie. Daddy has to go cut more sugarcane. And name some new animals."

"Animals," Sheitha says happily. She loves animals. "Sheitha go."

Adam smiles. "No, precious, Sheitha can't go. Little girls can't go."

"Sheitha *go!*"

"No," Adam says. He is still smiling, but he stands up and she tumbles off his lap. The food is ready. Eve turns with a coconut shell of salad just as Sheitha is picking herself up. The baby stands looking up at her father. Her small face is crumpled in disappointment, in disbelief, in anguish. Eve stops her turning motion and looks, her full attention on Sheitha's face.

I draw a deep breath.

The moment spins itself out, tough as spider thread. Eve breaks it. "Adam—can't you take her?"

He doesn't answer. Actually, he hasn't even heard her. He can't, in exactly the same way Eve cannot hear *Him* in the cool of the evening.

You could argue that this exempts him from fault.

Eve picks up the baby and stands beside the bower. Fragrance rises from the newly crushed flower petals where Adam was lying. When he and the boys have left again, I slither forward. Eve, the baby in her arms, has still not moved. Her head is bent. Sheitha is weeping, soft tears of vexation that will not, of course last very long. Not here. I don't have much time.

"Eve," I say. "Listen—"

I tell her how it will be for Sheitha after she marries Cain, who is not as sweet-tempered as his father. I tell her how it will be for Sheitha's daughter's daughter. I spare her nothing: not the expansion of the garden until the home bowers are insignificant. Not the debate over whether women have souls. Not foot-binding nor clitoridectomy nor suttee nor the word "chattel." Sheitha, I say. Sheitha and Sheitha's daughter and Sheitha's daughter's daughter ... I am hoarse before I'm done talking. Finally, I finish, saying for perhaps the fortieth or fiftieth time, "Knowledge is the only way to change it. Knowledge, and truth. Eve, listen—"

She goes with me to the tree. Her baby daughter in her arms, she goes with me. She chooses a bright red apple, and she chews her mouthful so completely that when she transfers it to Sheitha's lips, there is no chance the baby could choke on it. Together, they eat the whole thing.

I am tired. I don't wait around for the rest: Adam's

return, and his outrage that she has acted without him, his fear that now she knows things he does not. *His* arrival. I don't wait. I am too tired, and my gut twists as if I had swallowed something foul, or bitter. That happens sometimes, without my intending it. Sometimes I eat something with a vitamin I know I need, and it lies hard in my belly like pain.

This is not the way you heard the story.

But consider who eventually wrote that story down. Consider, too, who wiped up the ink or scrubbed the chisel or cleaned the printing office after the writing down was done. For centuries and centuries.

But not forever.

So this may not be the way you heard the story, but you, centuries and centuries hence, my sisters, know better. Finally. You know, yes, about Eve's screams on her childbed, and Sheitha's murder at the hands of her husband, and Sheitha's daughter's cursing of her rebellious mother as the girl climbed willingly onto her husband's funeral pyre, and *her* daughter's harlotry, and *her* daughter's forced marriage at age nine to a man who gained control of all her camels and oases. You know all that, all the things I didn't tell poor Eve would happen anyway. But you know, too—as Eve would not have, had it not been for me— that knowledge can bring change. You sit cross-legged at your holodecks or in your pilot chairs or on your Councils, humming, and you finally know. Finally—it took you so fucking *long* to digest the fruit of knowledge and shit it out where it could fertilize anything. But you did. You are not stupid. More—you know that stupidity is only the soul asleep. The awakened sleeper may stumble a long time in the dark, but eventually the light comes. Even here.

I woke Eve up.

I, the mother.

So that may not be the way you heard the story, but it is the way it happened. And now—finally, finally—you know.

And can forgive me.

Babbitt's Daughter

Phyllis Ann Karr

In "Babbitt's Daughter," Phyllis Ann Karr takes a wry
and loving look at two myths—one American, the
other Transylvanian. Sinclair Lewis's Babbitt would
hardly welcome Phyllis Ann Karr's Amarantha "whose
father was a Babbitt" with open arms—or veins. After
all, vampires aren't the sort of neighbors you want on
Main Street.

Or are they?

From Anne Rice, we have the image of the vampire
as rock musician. Phyllis Ann Karr gives us musicologists
and activists who never drink . . . wine and who leave
their victims—and her readers—laughing.

The question is: who has the last laugh?

"My father was a Babbitt!" Amarantha flashed back
at her host.

"Well? Isn't that in itself a rather remarkable accomplishment for a vampire?" Still smiling calmly,
Mendoza slipped his fingers beneath his guest's miniature snifter and carried it back to the table for a refill
with the dark cherry cordial he called homemade. "I
rest my case."

"No, you don't. You're getting ready to deliver more words of wisdom to help me cope with my bereavement."

"Is that what we're doing?" He looked around at her, fireplace light crimsoning his almost completely silver hair. Though he still moved like a man in the prime of life, he was an indeterminate number of years older than her father had been.

But then, Amarantha was no schoolgirl. Her own hair held quite a bit of silver.

"We're both mature enough to have read up on the recommended mental hygienics of coping with bereavement," Mendoza complimented her, returning her glass to the arm of her chair. "I thought we were simply reminiscing. But if you'd like another argument, consider that by living his life out of the closet, your father put himself up against two antagonistic mindsets: the one that assumes all vampires are automatically evil monsters, and the one that wants them that way—that believes any vampire who may genuinely prefer saintliness is somehow betraying his or her very nature."

"Saintliness!" she echoed in a mocking tone. "You never saw him really pig out."

It must have been the Christmas vacation of her frosh year at the University of Madison ... with a cozy little school of higher learning in her hometown, and both parents on its faculty, she had nevertheless insisted on going to the big education factory downstate, hopping home only on holidays.

Anyway, she remembered the night of some party or other between Christmas and New Year's—probably the Dean's annual bash. They'd gotten back well after midnight, most of the family going more or less straight to bed. After half an hour or so, Amarantha gave up the struggle to fall asleep and got up for a book and some warm milk.

She found her father at the refrigerator, filling a glass from the bottle of chicken blood.

"Father!"

"Amy." Smiling at her without the least sign of shame, he reached for the small bottle of human hemoglobin from the Bloodbank. "Enjoy the party?"

"Not as much as you did. *Jesus,* Father, you ate enough for the whole Coast Guard!"

He shivered and paused, then set the Bloodbank bottle beside his glass on the table, shut the fridge door gently but firmly, and turned to her. "Amy, don't throw His Name around carelessly."

"I wasn't. I was using It to wake your conscience up. Je-*eesh,* Father, how can you stand there raiding the refrigerator after the way you stuffed yourself silly all evening?"

"I did?"

"I can't even count the number of times you kept refilling your plate. It's a good thing they had so much on the buffet, or you wouldn't have left anything for anybody else. Jeesh, some people get embarrassed about how much their parents drink. With me, it's how much my father *eats!*"

"I'm sorry, Amy. I never intended to embarrass you."

"And please don't call me that! You don't like to be nicknamed. Neither do I."

He sat down at the table, opened the Bloodbank bottle, and inserted the medicine dropper. "I don't like my contemporaries calling me 'Clem.' I've never minded 'Pop' or 'Daddy' from my own children."

"Well, I don't like 'Amy' from anyone. My name is Amarantha."

To be fair, her baptismal name was Teresa, and while her mother, brother, and sister slipped back to it pretty regularly even after the formal announcement of her new chosen name, her father never did. Even though she knew how disappointed he'd been that she didn't like "Teresa" for everyday wear.

"Very well. Amarantha," he said now, squeezing three drops of human into his glass of chicken blood, hesitating, and adding two more.

She could tell he was angry. But so was she. "I don't know why your crosses didn't drive you crazy!"

"Well, they didn't." His hand went to the tiny crucifix earring in his pierced ear. "Although this is beginning to pinch now, with the temptation to turn you over my knee."

"For what? Being scandalized by my own father's *gluttony*?"

He got a spoon out of the drawer and stirred his snack briskly. "I'm sorry I scandalized you. It was a Christmas party. I wasn't aware I was filling my plate so often."

"Well, you were. You dress up like a movie dracula, why don't you act like one? Movie dracs never eat at all."

"No, they pig out on blood. If you've ever noticed, movie vampires drink more than—"

"At least they don't do it in public!"

He shot her a look of real anger, and for a moment—if he had been somebody else's father or even her own mother—she'd have been afraid he really would turn her over his knee. Instead, being the world's most conscientiously saintly vampire, he put his spoon down and said in a voice so quiet it hurt, "I already apologized for embarrassing you, Amarantha. It happens I was hungry. Or didn't you notice that our hostess kept 'fooling' me with glasses of tomato juice?"

"And you kept adding drops from people's thumbs.

Why the 'H' don't you just *tell* people when you see they aren't giving you real blood?''

"It's called being polite—"

"Oh, affirmative! And so you go and stuff yourself silly instead, and I suppose *that's* just 'being polite,' too, seeing you don't get any calories or nutrition or anything out of plain old human food." The words "plain old human" pushed one of his most sensitive buttons. She had done that on purpose, and by his response she knew how well she managed to hide feeling sorry about it.

"Above all other people," he answered slowly, "the members of my own family should know I'm as human as everybody else. If there's nothing but water around, a hungry human will try to fill up on water and create the illusion of a full stomach."

"A *very* full stomach—a gorged-to-bursting stomach. Jeesh, *Pop,* can you even guess how many ordinary human beings would just love to be able to pig out on everything in sight without putting on a millimeter around the waistline? If eating like that in front of a bunch of people who're going to have to diet their souls out after the holidays is being polite—"

"Amarantha!"

His hand was quivering. He set his glass down before any of its contents sloshed out. There was a tight click when the glass met the tabletop.

"I'm sorry," he went on stiffly. "I thought she was going to have real blood for me. I suppose that at the last minute she couldn't get it after all. If I'd known, I would have drunk a glass here at home beforehand. Following St. Paul's advice. Then you wouldn't have had to suffer through watching your father make a glutton out of himself. Which I did unconsciously—"

"Don't make it sound like you were sleep-eating or something! You were wide-awake every minute! Your usual charming self—"

"Daughter! You don't know what it's like—thank God!—being hungry in the middle of a feast, in the middle of fellow human beings enjoying mountains of food—gourmet food—and being the only one there who can't get anything out of it at all except flavor and texture and false satis—"

"No, I don't know what it's like! But I *want* to know! I want like *Hell* to know! Come *on,* Father, bite me!"

"I kept asking him and asking him," she complained, almost less to Mendoza than to herself, "and he kept telling me, 'Be sure you understand what you're asking for.' Lord, he was still telling me that the day I turned forty! And now ... it's too late."

"He knew the everydayness of it," said Mendoza. "He knew what it was, circumventing pure-food rules in order to buy raw animal blood, combing your hair or getting an eyelash out of your eye without being able to see yourself in a mirror, keeping the conscience quiet enough not to react to holy things, facing the occasional serious danger from bigots ..."

"I'd have been willing! Do you think I couldn't see all that, just from living in the same house? But you'd have thought I was begging for incest! Or the power to be a screen monster. Why couldn't he ever trust me?"

Mendoza shook his head. "Not that he didn't trust you. It was that he didn't fully trust himself. His professional life was music, his spiritual life was his family and his religion. He never felt he had the academic or scientific credentials to make his ideas about vampirism anything more than a hobby—an amateur's theory that explained his own case but might not work for anybody else. That's why he never made another vampire, not even when someone begged him for it. Not even you. Especially not the members of his own family. I'm sure your mother loved—knew him better than to ask."

"My mother ... thanks to her, we're only half Japanese, when we could have been Purebloods!"

"Do you think you'd have existed if your mother had married someone else? Chances are that this consciousness calling itself Amarantha Czarny Kato would never have come into being at all ... But if it had, why the mother's child any more than the father's?"

"She made us halfbloods, and he gave us the name of junior vampires without the substance. Have you got any idea what it's like growing up as a dracula's daughter? Especially when your home isn't even much different from your friends' homes?"

"Another accomplishment." Sipping his cordial, Mendoza gazed at the fireplace. "Giving you the normal, middle class childhood he had missed out on. How old was he when it happened to him? Ten? Eleven?"

"Eleven." Amarantha knew this piece of family history very well. "In the Minnemagantic town hospital on a Sunday in July ..."

The first thing he remembered was the accident. A perfect swan dive—anything, he thought it should've been nearly perfect this time, for a dive from the boat—and then a thud to his head about the time he was ready to start surfacing.

He didn't feel like he was breathing, but it was a kind of comfortable feeling. He was still floating, only not in water anymore. Now he was drifting along in the air above a bed in a semidarkened room with forest murals on the walls. There was a boy in the bed, all hooked up to some kind of monitor unit. That and the rollover bedside tray-tables and stuff like that told him it was a hospital room.

The boy in the bed looked terrible. Like some kind of Frankenstein's Monster. Blackened eyes, puffy cheeks, mouth hanging open ... It took him awhile to recognize himself. He wasn't sure whether the himself in the bed was breathing, either. If it mattered.

He must've bashed his head against something hard in the water. Too bad Wolf Lake wasn't one of those crystal-clear lakes you heard about where people could see all the way down to count the pebbles on the bottom ten meters below. Too bad it was one of those lakes where you lost sight of your hand when you held it under at arm's length, and just had to take it on trust that the water was clean and nontoxic and didn't have hard stuff on the bottom waiting to getcha.

He wondered dreamily how much of that water he'd swallowed before Uncle Buck and Ted and Omar got him out and rushed him here. He figured that was what must have happened. Too bad they'd gone to all that trouble. How come he could remember their names and not his own?

The monitor unit seemed to be doing things, but he didn't read Monitorese. Some kind of antigravity was tugging him up toward the ceiling. He just let himself go with the flow ... too relaxed to do anything else.

He floated through the ceiling as if it was mist, and found himself on a huge open plain. He remembered from somewhere that there should be some kind of long tunnel, but he was on an open plain, glowing with light that came from all around, even up from the "ground." He thought his Guardian Angel should be here, too, but he couldn't see anybody. He seemed to feel someone at his back, but whoever it was must have kept pivoting around with him when he turned.

What there were, were a lot of cities and lake resorts and elegant buildings and mountain mini-ranges and campgrounds dotting the plain in all directions, like the galaxy clusters at the Chicago Planetarium show, and every time he turned around, they seemed to get closer. Especially one that looked like … He thought it looked a little like the Original Disneyland he'd never gotten to visit.

And standing there at the gates, waving to him— Dad and Mom! Looking the way he could just barely remember them, kissing him good-bye the time they drove off to get killed by that crazy UPS driver, only even better than they'd looked when they kissed him good-bye, even happier. Glowing … like some of the light was coming from inside them.

He waved back. He started trying to run to them …

Something held him back. Whoever was standing behind him? Was whoever it was giving him the old Vulcan neck pinch?

He tried to hit it away. The pinch just tightened. Actually, it felt more like something biting him.

Mom and Dad left the gates and floated down to him.

"Oh, honey, you're still so young!" said Mom. Only she didn't exactly "say" it. The words glowed out of her, like the light, and reformed themselves in his head, tonal vibrations and all.

"What *is* it?" he wanted to know. "Mom, Dad, what's biting me?"

"Maybe you'd better get on back, son," Dad told him. "Or else a lot of people will be pretty unhappy about you for a while. Your Mom and I can wait."

Something hard came up against his mouth. He couldn't see it, any better than he could see whatever had been biting him, but he could feel it, and there was something on it.

It worked his lips apart and drops of sweet, warm, salty liquid started falling into his mouth. He swallowed and opened his eyes.

Just like that, he was back in the hospital bed with somebody bending over him. Someone shadowy, holding one wrist to his mouth and using the other dark-sleeved arm for a mask.

Just that one glimpse of the faceless somebody, and then he was in Christine Daaé's dressing room. He was Raoul de Chagny, watching Christine from the curtained inner room, and he was also the Phantom of the Opera, Erik himself, singing to her through the walls, and he may have been Christine, too. But mainly he was seeing things through Raoul's eyes, following Christine as she walked toward her back wall, the wall that was one huge mirror. He could see her front in the mirror better than he could see her back that was right in front of him. Her eyes were huge, and there were two trickles of blood at the corners of her mouth. Her skin was as pale gray as if they were in one of the old black-and-white movies instead of the original novel. He couldn't see himself in the mirror because he was right in back of her, and her reflection completely covered his.

The dressing room was longer and longer, like a football field ... like the time line of the history of the universe ... and they kept on walking, and walking, and walking, with her getting bigger and bigger in the mirror until he didn't see how she could get any bigger, and meanwhile he kept on singing his opera to her, the opera Erik was composing about Don Juan triumphing over all the powers of Hell ...

She was touching the giant mirror, putting her arms through it. He reached out to hug her from behind and pull her back—she shattered into a zillion Christines, each tiny new Christine a facet in a huge mirror-tile globe spinning around and around, faster and faster, tinkling till it white-noised out his music.

And then, when it stopped and the mirror wall settled down again, like the lake smoothing out ... *he couldn't see himself at all.*

He was in Erik's torture chamber, the little room

with six walls and every one of them an identical mirror, reflecting each other over and over again until nobody could ever count all the reflections. There was a whole crowd of people in there with him ... well, maybe just two or three, but they looked like a whole crowd, an endless mob of the same two or three faces reflected over and over everywhere ... except *he couldn't find his own face anywhere!* And he finally understood how a person could go crazy in the Phantom of the Opera's mirror torture chamber ...

Christine Daaé sang, "He becomes a living dead man."

Her voice woke him up. His mother's antique hand mirror with the pearly plastic frame was lying on the hospital bedside tray table. He reached for the mirror, picked it up trembling, made sure he had the mirror side toward him, and looked in.

He saw the dent his head was making in the pillow, and a little bloodstain on the pillowcase down near the lower edge. His head wasn't in the reflection at all.

Still watching the mirror, he used his other hand to feel his neck and the corners of his mouth. Blood, both places. He could see it on his fingers, but he couldn't see either it or his fingers in the mirror. Just the pillow changing shape as he moved around.

He popped his fingers in his mouth and licked them clean before anybody came in and saw them. He could feel his eyeteeth growing long and sharp already. The bloodstain on the pillowcase must have come out of his neck before any blood from the dark shape's wrist got into his mouth.

His mother's mirror slipped out of his hand and dropped to the floor. Its bounce echoed on and on and on ... like Christine Daaé's song in his brain. A vague recollection came to him that Aunt Cele had Mom's old hand mirror down in Indiana. That meant it couldn't be up here. He was still dreaming ...

It didn't make any difference. Some dreams were true. This one was. Not about his mother's mirror ... and maybe not about the blood on his pillow. But true in what it was telling him.

He had seen his own face for the last time in his life a few minutes ago when he'd been floating in the air above his body. All puffy and bruised—what a last sight to get of your own face! And that was it, that was the last he'd ever be able to see of it live ...

He guessed he'd have to buy a portrait from one of those sidewalk artists every so often.

It seemed a stupid thing to worry about on top of everything else, but ... He'd known Erik's whole *Don Juan Triumphant* when he was singing it in the dream, and the hospital people came rushing in just as he finally started trying to get it back. Well, maybe it would've been too late, anyway.

"I hadn't been aware he was an orphan at the time," Mendoza commented. "He missed out on a normal family childhood in more ways than one."

"I never had any paternal grandparents to go visit and be spoiled by, either. Thanks to that speeding UPS truck years before I was born ... And then to have a truck get *him*, too! Exactly the same way it would have gotten anybody else who happened to be in that crossing when it jumped the red light."

"A crossroads, of sorts," Mendoza said musingly. "To have spent most of his life under a mild phobia of the stake, and then ..."

"At least it wasn't driven through his heart until afterward." All the same, Amarantha shut her eyes for a moment, involuntarily reliving the horror of the desecration. And she hadn't even seen his body until after Farwell's Funeral Home had cosmeticized away all traces of that last indignity as well as most of what the speeding truck had done. "He wouldn't have cared

then, not when he was already dead," she reminded
her host and herself.

"No, I suppose not. Considering the instructions he
left for having his body cremated."

"He didn't even want to test whether or not he
could be brought back to life!" She wished he had left
them room to try resuscitating him. Dying in your
early seventies was premature even for ordinary people nowadays, and slowly as her father had been aging,
he could have looked forward to twenty or thirty more
years of fully active life.

"I think he came to welcome the irreversibility of
change," Mendoza remarked. "Once he became rec-
onciled to the fact that, as far as anyone has been able
to discover, there is no way to get back to not being
a vampire, any other than any of us can get back to
babyhood or adolescence or virginity . . . why look for
death to be any less permanent? Whatever happens
to our consciousness after death—and he for one believed that it survives the body—the way to grow is
by stepping from change to change, not by slipping
backward, even if and when slipping backward might
be possible."

She was only half listening. "Almost the only thing
we had left from my father's parents," she said, "was
an antique manger set that had been his grandmoth-
er's. Maybe even his great-grandmother's. I'm not sure
exactly what it's made of. Some kind of plaster, I
think. Lord, I used to love that old set! One of my
biggest thrills every Christmas was unwrapping the little figures and setting them up, one by one. Until that
one year . . . I must have been about six or seven. I
think it was during one of those phases Pop went
through now and then where he'd try wearing something else than the old vampire 'habit' for a day or
two. I seem to remember him in blue trousers and a
blue pullover sweater with snowflakes that evening.

Anyway, that'd explain why I didn't notice right away that he'd taken off his crosses ..."

He guessed that a thirty-seven-year-old tenured professor with three growing children should know better by now. Wearing anything else than his traditional Lugosi-style opera suit and cape had the tang of hypocrisy, and always seemed to bring on a major or minor crisis. Why did he keep deciding, every few years, that all the times before had been pure coincidence, and try again?

It didn't help that this time the first colleague he encountered in the faculty lounge of the Music School was Dave Groves.

"Say, old bloodsucker, what's happening? Planning to sneak up unsuspected on some new nick beneath the mistletoe, are we?"

"Well, you know. The eve of a new decade, time for a new image ..."

"Uh-*unh*, old bean." The know-it-all wink that was the younger professor's specialty. "New decade doesn't start till sixty-one. The year ending in 'zero' still belongs to the old decade. Take it from me, don't let that subject loose on your students. Stick with what you know."

"Thanks for the stray gem from your encyclopedic knowledge, Dave, but if I took a vote on it, I'd bet ninety-eight percent of my students would say the Sixties begin a little more than a week from now." Ordinarily, Clement would have shut his mouth on a comeback like that; but out of vampire habit he felt looser, more like everybody else—the people who could sin to their hearts' content without any inconvenient physical side effects.

"Ninety-eight percent?" Pushing up his lower lip, Groves shook his head. "No, I can't believe the level of misinformation is that high. Tell you what, I'll just take you up on that bet for ... oh, let's say a dollar or two."

"Let's say three," the vampire answered stiffly, and his miniature white-gold crucifix sent a twinge through his pierced earlobe at this display of stubborn pride. He ignored it.

Then he ran into Jane Hoffman in the hall and watched her expression flicker from lack of recognition to the kind of look that could still make him wonder, even after all these years of doing it mirrorless, if he'd combed his hair crooked or missed a patch of beard while shaving.

Without waiting for the tactful comment he could see she was trying to formulate about his change of dress, he fell back on his second line of defense: "Well, you know, my two oldest are getting to the age where it's hard enough figuring out what to get the old man for Christmas. Just thought I'd let them have the option other kids have of choosing Pop something loud and sporty."

The gray-haired doctor of music bestowed on him a sage nod. "I see. Very commendable. All the same, Dr. Czarny,"—Clement's doctorate was still pending, but Jane Hoffman's way of democratizing her title was giving it out gratis to almost every colleague—"if I might offer a word of fashion advice ... the silver filigree cross is striking on your usual outfit, but I wouldn't wear it with that sweater."

"No? I thought it matched the snowflakes pretty well."

"It's hardly visible against the pale blue. And when a person looks closely enough to see it, it seems ... out of place. Much too formal for its background. On your usual shirt, it's elegant. On that sweater, just an extraneous dangle of jewelry."

"I see. Thank you." Lifting the cross on its chain, he dropped it between his new sweater and the match-

ing blue shirt he wore beneath. Through a single layer
of thin cotton, it felt remarkably warm. He monitored
his thoughts, found angry resentment toward Dr.
Hoffman with her "fashion advice," and tried to leave
it behind in the echo of his footprints on the tile floor.
The whole reason he wore the cross was to help him
avoid anger, not rouse it.

His necklace and earring had both cooled by the
time he reached the lecture room, only to heat up
again in the stress of dealing with his "Music Appreci-
ation I" class. The Friday before Christmas break
turned out to be one of the worst days in the year he
could have chosen to break out of habit. Whether it
was the coming vacation that made the students act
more like high school than university freshmen and
sophomores, or whether his usual vampire costume
inspired more awe than he suspected, discipline fell
apart. A few of the naturally better-behaved kids complimented their prof on his new clothes, but most of
the students apparently took the change of costume
as a signal to go slaphappy.

It did not improve matters that seven of the thirty-
four—an easy twenty percent—chose to vote in favor
of beginning the new decade in 'sixty-one.

Discipline-wise, the day's second class was, if anything, worse. The kids didn't even quiet down when
he signaled his anger by making a show of removing
the crucifix from his ear and putting it away in the case
his oldest daughter had petit-pointed for it, usually a
surefire trick for reining them in. It seemed that when
he was out of vampire costume, they no longer so
much as pretended to take the vampirish temper
seriously.

And the earring had definitely needed removing
by then.

The third class comprised mostly juniors and se-
niors, but today they were the worst of all. He gave

up trying to siphon "Advanced Theory" into their brains and let the period disintegrate early into the 'sixty-versus'-sixty-one argument the grapevine had obviously prepared them to expect.

At least, when all three classes were added together, the total percentage voting for 'sixty-one fell several points. Not enough: all Groves needed was three percent who saw the new decade thing his way, and he still had more than quadruple that.

Meanwhile, between classes, Prof Czarny's office hours brought in one legitimate counseling problem, one simple headache—Bob Wilde arguing about his latest grade again (if Wilde would put half the time into studying that he put into arguing with every teacher about his grades . . .), and one frosh lad from Engineering School, not even a student the vampire had ever seen close-up before, wanting confidential tips on "how to give a girl a real, topflight hickey."

Somebody or other hit with this hickey business several times a year. Young women had even solicited him to give them one in person. Occasionally older women, too, and once—he still cringed to think of it— a young man. It could take half an hour to convince them that being a vampire did not automatically make someone an expert in hickeys, that, in fact, Professor Czarny, mindful of the awkwardness and possible danger from his fangs, had never given one to anybody. Today it took the full hour, and the engineering student left for his next class still looking unconvinced, as if he might come back.

It was immediately after that visit that Clement pulled the cross up from beneath his sweater and took it off completely. He wished he had taken it off an hour or two earlier. If things kept on the way they'd been going, he'd have to work twice as hard at self-restraint without the alarm system on his temper, but he thought the holy symbol was starting to blister his skin through the thin cloth shirt.

He knew from experience that the cloth itself would be undamaged. That was something, anyway.

Trying to unwind between his scheduled office hours and the late-afternoon opera committee meeting, he again encountered Dave Groves in the faculty lounge, where Groves seemed to spend the better part of almost every school day.

In one way, it was just as well. The vampire would have hated having this matter of the bet hanging over the entire Christmas break or, even worse, cropping up at some holiday party. But in another way, it was the last thing he needed to cap off the day's irritations.

"Oh, yes! David," he began at once, fumbling carefully with his money clip, before the younger man could broach the subject. "You won. Congratulations." He twitched out a pinchful of bills, eventually extracted three singles, and held them out between little finger and ring finger while putting the extra currency away with as much dignity as he could manage.

"I did?" Groves returned, pretending surprise but sounding smug about it as he accepted the money. "By how much?"

"It totaled out to fourteen percent seeing it your way."

"That high, eh? Well, I know you, Clem. You probably bent overbackward to be fair. Overstated my case until they thought they were voting the way *you* wanted." Another know-it-all wink. "You'd make a lousy courtroom lawyer, you old bloodsucker."

Actually, quite a few people had told Clement, throughout his life, that he'd have made a fine courtroom lawyer. They used to beg him, back in his student days, to go out for the Debate Team. Maybe the dracula costume had a lot to do with that, too; he certainly didn't seem to have the touch today. In fact, he suspected most of that fourteen percent had voted for 'sixty-one in order to annoy him, guessing or having heard where he'd put his money. But there was no way he would share that thought with Groves. "Thank you, David," he replied instead. "I take it as a compliment to be told how fair and impartial I am to an opponent's viewpoint. Might not be much good as a courtroom lawyer, but I'd have made a fine judge, wouldn't you say?"

It was one of the day's few victories-out-of-defeat. But it sent him to the opera committee meeting with a nagging doubt about taking too much pride in an irate comeback.

The meeting would have been grim enough if he'd gone into it with a quiet conscience. The Ives triumvirate obviously came prepared to do full battle for *Tannhäuser*: Dean Ives because he wanted his latest Met-material protégé in the lead, Grundman because he was the dean's pet yes-man, and Lomax because she was clearly itching to direct it in the same lurid style she had directed *Lulu* and *The Threepenny Opera*.

Dr. Hoffman sat back saying little except for the occasional comment to second whoever had spoken last. Clement found himself holding out alone for the piece that they should have done this December, and that Ives had been promising to do "next term" for the last three years, Rossini's *Cenerentola*.

"You just want to sing the valet," said Lomax.

"I do not! Tom Harringan would be almost ideal in that part." If they'd done it when Clement had first suggested it, they could have cast Rico Sforzi, who was born for such roles; but Sforzi had gone on to Juilliard last year.

"You did Papageno four or five years back," Lomax pointed out.

Dr. Hoffman put in, "Superbly, too. But only because Sforzi sprained his ankle the day before we opened."

"*La Cenerentola,*" said Dean Ives, "is more of a Christmas piece. I should have thought, Czarny, that you'd approve a highly moral work such as *Tannhäuser,* especially falling as close to Easter as this spring's opera will."

Moral? With the Venusburg sequence, and not impossibly the music contest as well, staged by Sally Lomax in the style of a skin flick? "If you want a piece with an edifying moral," Clement said carefully, hoping Lomax could restrain herself with Mozart, "let's do *The Marriage of Figaro.*"

"We just did *Mikado* this month," said the dean's yes-man Grundman, shaking his head. "Can't do two light comedies in a row."

"The whole theme of *Figaro* is forgiveness! You can't put it in the same category as *Mikado.* But if you want something heavy," Clement argued, "why not *Don Giovanni*?"

Lomax said, "You just want to sing the valet."

The vampire slipped off his rings and put them in his pocket, away from his skin. Even though silver and gold hadn't been counted as particularly sacred metals for years, the bands were starting to constrict and burn his fingers.

In the end, the committee compromised on *Tannhaüser* with a three to one vote, Dr. Hoffman abstaining.

Sunlight almost never gave Clement trouble but, considering his mood by the time he got out of the building, he was glad today was one of the shortest days of the year, with the sun already safely set. He hoped they weren't having spaghetti or anything else with garlic for dinner. Tonight, unless he could simmer down quickly, even garlic—forgotten though its ancient holy symbolism was—might react on him. And

he felt too tired _hitt's Daughter_
simmer down quick out of the anger groove and

Tired in mind and s out of the anger groove and
of angry energy that he in body he was so full
home in six minutes. the ten-minute walk

He opened the door and hear two oldest in the
dining room having a teenage squa about singing
stars as they slammed silverware on th ble. Shutting
his eyes, he shouted, "I'm home!" in som faint hope
of sidetracking the argument before it finishe the ru-
ination of his nerves.

"Daddy! Daddy!" That was Terry, his youngest,
pattering out to meet him on her first-grader's legs.

He stooped to sweep her up in his arms. Her little
fists hit the back of his neck with a stabbing, searing
pain.

He jerked, stifling a scream, desperate to keep his
grip on the child. Something hit the floor with more
of a crunch than a crash. The little girl gave a wail
that brought the rest of the family.

"Uh-oh," said Solly, picking up the pieces. "You're
gonna catch it now, Terry. The Christ Child from
Pop's old manger set. How often do we have to tell
you, don't run around with breakables in your hands!"

Oh. For a few confused seconds, Clement had wondered how his child could run around with anything
that hot in her bare fingers.

One of the last, most precious mementos they had
of his parents . . .

"Forget it, Solly," the vampire told his son. "Let
Terry alone. The key figure of a manger set is as much
a holy symbol as a crucifix is, and your father has had
a very hassling day. Don't make it any worse."

"He never punished me for it," Amarantha remembered softly. "Mother wasn't able to mend it, so we
had to heap a handkerchief up over a tiny little cloth

doll in the manger to m... we never found a re-
Child was all covered ...ry antique shop, second-
placement—we check... for years. But he never
hand store, and ya...
punished me."

Mendoza rem... ...d, "When he could get people to
accept him as ... ampire, they wouldn't accept him as
a human bei... I doubt that very many at all, outside
his own f... ...ily and closest friends, could ever accept
him a... both at once."

"I've just understood something," Amarantha went
on. "Losing that figurine must have cost him more
than it cost me. But he never even scolded me about
it. I think he took all the blame on himself." She rose.
"May I use your—"

"Down the hall and across from the bedroom."

When she came back to the combination living-din-
ing room, she observed, "You have a very nice mirror
in there."

"I'd have said a very ordinary one. It serves its
purpose."

"I was beginning to suspect ... You may call this
silly! ... only, when I didn't see mirrors anywhere else
in your home ..."

"Not everyone hangs them everywhere. People expect one above the bathroom sink, however. You always had one in each of your bathrooms, didn't you?"

"Yes," she admitted, "but we had four plain, ordinary people in the house. You live alone."

He smiled. "I have guests from time to time. More
cherry cordial?"

"No, thank you. My glass is still half-full." She sat
and sipped a moment in silence, lowering the level of
cordial by a millimeter or two, before speaking again.
"M. Mendoza, is my father's theory correct?"

"Most of it, I believe," he answered in a matter-of-
fact voice. "Possibly all of it."

"Then vampirism really *is* a state of heightened sensitivity to holiness?" She felt that her eyes were shining.

"Well, I never suffered quite as much inconvenience with religious symbols as your father did on his worst days. But then, I never developed conscience to such a fine, gnat-straining art."

"But you've spent your life being heroically good!" she protested. "Working for Greenpeace, Amnesty, all those movements for human and animal and planetary rights—"

"Only because I lacked the courage to do what my son and your father did—come out of the closet and live openly and honestly. It isn't that I lack a conscience, Amarantha. It's that I lacked whatever it takes to live life in its little, everyday, Babbitt fulfillments and frustrations. 'Heroism' has simply been my way of coping on a grand scale, quieting my conscience by overpaying for any petty little peccadillos I may commit."

"Your son . . ."

"In a manner of speaking. My foster son, if you prefer."

"Did he ever know it was you?"

"Not so far as I can tell. Anyway, I never confessed it to him. I've sometimes wondered if he ever had his secret suspicions, the way I used to step in and guardian-angel him from time to time. Never with advice about our condition, of course. He was my teacher there, whether or not he ever guessed that his theories might apply to me personally."

"He liked to think," Amarantha said slowly, "that whoever made him a vampire did it to save his life."

Her host shook his head. "I was just a teenager myself at the time, still experimenting, prowling around hospitals in search of meals I could sneak from comatose patients when nobody else was in the room.

Your father's blood had a good, fresh tang. I don't know if it was my drinking that almost pushed him over the edge, or if it was just coincidence, but when I noticed what the monitors were doing, I had an instant remorse attack. I jabbed my wrist vein and stuffed it in his mouth as an emergency measure to repair the damage I guessed I'd done."

She asked, "Then it was a complete accident, his being a vampire?"

"Oh, I'd probably already come across the idea that it's the sharing of blood between vampire and victim that does the trick, but I doubt I remembered it at the crucial moment. I think that giving him my vein to suck was simply the first way that occurred to my green brain to pour back some of the blood I'd just taken out of him. Crucifixes bothered me for several days afterward, especially when I heard that he'd gone vampire, too." Mendoza smiled. "My conscience may not be as fussy as your father's, but it's kept me out of any really serious evildoing ever since."

She finally admitted, "His got a little less fussy after the midlife crisis years. Enough to stop nagging him about having been pushed to the limit by other people. Still, to have a built-in alarm system ... That's all I ever wanted from him. To be forced to hold myself in check. Lord knows I don't *like* flying off the handle, saying hurtful things, weltering in angry thoughts ... Why wouldn't he ever trust me with the gift?"

Instead of repeating arguments, Mendoza asked, "After living with him, can you really think it makes it that easy?"

"M. Mendoza, you're as much my grandfather as his father. If it hadn't been for you, I'd never have been born."

"If it hadn't been for an infinity of circumstances, none of us would have been born, and a totally different set of people would be inhabiting the universe."

She had appropriated some of the old medical blood test lancets her father used to carry for soliciting drops from people's thumbs. She had a few in her pocket now. Pulling one out, she jabbed it into her thumb and squeezed half a dozen drops into her cherry cordial, then got up to set both glass and lancet on the table beside her host.

He looked at her. "Determined, aren't you?"

"It's what I've wanted ever since I was a little girl. If my father's theory is correct, this should work as well as any actual biting and body-to-body sucking."

"All that is needed is sharing the blood. The possible origin of all blood-brotherhood and sisterhood rituals . . . almost sacramental in its pure simplicity." He picked up her glass and frowned into it for several seconds, twirling it slowly by the stem. Setting it down at last, he ignored the lancet, got a case of needles from his pocket, extracted one, and used it on his thumb. He squeezed three or four drops into his own half-drunk cordial, laid the needle crosswise over the lancet, and touched the rim of his glass lightly to hers. The crystal ping sounded clear in the silent moment.

He lifted the glass with Amarantha's blood to his lips and drained it, wiped his lips on his handkerchief, and returned her gaze. After another moment, he nodded and gestured at her glass seasoned with his blood. "In my foster-grandfatherly way, I'm going to leave you alone five minutes with that and your father's memory. If you think that, wherever he is, he would be ready to trust you with 'the gift' now . . . the choice belongs to you."

Remedia Amoris

Judith Tarr

Readers know Judith Tarr as the author of meticulously researched and gorgeously crafted historical fantasies like *Alamut* and *The Dagger and the Cross*. More recently, she has moved into Macedon and Egypt with *Lord of the Two Lands* and *Throne of Isis*, about Alexander the Great and his equally charismatic descendant, Cleopatra.

Like Katharine Kerr, Judith is a writer who is usually so busy with novels that we don't get enough of her short fiction.

Fortunately, in her nonexistent spare time, she has remedied this situation to some degree; and readers are finding in short stories by Judith Tarr a wry, ribald, and even gonzo streak—nowhere more than here. I think that Ovid, her inspiration, would understand . . . if he wasn't laughing too hard.

I stumbled onto it. Staggered. Cock first and no mistake, skin full of the old Falernian, and Whatsername shrieking and whacking me with her thyrsus just hard enough to keep me good and hard, which was all in the game, and the old bitch-goddess should have known it.

Dear Mother Three-Face Hecate wouldn't know a good game if it tupped her from behind.

So there we were, tumbling on the grass, mooncup swelled and brimming over, me-cup getting near it, and Lalage, or was it Phyllis, paying top-of-the-lungs tribute to her Bacchante's vows. She was just about through the Third Twist-and-Shriek, and she'd winked at me once when the moon caught her eye. And the silence crashed down on us.

They ran up to thirteen in full coven. Tonight they were down to three, but three were enough when they were Threefold Hecate. Maiden was ripe-fig sweet and dripping honey, and when I was done with Phyllis I'd make a run for her. Mother was a little off the peak and bellyful of baby. Crone was Crone incarnate.

Maiden was horrified. Mother was indignant. Crone was in midcurse and not pleased to be interrupted. Maiden swept in and rescued Phyllis, or maybe Lalage, and fine thanks she got: Lalage, or maybe Phyllis, crowned her neatly with the thyrsus, told her what she could do with her maidenhead, and cut for the deep cover. Mother made a leap for the altar and raised a pitchy smoke. Crone stood over me—no will in me to move, even if I'd been able, and every bit of me as limp as the old hag's dugs. She reached out her staff and tested it. I couldn't even flinch.

Maiden came up behind her. "Faun," she said in the sweet severe way they have before they know a man. "Faun, you were mad to have come here."

My tongue was my own; just about all of me that was. "Fauns are mad by nature," I said. I tried to grin. Insouciance, old Silenus always told us, drives the ladies wild.

I don't think he meant this kind of wild.

Mother was chanting through her smokes and lighting them with bits of fire. The purple was particularly fine. It made me think of once-dyed Tyrian.

I told her so. She paid no attention to me. Crone prodded me again with her staff. No more life there than before. Maiden said, "You are a very shallow creature. Drunk as a sponge, raping anything that moves—have you no more use in life but that?"

"I eat," I said helpfully. "Lots. I play the pipes. I herd sheep for old Mopsus, up by Volaterrae, and I leave the ewes alone. Nymphs are better. And Bacchantes." I showed her my best smile. "And witches?"

She shuddered. "He is dreadful," she said.

Crone nodded with too much satisfaction. "And he profaned our rite." She stopped prodding my jewels, for which I was properly grateful, but her expression was nothing to comfort a poor lonely Faun. She turned round toward the altar. In a moment, so did Maiden.

They had their backs to me. I thought of crawling away. The best I managed was a flop onto my face and a scrabble in the grass. My tail hurt. My head hurt worse.

The three weird women raised their voices. Most of it was nonsense, and some was no language I ever knew, but enough was decent speech that I knew I'd not been forgotten. They were cursing me, as Mopsus would say, right proper. Starting with the tip of my left horn and working down to the point of my right hoof, with stops between. Somehow I was standing upright, and that meant all of me. Pipes in hand, too. Just about ready to play.

The marching-drums in my head had stopped. So had the throb in my tail. I felt . . . cool. And smooth. And chiseled clean. Marmoreal, for a fact.

"So mote it be," said Crone. She stood in front of me. She was smiling. I would have closed my eyes if I could. That was nothing I'd be doing, for a while.

"Be so," Crone said. "Be bound forever as the stonebrain that you are."

"It's only just," said Mother, "for a ravisher of maidens."

Maidens! I would have howled, if they'd left me with a voice. Those were good lusty Bacchantes, and fine chases they led, too, and all the Rites in order, and if a lad was new to it, then they'd help him along.

But Mother never heard me. "Stand for all of time as you stand now, with your phallus for a luck piece."

"Perhaps we should have made him a fountain," mused Crone. "He might have been more entertaining."

"Oh," said Maiden, and her voice could melt my heart, even turned to stone. "Oh, the poor thing. Were we too severe, do you think? Shouldn't we just let him stay for a while, and then let him go? He only did what Fauns are born to do."

"And who was first to curse him for it?" Mother inquired.

Maiden blushed and hung her head. "I let my temper get the better of it. I confess it. You helped me," she said. "Don't say you didn't."

"Very well," said Crone, and she was impatient, but even she was hardly proof against Maiden. "A witch who weakens her curse with codicils is a fool, but we are all born fools. You, Faun! For this Maiden's sake—and do remember it, if you are capable of such refinement—I offer you one escape. Marble you are, and marble you shall be, and your fate shall be to watch unsleeping, until two mortals shall come before you, and show themselves true lovers."

"None of this reckless ravishment," Mother said, "or she-wolf with her flesh for hire. True love, and true lovers, and goodwill toward you who watch."

"This is excessive!" Maiden protested. "Love

comes, and comes true, but goodwill for a marble Faun?"

"There's no changing it now," said Crone. "It's spoken and it's done. When true love comes, he shall be free."

Maiden sighed, but she had no more objections. I had a worldful, and a tongue as hopeless-heavy as only stone can be.

"Iron's worse," said Crone. She rubbed my best man—for luck, what else? And I felt it, no doubt about that, and not a whit of good it did me.

The moon was down. Dawn was coming. They went about their business, all three. Only Maiden looked back. She sighed. So would I have done, if I could. All those might-have-beens.

II

It was against nature. A Faun was never loot; a Faun did the looting. But a Faun was never marble, either, and here was I, and there were they, big flapping man-shaped vultures with a lust for statuary. Never a whisper of True Love, not that I'd seen any in my grove—Fauns stopped going there, once it got about that I'd chased my last sweet Bacchante, and witches didn't bring their lovers, except to give them to the goddess. I was a rack for their cloaks and a prop for their spells, and they rubbed me for luck when they left.

Then the men in armor came, and it was true, what Crone said. Marble was a cold still way to spend one's years, but iron was worse. They loaded me in a wagon and carried me away. Rubbing me, of course, for luck, and making comparisons. The sculpture was a jester, they said. Nobody was hung like that.

I could have shown them something, if they'd happened into the deep cover when there was a bacchanal.

The wagon creaked and rattled and came skinned-teeth close to chipping a piece off my left horn, but in the end it brought me whole into the City.

That was what they called it. The City. Roma Dea, Roma Mater—Old Rome she wasn't yet, and to listen to them you'd swear she'd never be. They set me up in the middle of her, in a garden as wide as half Campania, and I had my own glade in it, my own oak tree for shade, my own fountain to stand over. So Crone had her wish after all. I didn't piddle forever into a pool, but I stood in the middle of one. If the air was still, I could glimpse my reflection.

It stopped people rubbing me, which I was glad of. The few who tried, had to wade through the pool to do it, and they were too drunk to go halfway before they slipped and fell in.

A philosopher had a school for a while in my tree's shade. Most of what he said was arrant nonsense, but it made good chewing over. Two separate sets of assassins plotted under my nose. I never did learn whether they got their man. There were always poets yelling at the Muse, and mothers yelling at their children, and children yelling for the joy of it.

And lovers. Lovers in scores. Every one swore undying love, and every one left me as mutely marble as before. One hanged herself from a branch of my tree. That was a pity. She'd been a tender young thing till her father found out she'd been tumbling with his secretary. Since the secretary was supposed to be a eunuch, it was a scandal to put it mildly. He was a eunuch sure when they killed him. She told me all about it before she knotted up her mantle and threw it over the convenient branch; and not a word I could say to stop her. They buried her with the proper rites, but her ghost hung about still, not saying anything, just sitting by my pool and keeping me company.

While I was the witches' marble Faun, I'd soaked up enough sorcery to make me glow like the moon, and enough over that to damp me down again. Not that I could do much with it with no tongue to say the spells and no hands to make the gestures, but the sight it gave never left me. I could see the cords that bound the world. They ruled the moon in its course. They stirred the wind, and made my tree grow, and wove as rich as Arachne's web round the mortals who passed me by. Even I was part of it. On me it was like chains and light—chains for the curse, light for the magic I was steeped in. Nobody but witches, and I, could see it.

There were colors in it, every color that was and some that I'd never conceived of. When they were clearest, my world was calmest. When they went dark, I braced myself for the storm. They were blood-black when Cornelia hanged herself on my tree, knotted and tangled like a witch's hair.

Once she was a ghost, she saw the web as well as I. Sometimes she played with it. She could smooth a knot if it was not too tangled, and stroke a grey thread silver. She stopped a lovers' quarrel so, and they went away arm in arm, though they didn't set me free.

We settled in together, the ghost and I, and maybe she was happy—though if she had been, surely she'd have gone where the joyful dead go.

When the moon was full, the world's web was bright enough to run a revel by. A few had done it in my glade, but they'd grown tired, or the world was in one of its grey times. Those came, and mercifully went. The bloodred times were worse, and the black ones were worst of all; but grey had its own drab charmlessness. Everyone was stiffly proper then, the philosophers were all Stoics and the women were all chaste,

and when they noticed me at all, they disapproved.
"Greek luxury," they muttered. "Eastern corruption."
And I a good Italian Faun, straight out of Etruria.

This grey time was turning bloody. There was a new
cult, and the more of its believers they disposed of,
the more there seemed to be. They multiplied like a
Hydra's head, said the scholar who droned to his
yawning students under my tree. They were unshaka-
bly stubborn. They would not sacrifice peaceably to
any gods but theirs, and who was he to keep them all
to himself? The Senator who liked to walk through
my garden in his mob of friends and hangers-on, could
not see why they should be so obstinate. It was a
matter of form, no more. Sacrifice to Rome's gods,
give the nod to Rome's power, go about their business. There was nothing in it about *believing* in the
gods. A man's mind was his own. After all.

He'd never seen Triune Hecate in a snit, or spied
on chaste Diana while she rested from a hunt—and if
that was chastity, then mortals were worse fools than
I'd taken them for. She might guard her maidenhead
with chains of adamant, but she liked her slim young
lads, and her lissome lasses, too.

Not that he ever asked me. He went his way, and
I watched the sun go down, and the moon came up,
heavy and full. The world's web was as dark as wine,
and pulsed like a heart. Cornelia shivered under the
oak. Even the moon's light couldn't lure her as far as
the pool.

They came by ones and twos as the witches used to
do, ragged like the witches, too, and by the nick of
an ear or the gleam of a collar, more than one of
them was a slave. Some started when they saw me,
and made signs against evil. The same man always
comforted them. He was as ragged as the worst, the
top of his head shaved in the slave's tonsure, and one
ear missing. He sat beside my pool where Cornelia

liked to sit. He was obviously a city slave, and he had a gladiator's scars, but he carried a shepherd's crook. It made me think of Mopsus. Long dead, gods rest him, and he never had forgiven me for getting myself cursed the night before I was supposed to move his sheep to the winter pasture.

This was a strange shepherd. He said that mortals were his sheep. He was deadly earnest about it. When my glade was full and there were rustlings in the hedge that marked a posting of guards, he stood up.

Most of what he said was nonsense, and none of it was good philosophy. It dawned on me early that this was the cult the Senator spoke of, and meeting in his favorite garden, too. When the man with the crook had talked for a while, and told them all about the devil—by that he meant me—whom their god had vanquished, and done the maddest thing I'd seen yet, wrapped me in somebody's sweat-stinking cloak, they set up an altar. I waited to see who would die on it, but no one did. They took bread and called it flesh, and took wine and called it blood, and by grim black Styx they believed it.

Somewhere in their rite, Cornelia crept out from her shadow. She looked as starkly terrified as she had before she died, but there was hope in her face, too, and a desperate longing. I wanted to shout at her. I couldn't speak, no more than I could when she died. They ate their magicked bread and drank their magicked wine, and the web was throbbing and knotting, and its colors were mad. I don't think they even knew what powers they raised. My witches would have been appalled. Pure lack of discipline, and magic that snagged the world-web till it frayed.

Cornelia drifted like a leaf in a sharp wind, and no more power to stop herself, either. Just before she touched the altar, she hesitated; or the web held her, tangling around her. She reached through it. The priest was just raising the cup to his lips to drain the last of the wine—raw stuff, nothing like my good Falernian. Her shadow of a hand curved around the cup. He felt it, felt something; and started. A drop of the awful wine spilled on her wrist.

She went up like a torch. White light so bright even my eyes were dazzled. Her face—it showed no fear at all, no pain. Later I named it, to give my grief a center. Exultation.

The mortals never saw. She was gone, gone right out of the world, and they were oblivious. Their rite went on. The web was quieter now, as if Cornelia had taken some of its power with her. Its knots and tangles were smoother, and more of its gray was silver.

They took their altar and their magics, and relieved me of the ridiculous cloak, and went away. I had my glade to myself again. All to myself. No gentle ghost to sit by my pool and smile. No quiet undemanding company with eyes to see what I was.

The slave-fanatics never came back, either, not as they were that night. Their cult grew into Rome's cult, and all the old gods died. I felt them go as Cornelia had: like dry grass in a fire.

I was marble, and I was cursed. Even the name of their Christ had no power over that.

III

Roma Dea died, and Roma Mater shrank into a crone. My oak tree took Jupiter's last bolt and fell. My pool filled with weeds and disappeared. A thicket grew up around me. People stumbled on me now and then. A flock of sparrows had a kingdom in what had been my glade. The queen nested on my head. I'd have minded it more if I'd had any dignity left. As it was, I was only glad that the vine that twisted round my cock a-crowning was a thornless thing.

Lovers always managed to find me. It was part of my curse. They were particularly lusty along about the time their Latin stopped being Latin, but the curse said nothing about lust. The ones who came after them wore clothes that beggared belief, and stank to high heaven.

By the time they began to be clean again, some of them cleared away the thicket and evicted the queen sparrow from my head. I'd grown mossy with the years, but all my bits were still in place. They cleaned away the moss—not too gently, either—and put a roof over me, and had what they called salons. Which meant that they drank a great deal of bad wine, ate too much, and talked endlessly of nothing in particular. The women looked at me and giggled. The men eyed me sidelong, often with a glower. No rubbing me for luck in this age.

They still rutted as eagerly as human animals could, though they made a rite of protesting and calling it a sin. Sin was what the priest of that old cult had gone on about so endlessly. It had made no sense to me then. It made no sense now, however lengthy the explanations. The ones in black with the tiny circle of tonsure were the loudest in condemnation of lust, and the hottest in pursuit of it. I wondered what they would have said if I'd told them the truth about Diana. They disapproved of her divinity, but they made much of her chastity. She was more like them than they would ever want to know.

There were no true lovers. Or else the Crone had lied, and there was no escape from my curse. That would be like a witch. Small comfort that they were all dead, the lot of them, and Hecate too.

I was thinking so, one grey dim morning. For some reason I shivered inside.

The salons were long gone. The roof over me was still there, but it was crumbling. The sparrows had come back to nest in it. A cat or two made forays into their kingdom, but I'd learned a little through the years. I could think at the web that still bound the world, and shift it a little. Enough to keep out the cats, and to hold up the roof long after it should have fallen in.

This was the strangest age that I could remember. It seemed grey, grey as ash, with great clots of blood and corruption. But there was brightness in it, too. I'd never seen the web so complicated, or the colors so varied. Either mortals were swimming in blood or they were reveling in a golden age. The web said it was both. The grey in it was often silver, sometimes tarnished black, sometimes so bright it blinded. It was terrifying. Exhilarating. Men flew like birds. Men lived undersea like fish. Men sailed to the moon. They were like gods.

They were still men. They still came to my garden, and they still danced the old, old dance. They brought their music with them, trapped by magic in a box. It was a different magic than mine, cold metal magic, and they saw no wonder in it.

Often of a morning a lady came to sit on the stone bench near me and read her book, or write, or simply sit and think. Once in a while she talked to me, because, she said, I looked like intelligent company. She was writing a book on Old Rome. It was a stubborn thing, and it kept going off in unexpected directions. She liked an adventure, she said, and mostly she was glad to go where it took her, but at this rate she didn't think she'd ever finish it.

Every morning as she worked on her book, a gentleman walked briskly by. If she happened to notice him, she'd nod. He'd nod back. And off he'd go, and there she'd stay.

This was hardly a lonely place, though it was never crowded. My scholar had it to herself, mostly, but people wandered past, peering curiously at me and not seeming to see her at all.

On the morning that I marked by reflecting that the gods were dead, my scholar came as always. She had her satchel of books, and something new, that she showed me. More magic. A little box full of words, with a page that one wrote on without ever touching it. The world-web shimmered around it, but it always did where my scholar was. Her name was Cornelia. I thought it an interesting coincidence.

As she settled down with her books and her box, a dreadful cacophony startled her almost into dropping the box. A pair of this age's young lovers came entwined like a vine about an elm. Her hair was indescribable. His screamed pink so loud it made my eyes burn. Their music came out of a great gleaming thing full of bone-deep thumpings and mating-cat wails.

Cornelia's box of words was silent but for the click of the keys that made the words grow. She struggled on, with her neck bent at a stubborn angle and her fingers flying. The young lovers arranged themselves in front of my plinth, did something to their box that made it sound like mountains falling, and went at it as people did in this strange age. A great deal of kissing and groping, a symphony of moans drowned out in the tumult, and nothing like getting down to honest business. That was the Christians' innovation: tease oneself to insanity, and promise more for later. Later, when it came, was never what they hoped for.

Cornelia was angry. I could see the web darkening around her. Just before she could have moved, a brisk figure stepped in over the lovers, snapped something on the box, and stepped coolly out again. The silence was thunderous. The lovers unknotted. He had his hackles up. She had her shirt off. Sweet and almost ripe; but I'd seen better.

Her young man was all righteous indignation. The brisk gentleman looked down a noble nose at him and said, "You were disturbing the lady."

The boy swelled his pretty muscles and beetled his handsome brows.

"There is ample space in this garden for anyone who wishes to come there," the gentleman said. "I would advise you to find some of it, and not to trouble this lady further."

The lady said nothing through all of this. Neither did the girl on the grass. The boy blustered and sneered. It was a game, like the game of Faun and Bacchante.

He didn't seem to know it, but the gentleman did. When the boy gave up on words and transparently thought of fists, the gentleman said, "It does amaze me that you would bring your inamorata here. She can look at the Faun, after all, and compare."

The boy's fist went wild. The gentleman's cane caught his elbow as it flailed past. It seemed a light blow, a tap, no more, but the boy howled and collapsed.

They limped from the field, the boy clutching his arm and the girl her blouse, dragging their box. I applauded in my head.

"How heroic," Cornelia said. Her tone was acid.

The gentleman tucked his cane under his arm and bowed slightly. I'd seen his face a thousand times in a thousand years, an inescapably Roman face, big nose and thin mouth and uncompromising jaw. My Senator had looked like him, back when Christians were a thorn in the Empire's side.

"I really didn't need a rescue," said Cornelia. "Or a knight in shining armor."

Cornelia, it should be said, was not a Roman. She

came from somewhere that Rome had never heard of, on the other side of the world. She believed in independence. She didn't believe in thanking a man for doing what she could perfectly well have done for herself.

"Signora," said the gentleman, "whatever you needed, or thought you needed, I was offended by those barbarians."

"They weren't so bad," Cornelia said. "You did a terrible thing to that poor boy. She'll never let him forget that he's not as fine and upstanding as a Faun."

The gentleman looked shocked. Then he laughed. "Ah, but what man is? A man of parts would accept it. A young Goth with all his wits below his belt—he would never stop to think."

"I think he was solid Roman," Cornelia said. "And you, sir?"

"Giuliano," he said, bowing. "Giuliano Cavalli."

"Signor Cavalli," said Cornelia. She'd softened a bit. She liked him, I thought. So did I. He talked like a book, as she would have said, but he was old enough to do it gracefully. He was a scholar, too, as it happened. Not of Old Rome but—he looked mildly embarrassed and slightly wicked—but of the new philosophy, the doctrine of signs and shadows.

"You're a literary theorist?" Cornelia had cooled again, but not as much as before.

"Theoretician," he said, "please. And one does make a game of it. *Ecce* Eco, *vale* Vergil . . ."

"And *sayonara Petrarca*?" Cornelia shook her head. He was smiling and nodding, looking as close to an amiable fool as a Roman could. She laughed, very much as if she didn't want to, and said, "I don't believe in theory. It gets in the way."

"But, Signora, if you use it properly, it sweeps away all obstacles, and there stands Meaning bare."

"Do I want to see Meaning naked? She's not a pretty sight at the best of times."

He sat down beside her. He was going to make a convert, I could see, or burst his heart trying. She was going to resist him to the utmost.

It was the strangest love dance I'd ever seen.

I listened, I could hardly help it. None of it made a great deal of sense. A Faun took the world as it was, and if he happened to be marble, and me, as it showed itself in the world-web.

They argued all morning and half the afternoon, and went away still arguing. Cornelia was looking ruffled. Signor Cavalli had lost his elegant aplomb. They were gloriously happy.

They came back, of course. Often. Cornelia had her book, still, and she insisted that she have an hour at least to glare at it before he came to distract her. Actually she did more than glare. She'd got through a particularly tangled thicket, and the rest, she told me, was looking almost simple. "Scary," she said. My grin was carved on my face, but she seemed to know I meant it."

He scared her too, but it was a wonderful terror. She called herself a fallow field. Now she was growing green. Blooming. And arguing, endlessly, delightedly arguing about everything under the sun.

Then they stopped coming. It rained for days, and my roof dripped and dribbled abominably. But the sun came back, and they didn't.

Mortals did that. Even mortal ghosts. I should have known better than to miss them; but a marble heart is as unreasonable as a living one. I'd actually been starting to understand Signor Cavalli's philosophy, which is proof that either it becomes comprehensible with enough time and explanation, or I was missing a piece of it.

The sun came and went more regularly than anything human. The moon swelled and shrank. My days stretched. I wondered if a marble Faun could die, just will himself to crumble away. My kind were all gone. Great Pan was ages dead, and there was nothing of my old world left.

And then, one morning, she was there. Cornelia with her books and her box of words, sitting on the bench she'd claimed for her own. She looked tired, worn to the bone. There was more grey in her hair than I remembered.

After a while her fingers slowed on the keys. A while longer and they stopped. She looked at me as if she'd never seen me before. I couldn't read her expression.

She put her word-box down on the bench and stood up. She stood in front of me. Without my plinth, I'd have been just a little smaller than she was.

"He died," she said. She was very, very calm. "I'd just begun to know him, and he died. Do you know how angry that makes me? Do you even begin to imagine how bloody *unfair* it is?"

Did I? I'd felt it when they were near me. I'd felt the marble softening, remembering—for a precious instant—the shape and feel of flesh.

"He was dying when I met him," she said. "He knew it. He was living on time he'd stolen from the monster in his body. He—we—stole a whole three months of it. Counting every blessed minute.

"Why couldn't I have died instead of him?"

She started to cry. Quiet at first, just the tears spilling over and running down her face. Then harder. Falling forward onto my cold flanks and howling in rage and loss, pounding marble that bruised her poor fists, raking it till her nails broke and bled.

She couldn't hang herself. There was no oak to offer a branch. But hanging wasn't the only way to take a life. She'd tear herself to pieces in front of me, and never a thing I could do to stop her.

Never.

I didn't know what it was that swelled inside of me. It felt like fire, but with edges like a sword, and it was black, and red, and grey, grey, grey. My freedom had been in front of me. One day, one more day, and I would have known it, and give it its name.

Death had taken it from me. Death and Chance, and Fate with her Crone's face, laughing at the poor ensorcelled fool. I'd be marble forever, and no hope of breaking free.

And to what? the wind seemed to ask. It was small and cold, nosing about in corners. This was no world for a goatfoot monster out of a long-discredited myth. I wasn't even authentic. I should have had a horse's tail and horse's ears, and spoken country Greek.

Great Pan is dead, the wind moaned. Mocking me. No more Bacchae, no more choruses. No more love-games in the deep coverts. They were gone, all gone, and I was marble, and mad.

The web was black, shot with lightnings. Jove was dead, too, and Pluto in his Underworld, and Hecate of the three faces, whose servants had laid the curse on me. Signor Cavalli was dead, who had had three months' true love before he died, and that was more than I would ever have.

Oh, Faun, the wind said, and now it aped the Maiden's voice, and now the Crone's. *How you have changed!*

Years out of count, and a marble heart, and no hope, no hope ever, of everything else. I'd been stone-simple. Stone-stupid, too. I'd paid, and paid, and paid. I'd never stop paying.

Cornelia had stopped pummeling me. She was still crying. Still holding tight, arms around my knees as if

I'd been a king and she a suppliant. Begging me to change the world. To bring back the dead.

The witches had done that, but it was a grim thing, and the dead were never glad to be called back. The web hated it; turned black and rotted where the undead were.

And did I care for that? I was a cursed thing. I should have been long dead myself. Let him come back. Let Cornelia be happy. I'd give my life and substance for him—life stretched out of all natural measure, substance as cold as Hades' heart.

The web was thrumming. She didn't know. Couldn't. I didn't care. It was full of magic. I poured it all out of me. All. Every drop. While she clung to me and wept, and the wind fled shrieking, and the web caught fire.

I tore it from top to bottom. "Giuliano!" I thundered in a voice I'd never known I had. "Giuliano Cavalli!"

He came out of the shadows, moving slowly. His shape was firm still, only a little blurred around the edges. He didn't have the terrible blood-hunger. Not yet. Though when he saw Cornelia, his nostrils flared at the blood-warm scent of her. He licked his lips. And cried out in horror.

"No! No, I am dead, let me be!"

I was merciless. "She mourns for you. Come back to this life. Take this flesh. Live."

He looked at me. He was dead. He could measure the depth of my meaning. As opposed to Meaning, which the dead understand completely, and reckon absolute idiocy.

"No."

That was Cornelia. Her voice was rough with tears, but there was no yielding in it. "I'm not that selfish. Let him go."

"You are damnably independent," said Signor Cavalli, and he sounded so much like his old self that she gasped.

But she wouldn't weaken even for that. "Go," she said. "Have peace. I'll be with you soon enough, as the world goes. Then we'll have all of time to be together."

"If by then you want it," he said.

She let go of me and planted her fists on her hips. "Giuliano Cavalli, if you think I'm going to forget you for one moment of this life *or* the next, then you're a worse idiot than I ever took you for."

"But you are young," he said, "and beautiful still, with a heart that needs so much to love, and a body that pays all tribute to it. God forbid that you live your life a widow, and die a withered and shriveled thing."

"What, you won't want me then?" She was wonderfully angry. "Now that's a pity, because you'll have me—whether I turn into a nun or take a dozen lovers a year. You're the one I want to spend my death with."

"Alive still, and you know that?"

"I know it." She clapped her hands together. "Now go. Rest. Wait for me."

He hovered. His substance was thinning for all that I could do, shredding like a fog in a sudden wind. He held out his arms. "Wait," he said like an echo. "Wait for me."

She wouldn't touch him. Wouldn't reach, wouldn't soften. "Go," she said.

He went.

The web was still, grey shading to silver. Its shadows were black. Its knots were almost smooth.

I fell off my plinth.

Marble shattered. Flesh bruised. It hurt. It hurt like blessed Hades.

Cornelia stood over me. Her face blurred and

shifted and broke into threes. Maiden Mother Crone, every face of woman, and who but me had said that Hecate was dead?

She helped me up. She was too stunned, I think, to notice the horns or the goatfeet, or the marble dust that sifted and fell when I moved. My cock wasn't crowing, by the dead gods' mercy. He hid in his dusty thicket and hoped we'd all forget him—such trouble as he'd got us into.

She pinked herself on a horn, brushing dust out of my hair. That brought her to herself. She stared at me.

I'd worn a grin so long, I'd forgotten how to start one. I backed away instead. I still had my pipes in my hand. I let them fall. They dangled by the string around my neck, bumping my flanks. My tail was clamped tight.

"There," she said as if I'd been one of the million Roman cats. "There."

I stopped. She came toward me slowly. Her face had a blank look, as if it didn't quite know what to do with itself. She touched me. I started. My back went flat against a wall I'd forgotten was there.

"It was you," she said. "Calling up the dead."

I couldn't duck. I'd have gored her: she was that close. Her hands were on my shoulders, holding me as fast as any curse.

"I think I'm supposed to do something," she said. Her brow wrinkled, as if she strained to catch a voice she couldn't quite hear. All at once her face cleared. She nodded. "Yes. Yes, I can do that."

She looked at me and my puzzlement, and smiled. It was dazzling. "Look," she said gently. She pulled me around. I came as meek as a ram to the altar. She held me so that I couldn't help but see.

Web. Light. Gate. Pillars and lintel, and on the other side . . .

"There," she said. Her voice was Cornelia's, it always had been. It was Maiden's, too, and Mother's, and Crone's. "There they all went, all your people. Shallow silly things, the lot of them, but they had their charm. Even you. They're waiting for you."

My voice found itself. It was rusty. "Oh, they are? There aren't any more bacchanals, then? Or grapes to grow and press into wine? Or sheep to herd? Or woods to run through with the barefooted Bacchae?"

"All of those remain," said Cornelia-goddess. "They're just not in this earth any longer. Any more than Giuliano is." She caught on that, but she rallied in an eye blink. "The gate's open. Go on."

She let me go. I scampered toward the shining gate.

Just outside of it, I stopped. I don't know what it was. A sparrow twittering. A cloud across the sun. Cornelia being a goddess and being a woman with marble dust on her hands, watching me go.

I turned around and went back to her. Past her. Climbed up on the plinth I'd stood on for so long, and said, "I don't think so."

We Fauns used to boast that we could knock even a goddess off her stride. I did it then, no doubt about it. She was speechless.

"Look here," I said. "I've been a piece of statuary for longer than some of us got to be gods. I'm used to it. I'd be the odd Faun out, out there. I'm the one who got trapped. I'm the one who changed."

"We can undo that," Cornelia said. She sounded like Maiden-remorseful.

I shook my head. "Even you can't put the lid back on that box. I'm not simple anymore. The next time I tried to chase a Bacchante, I'd stop to wonder about it, and then I'd wander off course, and before I knew it, I'd be teaching philosophy to the sheep."

"They would be *your* sheep," she said.

I swept my arm around. "So is this my place, and those my sparrows." I took a deep breath. Air felt good, so good, in lungs that weren't airless marble. "Put the curse back."

She wouldn't move.

"All right then," I said. I was getting angry. I picked up my pipes. I knew the notes that would shift the web. This, and this, and this. One-two-three, up-down-swoop, slow, slow, sudden trill like a sparrow's twitter. Then slow again. And slower. And slower yet. As the cool smooth stillness spread over me. As the air died from my lungs, and my lungs set into stone. This eon I wouldn't be a grinning idiot. I'd be a dancing Faun, piping down the long years. And maybe, when the moon was full, and the web was all a shimmer and a shadow, someone would have ears to hear; and I'd fill the night with music.

Cornelia put her arms around my marble middle. Her eyes were full of tears. And not for herself, or for Giuliano. For me.

I couldn't tell her not to cry. She stopped after a while. And kissed me just about *there,* and if I could have blushed, I would have. She did it for me, a splendid, scarlet blaze of it. "I won't forget," she said. "What you tried to do for me. Because—because you loved me."

That was Threefold Goddess, and Woman, too. Stating the obvious as if she'd just invented it. I couldn't shrug, or tell her not to be silly. So I waited till she went away, and then I played a run on my pipe. The wind was pleased to help me with it. The sparrows were back, squabbling over a crust someone had dropped. The world rode in its web, wobbling and tottering but never quite falling over. My world, when it came to it, and my choice, too. What's a Faun if he can't pick the story he wants to be in?

The Bargain

Katharine Kerr

Katharine Kerr, best known for her Deverry series, rarely writes short fiction. "The Bargain" is thus a very rare event and a very special story. And even now, I'm wondering if Kit has managed to get out of committing short fiction yet again—I've got my suspicion that "The Bargain," a story of Deverry, is a ballad written in the form of prose. Certainly, it has the wry Celtic wisdom on which Kit has built her reputation.

A long time ago, when Deverry men first sailed west to the province they called Elditiña, but which we know today as Eldidd, there lived a man named Paran of Aberwyn. Half scribe and half hunter, he was the son of a merchant house but a restless soul who preferred to explore new territory rather than haggle in the marketplace. All alone he traveled wild places and lived out of his pack like a pedlar, but he carried dry chunks of ink, a stone for grinding them with water, bunches of river reeds that he could cut into pens, and strips of parchment. Since in those days there were no lodestones and astrolabes, his maps were rough, of

287

course. He squinted out the directions from the sun and estimated the distances from how far and fast he'd been walking, but he always put in plenty of land-marks—watercourses and suchlike—so that others could follow him. Both the merchant guilds and the noble lords paid high for those maps and the stories he told to go with them.

On one of his trips west, however, Paran ended up with a fair bit more than he'd bargained for. After about a week's walk on foot to the west of Aberwyn, he came to a place where, through a tangle of sapling hazels and fern, he saw a river flowing silently, clear water over white sand. The path he'd been following, a deer trail or so he assumed then, turned to skirt the water and lead deeper into the trees. At the bank itself, he found a clearing, a sunny luxury after days in the wild forest. He swung his heavy pack off his shoulders and laid it down for a good stretch of his sore back. To either hand the river ran through a tun-nel of trees that promised hard walking ahead. Nearby, the *pock pock pock* loud in the drowsy sum-mer day, a woodpecker hammered an oak.

"Good morrow, little carpenter," Paran remarked.

The bird ignored the sound of his voice—puzzling, that. He sat down by his pack, unlaced the leather sack at the top of the wooden frame, and took out a long roll of parchment, scratched and spotted with his map and his notes. He was just having a look at how far he'd come when he heard the barest trace of a sound behind him. He was on his feet and turning in an instant, his hand reaching for the hilt of his sword, but he drew it only to find himself facing an archer, his horn bow drawn, an arrow nocked and ready, out of reach at the forest edge. When Paran let his sword fall and raised his hands in the air, the archer smiled. He was a pale young man, with a long tangle of hair so blond it was nearly white, and boyish-slender with long, narrow fingers. Barefoot, he wore a knee-length tunic of fine pale buckskin, belted in with the quiver of arrows slung at his hip. Around his neck on thongs hung a collection of tiny leather pouches and what seemed to be carved bone charms or decorations. When he spoke quickly in a melodious, lilting, and utterly unknown language, Paran gave a helpless sort of shrug.

"My apologies, lad, but I don't understand."

The archer cocked his head in surprise, looked Paran over for a moment, then whistled three sharp notes. From a far distance they heard first one answering whistle, then another. Two more archers stepped out of the forest, and when the three of them strolled over to inspect their prize, Paran was in for the shock of his life. Their eyes were dark purple, and the enormous irises were slit vertically with pupils like those of cats. Their ears were abnormally long, too, and curled to delicate points like seashells. They in their turn were pointing out his eyes and ears to each other and chattering away about them, too, from the sound of it.

"Uh, I mean you no harm. Truly I don't."

The three of them smiled in a rather unpleasant way.

"And what have we here?"

The voice seemed to speak in Paran's language, but the young men called out a greeting in their own. As she materialized between two trees, the woman looked as blonde and boyish as her companions, dressed much like them, too, but when Paran tried to look at her face, her image swam and flickered, as if he'd drunk himself blind. She seemed to age, her tunic changing back and forth from blue to green to gray; then she suddenly was young again. The archers, however, stayed as visible and substantial as himself as they stared at the woman in awe, lips half-parted.

"This is a strange deer you've caught in my forest," she said to them, then turned to Paran. "Who are you?"

"Paran of Aberwyn, my lady. Do you know the place? It's a little town down by the sea."

"I don't, and the sea means naught to me. What are you doing here?"

"Just seeing what I can see. I'm a curious man, my lady, and no man of my race has ever been here."

"I'm well aware of that, my thanks."

She studied him with narrow eyes, cold now and yellow as a snake's, and her lips were tight, too, perhaps in rage, perhaps in contempt—it was hard to tell with her constant shape-shifting—yet of one thing he was sure, that he'd never seen a woman so beautiful or so dangerous. If she gave the word, the archers would fill him with arrows like a leather target at a festival.

"I swear it, my lady. I mean you not the slightest harm."

"No doubt, but harm can come without a meaning behind it. Your people are the ones who are taking slaves from the river villages, aren't you?"

"Are those your vassals? I'll swear to you on the gods of my people that I've naught to do with that. My kind of clan doesn't need bondmen. We don't have any lands."

"They're not mine, but they're gentle souls who do no harm and make their tools out of stones. Your people stink of blood and iron." She turned old, very old, old beyond belief yet still beautiful, and her heavy cloak was gray with mourning. "How much have you killed in my woods?"

"Some squirrels, some hares, and some fish from the river. Forgive me: I didn't know I was poaching. I didn't know anyone lived out here."

"And what will you give me in return?"

"Anything of mine you desire." Paran pointed at his pack. "Look through it, or take it all if you want."

Suddenly she was young again, with a smile as disdainful as any highborn lady's in Elditiña. Her beauty seemed to hang around her like a cloud of scent or crackle in the air like heat lightning: he found himself struggling for words, and him a man who'd always been able to talk his way out of anything before.

"Keep your greasy trinkets," she said. "I want the truth for my dues. What truly made you come here?"

"A change from the merchants of Aberwyn. They wish to find out what lies in this country because they wish to trade. Naught more—only to caravan goods back and forth in peace."

"But who comes behind them? Those blood-soaked men who build the ugly stone towers and take slaves?"

Paran could only nod in agreement. Like most common-born men in Eldidd, he had never approved of making bondmen out of people who were neither criminals nor debtors. It infuriated him that he was on the edge of paying for the arrogance of lords.

"If I have you killed," she said in a musing sort of voice. "No doubt someone else will come, sooner or later. I have no desire to be as cruel as your folk, Paran of Aberwyn. You walk out of my forest alive if you leave today."

"I will, then. I'll even walk hungry to spare your game."

"No need of that, as long as you take only what you truly need to feed yourself."

With a smile she laid a slender hand on his cheek, her fingers oddly cool and smooth; she even allowed him to turn his head and kiss her fingers. Then she was gone; they were all gone; there was only the clearing, the sunlight, his pack and his sword lying in grass. Something else had been there, not but a moment before—Paran couldn't remember what. Deer, perhaps? Birds? A badger? He shrugged the wondering away. Whatever it was, he'd gone far enough into this useless forest, and it was time to head back to Aberwyn.

Yet when he knelt to retrieve his pack, he found his map. As he picked it up and read his notes, the memory came back to him, sharp and clear, and he laughed in triumph. Dweomer the lady had, strange and powerful dweomer, but she knew nothing of the ways of men, who write things down to outlast their remembering. Of course, if he told this story of a sorceress in the woods and her cat-eyed servants, no one was going to believe him anyway. As he set off, he was wondering just how to phrase the thing to the merchant guild of Aberwyn, or if he should say anything at all.

Five men on horseback, and a couple of mules carrying supplies—the effort seemed more than one stinking bondman was worth, but at stake was the honor of the thing, Addaric decided. This snot-faced Grunno belonged to Lord Cadlomar, and if he had the gall to go sneaking off, then Addaric would fetch him back for his lordship if it took him a fortnight. They took the hounds to Grunno's hut and let the dogs sniff his greasy blankets while his filthy woman watched, gasping for breath with a sound like mice chittering. When they brought the dogs to the edge of the village, they picked up the scent at once and went baying across the pastureland with the riders trotting after, the kennelmaster first, then the four men from the warband. The boy with the mules followed as best he could.

At the edge of the pasture, the ground turned rough with rock and burrow, and Omillo, the kennelmaster, called in the big black-and-gray boarhounds. Addaric rode up to join him.

"He's got a good head start," Omillo said.

"So he does. But we've got horses. We'll get him, sure enough."

Yet that evening they reached the big river, so newly discovered that most people called it only "the one that flows into the Gwyn" or "the western one." Here in late summer it flowed so broad and shallow that a man could wade in it for miles and let it wash all his scent away. As they milled around on the riverbank, the hounds snapped at each other in sheer frustration.

"Well, young Addaric, which way do you think he went?"

"That's an easy one—upstream. Down would bring him right back to the Gwyn and settled land again."

On the morrow Addaric was proved right. Although they had to crisscross the river for a tedious ten miles before the hounds picked up the scent, find it they did. They sang out and raced away to the northwest while the men followed at a cavalry pace, walking and trotting, stopping frequently to rest the pack. Still they were moving far faster than a frightened man could run. Toward evening the hounds found a leather sack, which they grabbed and shook, growling.

"It must stink of the man," Addaric remarked. "Looks to me like he's run out of food, too."

The very next morning, for a few brief moments they thought they'd found their prey. As they traveled across wild meadowland, they saw far ahead of them a small shape that had to be a man walking. With a whoop of triumph they kicked their horses forward, but the whoop died when they realized that the fellow was coming calmly toward them, not running away. When they met, Addaric at first thought he was a pedlar, because he was carrying a heavy pack of the same sort that a traveling man would use, but there was not one out here to buy ribands and needles and trinkets. The fellow was imposing, too, a tall man with the raven-dark hair and cornflower blue eyes so common in the province, but tanned and tough with a calm if watchful look about him that seemed to say he'd faced worse trouble than five riders before.

"Good morrow, good sir," Addaric said. "You're a good long way from settled country."

"I could say the same of you, lad." He smiled to take any sting from the words. "My name's Paran of Aberwyn."

"Well, by the gods! Truly, good sir, I've heard of you. I'll wager we all have, and many a time, too. The bards all call you the bravest man in Elditiña, going off alone for months like that."

The men with him muttered their agreement and rode up close to get a good look at this famous person. Paran turned embarrassed.

"Er, just on my way home," he muttered, stepping back a little. "And what of you? What brings armed men to a wilderness?"

"Looking for an escaped bondman. One of my lord's men had the blasted gall to run away, and his lordship sent me to get him back again." Addaric couldn't help letting his pride sound in his voice, that Lord Cadlomar had placed him in charge. "Have you seen any trace of him?"

"I haven't, at that." Paran thought for a moment. "Now listen, lad. Before the day's over, you'll come to a forest, and a wild, huge one it is. Don't go in there. I swear it to you: that forest is no place to go a-hunting anything down. If you honor me, then for the love of our gods, let the poor bastard be."

When he stared directly into Addaric's eyes, the lad felt himself blushing and looked away.

"I've got my orders from our lord," he stammered.

"Lords have been given cut-down versions of truth's cloak before. Your bondman's only going to die in that forest, anyway, so stay out of it."

Perhaps some of the gods agreed with Paran. The hunters had ridden only a scant couple of miles when the sky began churning with gray clouds and the wind brought a smell of damp in the air, but the rain did hold off till evening, and by then they were within sight of the forest. For some time they'd seen it on the horizon like a second bank of clouds; just as the sunset turned the sky blood-colored they came within clear sight of it. The meadowland bordering the river stopped abruptly in a tangle of shrubby growth; then the trees began, a dark wall, stretching out and back farther than any of them could see or guess. The men paused their horses in a little knob and simply stared at it for a long time.

"I see what Paran meant," Addaric said. "We're going to have a hellish time in there."

"Are we turning back?" Matun, his closest friend in the warband, edged his horse up beside him.

"What? And lie to your lord? I'd rather die than that."

Yet the forest was so silent, so dark under the scarlet sky, that he felt his battle-hardened nerves run just a little cold. His nerves grew on him, too, after they'd made camp. Since they needed meat for the dogs, Omillo took a short hunting bow and one of the pack and started toward the forest to track them a deer. Addaric went with him some ways across the meadow.

"Be careful in there."

"What? And haven't I been hunting in our lord's service for a good twenty years now?"

"I was just thinking of Paran's warning. They say he knows wild country better than any man alive."

When Omillo walked into the trees, the forest seemed to cover him over like deep water. Addaric waited, pacing back and forth, until he returned, staggering under the weight of a three-month fawn while the dogs pranced around him and drooled in anticipation.

They'd no sooner reached the fire when the rain came, pouring down and dousing them and the flames both in a matter of minutes. Cursing and swearing, Omillo had to hack the fawn up in the dark while the dogs crowded round and whined, and the other men swore at the wet night ahead of them and the meager meals, too—they'd been looking forward to the roast meat. Although Addaric wanted to set a watch, everyone grumbled, and since he was young and only a temporary commander at that, he gave in. Yet he himself slept so restlessly, dreaming of voices in the forest and things creeping through tangled undergrowth, that he woke some two hours before dawn.

By then the rain had stopped, but he and his bedroll were soaked straight through. Since they'd all slept wet on many a campaign, the rest of the men were hunched up with their saddles over their heads and still asleep, but he got up, buckling his baldric over his shoulder and feeling the weight of the sword at his hip as a solid comfort. He walked away from the camp until he stood some twenty paces from the forest edge and thought of Grunno, somewhere in the ominous dark. He was probably so terrified that he'd be glad to go home and take his flogging.

"You'll never find him."

With a yelp Addaric spun round, but there was no one there. He heard laughter, then, coming from everywhere and nowhere, a woman's mocking-sweet laugh.

"You took a fawn from my woods. I'll have a price for that. What will you give me?"

"By the black ass of the Lord of Hell, show yourself, wench, and then maybe we'll talk about bargaining."

"Let me warn you somewhat. If a price isn't offered me, then I take what I want."

"Oh, will you now?" Addaric drew his sword. "Just try to steal from us."

She laughed again, a mocking ripple that blended with the riversound, grew loud, louder, until it seemed to ring in his head and deafen him.

"Hold your tongue! Stop that! I said stop it!"

The laughter died away. In the camp someone shouted. Matun and Omillo came running, swords in hand. But there was no one there, no woman, no speaker, only the wind, rising as the eastern sky began to turn gray. When Addaric told his story, everyone mocked and said he'd been having naught more than a nightmare. He felt the shame of their laughter burn his cheeks, and it ran through him and poisoned his stomach so badly that he couldn't eat breakfast.

The shame drove him into the forest, too, when the time came. Since there was no use in taking all five men to crash around and warn Grunno they were coming, Addaric left the others with the horses while he and Omillo took the two best hounds after their prey. As they walked across the last stretch of open land, Addaric felt a little coldness around his heart. He'd ridden to battle and never felt fear, but now the coldness tightened around his lungs and grew tendrils down into his stomach. For a moment he thought of turning back, but the shame of it forced him to walk into the silent darkness of the trees.

"Here's the deer track I found yesterday," Omillo said. "We can follow it a-ways and hope the dogs pick the scent out of the air."

Out of his saddlebags Omillo got Grunno's sack and let the hounds sniff it. For a moment they milled around, confused; then one of them growled and

headed straight off down the path. Although Addaric
tried to keep up with Omillo and the dogs, his baldric
kept catching on the shrubs and bracken. Once they
left the river behind, the path twisted through bush
and bracken until Addaric had no idea where the open
country lay. He felt things watching, eyes from among
the ferns, eyes above him in the leaves, and he heard
voices whispering in the rising wind. Once he thought
he felt a hand grab his arm, but it was only the twiggy
touch of a sapling. He drew his sword and cut the
thing clear through.

Ahead, as if at a signal, the hounds sang out and
leapt forward. With a shout, Omillo darted after. Addaric tripped, swore, got up, and hurled himself after,
but at that precise moment the rain broke again, pattering first on the canopy far above, then slashing
down like so many spears made of water. The wind
howled and shook the trees in a flurry of falling leaves.

"Omillo! Hold a minute! I can't see you."

He tripped again, or something tripped him. He felt
a clutch at his ankles and went down, sprawling into
the mucky-wet leaves on the deer trail. In the howl
of the wind he was sure he heard laughter. Yelling for
Omillo, he scrambled up, but the rain was sweeping
through the woods in a gray curtain. Stumbling and
swearing, he followed the path until he came to a fork.
When he found not a trace of man or dog on either
path, he had the grim thought that he'd expected no
less. No matter which he took, it would be the wrong
one. He was sure of that. For a long time he stood
there, the rain drenching his clothes and running down
the steel blade of his sword, simply stood and listened
to his heart pound.

"You won't trap me so easy, wench."

Addaric turned and went back the way he'd come,
but the rain had turned their tracks into mere mud
and leaf-mold, and in the driving grayness one thin

spot in the underbrush looked much like any other. Addaric knew he was lost not fifty yards after he started. He kept walking for want of anything else to do, used his sword to slash his way through bush and bracken alike for the sheer pleasure of venting his rage on the woods.

It wasn't only the rain that kept him company. He could feel eyes upon him, hear voices, and at times, he caught a glimpse of something moving out of the corner of his eye. Whenever he turned to look directly at this mysterious something, it would disappear. When the growling in his stomach told him it was well past noon, he sat down in the muck beneath a tree and choked back the tears that threatened to shame him.

"I'll just sit here. Curse it all, I should have done that in the first wretched place! Just sit here and let Omillo find me. He can give the dogs the scent from my saddle."

But the rain was washing the forest clean in a steady gray pour while the wind plucked at the leaves and sang of death by starving, death from cold, or perhaps even a worse death from the things that clustered round to mock him in the rustle of branch and leaf. All afternoon, as he sat there waiting, he saw them. In the water drops bright eyes gleamed, in the rough bark fingers pinched. Once, when he looked sharply to his left, he saw a tiny naked girl-child with a lizard hanging on her shoulder like a pet. Then she disappeared, if indeed anything had ever been there at all, and laughter rippled in the trees. Addaric gripped his sword hilt in both hands.

"I won't go mad. Even if I starve, I'll die sane. It's a battle, and curse you all to the hells, I'm going to win."

The voices snickered in disbelief.

At sunset he struggled to his feet on aching legs and braced himself against the trunk. As the rain died away, the voices around him grew hushed, expectant. Clutching his sword like a talisman, Addaric waited with them in the damp dark. It wasn't long before he saw a light moving among the trees, the distant, bobbing glow of a torch.

"Omillo! Omillo! I'm over here!"

"Oh, I know where you are, sure enough." It was the woman's voice that answered, full of her musical laughter.

With barely a sound they slipped through the trees and underbrush to surround him, the woman slender and boyish in her short gray cloak, but beautiful with moonbeam pale hair and violet eyes. With her were three young men in buckskin tunics, all armed with bows. By the light of the torch she carried, Addaric could see the glittering points of nocked arrows.

"I've come for the price of my fawn. What's your name, lad?"

"Addaric of Belglaedd."

"Addaric of Belglaedd? Addaric of Belglaedd, Addaric of Belglaedd."

All at once his head was swimming with a longing for sleep. As he leaned back against the tree, the weight of his sword seemed to pull his arm down of its own will.

"You called me a wench, too. I'll have repayment for that as well as the fawn. What will you offer me?"

"I'd die before I gave you one cursed thing."

She set her hands on her hips and frowned. All at once he realized that the torch hung above her in the air and flowed with the bluish light of something other than fire.

"You come to my woods hunting a man as if he were a deer. I shan't have that. And then you kill without offering me dues. I shan't have that, either. I'll take you as my price for the fawn."

When the archers snickered, she waved them into

silence. Addaric looked at the drawn bows and saw his death glittering on arrow points. With one last wrench of his will, he raised his sword, determined to drag her to the Otherlands with him.

"Oh, you utter lout, I'm not talking of killing you. How strange that the gods would make such a pretty lad but not give him any wits! You're coming with me, Addaric of Belglaedd, Addaric of Belglaedd, Addaric of Belglaedd."

Addaric tried to swing at her, but the sword fell from his hand as he crumpled into sleep. Dimly he was aware of being picked up, then carried a long way only to be laid down on something soft and warm. He heard her whispering his name three times again; then the sleep deepened to a welcome darkness that swallowed him whole.

When he woke, he found himself lying naked in soft blankets, and around him was the dim glow of sunlight filtering through the walls of a round tent, about ten feet across, made of hides stitched together with thongs. Leather cushions lay scattered on the floor, and brightly colored bags hung from the tent poles. He sat up, rubbing his eyes, realizing that his muscles no longer ached. In a blinding glare of sunlight, the woman pushed open the tent flaps and came in, carrying a wooden bowl. Once the flaps closed again, he could see her better in the dim light, her pale hair, unbound to fall down her back in a spill of gold, her delicate face. Her eyes were oddly hidden, so much so that he couldn't tell their color.

"I've brought you somewhat to eat," she announced.

She handed him the bowl, then sat down facing him and studied him so curiously that he bundled the blanket firmly around his waist.

"You people grow hair on your faces and on your chests. Fancy that."

Addaric had the annoying feeling that he was blushing. In the bowl he found a flat cake of some coarsely ground grain, smeared with wild honey, and slices of cold roast venison. While he ate, she clasped her arms around her knees and watched. She seemed younger than ever, a lass about his own age of nineteen, perhaps, and very pretty indeed.

"I've told you my name. Won't you tell me yours?"

"I won't, never. My people call me Melario. It means wood rose in their tongue. Or you may call me Briaclan, that means the same in yours."

When he finished the food, he handed her the bowl. With a smile of cold triumph she raised it high, then rose and with a ritual care set it outside the tent door. All at once he realized that he never should have eaten her food. Why, he wasn't exactly sure, but he felt the sting of an old tale at his mind. Too late, now: still smiling she came back to stand over him.

"And just what do you want with me?"

"Oh, come now. What kind of a man are you, that you can't guess?"

Since he thought she was setting him a riddle, he honestly tried to think of an answer, but with a laugh she unclasped her belt, then pulled off her tunic. Naked she was so beautiful that he could think of nothing but her body, glowing softly as if her flesh captured sunlight. Then she lay down next to him on the blanket and kissed him on the mouth.

Some two weeks later, Paran heard a very strange story about Addaric's disappearance. While in Aberwyn, he lived with his father, a widower, and his unmarried sister. They had one of the biggest houses in town, a two-story roundhouse set on a couple of acres where they kept a cow and three pigs, while a flock of chickens roamed among the greens and turnips in the kitchen garden. That particular afternoon he was working in the garden, in fact, when a horseman rode up to the gate in the earthen wall that surrounded the homestead. At the hysterical barking of the family dogs, Paran got up, dusting off the knees of his brigga, and recognized Matun from Lord Cadlomar's warband.

"Morrow, lad! What brings you here? My sister's down at the market with my father, if it's either love or commerce."

"Neither, truly, but a word with you."

"Come in, then. Ye gods, hounds! Will you stop your demon-get barking?"

Inside, the central fire smoldered under the smoke hole. In the curve of the round wall, under a row of tankards hanging from pegs, stood a big barrel of ale. Paran dipped them both out some drink and sat his guest down at the wooden table by the hearthstone.

"It's about Addaric," Matun said. "Did you hear that he was killed in that god-cursed forest you warned us about?"

"I hadn't, but it aches my heart to hear it now. What did he do, charge right in there?"

"Just that." Matun looked up, his eyes snapping rage. "He and the kennel master went in, but only Omillo came out. We searched and searched, and finally we found the place where he'd been killed. Here, you might have warned us about the blasted bears!"

"Bears? I didn't see any bears."

"But that's what got him. We found its tracks, and they were huge. It must have been an enormous bear, or so the kennel master said. There was a tuft of black fur caught on a thorn, too. Addaric's bloody sword was nearby."

"Did you ever find his body?"

Matun shook his head no. There were tears in his eyes.

"He was a good friend of yours, was he?"

"I loved him, and I don't give a pig's fart who knows it, either." He had a long swallow of ale. "I loved him better than that rotten little bitch he had in the village did, too, her and her cursed mincing and flirting with the rest of us lads." Then he did cry, dropping his face into his hands and sobbing aloud.

Paran got up and wandered to the doorway to look out while Matun got himself under control. He wondered very much about that huge black bear, very much indeed, because the only bears he'd ever seen to the west were small brown ones. He glanced back to find Matun sniffing into his sleeve and swallowing heavily, gave him an encouraging smile, and wandered back to the table again.

"So you came here to reproach me for your friend's death?"

"I did, but it seems stupid now. You did warn us about the forest, and even if you'd told us about the bears, that wouldn't have held Addaric back anyway. He was all keen to go into the cursed place because he felt shamed."

"And why did he feel shamed?"

"Oh, the night before he woke us all up. He said he heard someone talking to him, but when he got there, she was gone."

"She?"

"That's what he said. Some woman's voice."

"Oh, did he now? Well, lad, my heart truly aches for you and Addaric both. I only wish he'd listened to me and left the forest alone. I think me it's wilder than we can know."

For the rest of that day Paran tried to talk himself out of the idea that kept haunting him, but when his father and sister returned from the marketplace, he announced that he was leaving on the morrow to set off west again. He couldn't quite bring himself to say why.

Since he'd already traveled this stretch of country, Paran reached the forest with no trouble. Round about noon on a hot summer day, he even found the exact spot where Addaric and his men had camped, thanks to the scar left on the land by their fire pit and the bones of the fawn, scattered all over the meadow by the ravens and badgers. He shrugged off his pack, laid it down by the pit, and stood for a long time, shading his eyes with one hand and staring at the dark and silent wall of forest. Now that he'd come so far, he certainly wasn't about to turn round and go home again, but he had to admit that he was frightened, and more than fear, he felt futility. For all he knew, Addaric might be wandering through a ghost forest in the Otherlands.

"Well," he said to nothing in particular. "I might as well wait till the morrow, go in right at dawn, like, when there's a whole day's light ahead of me."

Yet, once the sun was well down and the not quite full moon rising, the sorceress came to him. Paran was on his knees, nursing a fire of gleaned deadfall, when he heard her laughing behind him.

"Good eve, my lady. Won't you join me at my fire?"

"You *are* a civil man, Paran of Aberwyn. Unlike some as I could mention."

Moving silently on bare feet, she came round and stood before him as he kneeled. That night she seemed more solid than he was remembering her, a young lass dressed in a boy's tunic, a hunting bow dangling carelessly in one hand.

"I suppose you've come to ask me to give him back," she said.

"Addaric? I have, at that. He's got kinfolk at home who love him and miss him, you see. It's for their sake I've come, to be honest, not so much for his."

"Civil and a good judge of character." She grinned,

revealing sharp-pointed teeth. "What will you give me in return?"

"What would you like? Gold and jewels? I'm not a rich man, and no more are Addaric's friends, but no doubt I could scrounge together a ransom once I know your demands."

"I have no use for that."

"Fine horses? Addaric's lord owes a legal blood price for the lad, two war-worthy geldings and a broodmare."

"No use for them, either. There's no fodder for horses in my forests."

"Well, then, won't you name me a price?"

"You."

Paran could only stare. All at once he understood what that tired old way of speaking, "feeling your blood run cold," meant in the flesh. She was smiling, staring down at the dirt scattered round the fire pit, drawing a pattern in it with her big toe like some shy country lass.

"What would you want with me?"

"I don't know, but I'll wager you're less boring than he is. He's a pretty lad, but your gods didn't give him much in the way of wits." She looked up, and suddenly her smile was all malice, her eyes cold and snakelike. "But that doesn't matter. I've named my price. Will you pay it or not?"

All at once he saw her as huge, towering over him, towering over the forest, swelling up the way a candle flame will do in a draught, and he knew that he'd been a fool to ever think her human and a sorceress.

"Are you a goddess, then?"

"Naught of the sort." She flickered back to a normal shape, as a candle flame will do when the door's been shut and the draft stopped. "This is my forest, and the folk who live here are mine to guard, but the gods are far, far above the likes of me." She smiled again, but briefly. "You haven't answered my question."

"If I just go away again, what will happen to Addaric?"

"He'll wander with my people till he dies."

Sitting on his heels Paran considered his tiny fire as if it could give him advice. For all that he loved hidden things, at that moment he found himself thirsting for his family's company and the familiar streets of Aberwyn. But he, at least, could learn from the lady, while Addaric would wander with her retinue like a tame beast.

"Well, I'll tell you," he said at last. "If I'm the prize you want, then you shall have me. But how will Addaric find his way home again? Without a guide, he'll wander around out here and starve to death. Can you take him home with your dweomer?"

"I can take him to the edge of his lord's fields, and surely even he can find his way back from there."

"I'm sure he will, my lady." Paran got to his feet, but he felt as if he were hauling up an enormous weight. "Done, then. That'll be our bargain. You take Addaric home, and I'll come with you."

She laughed, jiggling a few steps of a dance like a farm lass. For a brief moment she looked to be a lovely young lass, too, all golden and smiling as she held her arms out to him.

"Give me a kiss, Paran of Aberwyn."

"Whatever my lady wants."

"What? Don't you want to take one?"

When he said nothing, she scowled, staring into his eyes as if she were reading his thoughts.

"Well, then," she snapped. "I'll do the taking!"

Never in his life had he been kissed like that, with a passion as sweet as it was urgent. With a gasp he caught his breath and reached to kiss her again. She was gone. He stood alone by a dying fire under the spread of stars and heard her voice, flying round like a lark.

"All that will have to wait, since you value your blood kin more highly than me. You drive a hard bargain, Paran of Aberwyn. I hope you like the terms of it once you're home."

Across the meadow, the dark forest stretched like a rampart. Paran dropped to his knees and wept, just from the missing of her.

In the morning, with the first light of dawn, Addaric came stumbling out of the forest, and he was carrying a leather sack stuffed with food for their journey home, as well. He tossed the sack down, fell at Paran's feet, and threw his arms around his rescuer's knees so fervently that he nearly tumbled Paran to the ground.

"Thank the gods, oh thank the gods you came! How did you—what did you—that bitch! That wretched rotten bitch! How did you get the better of her?"

Paran nearly slapped him across the face, but he restrained himself.

"Get up, lad, get up. We've got a long walk ahead of us."

"Walk?" Addaric let him go and slouched back on his heels. "Walk? Walk the whole cursed way? Didn't you bring any horses?"

"I didn't at that. Now get up before I leave you here."

The long walk home improved neither Addaric's moral fiber nor his temper, and Paran was more than glad to leave him at his lord's door by the time they reached it. He was also glad to take the lord's reward, too, not so much for saving Addaric, as for enduring him on the walk home, and he gave the fine horses in question to his sister for her dowry. No one believed Addaric, of course, when he talked of being ensnared by a beautiful sorceress. The lad had just plain gotten himself lost, or so the popular opinion ran, and he was too piss-proud stubborn to admit the truth. For some months their adventure was the talk of Aberwyn, but by spring, the folk found other things to marvel over and, as folk will, forgot.

Paran, however, always remembered that kiss in the wild meadow. Torn as he was between fear and regret, her memory haunted his dreams for years, while awake he shuddered at the thought of her. Although his mapping took him back to her forest many a time, he never saw her or her strange shy people again, not even when he lingered by her river in hopes of catching a glimpse of her—not, of course, that he could admit he was lingering. During all those long years he never married, living alone in the roundhouse after his father died and his sister found a man of her own. Finally, when his hair had turned steel gray, and he knew that his legs were beginning to lose their spring, he gave away everything he owned and left Aberwyn for the west. When he never came back, most people believed that he'd died in the wilderness, eaten by bears, maybe, or drowned, more likely, or just plain starved to death somewhere in the wild.

The truth of the matter is, though, that he walked into her forest and found the circular clearing, not far from the river that we call Delonderiel, which was the place where first he'd seen her. He shrugged off his pack and stood for a moment, staring around at the silent trees.

"Lady?" he called. "My lady Briaclan, can you hear me? I've come as a suppliant. I'll sit here and starve myself at your doorstep, just as if you were a great lord who'd wronged me, and the last word I speak will be the name you told to young Addaric, all those years ago."

He stooped and turned out his pack, strewing the stuff about to show her that he carried not a morsel of food, then sat down cross-legged in the grass. He'd barely settled himself, though, when she came strolling through the trees. She was wearing a dress of some pale stuff that shimmered round her like sunlight.

"So, you've come back to me, have you, Paran of Aberwyn?"

"I've come back many a time. You never showed yourself."

"You never asked, nor did you call to me, nor say one word about me. Why?"

"Why didn't you ever call out to me?"

"I asked my question first, and so you answer first."

"Fair enough. I was afraid that I'd love you more than any man should love a woman, and then I'd be a different man."

"Odd, that. I was afraid I'd love you more than one of my kind should love a mortal, and then I'd have changed beyond thinking. I'd say our answers are much alike."

"And I'd say the same." He looked away with a sigh for the foolishness of pride. "Is it too late for you to have me back?"

"Never. Come here."

Hand in hand they walked off through the woods, and never once did he look back nor think of his pack and his gear, lying scattered over the grass. And some say that thanks to the lady's great dweomer, Paran is still alive, wandering with her and her people under the wheel of the sky, but as to the truth of that, I couldn't say.

ROC

EXCITING FANTASY

☐ **THE OAK ABOVE THE KINGS A book of the Keltiad, Volume II of** *The Tales of Arthur* **by Patricia Kennealy-Morrison.** A fair and wondrous realm of Celtic myth which creates a faraway star empire that is at the same time both strangely familiar and utterly strange.
(453522—$17.95)

☐ **KNIGHTS OF THE BLOOD created by Katherine Kurtz and Scott MacMillan.** A Los Angeles policeman is out to solve an unsolved mystery— that would pitch him straight into the dark and terrifying world of the vampire. (452569—$4.99)

☐ **KNIGHTS OF THE BLOOD:** *At Sword's Point* **by Katherine Kurtz and Scott MacMillan.** A generation of Nazi vampires has evolved with a centuries-old agenda hell-bent on world domination, and the only way LAPD Detective John Drummond can save himself is to grab a sword and commit bloody murder. (454073—$4.99)

☐ **PRIMAVERA by Francesca Lia Block.** Primavera flees her home on a horse-headed motorcycle that takes her to the magical city of Elysia, land of carnivals and circuses, of magic and music, where growing old was the only crime. But if the city has its way, she may never find her way back home. (453239—$4.50)

*Prices slightly higher in Canada

Buy them at your local bookstore or use this convenient coupon for ordering.

PENGUIN USA
P.O. Box 999 — Dept. #17109
Bergenfield, New Jersey 07621

Please send me the books I have checked above.
I am enclosing $_____ (please add $2.00 to cover postage and handling). Send check or money order (no cash or C.O.D.'s) or charge by Mastercard or VISA (with a $15.00 minimum). Prices and numbers are subject to change without notice.

Card #_____ Exp. Date _____
Signature_____
Name_____
Address_____
City _____ State _____ Zip Code _____

For faster service when ordering by credit card call **1-800-253-6476**

Allow a minimum of 4-6 weeks for delivery. This offer is subject to change without notice.

FANTASY FROM ROC

☐ **FLAMES OF THE DRAGON by Robin W. Bailey.** The domains of light had welcomed Robert and Eric, two brothers skilled in martial arts, when they were transported through a portal that linked the Catskill Mountains to a land where magic was real, where dragons soared the skies, where black unicorns wreaked death and destruction, and where angry ghosts roved among the living, seeking vengeance upon their slayers.   (452895—$4.99)

☐ **THE INNKEEPER'S SONG by Peter S. Beagle.** This is the story of young Tikat's search for the lover whose death and resurrection he witnessed ... A search that will lead him into a world of magic and mystery beyond his comprehension ... which sets him on the trail of three women who are blessed—or cursed—to undertake an impossible mission of their own.   (454146—$9.95)

☐ **METAL ANGEL by Nancy Springer.** He was a fallen angel, and he was going to make the mortal realm his own through the power of rock-and-roll!
                                          (453301—$4.99)

☐ **BLUE MOON RISING by Simon Green.** The dragon that Prince Rupert was sent out to slay turned out to be a better friend than anyone at the castle. And with the Darkwood suddenly spreading its evil, with the blue moon rising and the Wild Magic along with it, Rupert was going to need all the friends he could get....
                                          (450957—$5.50)

*Prices slightly higher in Canada

Buy them at your local bookstore or use this convenient coupon for ordering.

PENGUIN USA
P.O. Box 999 — Dept. #17109
Bergenfield, New Jersey 07621

Please send me the books I have checked above.
I am enclosing $_____ (please add $2.00 to cover postage and handling). Send check or money order (no cash or C.O.D.'s) or charge by Mastercard or VISA (with a $15.00 minimum). Prices and numbers are subject to change without notice.

Card #_____ Exp. Date _____
Signature_____
Name_____
Address_____
City _____ State _____ Zip Code _____

For faster service when ordering by credit card call **1-800-253-6476**

Allow a minimum of 4-6 weeks for delivery. This offer is subject to change without notice.

ROC ROC

FANTASTICS

☐ **THE ARCHITECTURE OF DESIRE by Mary Gentle.** Return to a medieval world of Scholar Soldiers and magic in this magnificent sequel to *Rats and Gargoyles.* "Miraculous!—*Washington Post Book World*
(453530—$4.99)

☐ **DR. DIMENSION: MASTERS OF SPACETIME by John DeChancie and David Bischoff.** Can a questionable robot actually help Dr. Dimension and his sidekick, Troy, escape the trash planet? (453549—$4.99)

☐ **SHADOWS FALL by Simon R. Green.** A town of amazing magicks, where the real and the imagined live side by side, where the Faerie of legend know the automatons of the future. (453638—$5.99)

☐ **THE SEVEN TOWERS: WIZARD AT MECQ by Rick Shelley.** A battle is brought to the heart of the Wizard Silvas' own domain—where he might find himself facing a foe beyond even his magical abilities to defeat.
(453611—$4.99)

*Prices slightly higher in Canada

Buy them at your local bookstore or use this convenient coupon for ordering.

PENGUIN USA
P.O. Box 999 — Dept. #17109
Bergenfield, New Jersey 07621

Please send me the books I have checked above.
I am enclosing $_____ (please add $2.00 to cover postage and handling). Send check or money order (no cash or C.O.D.'s) or charge by Mastercard or VISA (with a $15.00 minimum). Prices and numbers are subject to change without notice.

Card #_____ Exp. Date _____
Signature_____
Name_____
Address_____
City _____ State _____ Zip Code _____

For faster service when ordering by credit card call **1-800-253-6476**

Allow a minimum of 4-6 weeks for delivery. This offer is subject to change without notice.

▓ ROC

THE BEST IN SCIENCE FICTION
AND FANTASY

☐ **LARISSA by Emily Devenport.** Hook is a mean, backwater mining planet where the alien Q'rin rule. Taking the wrong side can get you killed and humans have little hope for escape. Larissa is a young woman with a talent for sports and knives. She's beating the aliens at their own harsh game until someone dies.   (452763—$4.99)

☐ **STARSEA INVADERS: SECOND CONTACT by G. Harry Stine.** Captain Corry discovers that the U.S.S. *Shenandoah* is at last going to be allowed to track down the alien invaders who are based beneath the sea—invaders who had long preyed upon Earth and its people—and this time they were going to bring one of the creatures back alive!
(453441—$4.99)

☐ **DEADLY QUICKSILVER LIES by Glen Cook.** Garrett comes to the rescue of a damsel in distress in a kingdom where the biggest con artists weren't human, and magic could beat any weapon.   (453050—$4.99)

☐ **MUTANT CHRONICLES:** *The Apostle of Insanity Trilogy:* **IN LUNACY by William F. Wu.** It was a time to conquer all fears and stand up against the tidal wave of the Dark Symmetry. Battles rage across our solar system as mankind and the Legions of Darkness fight for supremacy of the kingdom of Sol. But though there is unity against the common enemy, the five MegaCorporations that rule the worlds are fighting among themselves. The struggle for survival goes on.   (453174—$4.99)

*Prices slightly higher in Canada

Buy them at your local bookstore or use this convenient coupon for ordering.

PENGUIN USA
P.O. Box 999 — Dept. #17109
Bergenfield, New Jersey 07621

Please send me the books I have checked above.
I am enclosing $_____ (please add $2.00 to cover postage and handling). Send check or money order (no cash or C.O.D.'s) or charge by Mastercard or VISA (with a $15.00 minimum). Prices and numbers are subject to change without notice.

Card #_____ Exp. Date _____
Signature_____
Name_____
Address_____
City _____ State _____ Zip Code _____

For faster service when ordering by credit card call **1-800-253-6476**

Allow a minimum of 4-6 weeks for delivery. This offer is subject to change without notice.

① SIGNET SCIENCE FICTION   ROC ROC   (0451)

OUT OF THIS WORLD ANTHOLOGIES

☐ **PREDATORS edited by Ed Gorman & Martin H. Greenberg.** This compelling new collection from the editors of the bestselling *Stalkers* tells of worlds where evil waits and watches ... and kills. Each story will send chills up your spine, keep you burning the lights all night, and have you looking over your shoulder—just in case the Predator is there.   (452267—$4.99)

☐ **I SHUDDER AT YOUR TOUCH: *22 Tales of Sex and Horror* Edited by Michele Slung.** Features 22 daring writers who prefer to go too far, writers whose every tale will have you fighting back a scream ... and a cry of delight. Includes stories by Stephen King, Ruth Rendell, Clive Barker, and a host of others. Also available on audio cassette from Penguin HighBridge.

       (451600—$5.99)

☐ **SHUDDER AGAIN 22 Tales of Sex and Horror Edited by Michele Slung.** This assembled feast of sensual scariness dares to go beyond the bestselling *I Shudder at Your Touch*. Here are stories from 22 superb experts at turning the screws of terror even as they lift the veils of desire. See if you're able to distinguish between those echoing cries expressing the ultimate pleasure ... and the piercing screams of pure terror.   (453468—$5.99)

☐ **THE BRADBURY CHRONICLES: *Stories in Honor of Ray Bradbury* edited by William F. Nolan and Martin H. Greenberg.** This tribute to Bradbury's genius includes original fiction by Bradbury himself, Gregory Benford, Orson Scott Card, F. Paul Wilson, and 18 others.   (451953—$5.50)

Prices slightly higher in Canada

Buy them at your local bookstore or use this convenient coupon for ordering.

PENGUIN USA
P.O. Box 999 — Dept. #17109
Bergenfield, New Jersey 07621

Please send me the books I have checked above.
I am enclosing $_____ (please add $2.00 to cover postage and handling). **Send** check or money order (no cash or C.O.D.'s) or charge by Mastercard or VISA (with a $15.00 minimum). Prices and numbers are subject to change without notice.

Card #_____ Exp. Date _____
Signature_____
Name_____
Address_____
City _____ State _____ Zip Code _____

For faster service when ordering by credit card call **1-800-253-6476**

Allow a minimum of 4-6 weeks for delivery. This offer is subject to change without notice.

If you and/or a friend would like to receive the *ROC Advance*, a bimonthly newsletter featuring all the newest and hottest ROC books and authors, on a complimentary basis, please fill out this form and return it to:

ROC Books/Penguin USA
375 Hudson Street
New York, NY 10014

Your Address
Name _____
Street _____ Apt. # _____
City _____ State _____ Zip _____

Friend's Address
Name _____
Street _____ Apt. # _____
City _____ State _____ Zip _____